Thomas De Quincey

Memorials and Other Papers

Volume 1

Thomas De Quincey

Memorials and Other Papers
 Volume 1

ISBN/EAN: 9783337363857

Printed in Europe, USA, Canada, Australia, Japan

Cover: Foto ©Andreas Hilbeck / pixelio.de

More available books at **www.hansebooks.com**

FROM THE AUTHOR, TO THE AMERICAN EDITOR OF HIS WORKS.

These papers I am anxious to put into the hands of your house, and, so far as regards the U.S., of your house exclusively; not with any view to further emolument, but as an acknowledgment of the services which you have already rendered me; namely, first, in having brought together so widely scattered a collection—a difficulty which in my own hands by too painful an experience I had found from nervous depression to be absolutely insurmountable; secondly, in having made me a participator in the pecuniary profits of the American edition, without solicitation or the shadow of any expectation on my part, without any legal claim that I could plead, or equitable warrant in established usage, solely and merely upon your own spontaneous motion. Some of these new papers, I hope, will not be without their value in the eyes of those who have taken an interest in the original series. But at all events, good or bad, they are now tendered to the appropriation of your individual house, the Messrs. TICKNOR & FIELDS, according to the amplest extent of any power to make such a transfer that I may be found to possess by law or custom in America.

I wish this transfer were likely to be of more value. But the veriest trifle, interpreted by the spirit in which I offer it, may express my sense of the liberality manifested throughout this transaction by your honorable house.

Ever believe me, my dear sir,

Your faithful and obliged,

THOMAS DE QUINCEY.

CONTENTS OF VOLUME I.

EXPLANATORY NOTICES.

Many of the papers in my collected works were originally written under one set of disadvantages, and are now revised under another. They were written generally under great pressure as to time, in order to catch the critical periods of monthly journals; written oftentimes at a distance from the press (so as to have no opportunity for correction); and always written at a distance from libraries, so that very many statements, references, and citations, were made on the authority of my unassisted memory. Under such circumstances were most of the papers composed; and they are now reissued in a corrected form, sometimes even partially recast, under the distraction of a nervous misery which embarrasses my efforts in a mode and in a degree inexpressible by words. Such, indeed, is the distress produced by this malady, that, if the present act of republication had in any respect worn the character of an experiment, I should have shrunk from it in despondency. But the experiment, so far as there was any, had been already tried for me vicariously amongst the Americans; a people so nearly repeating our own in style of intellect, and in the composition of their reading class, that a success amongst them counts for a success amongst ourselves. For some few of the separate papers in these volumes I make pretensions of a higher cast. These pretensions I will explain hereafter. All the rest I resign to the reader's unbiased judgment, adding here, with respect to four of them, a few prefatory words—not of propitiation or deprecation, but simply in explanation as to points that would otherwise be open to misconstruction.

1. The paper on "Murder as one of the Fine Arts" [Footnote: Published in the "Miscellaneous Essays."] seemed to exact from me some account of Williams, the dreadful London murderer of the last generation; not only because the amateurs had so much insisted on his merit as the supreme of artists for grandeur of design and breadth of style; and because, apart from this momentary connection with my paper, the man himself merited a record for his matchless audacity, combined with so much of snaky subtlety, and even insinuating amiableness, in his demeanor; but also because, apart from the man himself, the works of the man (those two of them especially which so profoundly impressed the nation in 1812) were in themselves, for dramatic effect, the most impressive on record. Southey pronounced their preeminence when he said to me that they ranked amongst the few domestic events which, by the depth and the expansion of horror attending them, had risen to the dignity of a *national* interest. I may add that this interest benefited also by the mystery which invested the murders; mystery as to various points but especially as respected one important question, Had the murderer any accomplice? [Footnote: Upon a large overbalance of probabilities, it was, however, definitively agreed amongst amateurs that Williams must have been alone in these atrocities. Meantime, amongst the colorable presumptions on the other side was this:—Some hours after the last murder, a man was apprehended at Barnet (the first stage from London on a principal north road), encumbered with a quantity of plate. How he came by it, or whither he was going, he steadfastly refused to say. In the daily journals, which he was allowed to see, he read with eagerness the

police examinations of Williams; and on the same day which announced the catastrophe of Williams, he also committed suicide in his cell.] There was, therefore, reason enough, both in the man's hellish character, and in the mystery which surrounded him, for a Postscript [Footnote: Published in the "Note Book."] to the original paper; since, in a lapse of forty-two years, both the man and his deeds had faded away from the knowledge of the present generation; but still I am sensible that my record is far too diffuse. Feeling this at the very time of writing, I was yet unable to correct it; so little self-control was I able to exercise under the afflicting agitations and the unconquerable impatience of my nervous malady.

2. "War." [Footnote: Published in "Narrative and Miscellaneous Essays."]—In this paper, from having faultily adjusted its proportions in the original outline, I find that I have dwelt too briefly and too feebly upon the capital interest at stake. To apply a correction to some popular misreadings of history, to show that the criminal (because trivial) occasions of war are not always its true causes, or to suggest that war (if resigned to its own natural movement of progress) is cleansing itself and ennobling itself constantly and inevitably, were it only through its connection with science ever more and more exquisite, and through its augmented costliness,—all this may have its use in offering some restraint upon the levity of action or of declamation in Peace Societies. But all this is below the occasion. I feel that far grander interests are at stake in this contest. The Peace Societies are falsely appreciated, when they are described as merely deaf to the lessons of experience, and as too "*romantic*" in their expectations. The very opposite is, to *my* thinking, their criminal reproach. He that is romantic errs usually by too much elevation. He violates the standard of reasonable expectation, by drawing too

violently upon the nobilities of human nature. But, on the contrary, the Peace Societies would, if their power kept pace with their guilty purposes, work degradation for man by drawing upon his most effeminate and luxurious cravings for ease. Most heartily, and with my profoundest sympathy, do I go along with Wordsworth in his grand lyrical proclamation of a truth not less divine than it is mysterious, not less triumphant than it is sorrowful, namely, that amongst God's holiest instruments for the elevation of human nature is "mutual slaughter" amongst men; yes, that "Carnage is God's daughter." Not deriving my own views in this matter from Wordsworth,—not knowing even whether I hold them on the same grounds, since Wordsworth has left *his* grounds unexplained,—nevertheless I cite them in honor, as capable of the holiest justification. The instruments rise in grandeur, carnage and mutual slaughter rise in holiness, exactly as the motives and the interests rise on behalf of which such awful powers are invoked. Fighting for truth in its last recesses of sanctity, for human dignity systematically outraged, or for human rights mercilessly trodden under foot—champions of such interests, men first of all descry, as from a summit suddenly revealed, the possible grandeur of bloodshed suffered or inflicted. Judas and Simon Maccabćus in days of old, Gustavus Adolphus [Footnote: The Thirty Years' War, from 1618 to the Peace of Westphalia in 1648, was notoriously the last and the decisive conflict between Popery and Protestantism; the result of that war it was which finally enlightened all the Popish princes of Christendom as to the impossibility of ever suppressing the antagonist party by mere force of arms. I am not meaning, however, to utter any opinion whatever on the religious position of the two great parties. It is sufficient for entire sympathy with the royal Swede, that he fought for the freedom of conscience. Many an enlightened Roman Catholic, supposing only that he were not a Papist, would

have given his hopes and his confidence to the Protestant
king.] in modern days, fighting for the violated rights of
conscience against perfidious despots and murdering
oppressors, exhibit to us the incarnations of Wordsworth's
principle. Such wars are of rare occurrence. Fortunately they
are so; since, under the possible contingencies of human
strength and weakness, it might else happen that the
grandeur of the principle should suffer dishonor through
the incommensurate means for maintaining it. But such
cases, though emerging rarely, are always to be reserved in
men's minds as ultimate appeals to what is most divine in
man. Happy it is for human welfare that the blind heart of
man is a thousand times wiser than his understanding. An
arrière pensée should lie hidden in all minds—a holy reserve
as to cases which *may* arise similar to such as HAVE arisen,
where a merciful bloodshed [Footnote: "*Merciful bloodshed*"—
In reading either the later religious wars of the Jewish
people under the Maccabees, or the earlier under Joshua,
every philosophic reader will have felt the true and
transcendent spirit of mercy which resides virtually in such
wars, as maintaining the unity of God against Polytheism
and, by trampling on cruel idolatries, as indirectly opening
the channels for benign principles of morality through
endless generations of men. Here especially he will have read
one justification of Wordsworth's bold doctrine upon war.
Thus far he will destroy a wisdom working from afar, but,
as regards the immediate present, he will be apt to adopt the
ordinary view, namely, that in the Old Testament severity
prevails approaching to cruelty. Yet, on consideration, he
will be disposed to qualify this opinion. He will have
observed many indications of a relenting kindness and a
tenderness of love in the Mosaical ordinances. And recently
there has been suggested another argument tending to the
same conclusion. In the last work of Mr. Layard
('Discoveries in the Ruins of Nineveh and Babylon, 1853')

are published some atrocious monuments of the Assyrian cruelty in the treatment of military captives. In one of the plates of Chap xx., at page 456, is exhibited some unknown torture applied to the head, and in another, at page 458, is exhibited the abominable process, applied to two captives, of flaying them alive. One such case had been previously recorded in human literature, and illustrated by a plate. It occurs in a Dutch voyage to the islands of the East. The subject of the torment in that case as a woman who had been charged with some act of infidelity to her husband. And the local government, being indignantly summoned to interfere by some Christian strangers, had declined to do so, on the plea that the man was master within his own house. But the Assyrian case was worse. This torture was there applied, not upon a sudden vindictive impulse, but in cold blood, to a simple case apparently of civil disobedience or revolt. Now, when we consider how intimate, and how ancient, was the connection between Assyria and Palestine, how many things (in war especially) were transferred mediately through the intervening tribes (all habitually cruel), from the people on the Tigris to those on the Jordan, I feel convinced that Moses must have interfered most peremptorily and determinately, and not merely by verbal ordinances, but by establishing counter usages against this spirit of barbarity, otherwise it would have increased contagiously, whereas we meet with no such hellish atrocities amongst the children of Israel. In the case of one memorable outrage by a Hebrew tribe, the national vengeance which overtook it was complete and tearful beyond all that history has recorded] has been authorized by the express voice of God. Such a reserve cannot be dispensed with. It belongs to the principle of progress in man that he should forever keep open a secret commerce in the last resort with the spirit of martyrdom on behalf of man's most saintly interests. In proportion as the instruments for upholding or retrieving such saintly interests should come to be dishonored or less honored, would the inference be valid that those interests were shaking in their foundations. And any confederation or compact of nations for abolishing war would be the inauguration of a downward path for man.

A battle is by possibility the grandest, and also the meanest, of human exploits. It is the grandest when it is fought for godlike truth, for human dignity, or for human rights; it is the meanest when it is fought for petty advantages (as, by way of example, for accession of territory which adds nothing to the security of a frontier), and still more when it is fought simply as a gladiator's trial of national prowess. This is the principle upon which, very naturally, our British school-boys value a battle. Painful it is to add, that this is the principle upon which our adult neighbors the French seem to value a battle.

To any man who, like myself, admires the high-toned, martial gallantry of the French, and pays a cheerful tribute of respect to their many intellectual triumphs, it is painful to witness the childish state of feeling which the French people manifest on every possible question that connects itself at any point with martial pretensions. A battle is valued by them on the same principles, not better and not worse, as govern our own schoolboys. Every battle is viewed by the boys as a test applied to the personal prowess of each individual soldier; and, naturally amongst boys, it would be the merest hypocrisy to take any higher ground. But amongst adults, arrived at the power of reflecting and comparing, we look for something nobler. We English estimate Waterloo, not by its amount of killed and wounded, but as the battle which terminated a series of battles, having one common object, namely, the overthrow of a frightful tyranny. A great sepulchral shadow rolled away from the face of Christendom as that day's sun went down to his rest; for, had the success been less absolute, an opportunity would have offered for negotiation, and consequently for an infinity of intrigues through the feuds always gathering upon national jealousies amongst allied armies. The dragon would soon have healed his wounds; after which the prosperity of the despotism would have been greater than before. But, without reference to Waterloo in particular, *we*, on *our* part, find it impossible to contemplate any memorable battle otherwise than according to its tendency towards some commensurate object. To the French this must be impossible, seeing that no lofty (that is, no disinterested) purpose has ever been so much as counterfeited for a French war, nor therefore for a French battle. Aggression, cloaked at the very utmost in the garb of retaliation for counter aggressions on the part of the enemy, stands forward uniformly in the van of such motives as it is thought worth while to plead. But in French casuistry it is not held necessary to plead _any_thing; war justifies itself. To fight for the experimental purpose of trying the proportions of martial merit, but (to speak frankly) for the purpose of publishing and renewing to Europe the proclamation of French superiority—*that* is the object of French wars. Like the Spartan of old, the Frenchman would hold that a state of peace, and not a state of war, is the state which calls for apology; and that already from the first such an apology must wear a very suspicious aspect of paradox.

3. "The English Mail-Coach." [Footnote: Published in the "Miscellaneous Essays."]—This little paper, according to my original intention, formed part of the "Suspiria de Profundis," from which, for a momentary purpose, I did not scruple to detach it, and to publish it apart, as sufficiently intelligible even when dislocated from its place in a larger

whole. To my surprise, however, one or two critics, not carelessly in conversation, but deliberately in print, professed their inability to apprehend the meaning of the whole, or to follow the links of the connection between its several parts. I am myself as little able to understand where the difficulty lies, or to detect any lurking obscurity, as those critics found themselves to unravel my logic. Possibly I may not be an indifferent and neutral judge in such a case. I will therefore sketch a brief abstract of the little paper according to my own original design, and then leave the reader to judge how far this design is kept in sight through the actual execution.

Thirty-seven years ago, or rather more, accident made me, in the dead of night, and of a night memorably solemn, the solitary witness to an appalling scene, which threatened instant death, in a shape the most terrific, to two young people, whom I had no means of assisting, except in so far as I was able to give them a most hurried warning of their danger; but even *that* not until they stood within the very shadow of the catastrophe, being divided from the most frightful of deaths by scarcely more, if more at all, than seventy seconds.

Such was the scene, such in its outline, from which the whole of this paper radiates as a natural expansion. The scene is circumstantially narrated in Section the Second, entitled, "The Vision of Sudden Death."

But a movement of horror and of spontaneous recoil from this dreadful scene naturally carried the whole of that scene, raised and idealised, into my dreams, and very soon into a rolling succession of dreams. The actual scene, as looked down upon from the box of the mail, was transformed into a dream, as tumultuous and changing as a musical fugue. This troubled Dream is circumstantially reported in Section

the Third, entitled, "Dream-Fugue upon the Theme of
Sudden Death." What I had beheld from my seat upon the
mail,—the scenical strife of action and passion, of anguish
and fear, as I had there witnessed them moving in ghostly
silence; this duel between life and death narrowing itself to a
point of such exquisite evanescence as the collision neared,—
all these elements of the scene blended, under the law of
association, with the previous and permanent features of
distinction investing the mail itself, which features at that
time lay—1st, in velocity unprecedented; 2dly, in the power
and beauty of the horses: 3dly, in the official connection
with the government of a great nation; and, 4thly, in the
function, almost a consecrated function, of publishing and
diffusing through the land the great political events, and
especially the great battles during a conflict of unparalleled
grandeur. These honorary distinctions are all described
circumstantially in the FIRST or introductory section ("The
Glory of Motion"). The three first were distinctions
maintained at all times; but the fourth and grandest
belonged exclusively to the war with Napoleon; and this it
was which most naturally introduced Waterloo into the
dream. Waterloo, I understood, was the particular feature of
the "Dream-Fugue" which my censors were least able to
account for. Yet surely Waterloo, which, in common with
every other great battle, it had been our special privilege to
publish over all the land, most naturally entered the Dream
under the license of our privilege. If not—if there be
anything amiss—let the Dream be responsible. The Dream is
a law to itself; and as well quarrel with a rainbow for
showing, or for *not* showing, a secondary arch. So far as I
know, every element in the shifting movements of the
Dream derived itself either primarily from the incidents of
the actual scene, or from secondary features associated with
the mail. For example, the cathedral aisle derived itself from
the mimic combination of features which grouped

themselves together at the point of approaching collision, namely, an arrow-like section of the road, six hundred yards long, under the solemn lights described, with lofty trees meeting overhead in arches. The guard's horn, again—a humble instrument in itself—was yet glorified as the organ of publication for so many great national events. And the incident of the Dying Trumpeter, who rises from a marble bas-relief, and carries a marble trumpet to his marble lips for the purpose of warning the female infant, was doubtless secretly suggested by my own imperfect effort to seize the guard's horn, and to blow a warning blast. But the Dream knows best; and the Dream, I say again, is the responsible party.

4. "The Spanish Nun." [Footnote: Published in "Narrative and Miscellaneous Essays."]—There are some narratives, which, though pure fictions from first to last, counterfeit so vividly the air of grave realities, that, if deliberately offered for such, they would for a time impose upon everybody. In the opposite scale there are other narratives, which, whilst rigorously true, move amongst characters and scenes so remote from our ordinary experience, and through, a state of society so favorable to an adventurous cast of incidents, that they would everywhere pass for romances, if severed from the documents which attest their fidelity to facts. In the former class stand the admirable novels of De Foe; and, on a lower range, within the same category, the inimitable "Vicar of Wakefield;" upon which last novel, without at all designing it, I once became the author of the following instructive experiment. I had given a copy of this little novel to a beautiful girl of seventeen, the daughter of a statesman in Westmoreland, not designing any deception (nor so much as any concealment) with respect to the fictitious character of the incidents and of the actors in that famous tale. Mere accident it was that had intercepted those

explanations as to the extent of fiction in these points which in this case it would have been so natural to make. Indeed, considering the exquisite verisimilitude of the work meeting with such absolute inexperience in the reader, it was almost a duty to have made them. This duty, however, something had caused me to forget; and when next I saw the young mountaineer, I forgot that I *had* forgotten it. Consequently, at first I was perplexed by the unfaltering gravity with which my fair young friend spoke of Dr. Primrose, of Sophia and her sister, of Squire Thornhill, &c., as real and probably living personages, who could sue and be sued. It appeared that this artless young rustic, who had never heard of novels and romances as a bare possibility amongst all the shameless devices of London swindlers, had read with religious fidelity every word of this tale, so thoroughly life-like, surrendering her perfect faith and her loving sympathy to the different persons in the tale, and the natural distresses in which they are involved, without suspecting, for a moment, that by so much as a breathing of exaggeration or of embellishment the pure gospel truth of the narrative could have been sullied. She listened, in a kind of breathless stupor, to my frank explanation—that not part only, but the whole, of this natural tale was a pure invention. Scorn and indignation flashed from her eyes. She regarded herself as one who had been hoaxed and swindled; begged me to take back the book; and never again, to the end of her life, could endure to look into the book, or to be reminded of that criminal imposture which Dr. Oliver Goldsmith had practised upon her youthful credulity.

In that case, a book altogether fabulous, and not meaning to offer itself for anything else, had been read as genuine history. Here, on the other hand, the adventures of the Spanish Nun, which in every detail of time and place have since been sifted and authenticated, stood a good chance at one period of being classed as the most lawless of romances. It is, indeed, undeniable, and this arises as a natural result from the bold, adventurous character of the heroine, and from the unsettled state of society at that period in Spanish America, that a reader the most credulous would at times be startled with doubts upon what seems so unvarying a tenor of danger and lawless violence. But, on the other hand, it is also undeniable that a reader the most obstinately sceptical would be equally startled in the very opposite direction, on remarking that the incidents are far from being such as a romance-writer would have been likely to invent; since, if striking, tragic, and even appalling, they are at times repulsive. And it seems evident that, once putting himself to the cost of a wholesale fiction, the writer would have used his privilege more freely for his own advantage. Whereas the author of these memoirs clearly writes under the coercion and restraint of a *notorious reality*, that would not suffer him to ignore or to modify the leading facts. Then, as to the objection that few people or none have an experience presenting such uniformity of perilous adventure, a little closer attention shows that the experience in this case is *not* uniform; and so far otherwise, that a period of several years in Kate's South American life is confessedly suppressed; and on no other ground whatever than that this long parenthesis is *not* adventurous, not essentially differing from the monotonous character of ordinary Spanish life.

Suppose the case, therefore, that Kate's memoirs had been thrown upon the world with no vouchers for their authenticity beyond such internal presumptions as would have occurred to thoughtful readers, when reviewing the entire succession of incidents, I am of opinion that the person best qualified by legal experience to judge of evidence would finally have pronounced a favorable award; since it is easy to understand that in a world so vast as the Peru, the

Mexico, the Chili, of Spaniards during the first quarter of the seventeenth century, and under the slender modification of Indian manners as yet effected by the Papal Christianization of those countries, and in the neighborhood of a river-system so awful, of a mountain-system so unheard-of in Europe, there would probably, by blind, unconscious sympathy, grow up a tendency to lawless and gigantesque ideals of adventurous life; under which, united with the duelling code of Europe, many things would become trivial and commonplace experiences that to us home-bred English ("*qui musas colimus severiores*") seem monstrous and revolting.

Left, therefore, to itself, *my* belief is, that the story of the Military Nun would have prevailed finally against the demurs of the sceptics. However, in the mean time, all such demurs were suddenly and *officially* silenced forever. Soon after the publication of Kate's memoirs, in what you may call an early stage of her *literary* career, though two centuries after her *personal* career had closed, a regular controversy arose upon the degree of credit due to these extraordinary confessions (such they may be called) of the poor conscience-haunted nun. Whether these in Kate's original MS. were entitled "Autobiographic Sketches," or "Selections Grave and Gay," from the military experiences of a Nun, or possibly "The Confessions of a Biscayan Fire-Eater," is more than I know. No matter: confessions they were; and confessions that, when at length published, were absolutely mobbed and hustled by a gang of misbelieving (that is, *miscreant*) critics. And this fact is most remarkable, that the person who originally headed the incredulous party, namely, Senor de Ferrer, a learned Castilian, was the very same who finally authenticated, by *documentary* evidence, the extraordinary narrative in those parts which had most of all invited scepticism. The progress of the dispute threw the

decision at length upon the archives of the Spanish Marine.
Those for the southern ports of Spain had been transferred,
I believe, from Cadiz and St. Lucar to Seville; chiefly,
perhaps, through the confusions incident to the two French
invasions of Spain in our own day [1st, that under
Napoleon; 2dly, that under the Due d'Angoulęme].
Amongst these archives, subsequently amongst those of
Cuzco, in South America; 3dly, amongst the records of some
royal courts in Madrid; 4thly, by collateral proof from the
Papal Chancery; 5thly, from Barcelona—have been drawn
together ample attestations of all the incidents recorded by
Kate. The elopement from St. Sebastian's, the doubling of
Cape Horn, the shipwreck on the coast of Peru, the rescue of
the royal banner from the Indians of Chili, the fatal duel in
the dark, the astonishing passage of the Andes, the tragical
scenes at Tucuman and Cuzco, the return to Spain in
obedience to a royal and a papal summons, the visit to Rome
and the interview with the Pope—finally, the return to
South America, and the mysterious disappearance at Vera
Cruz, upon which no light was ever thrown—all these
capital heads of the narrative have been established beyond
the reach of scepticism: and, in consequence, the story was
soon after adopted as historically established, and was
reported at length by journals of the highest credit in Spain
and Germany, and by a Parisian journal so cautious and so
distinguished for its ability as the *Revue des Deux Mondes*.

I must not leave the impression upon my readers that this
complex body of documentary evidences has been searched
and appraised by myself. Frankly I acknowledge that, on the
sole occasion when any opportunity offered itself for such a
labor, I shrank from it as too fatiguing—and also as
superfluous; since, if the proofs had satisfied the compatriots
of Catalina, who came to the investigation with hostile
feelings of partisanship, and not dissembling their

incredulity,—armed also (and in Mr. de Ferrer's case conspicuously armed) with the appropriate learning for giving effect to this incredulity,—it could not become a stranger to suppose himself qualified for disturbing a judgment that had been so deliberately delivered. Such a tribunal of native Spaniards being satisfied, there was no further opening for demur. The ratification of poor Kate's memoirs is now therefore to be understood as absolute, and without reserve.

This being stated,—namely, such an attestation from competent authorities to the truth of Kate's narrative as may save all readers from my fair Westmoreland friend's disaster, —it remains to give such an answer, as without further research *can* be given, to a question pretty sure of arising in all reflective readers' thoughts—namely, does there anywhere survive a portrait of Kate? I answer—and it would be both mortifying and perplexing if I could *not—Yes*. One such portrait there is confessedly; and seven years ago this was to be found at Aix-la-Chapelle, in the collection of Herr Sempeller. The name of the artist I am not able to report; neither can I say whether Herr Sempeller's collection still remains intact, and remains at Aix-la-Chapelle.

But inevitably to most readers who review the circumstances of a case so extraordinary, it will occur that beyond a doubt *many* portraits of the adventurous nun must have been executed. To have affronted the wrath of the Inquisition, and to have survived such an audacity, would of itself be enough to found a title for the martial nun to a national interest. It is true that Kate had not taken the veil; she had stopped short of the deadliest crime known to the Inquisition; but still her transgressions were such as to require a special indulgence; and this indulgence was granted by a Pope to the intercession of a king—the greatest then reigning. It was a favor that could not have been asked by any greater man in this world, nor granted by any less. Had no other distinction settled upon Kate, this would have been enough to fix the gaze of her own nation. But her whole life constituted Kate's supreme distinction. There can be no doubt, therefore, that, from the year 1624 (that is, the last year of our James I.), she became the object of an admiration in her own country that was almost idolatrous. And this admiration was not of a kind that rested upon any partisan-schism amongst her countrymen. So long as it was kept alive by her bodily presence amongst them, it was an admiration equally aristocratic and popular, — shared alike by the rich and the poor, by the lofty and the humble. Great, therefore, would be the demand for her portrait. There is a tradition that Velasquez, who had in 1623 executed a portrait of Charles I. (then Prince of Wales), was amongst those who in the three or four following years ministered to this demand. It is believed, also, that, in travelling from Genoa and Florence to Rome, she sat to various artists, in order to meet the interest about herself already rising amongst the cardinals and other dignitaries of the Romish church. It is probable, therefore, that numerous pictures of Kate are yet lurking both in Spain and Italy, but not known as such. For, as the public consideration granted to her had grown out of merits and qualities purely personal, and was kept alive by no local or family memorials rooted in the land, or surviving herself, it was inevitable that, as soon as she herself died, all identification of her portraits would perish: and the portraits would thenceforwards be confounded with the similar memorials, past all numbering, which every year accumulates as the wrecks from household remembrances of generations that are passing or passed, that are fading or faded, that are dying or buried. It is well, therefore, amongst so many irrecoverable ruins, that, in the portrait at Aix-la-Chapelle,

we still possess one undoubted representation (and therefore
in some degree a means for identifying *other* representations)
of a female so memorably adorned by nature; gifted with
capacities so unparalleled both of doing and suffering; who
lived a life so stormy, and perished by a fate so unsearchably
mysterious.

THE ORPHAN HEIRESS

VISIT TO LAXTON.

My route, after parting from Lord Westport at Birmingham, lay, as I have mentioned in the "Autobiographic Sketches," through Stamford to Laxton, the Northamptonshire seat of Lord Carbery. From Stamford, which I had reached by some intolerable old coach, such as in those days too commonly abused the patience and long-suffering of Young England, I took a post-chaise to Laxton. The distance was but nine miles, and the postilion drove well, so that I could not really have been long upon the road; and yet, from gloomy rumination upon the unhappy destination which I believed myself approaching within three or four months, never had I weathered a journey that seemed to me so long and dreary. As I alighted on the steps at Laxton, the first dinner-bell rang; and I was hurrying to my toilet, when my sister Mary, who had met me in the portico, begged me first of all to come into Lady Carbery's [Footnote: Lady Carbery.—"To me, individually, she was the one sole friend that ever I could regard as entirely fulfilling the offices of an honest friendship. She had known me from infancy; when I was in my first year of life, she, an orphan and a great heiress, was in her tenth or eleventh."—See closing pages of "*Autobiographic Sketches*."] dressing-room, her ladyship having something special to communicate, which related (as

I understood her) to one Simon. "What Simon? Simon Peter?"—O, no, you irreverend boy, no Simon at all with an S, but Cymon with a C,—Dryden's Cymon,— "That whistled as he went for want of thought."'

This one indication was a key to the whole explanation that followed. The sole visitors, it seemed, at that time to Laxton, beside my sister and myself, were Lord and Lady Massey. They were understood to be domesticated at Laxton for a very long stay. In reality, my own private construction of the case (though unauthorized by anything ever hinted to me by Lady Carbery) was, that Lord Massey might probably be under some cloud of pecuniary embarrassments, such as suggested prudentially an absence from Ireland. Meantime, what was it that made him an object of peculiar interest to Lady Carbery? It was the singular revolution which, in one whom all his friends looked upon as sold to constitutional torpor, suddenly, and beyond all hope, had kindled a new and nobler life. Occupied originally by no shadow of any earthly interest, killed by *ennui*, all at once Lord Massey had fallen passionately in love with a fair young countrywoman, well connected, but bringing him no fortune (I report only from hearsay), and endowing him simply with the priceless blessing of her own womanly charms, her delightful society, and her sweet, Irish style of innocent gayety. No transformation that ever legends or romances had reported was more memorable. Lapse of time (for Lord Massey had now been married three or four years), and deep seclusion from general society, had done nothing, apparently, to lower the tone of his happiness. The expression of this happiness was noiseless and unobtrusive; no marks were there of vulgar uxoriousness—nothing that could provoke the sneer of the worldling; but not the less so entirely had the society of his young wife created a new principle of life within him, and evoked some nature

hitherto slumbering, and which, no doubt, would else have
continued to slumber till his death, that, at moments when
he believed himself unobserved, he still wore the aspect of an
impassioned lover.

"He beheld
A vision, and adored the thing he saw.
Arabian fiction never filled the world
With half the wonders that were wrought for *him*.
Earth breathed in one great presence of the spring
Her chamber window did surpass in glory
The portals of the dawn."

And in no case was it more literally realized, as daily almost
I witnessed, that

"All Paradise
Could, by the simple opening of a door,
Let itself in upon him."
[Footnote: Wordsworth's "Vandracour and Julia."]

For never did the drawing-room door open, and suddenly
disclose the beautiful figure of Lady Massey, than a mighty
cloud seemed to roll away from the young Irishman's brow.
At this time it happened, and indeed it often happened, that
Lord Carbery was absent in Ireland. It was probable,
therefore, that during the long couple of hours through
which the custom of those times bound a man to the
dinner-table after the disappearance of the ladies, his time
would hang heavily on his hands. To me, therefore, Lady
Carbery looked, having first put me in possession of the
case, for assistance to her hospitality, under the difficulties I
have stated. She thoroughly loved Lady Massey, as, indeed,

nobody could help doing; and for *her* sake, had there been no separate interest surrounding the young lord, it would have been most painful to her that through Lord Carbery's absence a periodic tedium should oppress her guest at that precise season of the day which traditionally dedicated itself to genial enjoyment. Glad, therefore, was she that an ally had come at last to Laxton, who might arm her purposes of hospitality with some powers of self-fulfilment. And yet, for a service of that nature, could she reasonably rely upon me? Odious is the hobble-de-hoy to the mature young man. Generally speaking, that cannot be denied. But in me, though naturally the shyest of human beings, intense commerce with men of every rank, from the highest to the lowest, had availed to dissipate all arrears of *mauvaise honte*; I could talk upon innumerable subjects; and, as the readiest means of entering immediately upon business, I was fresh from Ireland, knew multitudes of those whom Lord Massey either knew or felt an interest in, and, at that happy period of life, found it easy, with three or four glasses of wine, to call back the golden spirits which were now so often deserting me. Renovated, meantime, by a hot bath, I was ready at the second summons of the dinner-bell, and descended a new creature to the drawing-room. Here I was presented to the noble lord and his wife. Lord Massey was in figure shortish, but broad and stout, and wore an amiable expression of face. That I could execute Lady Carbery's commission, I felt satisfied at once. And, accordingly, when the ladies had retired from the dining-room, I found an easy opening, in various circumstances connected with the Laxton stables, for introducing naturally a picturesque and contrasting sketch of the stud and the stables at Westport. The stables and everything connected with the stables at Laxton were magnificent; in fact, far out of symmetry with the house, which, at that time, was elegant and comfortable, but not splendid. As usual in English establishments, all the appointments were complete, and carried to the same point of exquisite finish. The stud of hunters was first-rate and extensive; and the whole scene, at closing the stables for the night, was so splendidly arranged and illuminated, that Lady Carbery would take all her visitors once or twice a week to admire it. On the other hand, at Westport you might fancy yourself overlooking the establishment of some Albanian Pacha. Crowds of irregular helpers and grooms, many of them totally unrecognized by Lord Altamont, some half countenanced by this or that upper servant, some doubtfully tolerated, some *not* tolerated, but nevertheless slipping in by postern doors when the enemy had withdrawn, made up a strange mob as regarded the human element in this establishment. And Dean Browne regularly asserted that five out of six amongst these helpers he himself could swear to as active boys from Vinegar Hill. Trivial enough, meantime, in our eyes, was any little matter of rebellion that they might have upon their consciences. High treason we willingly winked at. But what we could *not* wink at was the systematic treason which they committed against our comfort, namely, by teaching our horses all imaginable tricks, and training them up in the way along which they should *not* go, so that when they were old they were very little likely to depart from it. Such a set of restive, hard-mouthed wretches as Lord Westport and I daily had to bestride, no tongue could describe. There was a cousin of Lord Westport's, subsequently created Lord Oranmore, distinguished for his horsemanship, and always splendidly mounted from his father's stables at Castle M'Garret, to whom our stormy contests with ruined tempers and vicious habits yielded a regular comedy of fun; and, in order to improve it, he would sometimes bribe Lord Westport's treacherous groom into misleading us, when floundering amongst bogs, into the interior labyrinths of these morasses. Deep, however, as the morass, was this man's remorse when, on leaving Westport, I gave him the heavy golden perquisite, which my mother (unaware of the tricks he had practised upon me) had by letter instructed me to give. He was a mere savage boy from the central bogs of Connaught, and, to the great amusement of Lord Westport, he persisted in calling me "your majesty" for the rest of that day; and by all other means open to him he expressed his penitence. But the dean insisted that, no matter for his penitence in the matter of the bogs, he had certainly carried a pike at Vinegar Hill; and probably had stolen a pair of boots at Furnes, when he kindly made a call at the Deanery, in passing through that place to the field of battle. It is always a pleasure to see the engineer of mischief "hoist with his own petard;" [Footnote: "Hamlet," but also "Ovid:"—"Lex nec justior ulla est, **Quam necis artifices arte perire sua."] and it happened that the horses assigned to draw a post-chariot carrying Lord Westport, myself, and the dean, on our return journey to Dublin, were a pair utterly ruined by a certain under-postilion, named Moran. This particular ruin did Mr. Moran boast to have contributed as his separate contribution to the general ruinations of the stables. And the particular object was, that *his* horses, and consequently himself, might be left in genial laziness. But, as Nemesis would have it, Mr. Moran was the charioteer specially appointed to this particular service. We were to return by easy journeys of twenty-five miles a day, or even less; since every such interval brought us to the house of some hospitable family, connected by friendship or by blood with Lord Altamont. Fervently had Lord Westport pleaded with his father for an allowance of four horses; not at all with any foolish view to fleeting aristocratic splendor, but simply to the luxury of rapid motion. But Lord Altamont was firm in resisting this petition at that time. The remote consequence was, that by way of redressing the violated

equilibrium to our feelings, we subscribed throughout
Wales to extort six horses from the astonished innkeepers,
most of whom declined the requisition, and would furnish
only four, on the plea that the leaders would only embarrass
the other horses; but one at Bangor, from whom we coolly
requested eight, recoiled from our demand as from a sort of
miniature treason. How so? Because in this island he had
always understood eight horses to be consecrated to royal
use. Not at all, we assured him; Pickford, the great carrier,
always horsed his wagons with eight. And the law knew of
no distinction between wagon and post-chaise, coach-horse
or cart-horse. However, we could not compass this point of
the eight horses, the double *quadriga*, in one single instance;
but the true reason we surmised to be, not the pretended
puritanism of loyalty to the house of Guelph, but the
running short of the innkeeper's funds. If he had to meet a
daily average call for twenty-four horses, then it might well
happen that our draft upon him for eight horses at one pull
would bankrupt him for a whole day.

But I am anticipating. Returning to Ireland and Mr. Moran,
the vicious driver of vicious horses, the immediate
consequence to *him* of this unexpected limitation to a pair of
horses was, that all his knavery in one hour recoiled upon
himself. The horses whom he had himself trained to vice
and restiveness, in the hope that thus his own services and
theirs might be less in request, now became the very curse of
his life. Every morning, duly as an attempt was made to put
them in motion, they began to back, and no arts, gentle or
harsh, would for a moment avail to coax or to coërce them
into the counter direction. Could retrogression by any
metaphysics have been translated into progress, we excelled
in that; it was our *forte*; we could have backed to the North
Pole. That might be the way to glory, or at least to
distinction — *sic itur ad astra*; unfortunately, it was not the

way to Dublin. Consequently, on *every* day of our journey—
and the days were ten—not once, but always, we had the
same deadly conflict to repeat; and this being always
unavailing, found its solution uniformly in the following
ultimate resource. Two large-boned horses, usually taken
from the plough, were harnessed on as leaders. By main
force they hauled our wicked wheelers into the right
direction, and forced them, by pure physical superiority,
into working. We furnished a joyous and comic spectacle to
every town and village through which we passed. The
whole community, men and children, came out to assist at
our departure; and all alike were diverted, but not the less
irritated, by the demoniac obstinacy of the brutes, who
seemed under the immediate inspiration of the fiend.
Everybody was anxious to share in the scourging which
was administered to them right and left; and once propelled
into a gallop (or such a gallop as our Brobdignagian leaders
could accomplish), they were forced into keeping it up. But,
without rehearsing all the details of the case, it may be
readily conceived that the amount of trouble distributed
amongst our whole party was enormous. Once or twice the
friends at whose houses we slept were able to assist us. But
generally they either had no horses, or none of the
commanding power demanded. Often, again, it happened, as
our route was very circuitous, that no inns lay in our
neighborhood; or, if there *were* inns, the horses proved to be
of too slight a build. At Ballinasloe, and again at Athlone,
half the town came out to help us; and, having no suitable
horses, thirty or forty men, with shouts of laughter, pulled
at ropes fastened to our pole and splinter-bar, and compelled
the snorting demons into a flying gallop. But, naturally, a
couple of miles saw this resource exhausted. Then came the
necessity of "drawing the covers," as the dean called it; that
is, hunting amongst the adjacent farmers for powerful
cattle. This labor (O, Jupiter, thanks be for *that!*) fell upon

Mr. Moran. And sometimes it would happen that the horses, which it had cost him three or four hours to find, could be spared only for four or five miles. Such a journey can rarely have been accomplished. Our zigzag course had prolonged it into from two hundred and thirty to two hundred and fifty miles; and it is literally true that, of this entire distance from Westport House to Sackville-street, Dublin, not one furlong had been performed under the spontaneous impulse of our own horses. Their diabolic resistance continued to the last. And one may venture to hope that the sense of final subjugation to man must have proved penally bitter to the horses. But, meantime, it vexes one that such wretches should be fed with good old hay and oats; as well littered down also in their stalls as a prebendary; and by many a stranger, ignorant of their true character, should have been patted and caressed. Let us hope that a fate, to which more than once they were nearly forcing *us*, namely, regress over a precipice, may ultimately have been their own. Once I saw such another case dramatically carried through to its natural crisis in the Liverpool Mail. It was on the stage leading into Lichfield; there was no conspiracy, as in our Irish case; one horse only out of the four was the criminal; and, according to the queen's bench (Denman, C. J.), there is no conspiracy competent to one agent; but he was even more signally under a demoniac possession of mutinous resistance to man. The case was really a memorable one. If ever there was a distinct proclamation of rebellion against man, it was made by that brutal horse; and I, therefore, being a passenger on the box, took a note of the case; and on a proper occasion I may be induced to publish it, unless some Houynhm should whinny against me a chancery injunction.

From these wild, Tartar-like stables of Connaught, how vast was the transition to that perfection of elegance, and of adaptation between means and ends, that reigned from centre to circumference through the stables at Laxton! *I*, as it happened, could report to Lord Massey their earlier condition; he to me could report their immediate changes. I won him easily to an interest in my own Irish experiences, so fresh, and in parts so grotesque, wilder also by much in Connaught than in Lord Massey's county of Limerick; whilst he (without affecting any delight in the hunting systems of Northamptonshire and Leicestershire) yet took pleasure in explaining to me those characteristic features of the English midland hunting as centralized at Melton, which even then gave to it the supreme rank for brilliancy and unity of effect amongst all varieties of the chase. [Footnote: If mere names were allowed to dazzle the judgment, how magnificent to a gallant young Englishman of twenty seems at first the *tiger-hunting* of India, which yet (when examined searchingly) turns out the meanest and most *cowardly* mode of hunting known to human experience. *Buffalo-hunting* is much more dignified as regards the courageous exposure of the hunter; but, from all accounts, its excitement is too momentary and evanescent; one rifle-shot, and the crisis is past. Besides that, the generous and honest character of the buffalo disturbs the cordiality of the sport. The very opposite reason disturbs the interest of lion-hunting, especially at the Cape. The lion is everywhere a cowardly wretch, unless when sublimed into courage by famine; but, in southern Africa, he is the most currish of enemies. Those who fancied so much adventurousness in the lion conflicts of Mr. Gordon Cumming appear never to have read the missionary travels of Mr. Moffat. The poor missionary, without any arms whatever, came to think lightly of half a dozen lions seen drinking through the twilight at the very same pond or river as himself. Nobody can have any wish to undervalue the adventurous gallantry of Mr. G. Cumming. But, in the single case of the Cape lion, there is an unintentional advantage taken from the traditional name of lion, as though the Cape lion were such as that which ranges the torrid zone.]

Horses had formed the natural and introductory topic of conversation between us. What we severally knew of Ireland, though in different quarters,—what we both knew of Laxton, the barbaric splendor, and the civilized splendor, —had naturally an interest for us both in their contrasts (at one time so picturesque, at another so grotesque), which illuminated our separate recollections. But my quick instinct soon made me aware that a jealousy was gathering in Lord Massey's mind around such a topic, as though too ostentatiously levelled to his particular knowledge, or to his *animal* condition of taste. But easily I slipped off into another key. At Laxton, it happened that the library was excellent. Founded by whom, I never heard; but certainly, when used by a systematic reader, it showed itself to have been systematically collected; it stretched pretty equably through two centuries,—namely, from about 1600 to 1800,—and might, perhaps, amount to seventeen thousand volumes. Lord Massey was far from illiterate; and his interest in books was unaffected, if limited, and too often interrupted, by defective knowledge. The library was dispersed through six or seven small rooms, lying between the drawing-room in one wing, and the dining-room in the opposite wing. This dispersion, however, already furnished the ground of a rude classification. In some one of these rooms was Lord Massey always to be found, from the forenoon to the evening. And was it any fault of *his* that his daughter, little Grace, about two years old, pursued him down from her nursery every morning, and insisted upon seeing innumerable pictures, lurking (as she had discovered) in many different recesses of the library? More and more from this quarter it was that we drew the materials of our daily after-dinner conversation. One great discouragement arises commonly to the student, where the particular library in which he reads has been so disordinately collected that he cannot *pursue* a subject once started. Now, at Laxton, the books had been so judiciously brought together, so many hooks and eyes connected them, that the whole library formed what one might call a series of *strata*, naturally allied, through which you might quarry your way consecutively for many months. On rainy days, and often enough one had occasion to say through rainy weeks, what a delightful resource did this library prove to both of us! And one day it occurred to us, that, whereas the stables and the library were both jewels of attraction, the latter had been by much the least costly. Pretty often I have found, when any opening has existed for making the computation, that, in a library containing a fair proportion of books illustrated with plates, about ten shillings a volume might be taken as expressing, upon a sufficiently large number of volumes, small and great, the fair average cost of the whole. On this basis, the library at Laxton would have cost less than nine thousand pounds. On the other hand, thirty-five horses (hunters, racers, roadsters, carriage-horses, etc.) might have cost about eight thousand pounds, or a little more. But the library entailed no permanent cost beyond the annual loss of interest; the books did not eat, and required no aid from veterinary [Footnote: "*Veterinary*."—By the way, whence comes this odd-looking word? The word *veterana* I have met with in monkish writers, to express *domesticated quadrupeds*; and evidently from that word must have originated the word *veterinary*. But the question is still but one step removed; for, how came *veterana* by that acceptation in rural economy?] surgeons; whereas, for the horses, not only such ministrations were intermittingly required, but a costly permanent establishment of grooms and helpers. Lord

Carbery, who had received an elaborate Etonian education, was even more earnestly a student than his friend Lord Massey, who had probably been educated at home under a private tutor. He read everything connected with general politics (meaning by *general* not personal politics) and with social philosophy. At Laxton, indeed; it was that I first saw Godwin's "Political Justice;" not the second and emasculated edition in *octavo*, but the original *quarto* edition, with all its virus as yet undiluted of raw anti-social Jacobinism.

At Laxton it was that I first saw the entire aggregate labors, brigaded, as it were, and paraded as if for martial review, of that most industrious benefactor to the early stages of our English historical literature, Thomas Hearne. Three hundred guineas, I believe, had been the price paid cheerfully at one time for a complete set of Hearne. At Laxton, also, it was that first I saw the total array of works edited by Dr. Birch. It was a complete *armilustrium*, a *recognitio*, or mustering, as it were, not of pompous Praetorian cohorts, or unique guardsmen, but of the yeomanry, the militia, or what, under the old form of expression, you might regard as the *trained bands* of our literature—the fund from which ultimately, or in the last resort, students look for the materials of our vast and myriad-faced literature. A French author of eminence, fifty years back, having occasion to speak of our English literature collectively, in reference to the one point of its *variety*, being also a man of honor, and disdaining that sort of patriotism which sacrifices the truth to nationality, speaks of our pretensions in these words: *Les Anglois qui ont une littérature infiniment plus variée que la nôtre.* This fact is a feature in our national pretensions that could ever have been regarded doubtfully merely through insufficient knowledge. Dr. Johnson, indeed, made it the distinguishing merit of the French, that they "have a book upon every subject." But Dr.

Johnson was not only capricious as regards temper and variable humors, but as regards the inequality of his knowledge. Incoherent and unsystematic was Dr. Johnson's information in most cases. Hence his extravagant misappraisement of Knolles, the Turkish historian, which is exposed so severely by Spittler, the German, who, again, is himself miserably superficial in his analysis of English history. Hence the feeble credulity which Dr. Johnson showed with respect to the forgery of De Foe (under the masque of Captain Carleton) upon the Catalonian campaign of Lord Peterborough. But it is singular that a literature, so unrivalled as ours in its compass and variety, should not have produced any, even the shallowest, manual of itself. And thus it happens, for example, that writers so laborious and serviceable as Birch are in any popular sense scarcely known. I showed to Lord Massey, among others of his works, that which relates to Lord Worcester's (that is, Lord Glamorgan's) negotiations with the Papal nuncio in Ireland, about the year 1644, &c. Connected with these negotiations were many names amongst Lord Massey's own ancestors; so that here he suddenly alighted upon a fund of archćologic memorabilia, connecting what interested him as an Irishman in general with what most interested him as the head of a particular family. It is remarkable, also, as an indication of the *general* nobility and elevation which had accompanied the revolution in his life, that concurrently with the constitutional torpor previously besetting him, had melted away the intellectual torpor under which he had found books until recently of little practical value. Lady Carbery had herself told me that the two revolutions went on simultaneously. He began to take an interest in literature when life itself unfolded a new interest, under the companionship of his youthful wife. And here, by the way, as subsequently in scores of other instances, I saw broad evidences of the credulity with which we have adopted into

our grave political faith the rash and malicious sketches of
our novelists. With Fielding commenced the practice of
systematically traducing our order of country gentlemen.
His picture of Squire Western is not only a malicious, but
also an incongruous libel. The squire's ordinary language is
impossible, being alternately bookish and absurdly rustic.
In reality, the conventional dialect ascribed to the rustic
order in general—to peasants even more than to gentlemen
—in our English plays and novels, is a childish and
fantastic babble, belonging to no form of real breathing life;
nowhere intelligible; not in *any* province; whilst, at the same
time, all provinces—Somersetshire, Devonshire, Hampshire
—are confounded with our midland counties; and positively
the diction of Parricombe and Charricombe from Exmoor
Forest is mixed up with the pure Icelandic forms of the
English lakes, of North Yorkshire, and of Northumberland.
In Scotland, it needs but a slight intercourse with the
peasantry to distinguish various dialects—the Aberdonian
and Fifeshire, for instance, how easily distinguished, even
by an English alien, from the western dialects of Ayrshire,
&c.! And I have heard it said, by Scottish purists in this
matter, that even Sir Walter Scott is chargeable with
considerable licentiousness in the management of his
colloquial Scotch. Yet, generally speaking, it bears the
strongest impress of truthfulness. But, on the other hand,
how false and powerless does this same Sir Walter become,
when the necessities of his tale oblige him at any time to
come amongst the English peasantry! His magic wand is
instantaneously broken; and he moves along by a babble of
impossible forms, as fantastic as any that our London
theatres have traditionally ascribed to English rustics, to
English sailors, and to Irishmen universally. Fielding is
open to the same stern criticism, as a deliberate falsehood-
monger; and from the same cause—want of energy to face
the difficulty of mastering a real living idiom. This defect in

language, however, I cite only as one feature in the complex falsehood which disfigures Fielding's portrait of the English country gentleman. Meantime the question arises, Did he mean his Squire Western for a *representative* portrait? Possibly not. He might design it expressly as a sketch of an individual, and by no means of a class. And the fault may be, after all, not in *him*, the writer, but in *us*, the falsely interpreting readers. But, be that as it may, and figure to ourselves as we may the rustic squire of a hundred to a hundred and fifty years back (though manifestly at utter war, in the portraitures of our novelists, with the realities handed down to us by our Parliamentary annals), on that *arena* we are dealing with objects of pure speculative curiosity. Far different is the same question, when practically treated for purposes of present legislation or philosophic inference. One hundred years ago, such was the difficulty of social intercourse, simply from the difficulty of locomotion (though even then this difficulty was much lowered to the English, as beyond comparison the most equestrian of nations), that it is possible to imagine a shade of difference as still distinguishing the town-bred man from the rustic; though, considering the multiplied distribution of our assize towns, our cathedral towns, our sea-ports, and our universities, all so many recurring centres of civility, it is not very easy to imagine such a thing in an island no larger than ours. But can any human indulgence be extended to the credulity which assumes the same possibility as existing for us in the very middle of the nineteenth century? At a time when every week sees the town banker drawn from our rural gentry; railway directors in every quarter transferring themselves indifferently from town to country, from country to town; lawyers, clergymen, medical men, magistrates, local judges, &c., all shifting in and out between town and country; rural families all intermarrying on terms of the widest freedom with town families; all again, in the persons of their children, meeting for study at the same schools, colleges, military academies, &c.; by what furious forgetfulness of the realities belonging to the case, has it been possible for writers in public journals to persist in arguing national questions upon the assumption of a bisection in our population—a double current, on the one side steeped to the lips in town prejudices, on the other side traditionally sold to rustic views and doctrines? Such double currents, like the Rhone flowing through the Lake of Geneva, and yet refusing to intermingle, probably *did* exist, and had an important significance in the Low Countries of the fifteenth century, or between the privileged cities and the unprivileged country of Germany down to the Thirty Years' War; but, for us, they are in the last degree fabulous distinctions, pure fairy tales; and the social economist or the historian who builds on such phantoms as that of a rustic aristocracy still retaining any substantial grounds of distinction from the town aristocracies, proclaims the hollowness of any and all his doctrines that depend upon such assumptions. Lord Carbery was a thorough fox-hunter. The fox-hunting of the adjacent county of Leicestershire was not then what it is now. The state of the land was radically different for the foot of the horse, the nature and distribution of the fences was different; so that a class of horses thoroughly different was then required. But then, as now, it offered the finest exhibition of the fox-chase that is known in Europe; and then, as now, this is the best adapted among all known varieties of hunting to the exhibition of adventurous and skilful riding, and generally, perhaps, to the development of manly and athletic qualities. Lord Carbery, during the season, might be immoderately addicted to this mode of sporting, having naturally a pleasurable feeling connected with his own reputation as a skilful and fearless horseman. But, though the chases were in those days longer than they are at present, small was the amount of time really abstracted from that which he had disposable for general purposes; amongst which purposes ranked foremost his literary pursuits. And, however much he transcended the prevailing conception of his order, as sketched by satiric and often ignorant novelists, he might be regarded, in all that concerned the liberalization of his views, as pretty fairly representing that order. Thus, through every *real* experience, the crazy notion of a rural aristocracy flowing apart from the urban aristocracy, and standing on a different level of culture as to intellect, of polish as to manners, and of interests as to social objects, a notion at all times false as a fact, now at length became with all thoughtful men monstrous as a possibility.

Meantime Lord Massey was reached by reports, both through Lady Carbery and myself, of something which interested him more profoundly than all earthly records of horsemanship, or any conceivable questions connected with books. Lady Carbery, with a view to the amusement of Lady Massey and my sister, for both of whom youth and previous seclusion had created a natural interest in all such scenes, accepted two or three times in every week dinner invitations to all the families on her visiting list, and lying within her winter circle, which was measured, by a radius of about seventeen miles. For, dreadful as were the roads in those days, when the Bath, the Bristol, or the Dover mail was equally perplexed oftentimes to accomplish Mr. Palmer's rate of seven miles an hour, a distance of seventeen was yet easily accomplished in one hundred minutes by the powerful Laxton horses. Magnificent was the Laxton turn-out; and in the roomy travelling coach of Lady Carbery, made large enough to receive upon occasion even a bed, it would have been an idle scruple to fear the crowding a party which mustered only three besides myself. For Lord Massey uniformly declined joining us; in which I believe

that he was right. A schoolboy like myself had fortunately
no dignity to lose. But Lord Massey, a needy Irish peer (or,
strictly speaking, since the Union no peer at all, though still
an hereditary lord), was bound to be trebly vigilant over his
surviving honors. This he owed to his country as well as to
his family. He recoiled from what he figured to himself (but
too often falsely figured) as the haughty and disdainful
English nobility—-all so rich, all so polished in manner, all
so punctiliously correct in the ritual of *bienséance*. Lord
Carbery might face them gayly and boldly: for *he* was rich,
and, although possessing Irish estates and an Irish
mansion, was a thorough Englishman by education and
early association. "But I," said Lord Massey, "had a careless
Irish education, and am never quite sure that I may not be
trespassing on some mysterious law of English good-
breeding." In vain I suggested to him that most of what
passed amongst foreigners and amongst Irishmen for
English *hauteur* was pure reserve, which, among all people
that were bound over by the inevitable restraints of their
rank (imposing, it must be remembered, jealous duties as
well as privileges), was sure to become the operative feeling.
I contended that in the English situation there was no
escaping this English reserve, except by great impudence
and defective sensibility; and that, if examined, reserve was
the truest expression of respect towards those who were its
objects. In vain did Lady Carbery back me in this
representation. He stood firm, and never once accompanied
us to any dinner-party. Northamptonshire, I know not
why, is (or then was) more thickly sown with aristocratic
families than any in the kingdom. Many elegant and pretty
women there naturally were in these parties; but
undoubtedly our two Laxton baronesses shone
advantageously amongst them. A boy like myself could lay
no restraint upon the after-dinner feelings of the gentlemen;
and almost uniformly I heard such verdicts passed upon the

personal attractions of both, but especially Lady Massey, as
tended greatly to soothe the feelings of Lord Massey. It is
singular that Lady Massey universally carried off the palm
of unlimited homage. Lady Carbery was a regular beauty,
and publicly known for such; both were fine figures, and
apparently not older than twenty-six; but in her Irish friend
people felt something more thoroughly artless and feminine
—for the masculine understanding of Lady Carbery in some
way communicated its commanding expression to her
deportment. I reported to Lord Massey, in terms of
unexceptionable decorum, those flattering expressions of
homage, which sometimes from the lips of young men,
partially under the influence of wine, had taken a form
somewhat too enthusiastic for a literal repetition to a
chivalrous and adoring husband.

Meantime, the reader has been kept long enough at Laxton
to warrant me in presuming some curiosity or interest to
have gathered within his mind about the mistress of the
mansion. Who was Lady Carbery? what was her present
position, and what had been her original position, in
society? All readers of Bishop Jeremy Taylor [Footnote: The
Life of Jeremy Taylor, by Reginald Heber, Bishop of Calcutta,
is most elaborately incorrect. From want of research, and a
chronology in some places thoroughly erroneous, various
important facts are utterly misstated; and what is most to be
regretted, in a matter deeply affecting the bishop's candor
and Christian charity, namely, a controversial
correspondence with a Somersetshire Dissenting clergyman,
the wildest misconception has vitiated the entire result. That
fractional and splintered condition, into which some person
had cut up the controversy with a view to his own more
convenient study of its chief elements, Heber had
misconceived as the actual form in which these parts had
been originally exchanged between the disputants—a

blunder of the worst consequence, and having the effect of translating general expressions (such as recorded a moral indignation against ancient fallacies or evasions connected with the dispute) into direct ebullitions of scorn or displeasure personally against his immediate antagonist. And the charge of intolerance and defective charity becomes thus very much stronger against the poor bishop, because it takes the shape of a confession extorted by mere force of truth from an else reluctant apologist, that would most gladly have denied everything that he *could* deny. The Life needs more than ever to be accurately written, since it has been thus chaotically mis-narrated by a prelate of so much undeniable talent. I once began a very elaborate life myself, and in these words: "Jeremy Taylor, the most eloquent and the subtlest of Christian philosophers, was the son of a barber, and the son-in-law of a king,"—alluding to the tradition (imperfectly verified, I believe) that he married an illegitimate daughter of Charles I. But this sketch was begun more than thirty years ago; and I retired from the labor as too overwhelmingly exacting in all that related to the philosophy and theology of that man so "myriad-minded," and of that century so anarchical.] must be aware of that religious Lady Carbery, who was the munificent (and, for her kindness, one might say the filial) patroness of the all-eloquent and subtle divine. She died before the Restoration, and, consequently, before her spiritual director could have ascended the Episcopal throne. The title of Carbery was at that time an earldom; the earl married again, and his second countess was also a devout patroness of Taylor. Having no peerage at hand, I do not know by what mode of derivation the modern title of the nineteenth century had descended from the old one of the seventeenth. I presume that some collateral branch of the original family had succeeded to the barony when the limitations of the original settlement had extinguished the earldom. But to me, who saw revived another religious Lady Carbery, distinguished for her beauty and accomplishments, it was interesting to read of the two successive ladies who had borne that title one hundred and sixty years before, and whom no reader of Jeremy Taylor is ever allowed to forget, since almost all his books are dedicated to one or other of the pious family that had protected him. Once more there was a religious Lady Carbery, supporting locally the Church of England, patronizing schools, diffusing the most extensive relief to every mode of indigence or distress. A century and a half ago such a Lady Carbery was in South Wales, at the "Golden Grove;" now such another Lady Carbery was in central England, at Laxton. The two cases, divided by six generations, interchanged a reciprocal interest, since in both cases it was young ladies, under the age of thirty, that originated the movement, and in both cases these ladies bore the same title; and I will therefore retrace rapidly the outline of that contemporary case so familiarly known to myself.

Colonel Watson and General Smith had been amongst the earliest friends of my mother's family. Both served for many years in India: the first in the Company's army, the other upon the staff of the king's forces in that country. Each, about the same time, made a visit to England, and each of them, I believe, with the same principal purpose of providing for the education of his daughter; for each happened to have one sole child, which child, in each case, was a girl of singular beauty; and both of these little ladies were entitled to very large fortunes. The colonel and the general, being on brotherly terms of intimacy, resolved to combine their plans for the welfare of their daughters. What they wanted was, not a lady that could teach them any special arts or accomplishments—all these could be purchased;—but the two qualifications indispensable for the difficult situation of lady-superintendent over two children so singularly separated from all relatives whatever, were, in the first place, knowledge of the world, and integrity for keeping at a distance all showy adventurers that might else offer themselves, with unusual advantages, as suitors for the favor of two great heiresses; and, secondly, manners exquisitely polished. Looking to that last requisition, it seems romantic to mention, that the lady selected for the post, with the fullest approbation of both officers, was one who began life as the daughter of a little Lincolnshire farmer. What her maiden name had been, I do not at this moment remember; but this name was of very little importance, being soon merged in that of Harvey, bestowed on her at the altar by a country gentleman. The squire—not very rich, I believe, but rich enough to rank as a matrimonial prize in the lottery of a country girl, whom one single step of descent in life might have brought within sight of menial service—had been captivated by the young woman's beauty; and this, at that period, when accompanied by the advantages of youth, must have been resplendent. I, who had known her all my life, down to my sixteenth year (during which year she died), and who naturally, therefore, referred her origin back to some remote ancestral generation, nevertheless, in her sole case, was made to feel that there might be some justification for the Church of England discountenancing in her Liturgy, "marriage with your great-grandmother; neither shalt thou marry thy great-grandfather's widow." She, poor thing! at that time was thinking little of marriage; for even then, though known only to herself and her *femme de chambre*, that dreadful organic malady (cancer) was raising its adder's crest, under which finally she died. But, in spite of languor interchanging continually with disfiguring anguish, she still impressed one as a regal beauty. Her person, indeed, and figure, *would* have tended towards such a standard; but all was counteracted, and thrown back into the mould of sweet natural womanhood, by the cherubic beauty of her features. These it was—these features, so purely childlike—that reconciled me in a moment of time to great-grandmotherhood. The stories about Ninon de l'Enclos are French fables—speaking plainly, are falsehoods; and sorry I am that a nation so amiable as the French should habitually disregard truth, when coming into collision with their love for the extravagant. But, if anything could reconcile me to these monstrous old fibs about Ninon at ninety, it would be the remembrance of this English enchantress on the high-road to seventy. Guess, reader, what she must have been at twenty-eight to thirty-two, when she became the widow of the Gerenian horseman, Harvey. How bewitching she must have looked in her widow's caps! So had once thought Colonel Watson, who happened to be in England at that period; and to the charming widow this man of war propounded his hand in marriage. This hand, this martial hand, for reason inexplicable to me, Mrs. Harvey declined;

and the colonel bounced off in a rage to Bengal. There were others who saw young Mrs. Harvey, as well as Colonel Watson. And amongst them was an ancient German gentleman, to what century belonging I do not know, who had every possible bad quality known to European experience, and a solitary good one, namely, eight hundred thousand pounds sterling. The man's name was Schreiber. Schreiber was an aggregate resulting from the conflux of all conceivable bad qualities. That was the elementary base of Schreiber; and the superstructure, or Corinthian decoration of his frontispiece, was, that Schreiber cultivated one sole science, namely, the science of taking snuff. Here were two separate objects for contemplation: one, bright as Aurora—that radiant Koh-i-noor, or mountain of light—the eight hundred thousand pounds; the other, sad, fuscous, begrimed with the snuff of ages, namely, the most ancient Schreiber. Ah! if they *could* have been divided—these twin yoke-fellows—and that ladies might have the privilege of choosing between them! For the moment there was no prudent course open to Mrs. Harvey, but that of marrying Schreiber (which she did, and survived); and, subsequently, when the state of the market became favorable to such "conversions" of stock, then the new Mrs. Schreiber parted from Schreiber, and disposed of her interest in Schreiber at a settled rate in three per cent. consols and terminable annuities; for every *coupon* of Schreiber receiving a *bonus* of so many thousand pounds, paid down according to the rate agreed on by the lawyers of the two parties; or, strictly speaking, *quarrelled on* between the adverse factions; for agreement it was hard to effect upon any point. The deadly fear which had been breathed into him by Mrs. Schreiber's scale of expenditure in a Park Lane house proved her most salutary ally. Coerced by this horrid vision, Schreiber consented (which else he never would have done) to grant her an allowance, for life, of about two thousand per annum. Could *that* be reckoned an anodyne for the torment connected with a course of Schreiber? I pretend to no opinion.

Such were the facts: and exactly at this point in her career had Mrs. Schreiber arrived, when, once more, Colonel Watson and General Smith were visiting England, and for the last time, on the errand of settling permanently some suitable establishment for their two infant daughters. The superintendence of this they desired to devolve upon some lady, qualified by her manners and her connections for introducing the young ladies, when old enough, into general society. Mrs. Schreiber was the very person required. Intellectually she had no great pretensions; but these she did not need: her character was irreproachable, her manners were polished, and her own income placed her far above all mercenary temptations. She had not thought fit to accept the station of Colonel Watson's wife, but some unavowed feeling prompted her to undertake, with enthusiasm, the duties of a mother to the colonel's daughter. Chiefly on Miss Watson's account it was at first that she extended her maternal cares to General Smith's daughter; but very soon so sweet and winning was the disposition of Miss Smith that Mrs. Schreiber apparently loved *her* the best.

Both, however, appeared under a combination of circumstances too singularly romantic to fail of creating an interest that was universal. Both were solitary children, unchallenged by any relatives. Neither had ever known what it was to taste of love, paternal or maternal. Their mothers had been long dead—not consciously seen by either; and their fathers, not surviving their last departure from home long enough to see them again, died before returning from India. What a world of desolation seemed to exist for them! How silent was every hall into which, by natural right, they should have had entrance! Several people, kind, cordial people, men and women, were scattered over England, that, during their days of infancy, would have delighted to receive them; but, by some fatality, when they reached their fifteenth year, and might have been deemed old enough to undertake visits, all of these paternal friends, except two, had died; nor had they, by that time, any relatives at all that remained alive, or were eligible as associates. Strange, indeed, was the contrast between the silent past of their lives and that populous future to which their large fortunes would probably introduce them. Throw open a door in the rear that should lay bare the long vista of chambers through which their childhood might symbolically be represented as having travelled—what silence! what solemn solitude! Open a door in advance that should do the same figurative office for the future— suddenly what a jubilation! what a tumult of festal greetings!

But the succeeding stages of life did not, perhaps, in either case fully correspond to the early promise. Rank and station the two young ladies attained; but rank and station do not always throw people upon prominent stages of action or display. Many a family, possessing both rank and wealth, and not undistinguished possibly by natural endowments of an order fitted for brilliant popularity, never emerge from obscurity, or not into any splendor that can be called national; sometimes, perhaps, from a temper unfitted for worthy struggles in the head of the house; possibly from a haughty, possibly a dignified disdain of popular arts, hatred of petty rhetoric, petty sycophantic courtships, petty canvassing tricks; or again, in many cases, because accidents of ill-luck have intercepted the fair proportion of success due to the merits of the person; whence, oftentimes, a hasty self- surrender to impulses of permanent disgust. But, more

frequently than any other cause, I fancy that impatience of
the long struggle required for any distinguished success
interferes to thin the ranks of competitors for the prizes of
public ambition. Perseverance is soon refrigerated in those
who fall back under any result, defeated or not defeated,
upon splendid mansions and luxuries of every kind, already
far beyond their needs or their wishes. The soldier described
by the Roman satirist as one who had lost his purse, was
likely enough, under the desperation of his misfortune, to
see nothing formidable in any obstacle that crossed his path
towards another supplementary purse; whilst the very same
obstacle might reasonably alarm one who, in retreating, fell
back under the battlements of twenty thousand per annum.
In the present case, there was nothing at all to move wonder
in the final result under so continual a siege of temptation
from the seductions of voluptuous ease; the only wonder is,
that one of the young ladies, namely, Miss Watson, whose
mind was masculine, and in some directions aspiring,
should so readily have acquiesced in a result which she
might have anticipated from the beginning.

Happy was the childhood, happy the early dawn of
womanhood, which these two young ladies passed under
the guardianship of Mrs. Schreiber. Education in those days
was not the austere old lady that she is now. At least, in the
case of young ladies, her exactions were merciful and
considerate. If Miss Smith sang pretty well, and Miss
Watson *very* well, and with the power of singing difficult
part music at sight, they did so for the same reason that the
lark sings, and chiefly under the same gentle tuition — that
of nature, glad almighty nature, breathing inspiration from
her Delphic tripod of happiness, and health, and hope. Mrs.
Schreiber pretended to no intellectual gifts whatever; and
yet, practically, she was wiser than many who have the
greatest. First of all other tasks which she imposed upon her

wards, was that of daily exercise, and exercise carried to *excess*. She insisted upon four hours' exercise daily; and, as young ladies walk fast, *that* would have yielded, at the rate of three and a half miles per hour, thirteen plus one third miles. But only two and a half hours were given to walking; the other one and a half to riding. No day was a day of rest; absolutely none. Days so stormy that they "kept the raven to her nest," snow the heaviest, winds the most frantic, were never listened to as any ground of reprieve from the ordinary exaction. I once knew (that is, not personally, for I never saw her, but through the reports of her many friends) an intrepid lady, [Footnote: If I remember rightly, some account is given of this palćstric lady and her stern Pćdo-gymnastics, in a clever book on household medicine and surgery under circumstances of inevitable seclusion from professional aid, written about the year 1820-22, by Mr. Haden, a surgeon of London.] living in the city of London (that is, technically the *city*, as opposed to Westminster, etc., Mary-le-bone, etc.), who made a point of turning out her newborn infants for a pretty long airing, even on the day of their birth. It made no difference to her whether the month were July or January; good, undeniable air is to be had in either month. Once only she was baffled, and most indignant it made her, because the little thing chose to be born at half-past nine P. M.; so that, by the time its toilet was finished, bonnet and cloak all properly adjusted, the watchman was calling "Past eleven, and a cloudy night;" upon which, most reluctantly, she was obliged to countermand the orders for that day's exercise, and considered herself, like the Emperor Titus, to have lost a day. But what came of the London lady's or of Mrs. Schreiber's Spartan discipline? Did the little blind kittens of Gracechurch-street, who were ordered by their penthesiléan mamma, on the very day of their nativity, to face the most cruel winds—did *they*, or did Mrs. Schreiber's wards, justify,

in after life, this fierce discipline, by commensurate results of
hardiness? In words written beyond all doubt by
Shakspeare, though not generally recognized as his, it
might have been said to any one of this Amazonian brood,
— "Now mild may be thy life; For a more blust'rous birth
had never babe. Quiet and gentle be thy temperature; For
thou'rt the rudeliest welcomed to this world That e'er was
woman's child. Happy be the sequel! Thou hast as chiding a
nativity As fire, air, water, earth, and heaven, can make, To
herald thee from darkness!"—*Pericles, Act III.*

As to the city kittens, I heard that the treatment prospered;
but the man who reported this added, that by original
constitution they were as strong as Meux's dray-horses; and
thus, after all, they may simply illustrate the old logical
dictum ascribed to some medical man, that the reason why
London children of the wealthier classes are noticeable even
to a proverb for their robustness and bloom, is because
none but those who are already vigorous to excess, and
who start with advantages of health far beyond the average
scale, have much chance of surviving that most searching
quarantine, which, in such [Footnote: For myself,
meantime, I am far from assenting to all the romantic abuse
applied to the sewerage and the church-yards of London,
and even more violently to the river Thames. As a tidal
river, even: beyond the metropolitan bridges, the Thames
undoubtedly does much towards cleansing the atmosphere,
whatever may be the condition of its waters. And one most
erroneous postulate there is from which the *Times* starts in
all its arguments, namely, this, that supposing the Thames
to be even a vast sewer, in short, the *cloaca maxima* of
London, there is in that arrangement of things any special
reproach applying to our mighty English capital. On the
contrary, *all* great cities that ever were founded have sought
out, as their first and elementary condition, the adjacency of

some great cleansing river. In the long process of development through which cities pass, commerce and other functions of civilization come to usurp upon the earlier functions of such rivers, and sometimes (through increasing efforts of luxurious refinement) may come entirely to absorb them. But, in the infancy of every great city, the chief function for which she looks to her river is that of purification. Be thou my huge *cloaca*, says infant Babylon to the Euphrates, says infant Nineveh to the Tigris, says infant Rome to the Tiber. So far is that reproach from having any special application to London. Smoke is not unwholesome; in many circumstances it is salubrious, as a counter-agent to worse influences. Even sewerage is chiefly insalubrious from its moisture, and not, in any degree yet demonstrated, from its odor.] an atmosphere, they are summoned to weather at starting. Coming, however, to the special case of Mrs. Schreiber's household, I am bound to report that in no instance have I known young ladies so thoroughly steeled against all the ordinary host of petty maladies which, by way of antithesis to the capital warfare of dangerous complaints, might be called the *guerilla* nosology; influenza, for instance, in milder forms, catarrh, headache, toothache, dyspepsia in transitory shapes, etc. Always the spirits of the two girls were exuberant; the enjoyment of life seemed to be intense, and never did I know either of them to suffer from *ennui*. My conscious knowledge of them commenced when I was about two years old, they being from ten to twelve years older. Mrs. Schreiber had been amongst my mother's earliest friends as Mrs. Harvey, and in days when my mother had opportunities of doing her seasonable services. And as there were three special advantages which adorned my mother, and which ranked in Mrs. Schreiber's estimate as the highest which earth could show, namely: 1°, that she spoke and wrote English with singular elegance; 2°, that her manners were eminently polished; and 3°, that, even in

that early stage of my mother's life, a certain tone of
religiosity, and even of ascetic devotion, was already diffused
as a luminous mist that served to exalt the coloring of her
morality. To this extent Mrs. Schreiber approved of religion;
but nothing of a sectarian cast could she have tolerated; nor
had she anything of that nature to apprehend from my
mother. Viewing my mother, therefore, as a pure model of
an English matron, and feeling for her, besides, a deeper
sentiment of friendship and affection than for anybody else
on her visiting list, it was natural enough that she should
come with her wards on an annual visit to "The Farm" (a
pretty, rustic dwelling occupied by my father in the
neighborhood of Manchester), and subsequently (when *that*
arose) to Greenhay. [Footnote: *"Greenhay."*—As this name
might, under a false interpretation, seem absurd as
including incongruous elements, I ought, in justification of
my mother, who devised the name, to have mentioned that
hay was meant for the old English word (derived from the
old French word *haie*) indicating a rural enclosure.
Conventionally, a *hay* or *haie* was understood to mean a
country-house within a verdant ring-fence, narrower than
a park: which word park, in Scotch use, means any
enclosure whatever, though not twelve feet square; but in
English use (witness Captain Burt's wager about Culloden
parks) means an enclosure measured by square miles, and
usually accounted to want its appropriate furniture, unless
tenanted by deer. By the way, it is a singular illustration of a
fact illustrated in one way or other every hour, namely, of
the imperfect knowledge which England possesses of
England, that, within these last eight or nine months, I saw
in the *Illustrated London News* an article assuming that the
red deer was unknown in England. Whereas, if the writer
had ever been at the English lakes during the hunting
season, he might have seen it actually hunted over
Martindale forest and its purlieus. Or, again, in Devonshire

and Cornwall, over Dartmoor, etc., and, I believe, in many other regions, though naturally narrowing as civilization widens. The writer is equally wrong in supposing the prevailing deer of our parks to be the *roe* deer, which are very little known. It is the *fallow* deer that chiefly people our parks. Red deer were also found at Blenheim, in Oxfordshire, when it was visited by Dr. Johnson, as may be seen in "Boswell."] As my father always retained a town-house in Manchester (somewhere in Fountain-street), and, though a plain, unpretending man, was literary to the extent of having written a book, all things were so arranged that there was no possibility of any commercial mementos ever penetrating to the rural retreat of his family; such mementos, I mean, as, by reviving painful recollections of that ancient Schreiber, who was or ought to be by this time extinct, would naturally be odious and distressing. Here, therefore, liberated from all jealousy of overlooking eyes, such as haunted persons of their expectations at Brighton, Weymouth, Sidmouth, or Bath, Miss Smith and Miss Watson used to surrender themselves without restraint to their glad animal impulses of girlish gayety, like the fawns of antelopes when suddenly transferred from tiger-haunted thickets to the serene preserves of secluded rajahs. On these visits it was, that I, as a young pet whom they carried about like a doll from my second to my eighth or ninth year, learned to know them; so as to take a fraternal interest in the succeeding periods of their lives. Their fathers I certainly had not seen; nor had they, consciously. These two fathers must both have died in India, before my inquiries had begun to travel in that direction. But, as old acquaintances of my mother's, both had visited The Farm before I was born; and about General Smith, in particular, there had survived amongst the servants a remembrance which seemed to us (that is to them and to myself) ludicrously awful, though, at that time, the practice was common throughout our Indian possessions. He had a Hindoo servant with him; and this servant every night stretched himself along the "sill" or outer threshold of the door; so that he might have been trodden on by the general when retiring to rest; and from this it was but a moderate step in advance to say that he *was* trodden on. Upon which basis many other wonders were naturally reared. Miss Smith's father, therefore, furnished matter for a not very amiable tradition; but Miss Smith herself was the sweetest-tempered and the loveliest of girls, and the most thoroughly English in the style of her beauty. Far different every way was Miss Watson. In person she was a finished beauty of the very highest pretensions, and generally recognized as such; that is to say, her figure was fine and queenly; her features were exquisitely cut, as regarded their forms and the correspondences of their parts; and usually by artists her face was said to be Grecian. Perhaps the nostrils, mouth, and forehead, might be so; but nothing could be less Grecian, or more eccentric in form and position, than the eyes. They were placed obliquely, in a way that I do not remember to have seen repeated in any other face whatever. Large they were, and particularly long, tending to an almond-shape; equally strange, in fact, as to color, shape, and position: but the remarkable position of these eyes would have absorbed your gaze to the obliteration of all other features or peculiarities in the face, were it not for one other even more remarkable distinction affecting her complexion: this lay in a suffusion that mantled upon her cheeks, of a color amounting almost to carmine. Perhaps it might be no more than what Pindar meant by the *porphyreon phos erotos,* which Gray has falsely [Footnote: Falsely, because poxphuxeos rarely, perhaps, means in the Greek use what we mean properly by *purple,* and *could* not mean it in the Pindaric passage; much oftener it denotes some shade of *crimson,* or else of *puniceus,* or blood-red. Gibbon was never

57

more mistaken than when he argued that all the endless disputing about the *purpureus* of the ancients might have been evaded by attending to its Greek designation, namely, *porphyry*-colored: since, said he, porphyry is always of the same color. Not at all. Porphyry, I have heard, runs through as large a gamut of hues as marble; but, if this should be an exaggeration, at all events porphyry is far from being so monochromatic as Gibbon's argument would presume. The truth is, colors were as loosely and latitudinarially distinguished by the Greeks and Romans as degrees of affinity and consanguinity are everywhere. *My son-in-law*, says a woman, and she means *my stepson*. *My cousin*, she says, and she means any mode of relationship in the wide, wide world. *Nos neveux*, says a French writer, and means not *our nephews*, but *our grandchildren*, or more generally *our descendants*.] translated as "the bloom of young desire, and PURPLE light of love." It was not unpleasing, and gave a lustre to the eyes, but it added to the eccentricity of the face; and by all strangers it was presumed to be an artificial color, resulting from some mode of applying a preparation more brilliant than rouge. But to us children, so constantly admitted to her toilet, it was well known to be entirely natural. Generally speaking, it is not likely to assist the effect of a young woman's charms, that she presents any such variety in her style of countenance as could naturally be called *odd*. But Miss Watson, by the somewhat scenical effect resulting from the harmony between her fine figure and her fine countenance, triumphed over all that might else have been thought a blemish; and when she was presented at court on occasion of her marriage, the king himself pronounced her, to friends of Mrs. Schreiber, the most splendid of all the brides that had yet given lustre to his reign. In such cases the judgments of rustic, undisciplined tastes, though marked by narrowness, and often by

involuntary obedience to vulgar ideals (which, for instance,
makes them insensible to all the deep sanctities of beauty
that sleep amongst the Italian varieties of the Madonna face),
is not without its appropriate truth. Servants and rustics all
thrilled in sympathy with the sweet English loveliness of
Miss Smith; but all alike acknowledged, with spontaneous
looks of homage, the fine presence and finished beauty of
Miss Watson. Naturally, from the splendor with which they
were surrounded, and the notoriety of their great
expectations,—so much to dazzle in one direction, and, on
the other hand, something for as tender a sentiment as pity,
in the fact of both from so early an age having been united
in the calamity of orphanage,—go where they might, these
young women drew all eyes upon themselves; and from the
audible comparisons sometimes made between them, it might
be imagined that if ever there were a situation fitted to
nourish rivalship and jealousy, between two girls, here it
might be anticipated in daily operation. But, left to
themselves, the yearnings of the female heart tend naturally
towards what is noble; and, unless where it has been tried
too heavily by artificial incitements applied to the pride, I do
not believe that women generally are disposed to any
unfriendly jealousy of each other. Why should they? Almost
every woman, when strengthened in those charms which
nature has given to her by such as she can in many ways
give to herself, must feel that she has her own separate
domain of empire unaffected by the most sovereign beauty
upon earth. Every man that ever existed has probably his
own peculiar talent (if only it were detected), in which he
would be found to excel all the rest of his race. And in every
female face possessing any attractions at all, no matter what
may be her general inferiority, there lurks some secret
peculiarity of expression—some mesmeric individuality—
which is valid within its narrower range—limited
superiority over the supreme of beauties within a narrow

circle. It is unintelligibly but mesmerically potent, this secret fascination attached to features oftentimes that are absolutely plain; and as one of many cases within my own range of positive experience, I remember in confirmation, at this moment, that in a clergyman's family, counting three daughters, all on a visit to my mother, the youngest, Miss F — — P— —, who was strikingly and memorably plain, never walked out on the Clifton Downs unattended, but she was followed home by a crowd of admiring men, anxious to learn her rank and abode; whilst the middle sister, eminently handsome, levied no such *visible* tribute of admiration on the public.

I mention this fact, one of a thousand similar facts, simply by way of reminding the reader of what he must himself have often witnessed; namely, that no woman is condemned by nature to any ignoble necessity of repining against the power of other women; her own may be far more confined, but within its own circle may possibly, measured against that of the haughtiest beauty, be the profounder. However, waiving the question thus generally put here, and as it specially affected these two young women that virtually were sisters, any question of precedency in power or display, when brought into collision with sisterly affection, had not a momentary existence. Each had soon redundant proofs of her own power to attract suitors without end; and, for the more or the less, *that* was felt to be a matter of accident. Never, on this earth, I am satisfied, did that pure sisterly love breathe a more steady inspiration than now into the hearts and through the acts of these two generous girls; neither was there any sacrifice which either would have refused *to* or *for* the other. The period, however, was now rapidly shortening during which they would have any opportunity for testifying this reciprocal love. Suitors were flocking around them, as rank as cormorants in a storm.

The grim old chancellor (one, if not both, of the young
ladies having been a ward in Chancery) had all his legal
jealousies awakened on their behalf. The worshipful order of
adventurers and *fortune-hunters*, at that time chiefly imported
from Ireland, as in times more recent from Germany, and
other moustachoed parts of the continent, could not live
under the raking fire of Mrs. Schreiber, on the one side,
with her female tact and her knowledge of life, and of the
chancellor, with his huge discretional power, on the other.
That particular chancellor, whom the chronology of the case
brought chiefly into connection with Miss Watson's
interests, was (if my childish remembrances do not greatly
mislead me) the iracund Lord Thurlow. Lovers and wooers
this grim lawyer regarded as the most impertinent order of
animals in universal zoology; and of these, in Miss Watson's
case, he had a whole menagerie to tend. Penelope, according
to some school-boy remembrance of mine, had one hundred
and eighteen suitors. These young ladies had almost as
many. Heavens! what a crew of Comus to follow or to lead!
And what a suitable person was this truculent old lord on
the woolsack to enact the part of shepherd—Corydon,
suppose, or Alphesibćus—to this goodly set of lambs! How
he must have admired the hero of the "Odyssey," who in one
way or other accounted for all the wooers that "sorned"
upon his house, and had a receipt for their bodies from the
grave-digger of Ithaca! But even this wily descendant of
Sisyphus would have found it no such easy matter to deal
with the English suitors, who were not the feeble
voluptuaries of the Ionian Islands, that suffered themselves
to be butchered as unresistingly as sheep in the shambles—
actually standing at one end of a banqueting-room to be
shot at with bows and arrows, not having pluck enough to
make a rush—but were *game* men; all young, strong, rich,
and in most cases technically "noble;" all, besides,
contending for one or other of two prizes a thousand times

better fitted to inspire romantic ardor than the poor, withered Penelope. One, by the way, amongst these suitors (I speak of those who addressed Miss Watson), merits a separate commemoration, as having drawn from Sheridan his very happiest *impromptu*—and an *impromptu* that was really such—(the rarest of all things from Sheridan). This was Lord Belgrave, eldest son of Lord Grosvenorthen an earl, but at some period, long subsequent to this, raised to the Marquisate of Westminster, a title naturally suggesting in itself a connection with the vast Grosvenor property, sweeping across the whole area of that most aristocratic region in the metropolis now called *Belgravia*, which was then a name unknown; and this Hesperian region had as yet no architectural value, and consequently no ground-rent value, simply because the world of fashion and distinction had as yet not expanded itself in that direction. In those days the territorial importance of this great house rested exclusively upon its connection with the county of Chester. In this connection it was that the young Viscount Belgrave had been introduced, by his family interest, into the House of Commons; he had delivered his maiden speech with some effect; and had been heard favorably on various subsequent occasions; on one of which it was that, to the extreme surprise of the house, he terminated his speech with a passage from Demosthenes—not presented in English, but in sounding Attic Greek. Latin is a privileged dialect in parliament. But Greek! It would not have been at all more startling to the usages of the house, had his lordship quoted Persic or Telinga. Still, though felt as something verging on the ridiculous, there was an indulgent feeling to a young man fresh from academic bowers, which would not have protected a mature man of the world. Everybody bit his lips, and as yet did *not* laugh. But the final issue stood on the edge of a razor. A gas, an inflammable atmosphere, was trembling sympathetically through the whole excited audience; all depended on a match being applied to this gas whilst yet in the very act of escaping. Deepest silence still prevailed; and, had any commonplace member risen to address the house in an ordinary business key, all would have blown over. Unhappily for Lord Belgrave, in that critical moment up rose the one solitary man, to wit, Sheridan, whose look, whose voice, whose traditional character, formed a prologue to what was coming. Here let the reader understand that, throughout the "Iliad," all speeches or commands, questions or answers, are introduced by Homer under some peculiar formula. For instance, replies are usually introduced thus:

"But him answering thus addressed the sovereign Agamemnon;"

or; in sonorous Greek:

"Ton d' apameibomenos prosephé kreion Agamemnon;"

or, again, according to the circumstances:

  "But him sternly surveying saluted the swift-footed Achilles;"
  "Ton d'ar', upodra idon, prosephé podas okus Achilleus."

This being premised, and that every one of the audience, though pretending to no Greek, yet, from his school-boy remembrances, was as well acquainted with these *formulé* as with the scriptural formula of *Verily, verily, I say unto you, &c.,* Sheridan, without needing to break its force by explanations, solemnly opened thus:

"Ton d' apameibomenos prosephé Sheridanios heros."_

Simply to have commenced his answer in Greek would have
sufficiently met the comic expectation then thrilling the
house; but, when it happened that this Greek (so suitable to
the occasion) was also the one sole morsel of Greek that
everybody in that assembly understood, the effect, as may be
supposed, was overwhelming, and wrapt the whole house
in what might be called a fiery explosion of laughter.
Meantime, as prizes in the matrimonial lottery, and prizes in
all senses, both young ladies were soon carried off. Miss
Smith, whose expectations I never happened to hear
estimated, married a great West India proprietor; and Miss
Watson, who (according to the popular report) would
succeed to six thousand a year on her twenty-first birthday,
married Lord Carbery. Miss Watson inherited also from her
father something which would not generally be rated very
highly, namely, a chancery lawsuit, with the East India
Company for defendant. However, if the company is a
potent antagonist, thus far it is an eligible one, that, in the
event of losing the suit, the honorable company is solvent;
and such an event, after some nine or ten years' delay, did
really befall the company. The question at issue respected
some docks which Colonel Watson had built for the
company in some Indian port. And in the end this lawsuit,
though so many years doubtful in its issue, proved very
valuable to Miss Watson; I have heard (but cannot vouch
for it) not less valuable than that large part of her property
which had been paid over without demur upon her twenty-
first birth-day. Both young ladies married happily; but in
marriage they found their separation, and in that separation
a shock to their daily comfort which was never replaced to
either. As to Miss Smith's husband, I did not know him; but
Lord Carbery was every way an estimable man; in some
things worthy of admiration; and his wife never ceased to

esteem and admire him. But she yearned for the society of her early friend; and this being placed out of her reach by the accidents of life, she fell early into a sort of disgust with her own advantages of wealth and station, which, promising so much, were found able to perform nothing at all in this first and last desire of her heart. A portrait of her friend hung in the drawing-room; but Lady Carbery did not willingly answer the questions that were sometimes prompted by its extraordinary loveliness. There are women to whom a female friendship is indispensable, and cannot be supplied by any companion of the other sex. That blessing, therefore, of her golden youth, turned eventually into a curse for her after-life; for I believe that, through one accident or another, they never met again after they became married women. To me, as one of those who had known and loved Miss Smith, Lady Carbery always turned the more sunny side of her nature; but to the world generally she presented a chilling and somewhat severe aspect—as to a vast illusion that rested upon pillars of mockery and frauds. Honors, beauty of the first order, wealth, and the power which follows wealth as its shadow—what could these do? what *had* they done? In proportion as they had settled heavily upon herself, she had found them to entail a load of responsibility; and those claims upon her she had labored to fulfil conscientiously; but else they had only precipitated the rupture of such ties as had given sweetness to her life.

From the first, therefore, I had been aware, on this visit to Laxton, that Lady Carbery had changed, and was changing. She had become religious; so much I knew from my sister's letters. And, in fact, this change had been due to her intercourse with my mother. But, in reality, her premature disgust with the world would, at any rate, have made her such; and, had any mode of monastic life existed for Protestants, I believe that she would before this have

entered it, supposing Lord Carbery to have consented.
People generally would have stated the case most
erroneously; they would have said that she was sinking
into gloom under religious influences; whereas the very
contrary was the truth; namely, that, having sunk into
gloomy discontent with life, and its miserable performances
as contrasted with its promises, she sought relief and
support to her wounded feelings from religion.

But the change brought with it a difficult trial to myself.
She recoiled, by natural temperament and by refinement of
taste, from all modes of religious enthusiasm. Enthusiasm is
a large word, and in many cases I could not go along with
her; but *canting* of all descriptions was odious to both of us
alike. To cultivate religious knowledge in an intellectual way,
she very well understood that she must study divinity. And
she relied upon me for assisting her. Not that she made the
mistake of ascribing to me any knowledge on that subject;
but I could learn; and, whatsoever I *had* learned, she knew,
by experience, that I could make abundantly plain to her
understanding. Wherever I did *not* understand, I was far too
sincere to dissemble that fact. Where I *did* understand, I
could enable *her* to understand.

On the subject of theology, it was not easy indeed for
anybody, man or boy, to be more ignorant than myself. My
studies in that field had been none at all. Nor was this any
subject for wonder, or (considering my age) for blame. In
reality, to make theology into a captivating study for the
young, it must be translated into controversial theology.
And in what way could such a polemic interest be evoked
except through political partisanship? But such partisanship
connects itself naturally with the irritability of sectarianism,
and but little with the majestic repose of a church such as
the Romish or the Anglican, founded upon the broad basis

of national majorities, and sheltered from danger, or the sense of danger, by state protection. Dissenters stand upon another footing. The Dissenter from the national church, whether in England or in France, is reminded by his own distinguishing religious opinions of the historic struggles through which those opinions have travelled. The doctrines which give to his own sect a peculiar denomination are also those which record its honorable political conflicts; so that his own connection, through his religious brotherhood, with the civil history of his country, furnishes a standing motive of pride for some acquaintance more or less with divinity; since it is by deviating painfully, conscientiously, and at some periods dangerously, from the established divinity, that his fathers have achieved their station in the great drama of the national evolution.

But, whilst I was ignorant of theology, as a direct and separate branch of study, the points are so many at which theology inosculates with philosophy, and with endless casual and random suggestions of the self-prompted reason, that inevitably from that same moment in which I began to find a motive for directing my thoughts to this new subject, I wanted not something to say that might have perplexed an antagonist, or (in default of such a vicious associate) that might have amused a friend, more especially a friend so predisposed to a high estimate of myself as Lady Carbery. Sometimes I did more than amuse her; I startled her, and I even startled myself, with distinctions that to this hour strike me as profoundly just, and as undeniably novel. Two out of many I will here repeat; and with the more confidence, that in these two I can be sure of repeating the exact thoughts; whereas, in very many other cases, it would not be so certain that they might not have been insensibly modified by cross-lights or disturbing shadows from intervening speculations.

1. Lady Carbery one day told me that she could not see any reasonable ground for what is said of Christ, and elsewhere of John the Baptist, that he opened his mission by preaching "repentance." Why "repentance"? Why then, more than at any other time? Her reason for addressing this remark to me was, that she fancied there might be some error in the translation of the Greek expression. I replied that, in my opinion, there was; and that I had myself always been irritated by the entire irrelevance of the English word, and by something very like cant, on which the whole burden of the passage is thrown. How was it any natural preparation for a vast spiritual revolution, that men should first of all acknowledge any special duty of repentance? The repentance, if any movement of that nature could intelligibly be supposed called for, should more naturally *follow* this great revolution—which, as yet, both in its principle and in its purpose, was altogether mysterious— than herald it, or ground it. In my opinion, the Greek word *metanoia* concealed a most profound meaning—a meaning of prodigious compass—which bore no allusion to any ideas whatever of repentance. The *meta* carried with it an emphatic expression of its original idea—the idea of transfer, of translation, of transformation; or, if we prefer a Grecian to a Roman apparelling, the idea of a *metamorphosis*. And this idea, to what is it applied? Upon what object is this idea of spiritual transfiguration made to bear? Simply upon the *noetic* or intellectual faculty—the faculty of shaping and conceiving things under their true relations. The holy herald of Christ, and Christ himself the finisher of prophecy, made proclamation alike of the same mysterious summons, as a baptism or rite of initiation; namely, *Metanoei*. Henceforth transfigure your theory of moral truth; the old theory is laid aside as infinitely insufficient; a new and spiritual revelation is established. *Metanoeite*—contemplate moral truth as radiating from a new centre; apprehend it

under transfigured relations.

John the Baptist, like other earlier prophets, delivered a message which, probably enough, he did not himself more than dimly understand, and never in its full compass of meaning. Christ occupied another station. Not only was he the original Interpreter, but he was himself the Author — Founder, at once, and Finisher — of that great transfiguration applied to ethics, which he and the Baptist alike announced as forming the code for the new and revolutionary era now opening its endless career. The human race was summoned to bring a transfiguring sense and spirit of interpretation (*metanoia*) to a transfigured ethics —an altered organ to an altered object. This is by far the grandest miracle recorded in Scripture. No exhibition of blank power — not the arresting of the earth's motion — not the calling back of the dead unto life, can approach in grandeur to this miracle which we all daily behold; namely, the inconceivable mystery of having written and sculptured upon the tablets of man's heart a new code of moral distinctions, all modifying — many reversing — the old ones. What would have been thought of any prophet, if he should have promised to transfigure the celestial mechanics; if he had said, I will create a new pole-star, a new zodiac, and new laws of gravitation; briefly, I will make new earth and new heavens? And yet a thousand times more awful it was to undertake the writing of new laws upon the spiritual conscience of man. *Metanoeite* (was the cry from the wilderness), wheel into a new centre your moral system; *geocentric* has that system been up to this hour — that is, having earth and the earthly for its starting-point; henceforward make it *heliocentric* (that is, with the sun, or the heavenly for its principle of motion).

2. A second remark of mine was, perhaps, not more

important, but it was, on the whole, better calculated to startle the prevailing preconceptions; for, as to the new system of morals introduced by Christ, generally speaking, it is too dimly apprehended in its great differential features to allow of its miraculous character being adequately appreciated; one flagrant illustration of which is furnished by our experience in Affghanistan, where some officers, wishing to impress Akhbar Khan with the beauty of Christianity, very judiciously repeated to him the Lord's Prayer and the Sermon on the Mount, by both of which the Khan was profoundly affected, and often recurred to them; but others, under the notion of conveying to him a more *comprehensive* view of the Scriptural ethics, repeated to him the Ten Commandments; although, with the sole exception of the two first, forbidding idolatry and Polytheism, there is no word in these which could have displeased or surprised a Pagan, and therefore nothing characteristic of Christianity. Meantime my second remark was substantially this which follows: What is a religion? To Christians it means, over and above a mode of worship, a dogmatic (that is, a doctrinal) system; a great body of doctrinal truths, moral and spiritual. But to the ancients (to the Greeks and Romans, for instance), it meant nothing of the kind. A religion was simply a *cultus*, a *thrćskeia*, a mode of ritual worship, in which there might be two differences, namely: 1. As to the particular deity who furnished the motive to the worship; 2. As to the ceremonial, or mode of conducting the worship. But in no case was there so much as a pretence of communicating any religious truths, far less any moral truths. The obstinate error rooted in modern minds is, that, doubtless, the moral instruction was bad, as being heathen; but that still it was as good as heathen opportunities allowed it to be. No mistake can be greater. Moral instruction had no existence even in the plan or intention of the religious service. The Pagan priest or flamen never

dreamed of any function like that of *teaching* as in any way
connected with his office. He no more undertook to teach
morals than to teach geography or cookery. He taught
nothing. What he undertook was, simply to *do*: namely, to
present authoritatively (that is, authorized and supported
by some civil community, Corinth, or Athens, or Rome,
which he represented) the homage and gratitude of that
community to the particular deity adored. As to morals or
just opinions upon the relations to man of the several
divinities, all this was resigned to the teaching of nature;
and for any polemic functions the teaching was resigned to
the professional philosophers—academic, peripatetic, stoic,
etc. By religion it was utterly ignored.

The reader must do me the favor to fix his attention upon
the real question at issue. What I say—what then I said to
Lady Carbery—is this: that, by failing to notice as a
differential feature of Christianity this involution of a
doctrinal part, we elevate Paganism to a dignity which it
never dreamed of. Thus, for instance, in the Eleusinian
mysteries, what was the main business transacted? I, for my
part, in harmony with my universal theory on this subject,
—namely, that there could be no doctrinal truth delivered in
a Pagan religion,—have always maintained that the only
end and purpose of the mysteries was a more solemn and
impressive worship of a particular goddess. Warburton, on
the other hand, would insist upon it that some great
affirmative doctrines, interesting to man, such as the
immortality of the soul, a futurity of retribution, &c., might
be here commemorated. And now, nearly a hundred years
after Warburton, what is the opinion of scholars upon this
point? Two of the latest and profoundest I will cite:—1.
Lobeck, in his "Aglaophamus," expressly repels all such
notions; 2. Otfried Mueller, in the twelfth chapter, twenty-
fourth section, of his "Introduction to a System of

Mythology," says: "I have here gone on the assumption which I consider unavoidable, that there was no regular instruction, no dogmatical communication, connected with the Grecian worship in general. *There could be nothing* of the kind introduced into the public service from the way in which it was conducted, for the priest *did not address the people at all.*" These opinions, which exactly tallied with my own assertion to Lady Carbery, that all religion amongst the Pagans resolved itself into a mere system of ceremonial worship, a pompous and elaborate *cultus*, were not brought forward in Germany until about ten or twelve years ago; whereas, my doctrine was expressly insisted on in 1800; that is, forty years earlier than any of these German writers had turned their thoughts in that direction.

Had I, then, really all that originality on this subject which for many years I secretly claimed? Substantially I had, because this great distinction between the modern (or Christian) idea of "a religion" and the ancient (or Pagan) idea of "a religion," I had nowhere openly seen expressed in words. To myself exclusively I was indebted for it. Nevertheless, it is undeniable that this conception must have been long ago germinating in the world, and perhaps bearing fruit. This is past all denial, since, about thirteen or fourteen years ago, I read in some journal (a French journal, I think) this statement: namely, that some oriental people— Turks, according to my present impression, but it might have been Arabs—make an old traditional distinction (so said the French journal) between what they call "religions of the book" and all other religions. The religions of the book, according to them, are three, all equally founded upon written and producible documents, namely: first, the Judaic system, resting upon the Pentateuch, or more truly, I should imagine, upon the Law and the Prophets; secondly, the Christian system, resting upon the Old and New

Testaments; thirdly, the Mahometan system, resting confessedly upon the Koran. The very meaning, therefore, of styling these systems, by way of honorable distinction, *religions of the book*, is, not that accidentally they had written vouchers for their creed, whereas the others had only oral vouchers, but that they severally offer to men's acceptance a large body of philosophic truth, such as requires and presupposes a book. Whereas the various religions contradistinguished from these three—namely, the whole body of Pagan idolatries—are mere forms of adoration addressed to many different divinities; and the brief reason why they are essentially opposed to religions of the book is, not that they *have* not, but logically that they *cannot* have, books or documents, inasmuch as they have no truths to deliver. They do not profess to teach anything whatsoever. What they profess, as their justifying distinction, is, to adore a certain deity, or a certain collective Pantheon, according to certain old authorized forms—authorized, that is to say, by fixed, ancient, and oftentimes local traditions.

What was the great practical inference from the new distinction which I offered? It was this: that Christianity (which included Judaism as its own germinal principle, and Islamism as its own adaptation to a barbarous and imperfect civilization) carried along with itself its own authentication; since, whilst other religions introduced men simply to ceremonies and usages, which could furnish no aliment or material for their intellect, Christianity provided an eternal *paléstra* or place of exercise for the human understanding vitalized by human affections: for every problem whatever, interesting to the human intellect, provided only that it bears a *moral* aspect, immediately passes into the field of religious speculation. Religion had thus become the great organ of human culture. Lady Carbery advanced half-way to meet me in these new views, finding my credentials as a

theologian in my earnestness and my sincerity. She herself
was painfully and sorrowfully in earnest. She had come at
this early age of seven or eight and twenty, to the most
bitter sense of hollowness, and (in a philosophic sense) of
treachery as under-lying all things that stood round her; and
she sought escape, if escape there were, through religion.
Religion was to be sought in the Bible. But was the Bible
intelligible at the first glance? Far from it. Search the
Scriptures, was the cry in Protestant lands amongst all
people, however much at war with each other. But I often
told her that this was a vain pretence, without some
knowledge of Greek. Or perhaps not always and absolutely
a pretence; because, undoubtedly, it is true that oftentimes
mere ignorant simplicity may, by bringing into direct
collision passages that are reciprocally illustrative, restrain
an error or illuminate a truth. And a reason, which I have
since given in print (a reason additional to Bentley's), for
neglecting the thirty thousand various readings collected by
the diligence of the New Testament collators, applied also to
this case, namely: That, first, the transcendent nature, and,
secondly, the *recurrent* nature, of Scriptural truths cause them
to surmount verbal disturbances. A doctrine, for instance,
which is sowed broadcast over the Scriptures, and recurs,
on an average, three times in every chapter, cannot be
affected by the casual inaccuracy of a phrase, since the
phrase is continually varied. And, therefore, I would not
deny the possibility of an effectual searching by very
unlearned persons. Our authorized translators of the Bible
in the Shakspearian age were not in any exquisite sense
learned men; they were very able men, and in a better sense
able than if they had been philologically profound scholars,
which at that time, from the imperfect culture of philology,
they could not easily have been; men they were whom
religious feeling guided correctly in choosing their
expressions, and with whom the state of the language in

some respects cooperated, by furnishing a diction more homely, fervent, and pathetic, than would now be available. For their apostolic functions English was the language most in demand. But in polemic or controversial cases Greek is indispensable. And of this Lady Carbery was sufficiently convinced by my own demur on the word *metanoia*. If I were right, how profoundly wrong must those have been whom my new explanation superseded. She resolved, therefore, immediately on my suggesting it, that she would learn Greek; or, at least, that limited form of Greek which was required for the New Testament. In the language of Terence, dictum factum—no sooner said than done. On the very next morning we all rode in to Stamford, our nearest town for such a purpose, and astounded the bookseller's apprentice by ordering four copies of the Clarendon Press Greek Testament, three copies of Parkhurst's Greek and English Lexicon, and three copies of some grammar, but what I have now forgotten. The books were to come down by the mail-coach without delay. Consequently, we were soon at work. Lady Massey and my sister, not being sustained by the same interest as Lady Carbery, eventually relaxed in their attention. But Lady Carbery was quite in earnest, and very soon became expert in the original language of the New Testament.

I wished much that she should have gone on to the study of Herodotus. And I described to her the situation of the vivacious and mercurial Athenian, in the early period of Pericles, as repeating in its main features, for the great advantage of that Grecian Froissart, the situation of Adam during his earliest hours in Paradise, himself being the describer to the affable archangel. The same genial climate there was; the same luxuriation of nature in her early prime; the same ignorance of his own origin in the tenant of this lovely scenery; and the same eager desire to learn it.

[Footnote: "About me round I saw Hill, dale, and shady woods, and sunny plains, And liquid lapse of murmuring streams; by these Creatures that lived and moved, and walked or flew; Birds on the branches warbling; all things smiled; With fragrance and with joy my heart o'erflowed. Myself I then perused, and limb by limb Surveyed, and sometimes went, and sometimes ran With supple joints, as lively vigor led; *But who I was or where, or from what cause,* Knew not."—*Paradise Lost,* Book viii. The *who,* the *where* (in any extended sense, that is, as regarded the *external* relations of his own country), and the *from what cause*—all these were precisely what the Grecian did *not* know, and first learned from Herodotus.] The very truth, and mere facts of history, reaching Herodotus through such a haze of remote abstraction, and suffering a sort of refraction at each translation from atmosphere to atmosphere, whilst continually the uninteresting parts dropped away as the whole moved onwards, unavoidably assumed the attractions of romance. And thus it has happened that the air of marvellousness, which seems connected with the choice and preferences of Herodotus, is in reality the natural gift of his position. Culling from a field of many nations and many generations, reasonably he preferred such narratives as, though possible enough, wore the coloring of romance. Without any violation of the truth, the mere extent of his field as to space and time gave him great advantages for the wild and the marvellous. Meantime, this purpose of ours with regard to Herodotus was defeated. Whilst we were making preparations for it, suddenly one morning from his Limerick estate of Carass returned Lord Carbery. And, by accident, his welcome was a rough one; for, happening to find Lady Carbery in the breakfast-room, and naturally throwing his arm about her neck to kiss her, "Ruffian," a monster of a Newfoundland dog, singularly beautiful in his coloring, and almost as powerful as a leopard, flew at him vindictively as at a stranger committing an assault, and his mistress had great difficulty in calling him off. Lord Carbery smiled a little at our Greek studies; and, in turn, made us smile, who knew the original object of these studies, when he suggested mildly that three or four books of the "Iliad" would have been as easily mastered, and might have more fully rewarded our trouble. I contented myself with replying (for I knew how little Lady Carbery would have liked to plead the *religious* motive to her husband), that Parkhurst (and there was at that time no other Greek-*English* Lexicon) would not have been available for Homer; neither, it is true, would he have been available for Herodotus. But, considering the simplicity and uniformity of style in both these authors, I had formed a plan (not very hard of execution) for interleaving Parkhurst with such additional words as might have been easily mustered from the special dictionaries (Grćco-Latin) dedicated separately to the service of the historian and of the poet. I do not believe that more than fifteen hundred *extra* words would have been required; and these, entered at the rate of twenty per hour, would have occupied only ten days, for seven and a half hours each. However, from one cause or other, this plan was never brought to bear. The preliminary labor upon the lexicon always enforced a delay; and any delay, in such case, makes an opening for the irruption of a thousand unforeseen hindrances, that finally cause the whole plan to droop insensibly. The time came at last for leaving Laxton, and I did not see Lady Carbery again for nearly an entire year.

In passing through the park-gates of Laxton, on my departure northward, powerfully, and as if "with the might of waters," my mind turned round to contemplate that strange enlargement of my experience which had happened to me within the last three months. I had seen, and become familiarly acquainted with, a young man, who had in a

manner died to every object around him, had died an
intellectual death, and suddenly had been called back to life
and real happiness—had been, in effect, raised from the dead
—by the accident of meeting a congenial female companion.
But, secondly, that very lady from whose lips I first heard
this remarkable case of blight and restoration, had herself
passed through an equal though not a similar blight, and
was now seeking earnestly, though with what success I
could never estimate, some similar restoration to some new
mode of hopeful existence, through intercourse with
religious philosophy. What vast revolutions (vast for the
individual) within how narrow a circle! What blindness to
approaching catastrophes, in the midst of what nearness to
the light! And for myself, whom accident had made the
silent observer of these changes, was it not likely enough
that I also was rushing forward to court and woo some
frantic mode of evading an endurance that by patience
might have been borne, or by thoughtfulness might have
been disarmed? Misgivingly I went forwards, feeling forever
that, through clouds of thick darkness, I was continually
nearing a danger, or was myself perhaps wilfully provoking
a trial, before which my constitutional despondency would
cause me to lie down without a struggle.

II.

THE PRIORY.

To teach is to learn: according to an old experience, it is the
very best mode of learning—the surest, and the shortest.
And hence, perhaps, it may be, that in the middle ages by
the monkish word *scholaris* was meant indifferently he that
learned and he that taught. Never in any equal number of

months had my understanding so much expanded as
during this visit to Laxton. The incessant demand made
upon me by Lady Carbery for solutions of the many
difficulties besetting the study of divinity and the Greek
Testament, or for such approximations to solutions as my
resources would furnish, forced me into a preternatural
tension of all the faculties applicable to that purpose. Lady
Carbery insisted upon calling me her "Admirable Crichton;"
and it was in vain that I demurred to this honorary title
upon two grounds: first, as being one towards which I had
no natural aptitudes or predisposing advantages; secondly
(which made her stare), as carrying with it no real or
enviable distinction. The splendor supposed to be connected
with the attainments of Crichton I protested against, as
altogether imaginary. How far that person really had the
accomplishments ascribed to him, I waived as a question not
worth investigating. My objection commenced at an earlier
point: real or not real, the accomplishments were, as I
insisted, vulgar and trivial. Vulgar, that is, when put
forward as exponents or adequate expressions of intellectual
grandeur. The whole rested on a misconception; the limitary
idea of knowledge was confounded with the infinite idea of
power. To have a quickness in copying or mimicking other
men, and in learning to do dexterously what *they* did
clumsily,—ostentatiously to keep glittering before men's eyes
a thaumaturgic versatility such as that of a rope-dancer, or
of an Indian juggler, in petty accomplishments,—was a
mode of the very vulgarest ambition: one effort of
productive power,—a little book, for instance, which should
impress or should agitate several successive generations of
men, even though far below the higher efforts of human
creative art—as, for example, the "De Imitatione Christi," or
"The Pilgrim's Progress," or" Robinson Crusoe," or "The
Vicar of Wakefield,"—was worth any conceivable amount of
attainments when rated as an evidence of anything that

could justly denominate a man "admirable." One felicitous ballad of forty lines might have enthroned Crichton as really admirable, whilst the pretensions actually put forward on his behalf simply install him as a cleverish or dexterous ape. However, as Lady Carbery did not forego her purpose of causing me to shine under every angle, it would have been ungrateful in me to refuse my cooperation with her plans, however little they might wear a face of promise. Accordingly I surrendered myself for two hours daily to the lessons in horsemanship of a principal groom who ranked as a first-rate rough-rider; and I gathered manifold experiences amongst the horses—so different from the wild, hard-mouthed horses at Westport, that were often vicious, and sometimes trained to vice. Here, though spirited, the horses were pretty generally gentle, and all had been regularly broke. My education was not entirely neglected even as regarded sportsmanship; that great branch of philosophy being confided to one of the keepers, who was very attentive to me, in deference to the interest in myself expressed by his idolized mistress, but otherwise regarded me probably as an object of mysterious curiosity rather than of sublunary hope.

Equally, in fact, as regarded my physics and my metaphysics,—in short, upon all lines of advance that interested my ambition,—I was going rapidly ahead. And, speaking seriously, in what regarded my intellectual expansion, never before or since had I been so distinctly made aware of it. No longer did it seem to move upon the hour-hand, whose advance, though certain, is yet a pure matter of inference, but upon the seconds'-hand, which *visibly* comes on at a trotting pace. Everything prospered, except my own present happiness, and the possibility of any happiness for some years to come. About two months after leaving Laxton, my fate in the worst shape I had anticipated

was solemnly and definitively settled. My guardians agreed
that the most prudent course, with a view to my pecuniary
interests, was to place me at the Manchester Grammar
School; not with a view to further improvement in my
classical knowledge, though the head-master was a sound
scholar, but simply with a view to one of the school
exhibitions. [Footnote: "*Exhibitions*."—This is the technical
name in many cases, corresponding to the *bursé* or *bursaries*
of the continent; from which word *bursé* is derived, I
believe, the German term *Bursch*,—that is, a bursarius, or
student, who lives at college upon the salary allowed by
such a bursary. Some years ago the editor of a Glasgow
daily paper called upon Oxford and Cambridge, with a
patronizing flourish, to imitate some one or more of the
Scottish universities in founding such systems of aliment for
poor students otherwise excluded from academic
advantages. Evidently he was unaware that they had existed
for centuries before the state of civilization in Scotland had
allowed any opening for the foundation of colleges or
academic life. Scottish bursaries, or exhibitions (a term
which Shakspeare uses, very near the close of the first act in
the "Two Gentlemen of Verona," as the technical expression
in England), were few, and not generally, I believe, exceeding
ten pounds a-year. The English were many, and of more
ancient standing, and running from forty pounds to one
hundred pounds a-year. Such was the simple difference
between the two countries: otherwise they agreed
altogether.] Amongst the countless establishments, scattered
all over England by the noble munificence of English men
and English women in past generations, for connecting the
provincial towns with the two royal universities of the land,
this Manchester school was one; in addition to other great
local advantages (namely, *inter alia*, a fine old library and an
ecclesiastical foundation, which in this present generation
has furnished the materials for a bishopric of Manchester,

with its deanery and chapter), this noble foundation secured
a number of exhibitions at Brasenose College, Oxford, to
those pupils of the school who should study at Manchester
for three consecutive years. The pecuniary amount of these
exhibitions has since then increased considerably through
the accumulation of funds, which the commercial character
of that great city had caused to be neglected. At that time, I
believe each exhibition yielded about forty guineas a-year,
and was legally tenable for seven successive years. Now, to
me this would have offered a most seasonable advantage,
had it been resorted to some two years earlier. My small
patrimonial inheritance gave to me, as it did to each of my
four brothers, exactly one hundred and fifty pounds a-year:
and to each of my sisters exactly one hundred pounds a-
year. The Manchester exhibition of forty guineas a-year
would have raised this income for seven years to a sum close
upon two hundred pounds a-year. But at present I was half-
way on the road to the completion of my sixteenth year.
Commencing my period of pupilage from that time, I should
not have finished it until I had travelled half-way through
my nineteenth year. And the specific evil that already
weighed upon me with a sickening oppression was the
premature expansion of my mind; and, as a foremost
consequence, intolerance of boyish society. I ought to have
entered upon my *triennium* of school-boy servitude at the age
of thirteen. As things were, —a delay with which I had
nothing to do myself, —this and the native character of my
mind had thrown the whole arrangement awry. For the
better half of the three years I endured it patiently. But it
had at length begun to eat more corrosively into my peace
of mind than ever I had anticipated. The head-master was
substantially superannuated for the duties of his place. Not
that intellectually he showed any symptoms of decay: but in
the spirits and physical energies requisite for his duties he
did: not so much age, as disease, it was that incapacitated

him. In the course of a long day, beginning at seven A. M. and stretching down to five P. M., he succeeded in reaching the further end of his duties. But how? Simply by consolidating pretty nearly into one continuous scene of labor the entire ten hours. The full hour of relaxation which the traditions of this ancient school and the by-laws had consecrated to breakfast was narrowed into ten, or even seven minutes. The two hours' interval, in like manner prescribed by the old usages from twelve to two P. M., was pared down to forty minutes, or less. In this way he walked conscientiously through the services of the day, fulfilling to the letter every section the minutest of the traditional rubric. But he purchased this consummation at the price of all comfort to himself: and, having done *that*, he felt himself the more entitled to neglect the comfort of others. The case was singular: he neither showed any indulgence to himself more than to others (which, however, could do nothing towards indemnifying others for the severe confinement which his physical decay inflicted upon them—a point wholly forgotten by him); nor, secondly, in thus tenaciously holding on to his place did he (I am satisfied) govern himself by any mercenary thought or wish, but simply by an austere sense of duty. He discharged his public functions with constant fidelity, and with superfluity of learning; and felt, perhaps not unreasonably, that possibly the same learning united with the same zeal might not revolve as a matter of course in the event of his resigning the place. I hide from myself no part of the honorable motives which might (and probably *did*) exclusively govern him in adhering to the place. But not by one atom the less did the grievous results of his inability to grapple with his duties weigh upon all within his sphere, and upon myself, by cutting up the time available for exercise, most ruinously.

Precisely at the worst crisis of this intolerable darkness (for such, without exaggeration, it was in its effects upon my spirits) arose, and for five or six months steadily continued, a consolation of that nature which hardly in dreams I could have anticipated. For even in dreams would it have seemed reasonable, or natural, that Laxton, with its entire society, should transfer itself to Manchester? Some mighty caliph, or lamp-bearing Aladdin, might have worked such marvels: but else who, or by what machinery? Nevertheless, without either caliph or Aladdin, and by the most natural of mere human agencies, this change was suddenly accomplished.

Mr. White, whom I have already had occasion to mention elsewhere, was in those days the most eminent surgeon by much in the north of England. He had by one whole generation run before the phrenologists and craniologists,— having already measured innumerable skulls amongst the omnigenous seafaring population of Liverpool, illustrating all the races of men,—and was in society a most urbane and pleasant companion. On my mother's suggestion, he had been summoned to Laxton, in the hope that he might mitigate the torments of Mrs. Schreiber's malady. If I am right in supposing that to have been cancer, I presume that he could not have added much to the prescriptions of the local doctor. And yet, on the other hand, it is a fact—so slowly did new views travel in those days, when scientific journals were few, and roads were heavy—that ten years later than this period I knew a case, namely, the case of a butcher's wife in Somersetshire who had never enjoyed the benefit of hemlock in relieving the pangs of a cancerous complaint, until an accident brought Mr. Hey, son to the celebrated Hey of Leeds, into the poor woman's neighborhood.

What might be the quality or the extent of that relief with which Mr. White was able to crown the expectations of poor

Mrs. Schreiber, I do not know; but that the relief could not have been imaginary is certain, for he was earnestly invited to repeat his visits, costly as unavoidably they were. Mrs. Schreiber did not reside at Laxton. Tenderly as she loved Lady Carbery, it did not seem consistent with her dignity that she should take a station that might have been grossly misinterpreted; and accordingly she bought or hired a miniature kind of villa, called *Tixover*, distant about four miles from Laxton. A residence in such a house, so sad and silent at this period of affliction for its mistress, would have offered too cheerless a life to Mr. White. He took up his abode, therefore, at Laxton during his earliest visit; and this happened to coincide with that particular visit of my own during which I was initiating Lady Carbery into the mysteries of New Testament Greek. Already as an infant I had known Mr. White; but now, when daily riding over to Tixover in company, and daily meeting at breakfast and dinner, we became intimate. Greatly I profited by this intimacy; and some part of my pleasure in the Laxton plan of migration to Manchester was drawn from the prospect of renewing it. Such a migration was suggested by Mr. White himself; and fortunately he *could* suggest it without even the appearance of any mercenary views. His interest lay the other way. The large special retainer, which it was felt but reasonable to pay him under circumstances so peculiar, naturally disturbed Mr. White; whilst the benefits of visits so discontinuous became more and more doubtful. He proposed it, therefore, as a measure of prudence, that Mrs. Schreiber should take up her abode in Manchester. This counsel was adopted; and the entire Laxton party in one week struck their Northamptonshire tents, dived, as it were, into momentary darkness, by a loitering journey of stages, short and few, out of consideration for the invalid, and rose again in the gloomy streets of Manchester.

Gloomy they were at that time—mud below, smoke above—
for no torch of improvement had yet explored the ancient
habitations of this Lancashire capital. Elsewhere I have
expressed the inexhaustible admiration which I cherish for
the *moral* qualities, the unrivalled energy and perseverance,
of that native Lancashire population, as yet not much
alloyed with Celtic adulteration. My feelings towards them
are the same as were eloquently and impressively avowed by
the late eminent Dr. Cooke Taylor, after an *official* inquiry
into their situation. But in those days the Manchester
people realized the aspiration of the noble Scythian; not the
place it was that glorified *them*, but they that glorified the
place. No great city (which technically it then was not, but
simply a town or large village) could present so repulsive an
exterior as the Manchester of that day. Lodgings of *any* sort
could with difficulty be obtained, and at last only by
breaking up the party. The poor suffering lady, with her two
friends, Lady Carbery and my mother, hired one house,
Lord and Lady Massey another, and two others were
occupied by attendants—all the servants, except one lady's-
maid, being every night separated by a quarter of a mile
from their mistresses. To me, however, all these discomforts
were scarcely apparent in the prodigious revolution for the
better which was now impressed upon the tenor of my daily
life. I lived in the house of the head-master; but every night
I had leave to adjourn for four or five hours to the drawing-
room of Lady Carbery. Her anxiety about Mrs. Schreiber
would not allow of her going abroad into society, unless
upon the rarest occasions. And I, on my part, was too
happy in her conversation—so bold, so novel, and so
earnest—voluntarily to have missed any one hour of it.

Here, by the way, let me mention that on this occasion arose a case of pretended *"tuft-hunting,"* which I, who stood by a silent observer, could not but feel to involve a malicious calumny. Naturally it happened that coroneted carriages, superb horses, and numerous servants, in a town so unostentatious and homely as the Manchester of that day, drew the public gaze, and effectually advertised the visit of the Laxton ladies. Respect for the motive which had prompted this visit coöperated with admiration for the distinguished personal qualities of Lady Carbery, to draw upon her from several leading families in the town such little services and attentions as pass naturally, under a spontaneous law of courtesy, between those who are at home and those who suffer under the disadvantages of *strangership.* The Manchester people, who made friendly advances to Lady Carbery, did so, I am persuaded, with no ulterior objects whatsoever of pressing into the circle of an aristocratic person; neither did Lady Carbery herself interpret their attentions in any such ungenerous spirit, but accepted them cordially, as those expressions of disinterested goodness which I am persuaded that in reality they were. Amongst the families that were thus attentive to her, in throwing open for her use various local advantages of baths, libraries, picture-galleries, etc., were the wife and daughters of Mr. White himself. Now, one of these daughters was herself the wife of a baronet, Sir Richard Clayton, who had honorably distinguished himself in literature by translating and *improving* the work of Tenhove the Dutchman (or Belgian?) upon the house of the *De' Medici*—a work which Mr. Roscoe considered "the most engaging work that has, perhaps, ever appeared on a subject of literary history." Introduced as Lady Clayton had been amongst the elite of our aristocracy, it could not be supposed that she would be at all solicitous about an introduction to the wife of an Irish nobleman, simply *as* such, and apart from her personal endowments. Those endowments, it is true,—namely, the beauty and the talents of Lady Carbery, made known in Manchester through Mr. White's report of them, and combined with the knowledge of her generous devotion to her dying friend, secluding her steadily from all society through a period of very many months,—did, and reasonably might, interest many Manchester people on her behalf. In all this there was nothing to be ashamed of; and, judging from what personally I witnessed, this seems to have been the true nature and extent of the "tuft-hunting;" and I have noticed it at all simply because there is a habit almost national growing up amongst us of imputing to each other some mode of unmanly prostration before the aristocracy, but with as little foundation for the charge generally, I believe, as I am satisfied there was in this particular instance.

Mr. White possessed a museum—formed chiefly by himself, and originally, perhaps, directed simply to professional objects, such as would have little chance for engaging the attention of females. But surgeons and speculative physicians, beyond all other classes of intellectual men, cultivate the most enlarged and liberal curiosity; so that Mr. White's museum furnished attractions to an unusually large variety of tastes. I had myself already seen it; and it struck me that Mr. White would be gratified if Lady Carbery would herself ask to see it; which accordingly she did; and thus at once removed the painful feeling that he might be extorting from her an expression of interest in his collection which she did not really feel.

Amongst the objects which gave a scientific interest to the collection, naturally I have forgotten one and all—first, midst, and last; for this is one of the cases in which we all

felicitate ourselves upon the art and gift of forgetting; that
art which the great Athenian [Footnote: "The great
Athenian"—Themistocles.] noticed as amongst the *desiderata*
of human life—that gift which, if in some rare cases it
belongs only to the regal prerogatives of the grave,
fortunately in many thousands of other cases is accorded by
the treachery of a human brain. Heavens! what a curse it
were, if every chaos, which is stamped upon the mind by
fairs such as that London fair of St. Bartholomew in years
long past, or by the records of battles and skirmishes
through the monotonous pages of history, or by the
catalogues of libraries stretching over a dozen measured
miles, could not be erased, but arrayed itself in endless files
incapable of obliteration, as often as the eyes of our human
memory happened to throw back their gaze in that
direction! Heaven be praised, I have forgotten everything;
all the earthly trophies of skill or curious research; even the
érolithes, that might possibly *not* be earthly, but presents
from some superior planet. Nothing survives, except the
humanities of the collection; and amongst these, two only I
will molest the reader by noticing. One of the two was a
mummy; the other was a *skeleton.* I, that had previously seen
the museum, warned Lady Carbery of both; but much it
mortified us that only the skeleton was shown. Perhaps the
mummy was too closely connected with the personal
history of Mr. White for exhibition to strangers; it was that
of a lady who had been attended medically for some years by
Mr. White, and had owed much alleviation of her sufferings
to his inventive skill. She had, therefore, felt herself called
upon to memorialize her gratitude by a very large bequest—
not less (I have heard) than twenty-five thousand pounds;
but with this condition annexed to the gift—that she
should be embalmed as perfectly as the resources in that art
of London and Paris could accomplish, and that once a year
Mr. White, accompanied by two witnesses of credit, should

withdraw the veil from her face. The lady was placed in a common English clock-case, having the usual glass face; but a veil of white velvet obscured from all profane eyes the silent features behind. The clock I had myself seen, when a child, and had gazed upon it with inexpressible awe. But, naturally, on my report of the case, the whole of our party were devoured by a curiosity to see the departed fair one. Had Mr. White, indeed, furnished us with the key of the museum, leaving us to our own discretion, but restricting us only (like a cruel Bluebeard) from looking into any ante-room, great is my fear that the perfidious question would have arisen amongst us—what o'clock it was? and all possible ante-rooms would have given way to the just fury of our passions. I submitted to Lady Carbery, as a liberty which might be excused by the torrid extremity of our thirst after knowledge, that she (as our leader) should throw out some angling question moving in the line of our desires; upon which hint Mr. White, if he had any touch of indulgence to human infirmity—unless Mount Caucasus were his mother, and a she-wolf his nurse—would surely relent, and act as his conscience must suggest. But Lady Carbery reminded me of the three Calendars in the "Arabian Nights," and argued that, as the ladies of Bagdad were justified in calling upon a body of porters to kick those gentlemen into the street, being people who had abused the indulgences of hospitality, much more might Mr. White do so with us; for the Calendars were the children of kings (Shahzades), which we were not; and had found their curiosity far more furiously irritated; in fact, Zobeide had no right to trifle with any man's curiosity in that ferocious extent; and a counter right arose, as any chancery of human nature would have ruled, to demand a solution of what had been so maliciously arranged towards an anguish of insupportable temptation. Thus, however, it happened that the mummy, who left such valuable legacies, and founded such bilious fevers of curiosity, was not seen by us; nor even the miserable clock-case.

The mummy, therefore, was not seen; but the skeleton was. Who was he? It is not every day that one makes the acquaintance of a skeleton; and with regard to such a thing —thing, shall one say, or person?—there is a favorable presumption from beforehand; which is this: As he is of no use, neither profitable nor ornamental to any person whatever, absolutely *de trop* in good society, what but distinguished merit of some kind or other could induce any man to interfere with that gravitating tendency that by an eternal *nisus* is pulling him below ground? Lodgings are dear in England. True it is that, according to the vile usage on the continent, one room serves a skeleton for bed-room and sitting-room; neither is his expense heavy, as regards wax-lights, fire, or "bif-steck." But still, even a skeleton is chargeable; and, if any dispute should arise about his maintenance, the parish will do nothing. Mr. White's skeleton, therefore, being costly, was presumably meritorious, before we had seen him or heard a word in his behalf. It was, in fact, the skeleton of an eminent robber, or perhaps of a murderer. But I, for my part, reserved a faint right of suspense. And as to the profession of robber in those days exercised on the roads of England, it was a liberal profession, which required more accomplishments than either the bar or the pulpit: from the beginning it presumed a most bountiful endowment of heroic qualifications— strength, health, agility, and exquisite horsemanship, intrepidity of the first order, presence of mind, courtesy, and a general ambidexterity of powers for facing all accidents, and for turning to a good account all unlooked-for contingencies. The finest men in England, physically speaking, throughout the eighteenth century, the very noblest specimens of man considered as an animal, were beyond a doubt the mounted robbers who cultivated their profession on the great leading roads, namely, on the road from London to York (technically known as "the great north road"); on the road west to Bath, and thence to Exeter and Plymouth; north-westwards from London to Oxford, and thence to Chester; eastwards to Tunbridge; southwards by east to Dover; then inclining westwards to Portsmouth; more so still, through Salisbury to Dorsetshire and Wilts. These great roads were farmed out as so many Roman provinces amongst pro-consuls. Yes, but with a difference, you will say, in respect of moral principles. Certainly with a difference; for the English highwayman had a sort of conscience for gala-days, which could not often be said of the Roman governor or procurator. At this moment we see that the opening for the forger of bank-notes is brilliant; but practically it languishes, as being too brilliant; it demands an array of talent for engraving, etc., which, wherever it exists, is sufficient to carry a man forward upon principles reputed honorable. Why, then, should *he* court danger and disreputability? But in that century the special talents which led to distinction upon the high road had oftentimes no career open to them elsewhere. The mounted robber on the highways of England, in an age when all gentlemen travelled with fire-arms, lived in an element of danger and adventurous gallantry; which, even from those who could least allow him any portion of their esteem, extorted sometimes a good deal of their unwilling admiration. By the necessities of the case, he brought into his perilous profession some brilliant qualities—intrepidity, address, promptitude of decision; and, if to these he added courtesy, and a spirit (native or adopted) of forbearing generosity, he seemed almost a man that merited public encouragement; since very plausibly it might be argued that his profession was sure to exist; that, if he were removed, a successor would inevitably arise, and that successor might or might *not* carry the same liberal and humanizing temper into his practice. The man whose skeleton was now before us had ranked amongst the most chivalrous of his order, and was regarded by some people as vindicating the national honor in a point where not very long before it had suffered a transient eclipse. In the preceding generation, it had been felt as throwing a shade of disgrace over the public honor, that the championship of England upon the high road fell for a time into French hands; upon French prowess rested the burden of English honor, or, in Gallic phrase, of English *glory*. Claude Duval, a French man of undeniable courage, handsome, and noted for his chivalrous devotion to women, had been honored, on his condemnation to the gallows, by the tears of many ladies who attended his trial, and by their sympathizing visits during his imprisonment. But the robber represented by the skeleton in Mr. White's museum (whom let us call X, since his true name has perished) added to the same heroic qualities a person far more superb. Still it was a dreadful drawback from his pretensions, if he had really practised as a murderer. Upon what ground did that suspicion arise? In candor (for candor is due even to a skeleton) it ought to be mentioned that the charge, if it amounted to so much, arose with a lady from some part of Cheshire—the district of Knutsford, I believe;—but, wherever it was, in the same district, during the latter part of his career, had resided our X. At first he was not suspected even as a robber—as yet not so much as suspected of being suspicious; in a simple rustic neighborhood, amongst good-natured peasants, for a long time he was regarded with simple curiosity, rather than suspicion; and even the curiosity pointed to his horse more than to himself. The robber had made himself popular amongst the kind-hearted rustics by his general courtesy. Courtesy and the spirit of neighborliness go a great way amongst country people; and the worst construction of the case was, that he might be an embarrassed gentleman from Manchester or Liverpool, hiding himself from his creditors, who are notoriously a very immoral class of people. At length, however, a violent suspicion broke loose against him; for it was ascertained that on certain nights, when, perhaps, he had *extra* motives for concealing the fact of having been abroad, he drew woollen stockings over his horse's feet, with the purpose of deadening the sound in riding up a brick-paved entry, common to his own stable and that of a respectable neighbor. Thus far there was a reasonable foundation laid for suspicion; but suspicion of what? Because a man attends to the darning of his horse's stockings, why must he be meditating murder? The fact is— and known from the very first to a select party of amateurs —that X, our superb-looking skeleton, did, about three o'clock on a rainy Wednesday morning, in the dead of winter, ride silently out of Knutsford; and about forty-eight hours afterwards, on a rainy Friday, silently and softly did that same superb blood-horse, carrying that same blood-man, namely, our friend the superb skeleton, pace up the quiet brick entry, in a neat pair of socks, on his return.

During that interval of forty-eight hours, an atrocious murder was committed in the ancient city of Bristol. By whom? That question is to this day unanswered. The scene of it was a house on the west side of the College Green, which is in fact that same quadrangle planted with trees, and having on its southern side the Bristol Cathedral, up and down which, early in the reign of George III., Chatterton walked in jubilant spirits with fair young women of Bristol; up and down which, some thirty years later, Robert Southey and S. T. C. walked with young Bristol belles from a later generation. The subjects of the murder were an elderly lady bearing some such name as Rusborough, and her female servant. Mystery there was none as to the motive of the murder—manifestly it was a hoard of money that had attracted the assassin; but there was great perplexity as to the agent or agents concerned in the atrocious act, and as to the mode by which an entrance, under the known precautions of the lady, could have been effected. Because a thorough-bred horse could easily have accomplished the distance to and fro (say three hundred miles) within the forty-eight hours, and because the two extreme dates of this forty-eight hours' absence tallied with the requisitions of the Bristol tragedy, it did not follow that X must have had a hand in it. And yet, had these coincidences *then* been observed, they would certainly—now that strong suspicions had been directed to the man from the extraordinary character of his nocturnal precautions— not have passed without investigation. But the remoteness of Bristol, and the rarity of newspapers in those days, caused these indications to pass unnoticed. Bristol knew of no such Knutsford highwayman—Knutsford knew of no such Bristol murder. It is singular enough that these earlier grounds of suspicion against X were not viewed as such by anybody, until they came to be combined with another and final ground. Then the presumptions seemed conclusive. But, by that time, X himself had been executed for a robbery; had been manufactured into a skeleton by the famous surgeon, Cruickshank, assisted by Mr. White and other pupils. All interest in the case had subsided in Knutsford, that could now have cleared up the case satisfactorily; and thus it happened that to this day the riddle, which was read pretty decisively in a northern county, still remains a riddle in the south. When I saw the College Green house in 1809-10, it was apparently empty, and, as I was told, had always been empty since the murder: forty years had not cicatrized the bloody remembrance; and, to this day, perhaps, it remains amongst the gloomy traditions of Bristol.

But whether the Bristol house has or has not shaken off
that odor of blood which offended the nostrils of tenants, it
is, I believe, certain that the city annals have not shaken off
the mystery: which yet to certain people in Knutsford, as I
have said, and to us the spectators of the skeleton,
immediately upon hearing one damning fact from the lips of
Mr. White, seemed to melt away and evaporate as
convincingly as if we had heard the explanation issuing in
the terms of a confession from the mouth of the skeleton
itself. What, then, *was* the fact? With pain, and reluctantly,
we felt its force, as we looked at the royal skeleton, and
reflected on the many evidences which he had given of
courage, and perhaps of other noble qualities. The ugly fact
was this: In a few weeks after the College Green tragedy,
Knutsford, and the whole neighborhood as far as
Warrington (the half-way town between Liverpool and
Manchester), were deluged with gold and silver coins,
moidores, and dollars, from the Spanish mint of Mexico, etc.
These, during the frequent scarcities of English silver
currency, were notoriously current in England. Now, it is
an unhappy fact, and subsequently became known to the
Bristol and London police, that a considerable part of poor
Mrs. Rusborough's treasure lay in such coins, gold and
silver, from the Spanish colonial mints.

Lady Carbery at this period made an effort to teach me
Hebrew, by way of repaying in *kind* my pains in teaching
Greek to *her*. Where, and upon what motive, she had herself
begun to learn Hebrew, I forget: but in Manchester she had
resumed this study with energy on a casual impulse derived
from a certain Dr. Bailey, a clergyman of this city, who had
published a Hebrew Grammar. The doctor was the most
unworldly and guileless of men. Amongst his orthodox
brethren he was reputed a "Methodist;" and not without
reason; for some of his Low-Church views he pushed into

practical extravagances that looked like fanaticism, or even like insanity. Lady Carbery wished naturally to testify her gratitude for his services by various splendid presents: but nothing would the good doctor accept, unless it assumed a shape that might be available for the service of the paupers amongst his congregation. The Hebrew studies, however, notwithstanding the personal assistance which we drew from the kindness of Dr. Bailey, languished. For this there were several reasons; but it was enough that the systematic vagueness in the pronunciation of this, as of the other Oriental languages, disgusted both of us. A word which could not be pronounced with any certainty, was not in a true sense possessed. Let it be understood, however, that it was not the correct and original pronunciation that we cared for—*that* has perished probably beyond recall, even in the case of Greek, in spite of the Asiatic and the Insular Greeks—what we demanded in vain was any pronunciation whatever that should be articulate, apprehensible, and intercommunicable, such as might differentiate the words: whereas a system of mere vowels too inadequately strengthened by consonants, seemed to leave all words pretty nearly alike. One day, in a pause of languor amongst these arid Hebrew studies, I read to her, with a beating heart, "The Ancient Mariner." It had been first published in 1798; and, about this time (1801), was re-published in the first *two*-volume edition of "The Lyrical Ballads." Well I knew Lady Carbery's constitutional inaptitude for poetry; and not for the world would I have sought sympathy from her or from anybody else upon that part of the L. B. which belonged to Wordsworth. But I fancied that the wildness of this tale, and the triple majesties of Solitude, of Mist, and of the Ancient Unknown Sea, might have won her into relenting; and, in fact, she listened with gravity and deep attention. But, on reviewing afterwards in conversation such passages as she happened to remember, she laughed at

the finest parts, and shocked me by calling the mariner
himself "an old quiz;" protesting that the latter part of his
homily to the wedding guest clearly pointed him out as the
very man meant by Providence for a stipendiary curate to
the good Dr. Bailey in his over-crowded church. [Footnote:
St. James', according to my present recollection.] With an
albatross perched on his shoulder, and who might be
introduced to the congregation as the immediate organ of
his conversion, and supported by the droning of a bassoon,
she represented the mariner lecturing to advantage in
English; the doctor overhead in the pulpit enforcing it in
Hebrew. Angry I was, though forced to laugh. But of what
use is anger or argument in a duel with female criticism?
Our ponderous masculine wits are no match for the
mercurial fancy of women. Once, however, I had a triumph:
to my great surprise, one day, she suddenly repeated by
heart, to Dr. Bailey, the beautiful passage—

"It ceased, yet still the sails made on," &c.

asking what he thought of *that?* As it happened, the simple,
childlike doctor had more sensibility than herself; for,
though he had never in his whole homely life read more of
poetry than he had drunk of Tokay or Constantia,—in fact,
had scarcely heard tell of any poetry but Watts' Hymns,—he
seemed petrified: and at last, with a deep sigh, as if
recovering from the spasms of a new birth, said, "I never
heard anything so beautiful in my whole life."

During the long stay of the Laxton party in Manchester,
occurred a Christmas; and at Christmas—that is, at the
approach of this great Christian festival, so properly
substituted in England for the Pagan festival of January and
the New Year—there was, according to ancient usage, on the
breaking up for the holidays, at the Grammar School, a

solemn celebration of the season by public speeches. Among
the six speakers, I, of course (as one of the three boys who
composed the head class), held a distinguished place; and it
followed, also, as a matter of course, that all my friends
congregated on this occasion to do me honor. What I had to
recite was a copy of Latin verses (Alcaics) on the recent
conquest of Malta. *Melite Britannis Subacta* —this was the title
of my worshipful nonsense. The whole strength of the
Laxton party had mustered on this occasion. Lady Carbery
made a point of bringing in her party every creature whom
she could influence. And, probably, there were in that
crowded audience many old Manchester friends of my
father, loving his memory, and thinking to honor it by
kindness to his son. Furious, at any rate, was the applause
which greeted me: furious was my own disgust. Frantic
were the clamors as I concluded my nonsense. Frantic was
my inner sense of shame at the childish exhibition to which,
unavoidably, I was making myself a party. Lady Carbery
had, at first, directed towards me occasional glances,
expressing a comic sympathy with the thoughts which she
supposed to be occupying my mind. But these glances
ceased; and I was recalled by the gloomy sadness in her
altered countenance to some sense of my own extravagant
and disproportionate frenzy on this occasion: from the
indulgent kindness with which she honored me, her
countenance on this occasion became a mirror to my own.
At night she assured me, when talking over the case, that
she had never witnessed an expression of such settled
misery, and also (so she fancied) of misanthropy, as that
which darkened my countenance in those moments of
apparent public triumph, no matter how trivial the
occasion, and amidst an uproar of friendly felicitation. I look
back to that state of mind as almost a criminal reproach to
myself, if it were not for the facts of the case. But, in excuse
for myself, this fact, above all others, ought to be mentioned

—that, over and above the killing oppression to my too sensitive system of the monotonous school tasks, and the ruinous want of exercise, I had fallen under medical advice the most misleading that it is possible to imagine. The physician and the surgeon of my family were men too eminent, it seemed to me, and, consequently, with time too notoriously bearing a high pecuniary value, for any school-boy to detain them with complaints. Under these circumstances, I threw myself for aid, in a case so simple that any clever boy in a druggist's shop would have known how to treat it, upon the advice of an old, old apothecary, who had full authority from my guardians to run up a most furious account against me for medicine. This being the regular mode of payment, inevitably, and unconsciously, he was biased to a mode of treatment; namely, by drastic medicines varied without end, which fearfully exasperated the complaint. This complaint, as I now know, was the simplest possible derangement of the liver, a torpor in its action that might have been put to rights in three days. In fact, one week's pedestrian travelling amongst the Caernarvonshire mountains effected a revolution in my health such as left me nothing to complain of.

An odd thing happened by the merest accident. I, when my Alcaics had run down their foolish larum, instead of resuming my official place as one of the trinity who composed the head class, took a seat by the side of Lady Carbery. On the other side of her was seated a stranger: and this stranger, whom mere chance had thrown next to her, was Lord Belgrave, her old and at one time (as some people fancied) favored suitor. In this there was nothing at all extraordinary. Lord Grey de Wilton, an old *alumnus* of this Manchester Grammar School, and an *alumnus* during the early reign of this same *Archididascalus*, made a point of showing honor to his ancient tutor, especially now when reputed to be decaying; and with the same view he brought Lord Belgrave, who had become his son-in-law after his rejection by Lady Carbery. The whole was a very natural accident. But Lady Carbery was not sufficiently bronzed by worldly habits to treat this accident with *nonchalance.* She did not *to the public eye* betray any embarrassment; but afterwards she told me that no incident could have been more distressing to her.

Some months after this, the Laxton party quitted Manchester, having no further motive for staying. Mrs. Schreiber was now confessedly dying: medical skill could do no more for her; and this being so, there was no reason why she should continue to exchange her own quiet little Rutlandshire cottage for the discomforts of smoky lodgings. Lady Carbery retired like some golden pageant amongst the clouds; thick darkness succeeded; the ancient torpor reestablished itself; and my health grew distressingly worse. Then it was, after dreadful self-conflicts, that I took the unhappy resolution of which the results are recorded in the "Opium Confessions." At this point, the reader must understand, comes in that chapter of my life; and for all which concerns that delirious period I refer him to those "Confessions." Some anxiety I had, on leaving Manchester, lest my mother should suffer too much from this rash step; and on that impulse I altered the direction of my wanderings; not going (as I had originally planned) to the English Lakes, but making first of all for St. John's Priory, Chester, at that time my mother's residence. There I found my maternal uncle, Captain Penson, of the Bengal establishment, just recently come home on a two years' leave of absence; and there I had an interview with my mother. By a temporary arrangement I received a weekly allowance, which would have enabled me to live in *any* district of Wales, either North or South; for Wales, both North and

South, is (or at any rate *was*) a land of exemplary cheapness.
For instance, at Talyllyn, in Merionethshire, or anywhere off
the line of tourists, I and a lieutenant in our English navy
paid sixpence uniformly for a handsome dinner; sixpence, I
mean, apiece. But two months later came a golden
blockhead, who instructed the people that it was "sinful" to
charge less than three shillings. In Wales, meantime, I
suffered grievously from want of books; and fancying, in my
profound ignorance of the world, that I could borrow
money upon my own expectations, or, at least, that I could
do so with the joint security of Lord Westport (now Earl of
Altamont, upon his father's elevation to the Marquisate of
Sligo), or (failing *that*) with the security of his amiable and
friendly cousin, the Earl of Desart, I had the unpardonable
folly to quit the deep tranquillities of North Wales for the
uproars, and perils, and the certain miseries, of London. I
had borrowed ten guineas from Lady Carbery; and at that
time, when my purpose was known to nobody, I might
have borrowed any sum I pleased. But I could never again
avail myself of that resource, because I must have given
some address, in order to insure the receipt of Lady
Carbery's answer; and in that case, so sternly conscientious
was she, that, under the notion of saving me from ruin, my
address would have been immediately communicated to my
guardians, and by them would have been confided to the
unrivalled detective talents, in those days, of Townsend, or
some other Bow-street officer.

* * * * *

That episode, or impassioned parenthesis in my life, which
is comprehended in "The Confessions of the Opium-Eater,"
had finished; suppose it over and gone, and once more, after
the storms of London, suppose me resting from my dreadful
remembrances, in the deep monastic tranquillity, of St.

John's Priory; and just then, by accident, with no associates
except my mother and my uncle. What was the Priory like?
Was it young or old, handsome or plain? What was my
uncle the captain like? Young or old, handsome or plain?
Wait a little, my reader; give me time, and I will tell you all.
My uncle's leave of absence from India had not expired; in
fact, it had nine or ten months still to run; and this accident
furnished us all with an opportunity of witnessing his
preternatural activity. One morning early in April of the
year 1803, a gentleman called at the Priory, and mentioned,
as the news of the morning brought down by the London
mail, that there had been a very hot and very sudden "press"
along the Thames, and simultaneously at the outports.
Indeed, before this the spiteful tone of Sebastiani's Report,
together with the arrogant comment in the *Moniteur* on the
supposed inability of Great Britain to contend "single-
handed" with France; and, finally, the public brutality to
our ambassador, had prepared us all for war. But, then,
might not all this blow over? No; apart from any choice or
preference of war on the part of Napoleon, his very existence
depended upon war. He lived by and through the army.
Without a succession of wars and martial glories in reserve
for the army, what interest had *they* in Napoleon? This was
obscurely acknowledged by everybody. More or less
consciously perceived, a feeling deep and strong ran
through the nation that it was vain to seek expedients or
delays; a mighty strife had to be fought out, which could
not be evaded. Thence it was that the volunteer system was
so rapidly and earnestly developed. As a first stage in the
process of national enthusiasm, this was invaluable. The
first impulse drew out the material.

Next, as might have been foreseen, came an experience
which taught us seasonably that these redundant materials,
crude and miscellaneous, required a winnowing and sifting,

which very soon we had; and the result was, an incomparable militia. Chester shone conspicuously in this noble competition. But here, as elsewhere, at first there was no cavalry. Upon that arose a knot of gentlemen, chiefly those who hunted, and in a very few hours laid the foundation of a small cavalry force. Three troops were raised in the *city* of Chester, one of the three being given to my uncle. The whole were under the command of Colonel Dod, who had a landed estate in the county, and who (like my uncle) had been in India. But Colonel Dod and the captains of the two other troops gave comparatively little aid. The whole working activities of the system rested with my uncle. Then first I saw energy: then first I knew what it meant. All the officers of the three troops exchanged dinner-parties with each other; and consequently they dined at the Priory often enough to make us acquainted with their characteristic qualities. That period had not yet passed away, though it was already passing, when gentlemen did not willingly leave the dinner-table in a state of absolute sobriety. Colonel Dod and my uncle had learned in Bengal, under the coërcion of the climate, habits of temperance. But the others (though few, perhaps, might be systematic drinkers) were careless in this respect, and drank under social excitement quite enough to lay bare the ruling tendencies of their several characters. Being English, naturally the majority were energetic, and beyond all things despised dreaming *fainéans* (such, for instance, as we find the politicians, or even the conspirators, of Italy, Spain, and Germany, whose whole power of action evaporates in talking, and histrionically gesticulating). Yet still the best of them seemed inert by comparison with my uncle, and to regard *his* standard of action and exertion as trespassing to a needless degree upon ordinary human comfort.

Commonplace, meantime, my uncle was in the character of

his intellect; there he fell a thousand leagues below my
mother, to whom he looked up with affectionate
astonishment. But, as a man of action, he ran so far ahead
of men generally, that he ceased to impress one as
commonplace. He, if any man ever did, realized the Roman
poet's description of being *natus rebus agendis*—sent into this
world not for talking, but for doing; not for counsel, but for
execution. On that field he was a portentous man, a
monster; and, viewing him as such, I am disposed to
concede a few words to what modern slang denominates his
"antecedents."

Two brothers and one sister (namely, my mother) composed
the household choir of children gathering round the hearth
of my maternal grand-parents, whose name was Penson. My
grandfather at one time held an office under the king; how
named, I once heard, but have forgotten; only this I
remember, that it was an office which conferred the title of
Esquire; so that upon each and all of his several coffins, lead,
oak, mahogany, he was entitled to proclaim himself an
Armiger; which, observe, is the newest, oldest, most classic
mode of saying that one is privileged to bear arms in a sense
intelligible only to the Herald's College. This *Armiger,* this
undeniable Squire, was doubly distinguished: first, by his
iron constitution and impregnable health; which were of
such quality, and like the sword of Michael, the warrior-
angel ("Paradise Lost," B. vi.), had "from the armory of God
been given him tempered so," that no insurance office,
trafficking in life-annuities, would have ventured to look
him in the face. People thought him good, like a cat, for
eight or nine generations; nor did any man perceive at what
avenue death could find, or disease could force, a practicable
breach; and yet, such anchorage have all human hopes, in
the very midst of these windy anticipations, this same
granite grandpapa of mine, not yet very far ahead of sixty,

being in fact three-score years and none, suddenly struck
his flag, and found himself, in his privileged character of
Armiger, needing those door (coffin-door) plates, which all
reasonable people had supposed to be reserved for the
manufacturing hands of some remote century. "*Armiger*, pack
up your traps"—"Collige sarcinas"—"Squire, you're wanted:"
these dreadful citations were inevitable; come they must; but
surely, as everybody thought, not in the eighteenth, or,
perhaps, even the nineteenth century. *Diis aliter visum.* My
grandfather, built for an *Conian* duration, did not come
within hail of myself; whilst his gentle partner, my
grandmother, who made no show of extra longevity, lived
down into my period, and had the benefit of my
acquaintance through half a dozen years. If she turned this
piece of good fortune to no great practical account, that
(you know) was no fault of mine. Doubtless, I was ready
with my advice, freely and gratuitously, if she had
condescended to ask for it. Returning to my grandfather: the
other distinguishing endowment, by which he was so
favorably known and remembered amongst his friends, was
the magical versatility of his talents, and his power of self-
accommodation to all humors, tempers, and ages.

"Omnis Aristippum decuit color, et status, et res."

And in allusion to this line from Horace it was, that
amongst his literary friends he was known familiarly by the
name of Aristippus. His sons, Edward and Thomas,
resembled him, by all accounts, in nothing; neither
physically, nor in moral versatility. These two sons of the
Squire, Edward and Thomas, through some traditional
prejudice in the family, had always directed their views to
the military profession. In such a case, the king's army is
naturally that to which a young man's expectations turn.
But to wait, and after all by possibility to wait in vain, did

not suit my fiery grandfather. The interest which he could put into motion was considerable; but it was more applicable to the service of the East India Company than to any branch of the home service. This interest was so exerted that in one day he obtained a lieutenantcy in the Company's service for each of his sons. About 1780 or 1781, both young men, aged severally sixteen and seventeen years, went out to join their regiments, both regiments being on the Bengal establishment. Very different were their fates; yet their qualifications ought to have been the same, or differing only as sixteen differs from seventeen; and also as sixteen overflowing with levity differs from seventeen prematurely thoughtful. Edward Penson was early noticed for his high principle, for his benignity, and for a thoughtfulness somewhat sorrowful, that seemed to have caught in childhood some fugitive glimpse of his own too brief career. At noonday, in some part of Bengal, he went out of doors bareheaded, and died in a few hours.

In 1800-1801, my mother had become dissatisfied with Bath as a residence; and, being free from all ties connecting her with any one county of England rather than another, she resolved to traverse the most attractive parts of the island, and, upon personal inspection, to select a home; not a ready-built home, but the ground on which she might herself create one; for it happened that amongst the few infirmities besetting my mother's habits and constitution of mind, was the costly one of seeking her chief intellectual excitement in architectural creations. She individually might be said to have built Greenhay; since to *her* views of domestic elegance and propriety my father had resigned *almost* everything. This was her *coup-d'essai*; secondly, she built the complement to the Priory in Cheshire, which cost about one thousand pounds; thirdly, Westhay, in Somersetshire, about twelve miles from Bristol, which, including the land attached to the house, cost twelve thousand five hundred pounds, not including subsequent additions; but this was built at the cost of my uncle; finally, Weston Lea, close to Bath, which being designed simply for herself in old age, with a moderate establishment of four servants (and some reasonable provision of accommodations for a few visitors), cost originally, I believe, not more than one thousand pounds—excluding, however, the cost of all after alterations.

It may serve to show how inevitably an amateur architect, without professional aid and counsel, will be defrauded, that the first of these houses, which cost six thousand pounds, sold for no more than twenty-five hundred pounds, and the third for no more than five thousand pounds. The person who superintended the workmen, and had the whole practical management of one amongst these four houses, was a common builder, without capital or education, and the greatest knave that personally I have known. It may illustrate the way in which lady architects, without professional aid, are and ever will be defrauded, that, after all was finished, and the entire wood-work was to be measured and valued, each party, of course, needing to be represented by a professional agent, naturally the knavish builder was ready at earliest dawn with *his* agent; but, as regarded my mother's interest, the task of engaging such an agent had been confided to a neighboring clergyman, —"evangelical," of course, and a humble sycophant of Hannah More, but otherwise the most helpless of human beings, baptized or infidel. He contented himself with instructing a young gentleman, aged about fifteen, to take his pony and ride over to a distant cathedral town, which was honored by the abode of a virtuous though drunken surveyor. This respectable drunkard he was to engage, and also with obvious discretion to fee beforehand. All which was done: the drunken surveyor had a sort of fits, it was understood, that always towards sunset inclined him to assume the horizontal posture. Fortunately, however, for that part of mankind whom circumstances had brought under the necessity of communicating with him, these fits were intermitting; so that, for instance, in the present case, upon a severe call arising for his pocketing the fee of ten guineas, he astonished his whole household by suddenly standing bolt upright as stiff as a poker; his sister remarking to the young gentleman that he (the visitor) was in luck that evening: it wasn't everybody that could get that length in dealing with Mr. X. O. However, it is distressing to relate that the fits immediately returned; and, with that degree of exasperation which made it dangerous to suggest the idea of a receipt; since that must have required the vertical attitude. Whether that attitude ever was recovered by the unfortunate gentleman, I do not know. Forty-and-four years have passed since then. Almost everybody connected with the case has had time to assume permanently the horizontal posture,—namely, that knave of a builder, whose knaveries (gilded by that morning sun of June) were controlled by nobody; that sycophantish parson; that young gentleman of fifteen (now, alas! fifty-nine), who must long since have sown his wild oats; that unhappy pony of eighteen (now, alas! sixty-two, if living; ah! venerable pony, that must (or mustest) now require thy oats to be boiled); in short, one and all of these venerabilities—knaves, ponies, drunkards, receipts—have descended, I believe, to chaos or to Hades, with hardly one exception. Chancery itself, though somewhat of an Indian juggler, could not play with such aerial balls as these.

On what ground it was that my mother quarrelled with the advantages of Bath, so many and so conspicuous, I cannot guess. At that time, namely, the opening of the nineteenth century, the old traditionary custom of the place had established for young and old the luxury of sedan-chairs. Nine tenths, at least, of the colds and catarrhs, those initial stages of all pulmonary complaints (the capital scourge of England), are caught in the transit between the door of a carriage and the genial atmosphere of the drawing-room. By a sedan-chair all this danger was evaded: your two chairmen marched right into the hall: the hall-door was closed; and not until then was the roof and the door of your chair opened: the translation was—from one room to another. To my mother, and many in her situation, the sedan-chair recommended itself also by advantages of another class. Immediately on coming to Bath her carriage was "laid up in ordinary." The trifling rent of a coach-house, some slight annual repairs, and the tax, composed the whole annual cost. At that time, and throughout the war, the usual estimate for the cost of a close carriage in London was three hundred and twenty pounds; since, in order to have the certain services of two horses, it was indispensable to keep three. Add to this the coachman, the wear-and-tear of harness, and the duty; and, even in Bath, a cheaper place than London, you could not accomplish the total service under two hundred and seventy pounds. Now, except the duty, all this expense was at once superseded by the sedan-chair—rarely costing you above ten shillings a week, that is, twenty-five guineas a year, and liberating you from all care or anxiety. The duty on four wheels, it is true, was suddenly exalted by Mr. Pitt's triple assessment from twelve guineas to thirty-six; but what a trifle by comparison with the cost of horses and coachman! And, then, no demands for money were ever met so cheerfully by my mother as those which went to support Mr. Pitt's policy against Jacobinism and Regicide. At present, after five years' sinecure existence, unless on the rare summons of a journey, this dormant carriage was suddenly undocked, and put into commission.

Taking with her two servants, and one of my sisters, my mother now entered upon a *periplus*, or systematic circumnavigation of all England; and in England only—through the admirable machinery matured for such a purpose, namely, inns, innkeepers, servants, horses, all first-rate of their class—it was possible to pursue such a scheme in the midst of domestic comfort. My mother's resolution was—to see all England with her own eyes, and to judge for herself upon the qualifications of each county, each town (not being a bustling seat of commerce), and each village (having any advantages of scenery), for contributing the main elements towards a home that might justify her in building a house. The qualifications insisted on were these five: good medical advice somewhere in the neighborhood; first-rate means of education; elegant (or, what most people might think, aristocratic) society; agreeable scenery: and so far the difficulty was not insuperable in the way of finding all the four advantages concentrated. But my mother insisted on a fifth, which in those days insured the instant shipwreck of the entire scheme; this was a church of England parish clergyman, who was to be strictly orthodox, faithful to the articles of our English church, yet to these articles as interpreted by Evangelical divinity. My mother's views were precisely those of her friend Mrs. Hannah More, of Wilberforce, of Henry Thornton, of Zachary Macaulay (father of the historian), and generally of those who were then known amongst sneerers as "the Clapham saints." This one requisition it was on which the scheme foundered. And the fact merits recording as an exposition of the broad religious difference between the England of that day and of this. At present, no difficulty would be found as to this fifth requisition. "Evangelical" clergymen are now sown broadcast; at that period, there were not, on an average, above six or eight in each of the fifty-two counties.

The conditions, as a whole, were in fact incapable of being realized; where two or three were attained, three or two failed. It was too much to exact so many advantages from any one place, unless London; or really, if any other place could be looked to with hope in such a chase, that place was Bath—the very city my mother was preparing to leave. Yet, had this been otherwise, and the prospect of success more promising, I have not a doubt that the pretty gem, which suddenly was offered at a price unintelligibly low, in the ancient city of Chester, would have availed (as instantly it *did* avail, and, perhaps, ought to have availed) in obscuring those five conditions of which else each separately for itself had seemed a *conditio sine qua non*. This gem was an ancient house, on a miniature scale, called the *Priory*; and, until the dissolution of religious houses in the earlier half of the sixteenth century, had formed part of the Priory attached to the ancient church (still flourishing) of St. John's. Towards the end of the sixteenth and through the first quarter of the seventeenth century, this Priory had been in the occupation of Sir Robert Cotton, the antiquary, the friend of Ben Jonson, of Coke, of Selden, etc., and advantageously known as one of those who applied his legal and historical knowledge to the bending back into constitutional moulds of those despotic twists which new interests and false counsels had developed in the Tudor and Stuart dynasties. It was an exceedingly pretty place; and the kitchen, upon the ground story, which had a noble groined ceiling of stone, indicated, by its disproportionate scale, the magnitude of the establishment to which once it had ministered. Attached to this splendid kitchen were tributary offices, etc. On the upper story were exactly five rooms: namely, a servants' dormitory, meant in Sir Robert's day for two beds [Footnote: The contrivance amongst our ancestors, even at haughty Cambridge and haughtier Oxford, was, that one bed rising six inches from the floor ran (in the day-time) under a loftier bed; it ran upon castors or little wheels. The learned word for a little wheel is *trochlea*; from which Grecian and Latin term comes the English word *truckle*-bed.] at the least; and a servants' sitting-room. These were shut off into a separate section, with a little staircase (like a ship's companion-ladder) and a little lobby of its own. But the principal section on this upper story had been dedicated to the use of Sir Robert, and consisted of a pretty old hall, lighted by an old monastic-painted window in the door of entrance; secondly, a rather elegant dining-room; thirdly, a bed-room. The glory of the house internally lay in the monastic kitchen; and, secondly, in what a Frenchman would have called, properly, Sir Robert's own *apartment* [Footnote: *Apartment.*—Our English use of the word "apartment" is absurd, since it leads to total misconceptions. We read in French memoirs innumerable of *the king's apartment*, of *the queen's apartment*, etc., and for us English the question arises, How? Had the king, had her majesty, only one room? But, my friend, they might have a thousand rooms, and yet have only one apartment. An apartment means, in the continental use, a section or *compartment* of an edifice.] of three rooms; but, thirdly and chiefly, in a pile of ruined archways, most picturesque so far as they went, but so small that Drury Lane could easily have found room for them on its stage. These stood in the miniature pleasure-ground, and were constantly resorted to by artists for specimens of architectural decays, or of nature working for the concealment of such decays by her ordinary processes of gorgeous floral vegetation. Ten rooms there may have been in the Priory, as offered to my mother for less than five hundred pounds. A drawing-room, bed-rooms, dressing-rooms, etc., making about ten more, were added by my mother for a sum under one thousand pounds. The same miniature scale was observed in all these additions. And, as the Priory was not within the walls of the city, whilst the river Dee, flowing immediately below, secured it from annoyance on one side, and the church, with its adjacent church-yard, insulated it from the tumults of life on all the other sides, an atmosphere of conventual stillness and tranquillity brooded over it and all around it forever.

Such was the house, such was the society, in which I now found myself; and upon the whole I might describe myself as being, according to the modern phrase, "in a false position." I had, for instance, a vast superiority, as was to have been expected, in bookish attainments, and in adroitness of logic; whilst, on the other hand, I was ridiculously short-sighted or blind in all fields of ordinary human experience. It must not be supposed that I regarded my own particular points of superiority, or that I used them, with any vanity or view to present advantages. On the contrary, I sickened over them, and labored to defeat them. But in vain I sowed errors in my premises, or planted absurdities in my assumptions. Vainly I tried such blunders as putting four terms into a syllogism, which, as all the world knows, ought to run on three; a tripod it ought to be, by all rules known to man, and, behold, I forced it to become a quadruped. Upon my uncle's military haste, and tumultuous energy in pressing his opinions, all such delicate refinements were absolutely thrown away. With disgust *I* saw, with disgust *he* saw, that too apparently the advantage lay with me in the result; and, whilst I worked like a dragon to place myself in the wrong, some fiend apparently so counterworked me, that eternally I was reminded of the Manx half-pennies, which lately I had continually seen current in North Wales, bearing for their heraldic distinction three human legs in armor, but so placed in relation to each other that always one leg is vertical and mounting guard on behalf of the other two, which, therefore, are enabled to sprawl aloft in the air—in fact, to be as absurdly negligent as they choose, relying upon their vigilant brother below, and upon the written legend or motto, STABIT QUOCUNQUE JECERIS (Stand it will upright, though you should fling it in any conceivable direction). What gave another feature of distraction and incoherency to my position was, that I still occupied the position of a reputed boy, nay, a child, in the estimate of my audience, and of a child in disgrace. Time enough had not passed since my elopement from school to win for me, in minds so fresh from that remembrance, a station of purification and assoilment. Oxford might avail to assoil me, and to throw into a distant retrospect my boyish trespasses; but as yet Oxford had not arrived. I committed, besides, a great fault in taking often a tone of mock seriousness, when the detection of the playful extravagance was left to the discernment or quick sympathy of the hearer; and I was blind to the fact, that neither my mother nor my uncle was distinguished by any natural liveliness of vision for the comic, or any toleration for the extravagant. My mother, for example, had an awful sense of conscientious fidelity in the payment of taxes. Many a respectable family I have known that would privately have encouraged a smuggler, and, in consequence, were beset continually by mock smugglers, offering, with airs of affected mystery, home commodities liable to no custom-house objections whatsoever, only at a hyperbolical price. I remember even the case of a duke, who bought in Piccadilly, under laughable circumstances of complex disguise, some silk handkerchiefs, falsely pretending to be foreign, and was so incensed at finding himself to have been committing no breach of law whatever, but simply to have been paying double the ordinary shop price, that he pulled up the *soi-disant* smuggler to Bowstreet, even at the certain price of exposure to himself. The charge he alleged against the man was the untenable one of *not* being a smuggler. My mother, on the contrary, pronounced all such attempts at cheating the king, or, as I less harshly termed it, cheating the tax-gatherer, as being equal in guilt to a fraud upon one's neighbor, or to direct appropriation of another man's purse. I, on my part, held, that government, having often defrauded me through its agent and creature the post-office, by monstrous over-charges on letters, had thus created in my behalf a right of retaliation. And dreadfully it annoyed my mother, that I, stating this right in a very plausible rule-of-three form—namely, As is the income of the said fraudulent government to my poor patrimonial income of one hundred and fifty pounds per annum, so is any one special fraud (as, for instance, that of yesterday morning, amounting to thirteen pence upon a single letter) to that equitable penalty which I am entitled to recover upon the goods and chattels (wherever found) of the ill-advised Britannic government. During the war with Napoleon, the income of this government ran, to all amounts, between fifty and seventy millions pounds sterling. Awful, therefore, seemed the inheritance of retaliation, inexhaustible the fund of reprisals, into which I stepped. Since, even a single case of robbery, such as I could plead by dozens, in the course of a few years, though no more than thirteen pence, yet multiplied into seventy million times two hundred and forty pence, *minus* one hundred and fifty pounds, made a very comfortable property. The right was clear; and the sole difficulty lay in asserting it; in fact, that same difficulty which beset the philosopher of old, in arguing with the Emperor Hadrian; namely, the want of thirty legions for the purpose of clearly pointing out to César where it was that the truth lay; the secret truth; that rarest of all "nuggets."

This counter-challenge of government, as the first mover in a system of frauds, annoyed, but also perplexed my mother exceedingly. For an argument that shaped itself into a rule-of-three illustration seemed really to wear too candid an aspect for summary and absolute rejection.

Such discussions wore to me a comic shape. But altogether serious were the disputes upon INDIA—a topic on separate grounds equally interesting to us all, as the mightiest of English colonies, and the superbest monument of demoniac English energy, revealing itself in such men as Clive, Hastings, and soon after in the two Wellesleys. To my mother, as the grave of one brother, as the home of another, and as a new centre from which Christianity (she hoped) would mount like an eagle; for just about that time the Bible Society was preparing its initial movements; whilst to my uncle India appeared as the *arena* upon which his activities were yet to find their adequate career. With respect to the Christianization of India, my uncle assumed a hope which he did not really feel; and in another point, more trying to himself personally, he had soon an opportunity for showing the sincerity of this deference to his spiritual-minded sister. For, very soon after his return to India, he received a civil appointment (*Superintendent of Military Buildings in Bengal*), highly lucrative, and the more so as it could be held conjointly with his military rank; but a good deal of its pecuniary advantages was said to lie in fees, or perquisites, privately offered, but perfectly regular and official, which my mother (misunderstanding the Indian system) chose to call "bribes." A very ugly word was *that*; but I argued that even at home, even in the courts at Westminster, in the very fountains of justice, private fees constituted one part of the salaries—a fair and official part, so long as Parliament had not made such fees illegal by commuting them for known and fixed equivalents.

It was mere ignorance of India, as I dutifully insisted against "Mamma," that could confound these regular oriental "nuzzers" with the clandestine wages of corruption. The *pot-de-vin* of French tradition, the pair of gloves (though at one time very costly gloves) to an English judge of assize on certain occasions, never was offered nor received in the light of a bribe. And (until regularly abolished by the legislature) I insisted—but vainly insisted—that these and similar *honoraria* ought to be accepted, because else you were lowering the prescriptive rights and value of the office, which you—a mere *locum tenens* for some coming successor —had no right to do upon a solitary scruple or crotchet, arising probably from dyspepsia. Better men, no doubt, than ever stood in *your* stockings, had pocketed thankfully the gifts of ancient, time-honored custom. My uncle, however, though not with the carnal recusancy which besieged the spiritual efforts of poor Cuthbert Headrigg, that incorrigible worldling, yet still with intermitting doubts, followed my mother's earnest entreaties, and the more meritoriously (I conceive), as he yielded, in a point deeply affecting his interest, to a system of arguments very imperfectly convincing to his understanding. He held the office in question for as much (I believe) as eighteen or nineteen years; and, by knowing old bilious Indians, who laughed immoderately at my uncle and my mother, as the proper growth of a priory or some such monastic establishment, I have been assured that nothing short of two hundred thousand pounds ought, under the long tenure of office, to have been remitted to England. But, then, said one of these gentlemen, if your uncle lived (as I have heard that he did) in Calcutta and Meer-ut, at the rate of four thousand pounds a year, *that* would account for a considerable share of a mine which else would seem to have been worked in vain. Unquestionably, my uncle's system of living was under no circumstances a self-denying one. To enjoy, and to make others enjoy—*that* was his law of action. Indeed, a more liberal creature, or one of more princely munificence, never lived.

It might seem useless to call back any fragment of conversations relating to India which passed more than fifty years ago, were it not for two reasons: one of which is this, —that the errors (natural at that time) which I vehemently opposed, not from any greater knowledge that I had, but from closer reflection, are even now the prevailing errors of the English people. My mother, for instance, uniformly spoke of the English as the subverters of ancient thrones. I, on the contrary, insisted that nothing political was ancient in India. Our own original opponents, the Rajahs of Oude and Bengal, had been all upstarts: in the Mysore, again, our more recent opponents, Hyder, and his son Tippoo, were new men altogether, whose grandfathers were quite unknown. Why was it that my mother, why is it that the English public at this day, connect so false an image—that of high, cloudy antiquity —with the thrones of India? It is simply from an old habit of associating the spirit of change and rapid revolution with the activities of Europe; so that, by a natural reaction of thought, the Orient is figured as the home of motionless monotony. In things religious, in habits, in costume, it *is* so. But so far otherwise in things political, that no instance can be alleged of any dynasty or system of government that has endured beyond a century or two in the East. Taking India in particular, the Mogul dynasty, established by Baber, the great-grandson of Timour, did not subsist in any vigor for two centuries; and yet this was by far the most durable of all established princely houses. Another argument against England urged by my mother (but equally urged by the English people at this day) was, that she had in no eminent sense been a benefactress to India; or, expressing it in words of later date, that the only memorials of our rule, supposing us suddenly ejected from India, would be vast heaps of champagne-bottles. I, on the other hand, alleged that our benefits, like all truly great and lasting benefits (religious benefits, for instance), must not be sought in external memorials of stone and masonry. Higher by far than the Mogul gifts of mile-stones, or travelling stations, or even roads and tanks, were the gifts of security, of peace, of law, and settled order. These blessings were travelling as fast as our rule advanced. I could not *then* appeal to the cases of Thuggee extirpated, of the Pindanees (full fifteen thousand bloody murderers) forever exterminated, or of the Marhattas bridled forever—a robber nation that previously had descended at intervals with a force of sometimes one hundred and fifty thousand troopers upon the afflicted province of Bengal, and Oude its neighbor; because these were events as yet unborn. But they were the natural extensions of that beneficent system on which I rested my argument. The two terrors of India at that particular time were Holkar and Scindiah (pronounced *Sindy*), who were soon cut short in their career by the hostilities which they provoked with us, but would else have proved, in combination, a deadlier scourge to India than either Hyder or his ferocious son. My mother, in fact, a great reader of the poet Cowper, drew from *him* her notions of Anglo-Indian policy and its effects. Cowper, in his "Task," puts the question,— "Is India free? and does she wear her plumed And jewelled turban with a smile of peace, Or do we grind her still?"

Pretty much the same authority it is which the British public of this day has for its craze upon the subject of English oppression amongst the Hindoos.

My uncle, meantime, who from his Indian experience should reasonably have known so much better, was disposed, from the mere passive habits of hearing and reading unresistingly so many assaults of this tone against our Indian policy, to go along with my mother. But he was too just, when forced into reflection upon the subject, not to bend at times to my way of stating the case for England. Suddenly, however, our Indian discussions were brought to a close by the following incident. My uncle had brought with him to England some Arabian horses, and amongst them a beautiful young Persian mare, called Sumroo, the gentlest of her race. Sumroo it was that he happened to be riding, upon a frosty day. Unused to ice, she came down with him, and broke his right leg. This accident laid him up for a month, during which my mother and I read to him by turns. One book, which one day fell to my share by accident, was De Foe's "Memoirs of a Cavalier." This book attempts to give a picture of the Parliamentary war; but in some places an unfair, and everywhere a most superficial account. I said so; and my uncle, who had an old craze in behalf of the book, opposed me with asperity; and, in the course of what he said, under some movement of ill-temper, he asked me, in a way which I felt to be taunting, how I could consent to waste my time as I did. Without any answering warmth, I explained that my guardians, having quarrelled with me, would not grant for my use anything beyond my school allowance of one hundred pounds per annum. But was it not possible that even this sum might by economy be made to meet the necessities of the case? I replied that, from what I had heard, very probably it was. Would I undertake an Oxford life upon such terms? Most gladly, I said. Upon that opening he spoke to my mother; and the result was, that, within seven days from the above conversation, I found myself entering that time-honored university.

OXFORD.

OXFORD.

It was in winter, and in the wintry weather of the year 1803, that I first entered Oxford with a view to its vast means of education, or rather with a view to its vast advantages for study. A ludicrous story is told of a young candidate for clerical orders—that, being asked by the bishop's chaplain if he had ever "been to Oxford," as a colloquial expression for having had an academic education, he replied, "No: but he had twice been to Abingdon:" Abingdon being only seven miles distant. In the same sense I might say that once before I had been at Oxford: but *that* was as a transient visitor with Lord W——, when we were both children. Now, on the contrary, I approached these venerable towers in the character of a student, and with the purpose of a long connection; personally interested in the constitution of the university, and obscurely anticipating that in this city, or at least during the period of my nominal attachment to this academic body, the remoter parts of my future life would unfold before me. All hearts were at this time occupied with the public interests of the country. The "sorrow of the time" was ripening to a second harvest. Napoleon had commenced his Vandal, or rather Hunnish War with Britain, in the spring of this year, about eight months before; and profound public interest it was, into which the very coldest hearts entered, that a little divided with me the else monopolizing awe attached to the solemn act of launching myself upon the world. That expression may seem too strong as applied to one who had already been for many months a houseless wanderer in Wales, and a solitary roamer in the streets of London. But in those situations, it must be remembered, I was an unknown, unacknowledged vagrant; and without money I could hardly run much risk, except of breaking my neck. The perils, the pains, the pleasures, or the obligations, of the world, scarcely exist in a proper sense for him who has no funds. Perfect weakness is often secure; it is by imperfect power, turned against its master, that men are snared and decoyed. Here in Oxford I should be called upon to commence a sort of establishment upon the splendid English scale; here I should share in many duties and responsibilities, and should become henceforth an object of notice to a large society. Now first becoming separately and individually answerable for my conduct, and no longer absorbed into the general unit of a family, I felt myself, for the first time, burthened with the anxieties of a man, and a member of the world.

Oxford, ancient mother! hoary with ancestral honors, time-honored, and, haply, it may be, time-shattered power—I owe thee nothing! Of thy vast riches I took not a shilling, though living amongst multitudes who owed to thee their daily bread. Not the less I owe thee justice; for that is a universal debt. And at this moment, when I see thee called to thy audit by unjust and malicious accusers—men with the hearts of inquisitors and the purposes of robbers—I feel towards thee something of filial reverence and duty. However, I mean not to speak as an advocate, but as a conscientious witness in the simplicity of truth; feeling neither hope nor fear of a personal nature, without fee, and without favor.

I have been assured from many quarters that the great body of the public are quite in the dark about the whole manner of living in our English universities; and that a considerable portion of that public, misled by the totally different constitution of universities in Scotland, Ireland, and generally on the continent, as well as by the different arrangements of collegiate life in those institutions, are in a state worse than ignorant (that is, more unfavorable to the truth)—starting, in fact, from prejudices, and absolute errors of fact, which operate most uncharitably upon their construction of those insulated statements, which are continually put forward by designing men. Hence, I can well believe that it will be an acceptable service, at this particular moment, when the very constitution of the two English universities is under the unfriendly revision of Parliament, when some roving commission may be annually looked for, under a contingency which I will not utter in words (for I reverence the doctrine of *euphćmismos*), far worse than Cromwellian, that is, merely personal, and to winnow the existing corporation from disaffection to the state—a Henry the Eighth commission of sequestration, and levelled at the very integrity of the institution—under such prospects, I can well believe that a true account of Oxford *as it is* (which will be valid also for Cambridge) must be welcome both to friend and foe. And instead of giving this account didactically, or according to a logical classification of the various items in the survey, I will give it historically, or according to the order in which the most important facts of the case opened themselves before myself, under the accidents of my own personal inquiry. No situation could be better adapted than my own for eliciting information; for, whereas most young men come to the university under circumstances of absolute determination as to the choice of their particular college, and have, therefore, no cause for search or inquiry, I, on the contrary, came thither in solitary

126

self-dependence, and in the loosest state of indetermination.

Though neither giving nor accepting invitations for the first two years of my residence, never but once had I reason to complain of a sneer, or indeed any allusion whatever to habits which might be understood to express poverty. Perhaps even then I had no reason to complain, for my own conduct in that instance was unwise; and the allusion, though a personality, and so far ill-bred, might be meant in real kindness. The case was this: I neglected my dress in one point habitually; that is, I wore clothes until they were threadbare—partly in the belief that my gown would conceal their main defects, but much more from carelessness and indisposition to spend upon a tailor what I had destined for a bookseller. At length, an official person, of some weight in the college, sent me a message on the subject through a friend. It was couched in these terms: That, let a man possess what talents or accomplishments he might, it was not possible for him to maintain his proper station, in the public respect, amongst so many servants and people, servile to external impressions, without some regard to the elegance of his dress.

A reproof so courteously prefaced I could not take offence at; and at that time I resolved to spend some cost upon decorating my person. But always it happened that some book, or set of books,—that passion being absolutely endless, and inexorable as the grave,—stepped between me and my intentions; until one day, upon arranging my toilet hastily before dinner, I suddenly made the discovery that I had no waistcoat (or *vest*, as it is now called, through conceit or provincialism), which was not torn or otherwise dilapidated; whereupon, buttoning up my coat to the throat, and drawing my gown as close about me as possible, I went into the public "hall" (so is called in Oxford the public eating-room) with no misgiving. However, I was detected; for a grave man, with a superlatively grave countenance, who happened on that day to sit next me, but whom I did not personally know, addressing his friend sitting opposite, begged to know if he had seen the last Gazette, because he understood that it contained an order in council laying an interdict upon the future use of waistcoats. His friend replied, with the same perfect gravity, that it was a great satisfaction to his mind that his majesty's government should have issued so sensible an order; which he trusted would be soon followed up by an interdict on breeches, they being still more disagreeable to pay for. This said, without the movement on either side of a single muscle, the two gentlemen passed to other subjects; and I inferred, upon the whole, that, having detected my manoeuvre, they wished to put me on my guard in the only way open to them. At any rate, this was the sole personality, or equivocal allusion of any sort, which ever met my ear during the years that I asserted my right to be as poor as I chose. And, certainly, my censors were right, whatever were the temper in which they spoke, kind or unkind; for a little extra care in the use of clothes will always, under almost any extremity of poverty, pay for so much extra cost as is essential to neatness and decorum, if not even to elegance. They were right, and I was wrong, in a point which cannot be neglected with impunity.

But, to enter upon my own history, and my sketch of Oxford life. — Late on a winter's night, in the latter half of December, 1803, when a snow-storm, and a heavy one, was already gathering in the air, a lazy Birmingham coach, moving at four and a half miles an hour, brought me through the long northern suburb of Oxford, to a shabby coach-inn, situated in the Corn Market. Business was out of the question at that hour. But the next day I assembled all the acquaintances I had in the university, or had to my own knowledge; and to them, in council assembled, propounded my first question: What college would they, in their superior state of information, recommend to my choice? This question leads to the first great characteristic of Oxford, as distinguished from most other universities. Before me at this moment lie several newspapers, reporting, at length, the installation in office (as Chancellor) of the Duke of Wellington. The original Oxford report, having occasion to mention the particular college from which the official procession moved, had said, no doubt, that the gates of University, the halls of University, &c., were at such a point of time thrown open. But most of the provincial editors, not at all comprehending that the reference was to an individual college, known by the name of University College, one of twenty-five such establishments in Oxford, had regularly corrected it into "gates of the University," &c. Here is the first misconception of all strangers. And this feature of Oxford it is which has drawn such exclamations of astonishment from foreigners. Lipsius, for example, protested with fervor, on first seeing this vast establishment of Oxford, that one college of this university was greater in its power and splendor, that it glorified and illustrated the honors of literature more conspicuously by the pomps with which it invested the ministers and machinery of education, than any entire university of the continent.

What is a university almost everywhere else? It announces
little more, as respects the academic buildings, than that
here is to be found the place of rendezvous—the exchange,
as it were, or, under a different figure, the *palćstra* of the
various parties connected with the prosecution of liberal
studies. This is their "House of Call," their general place of
muster and parade. Here it is that the professors and the
students converge, with the certainty of meeting each other.
Here, in short, are the lecture-rooms in all the faculties.
Well: thus far we see an arrangement of convenience—that
is, of convenience for one of the parties, namely, the
professors. To them it spares the disagreeable circumstances
connected with a private reception of their students at their
own rooms. But to the students it is a pure matter of
indifference. In all this there is certainly no service done to
the cause of good learning, which merits a state sanction, or
the aid of national funds. Next, however, comes an academic
library, sometimes a good one; and here commences a real
use in giving a national station to such institutions, because
their durable and monumental existence, liable to no flux or
decay from individual caprice, or accidents of life, and their
authentic station, as expressions of the national grandeur,
point them out to the bequests of patriotic citizens. They fall
also under the benefit of another principle—the conservative
feeling of amateurship. Several great collections have been
bequeathed to the British Museum, for instance—not chiefly
as a national institution, and under feelings of nationality,
but because, being such, it was also permanent; and thus
the painful labors of collecting were guaranteed from
perishing. Independently of all this, I, for my part, willingly
behold the surplus of national funds dedicated to the
consecration, as it were, of learning, by raising temples to its
honor, even where they answer no purpose of direct use.
Next, after the service of religion, I would have the service of

learning externally embellished, recommended to the affections of men, and hallowed by the votive sculptures, as I may say, of that affection, gathering in amount from age to age. *Magnificabo apostolatum meum* is a language almost as becoming to the missionaries and ministers of knowledge, as to the ambassadors of religion. It is fit that by pompous architectural monuments, that a voice may forever be sounding audibly in human ears of homage to these powers, and that even alien feelings may be compelled into secret submission to their influence. Therefore, amongst the number of those who value such things, upon the scale of direct proximate utility, rank not me: that *arithmetica officina* is in my years abominable. But still I affirm that, in our analysis of an ordinary university, or "college" as it is provincially called, we have not yet arrived at any element of service rendered to knowledge or education, large enough to call for very extensive national aid. Honor has thus far been rendered to the good cause by a public attestation, and that is well: but no direct promotion has been given to that cause, no impulse communicated to its progress, such that it can be held out as a result commensurate to the name and pretensions of a university. As yet there is nothing accomplished which is beyond the strength of any little commercial town. And as to the library in particular, besides that in all essential departments it might be bought, to order, by one day's common subscription of Liverpool or Glasgow merchants, students very rarely indeed have admission to its free use.

What other functions remain to a university? For those which I have mentioned of furnishing a point of rendezvous to the great body of professors and students, and a point of concentration to the different establishments of implements and machinery for elaborate researches [as, for instance, of books and MSS., in the first place; secondly, of maps, charts, and globes; and, thirdly, perhaps of the costly apparatus required for such studies as Sideral astronomy, galvanic chemistry or physiology, &c.]; all these are uses which cannot be regarded in a higher light than as conveniences merely incidental and collateral to the main views of the founders. There are, then, two much loftier and more commanding ends met by the idea and constitution of such institutions, and which first rise to a rank of dignity sufficient to occupy the views of a legislator, or to warrant a national interest. These ends are involved: 1st, in the practice of conferring *degrees*, that is, formal attestations and guarantees of competence to give advice, instruction, or aid, in the three great branches of liberal knowledge applicable to human life; 2d, in that appropriation of fixed funds to fixed professorships, by means of which the uninterrupted succession of public and authorized teachers is sustained in all the higher branches of knowledge, from generation to generation, and from century to century. By the latter result it is secured that the great well-heads of liberal knowledge and of severe science shall never grow dry. By the former it is secured that this unfailing fountain shall be continually applied to the production and to the *tasting* of fresh labors in endless succession for the public service, and thus, in effect, that the great national fountain shall not be a stagnant reservoir, but, by an endless *derivation* (to speak in a Roman metaphor!), applied to a system of national irrigation. These are the two great functions and qualifications of a collegiate incorporation: one providing to each separate generation its own separate rights of heirship to all the knowledge accumulated by its predecessors, and converting a mere casual life-annuity into an estate of inheritance—a mere fleeting *agonisma* into a *ktéma es ái*; the other securing for this eternal dowry as wide a distribution as possible: the one function regarding the dimension of *length* in the endless series of ages through which it propagates its gifts; the

other regarding the dimension of *breadth* in the large
application throughout any one generation of these gifts to
the public service. Here are grand functions, high purposes;
but neither one nor the other demands any edifices of stone
and marble; neither one nor the other presupposes any
edifice at all built with human hands. A collegiate
incorporation, the church militant of knowledge, in its
everlasting struggle with darkness and error, is, in this
respect, like the church of Christ—that is, it is always and
essentially invisible to the fleshly eye. The pillars of this
church are human champions; its weapons are great truths
so shaped as to meet the shifting forms of error; its armories
are piled and marshalled in human memories; its cohesion
lies in human zeal, in discipline, in childlike docility; and all
its triumphs, its pomps, and glories, must forever depend
upon talent, upon the energies of the will, and upon the
harmonious cooperation of its several divisions. Thus far, I
say, there is no call made out for *any* intervention of the
architect.

Let me apply all this to Oxford. Among the four functions
commonly recognized by the founders of universities, which
are—1st, to find a set of halls or places of meeting; 2d, to
find the implements and accessaries of study; 3d, to secure
the succession of teachers and learners; 4th, to secure the
profitable application of their attainments to the public
service. Of these four, the two highest need no buildings;
and the other two, which are mere collateral functions of
convenience, need only a small one. Wherefore, then, and to
what end, are the vast systems of building, the palaces and
towers of Oxford? These are either altogether superfluous,
mere badges of ostentation and luxurious wealth, or they
point to some fifth function not so much as contemplated by
other universities, and, at present, absolutely and
chimerically beyond their means of attainment. Formerly we

used to hear attacks upon the Oxford discipline as fitted to
the true *intellectual* purposes of a modern education. Those
attacks, weak and most uninstructed in facts, false as to all
that they challenged, and puerile as to what implicitly they
propounded for homage, are silent. But, of late, the battery
has been pointed against the Oxford discipline in its *moral*
aspects, as fitted for the government and restraint of young
men, or even as at all contemplating any such control. The
Beverleys would have us suppose, not only that the great
body of the students are a licentious crew, acknowledging
no discipline or restraints, but that the grave elders of the
university, and those who wield the nominal authority of
the place, passively resign the very shows of power, and
connive at general excesses, even when they do not
absolutely authorize them in their personal examples. Now,
when such representations are made, to what standard of a
just discipline is it that these writers would be understood
as appealing? Is it to some ideal, or to some existing and
known reality? Would they have England suppose that they
are here comparing the actual Oxford with some possible
hypothetic or imaginable Oxford, —with some ideal case,
that is to say, about which great discussions would arise as
to its feasibility, —or that they are comparing it with some
known standard of discipline actually realized and sustained
for generations, in Leipsic, suppose, or Edinburgh, or
Leyden, or Salamanca? This is the question of questions, to
which we may demand an answer; and, according to that
answer, observe the dilemma into which these furciferous
knaves must drop. If they are comparing Oxford simply
with some ideal and better Oxford, in some ideal and better
world, in that case all they have said—waiving its
falsehoods of fact—is no more than a flourish of rhetoric,
and the whole discussion may be referred to the shadowy
combats of scholastic declamation-mongers—those mock
gladiators, and *umbratiles doctores*. But if, on the other hand,

they pretend to take their station upon the known basis of some existing institution, —if they will pretend that, in this impeachment of Oxford, they are proceeding upon a silent comparison with Edinburgh, Glasgow, Jena, Leipsic, Padua, &c., —then are they self-exposed, as men not only without truth, but without shame. For now comes in, as a sudden revelation, and as a sort of *deus ex machina*, for the vindication of the truth, the simple answer to that question proposed above, Wherefore, and to what end, are the vast edifices of Oxford? A university, as universities are in general, needs not, I have shown, to be a visible body—a building raised with hands. Wherefore, then, is the *visible* Oxford? To what *fifth* end, refining upon the ordinary ends of such institutions, is the far-stretching system of Oxford *hospitia*, or monastic hotels, directed by their founders, or applied by their present possessors? Hearken, reader, to the answer:

These vast piles are applied to an end, absolutely indispensable to any even tolerable system of discipline, and yet absolutely unattainable upon any commensurate scale in any other university of Europe. They are applied to the personal settlement and domestication of the students within the gates and walls of that college to whose discipline they are amenable. Everywhere else the young men live *where* they please and *as* they please; necessarily distributed amongst the towns-people; in any case, therefore, liable to no control or supervision whatever; and in those cases where the university forms but a small part of a vast capital city, as it does in Paris, Edinburgh, Madrid, Vienna, Berlin, and Petersburg, liable to every mode of positive temptation and distraction, which besiege human life in high-viced and luxurious communities. Here, therefore, it is a mockery to talk of discipline; of a nonentity there can be no qualities; and we need not ask for the description of the discipline in situations where discipline there can be none. One slight anomaly I have heard of as varying *pro tanto* the uniform features of this picture. In Glasgow I have heard of an arrangement by which young academicians are placed in the family of a professor. Here, as members of a private household, and that household under the presiding eye of a conscientious, paternal, and judicious scholar, doubtless they would enjoy as absolute a shelter from peril and worldly contagion as parents could wish; but not *more* absolute, I affirm, than belongs, unavoidably, to the monastic seclusion of an Oxford college—the gates of which open to no egress after nine o'clock at night, nor after eleven to any ingress which is not regularly reported to a proper officer of the establishment. The two forms of restraint are, as respects the effectual amount of control, equal; and were they equally diffused, Glasgow and Oxford would, in this point, stand upon the same level of discipline. But it happens that the Glasgow case was a personal accident; personal, both as regarded him who volunteered the exercise of this control, and those who volunteered to appropriate its benefits; whereas the Oxford case belongs to the very system, is coextensive with the body of undergraduates, and, from the very arrangement of Oxford life, is liable to no decay or intermission.

Here, then, the reader apprehends the first great characteristic distinction of Oxford—that distinction which extorted the rapturous admiration of Lipsius as an exponent of enormous wealth, but which I now mention as applying, with ruinous effect, to the late calumnies upon Oxford, as an inseparable exponent of her meritorious discipline. She, most truly and severely an "Alma Mater" gathers all the juvenile part of her flock within her own fold, and beneath her own vigilant supervision. In Cambridge there is, so far, a laxer administration of this rule, that, when any college

overflows, undergraduates are allowed to lodge at large in
the town. But in Oxford this increase of peril and
discretionary power is thrown by preference upon the
senior graduates, who are seldom below the age of twenty-
two or twenty-three; and the college accommodations are
reserved, in almost their whole extent, for the most youthful
part of the society. This extent is prodigious. Even in my
time, upwards of two thousand persons were lodged within
the colleges; none having fewer than two rooms, very many
having three, and men of rank, or luxurious habits, having
often large suites of rooms. But that was a time of war,
which Oxford experience has shown to have operated most
disproportionably as a drain upon the numbers disposable
for liberal studies; and the total capacity of the university
was far from being exhausted. There are now, I believe,
between five and six thousand names upon the Oxford
books; and more than four thousand, I understand, of
constant residents. So that Oxford is well able to lodge, and
on a very sumptuous scale, a small army of men; which
expression of her great splendor I now mention (as I repeat)
purely as applying to the question of her machinery for
enforcing discipline. This part of her machinery, it will be
seen, is unique, and absolutely peculiar to herself. Other
universities, boasting no such enormous wealth, cannot be
expected to act upon her system of seclusion. Certainly, I
make it no reproach to other universities, that, not
possessing the means of sequestering their young men from
worldly communion, they must abide by the evils of a laxer
discipline. It is their misfortune, and not their criminal
neglect, which consents to so dismal a relaxation of
academic habits. But let them not urge this misfortune in
excuse at one time, and at another virtually disavow it.
Never let *them* take up a stone to throw at Oxford, upon this
element of a wise education; since in them, through that
original vice in their constitution, the defect of all means for

secluding and insulating their society, discipline is abolished by anticipation—being, in fact, an impossible thing; for the walls of the college are subservient to no purpose of life, but only to a purpose of convenience; they converge the students for the hour or two of what is called lecture; which over, each undergraduate again becomes *sui juris*, is again absorbed into the crowds of the world, resorts to whatsoever haunts he chooses, and finally closes his day at ——if, in any sense, at home—at a home which is not merely removed from the supervision and control, but altogether from the bare knowledge, of his academic superiors. How far this discipline is well administered in other points at Oxford, will appear from the rest of my account. But, thus far, at least, it must be conceded, that Oxford, by and through this one unexampled distinction—her vast disposable fund of accommodations for junior members within her own private cloisters—possesses an advantage which she could not forfeit, if she would, towards an effectual knowledge of each man's daily habits, and a control over him which is all but absolute.

This knowledge and this control is much assisted and concentrated by the division of the university into separate colleges. Here comes another feature of the Oxford system. Elsewhere the university is a single college; and this college is the university. But in Oxford the university expresses, as it were, the army, and the colleges express the several brigades, or regiments.

To resume, therefore, my own thread of personal narration. On the next morning after my arrival in Oxford, I assembled a small council of friends to assist me in determining at which of the various separate societies I should enter, and whether as a "commoner," or as a "gentleman commoner." Under the first question was couched the following latitude of choice: I give the names of the colleges, and the numerical account of their numbers, as it stood in January, 1832; for this will express, as well as the list of that day, (which I do not accurately know), the *proportions* of importance amongst them.

Mem.
1.
University
College
. . . .
207
2.
Balliol
"
. . . .
257
3.
Merton
"
. . . .
124
4.
Exeter
"
. . . .
299
5.
Oriel
"
. . . .
293
6.
Queen's
"

Then, besides these colleges, five *Halls*, as they are technically called, (the term *Hall* implying chiefly that they are societies not endowed, or not endowed with fellowships as the colleges are), namely:

Mem.
1.
St.
Mary
Hall.

. . . .
83
2.
Magdalen
"

. . . .
178
3.
New
Inn
"

. . . .
10
4.
St.
Alban
"

. . . .
41
5.
St.
Edmund
"

Such being the names, and general proportions on the scale of local importance, attached to the different communities, next comes the very natural question, What are the chief determining motives for guiding the selection amongst them? These I shall state. First of all, a man not otherwise interested in the several advantages of the colleges has, however, in all probability, some choice between a small society and a large one; and thus far a mere ocular inspection of the list will serve to fix his preference. For my part, supposing other things equal, I greatly preferred the most populous college, as being that in which any single member, who might have reasons for standing aloof from the general habits of expense, of intervisiting, etc., would have the best chance of escaping a jealous notice. However, amongst those "other things" which I presumed equal, one held a high place in my estimation, which a little inquiry showed to be very far from equal. All the colleges have chapels, but all have not organs; nor, amongst those which have, is the same large use made of the organ. Some preserve the full cathedral service; others do not. Christ Church, meantime, fulfilled *all* conditions: for the chapel here happens to be the cathedral of the diocese; the service, therefore, is full and ceremonial; the college, also, is far the most splendid, both in numbers, rank, wealth, and influence. Hither I resolved to go; and immediately I prepared to call on the head.

The "head," as he is called generically, of an Oxford college (his *specific* appellation varies almost with every college— principal, provost, master, rector, warden, etc.), is a greater man than the uninitiated suppose. His situation is generally felt as conferring a degree of rank not much less than episcopal; and, in fact, the head of Brazennose at that time, who happened to be the Bishop of Bangor, was not held to rank much above his brothers in office. Such being the rank of heads generally, *a fortiori*, that of Christ Church was to be had in reverence; and this I knew. He is always, *ex officio,* dean of the diocese; and, in his quality of college head, he only, of all deans that ever were heard of, is uniformly considered a greater man than his own diocesan. But it happened that the present dean had even higher titles to consideration. Dr. Cyril Jackson had been tutor to the Prince of Wales (George IV.); he had repeatedly refused a bishopric; and *that*, perhaps, is entitled to place a man one degree above him who has accepted one. He was also supposed to have made a bishop, and afterwards, at least, it is certain that lie made his own brother a bishop. All things weighed, Dr. Cyril Jackson seemed so very great a personage that I now felt the value of my long intercourse with great Dons in giving me confidence to face a lion of this magnitude.

Those who know Oxford are aware of the peculiar feelings which have gathered about the name and pretensions of Christ Church; feelings of superiority and leadership in the members of that college, and often enough of defiance and jealousy on the part of other colleges. Hence it happens that you rarely find yourself in a shop, or other place of public resort, with a Christ-Church man, but he takes occasion, if young and frivolous, to talk loudly of the Dean, as an indirect expression of his own connection with this splendid college; the title of *Dean* being exclusively attached to the headship of Christ Church. The Dean, as may be supposed, partakes in this superior dignity of his "House;" he is officially brought into connection with all orders of the British aristocracy—often with royal personages; and with the younger branches of the aristocracy his office places him

in a relation of authority and guardianship—exercised,
however, through inferior ministry, and seldom by direct
personal interference. The reader must understand that,
with rare exceptions, all the princes and nobles of Great
Britain, who choose to benefit by an academic education,
resort either to Christ Church College in Oxford, or to
Trinity College in Cambridge; these are the alternatives.
Naturally enough, my young friends were somewhat
startled at my determination to call upon so great a man; a
letter, they fancied, would be a better mode of application. I,
however, who did not adopt the doctrine that no man is a
hero to his valet, was of opinion that very few men indeed
are heroes to themselves. The cloud of external pomp, which
invests them to the eyes of the *attoniti* cannot exist to their
own; they do not, like Kehama, entering the eight gates of
Padalon at once, meet and contemplate their own
grandeurs; but, more or less, are conscious of acting a part.
I did not, therefore, feel the tremor which was expected of a
novice, on being ushered into so solemn a presence.

II.

OXFORD.

The Dean was sitting in a spacious library or study,
elegantly, if not luxuriously furnished. Footmen, stationed
as repeaters, as if at some fashionable rout, gave a
momentary importance to my unimportant self, by the
thundering tone of their annunciations. All the machinery
of aristocratic life seemed indeed to intrench this great Don's
approaches; and I was really surprised that so very great a
man should condescend to rise on my entrance. But I soon
found that, if the Dean's station and relation to the higher

orders had made him lofty, those same relations had given a peculiar suavity to his manners. Here, indeed, as on other occasions, I noticed the essential misconception, as to the demeanor of men of rank, which prevails amongst those who have no personal access to their presence. In the fabulous pictures of novels (such novels as once abounded), and in newspaper reports of conversations, real or pretended, between the king and inferior persons, we often find the writer expressing *his* sense of aristocratic assumption, by making the king address people without their titles. The Duke of Wellington, for instance, or Lord Liverpool, figures usually, in such scenes, as "Wellington," or "Arthur," and as "Liverpool." Now, as to the private talk of George IV. in such cases, I do not pretend to depose; but, speaking generally, I may say that the practice of the highest classes takes the very opposite course. Nowhere is a man so sure of his titles or official distinctions as amongst *them*; for, it is upon giving to every man the very extreme punctilio of his known or supposed claims, that they rely for the due observance of their own. Neglecting no form of courtesy suited to the case, they seek, in this way, to remind men unceasingly of what they expect; and the result is what I represent—that people in the highest stations, and such as bring them continually into contact with inferiors, are, of all people, the least addicted to insolence or defect of courtesy. Uniform suavity of manner is indeed rarely found, except in men of high rank. Doubtless this may arise upon a motive of self-interest, jealous of giving the least opening or invitation to the retorts of ill-temper or low breeding. But, whatever be its origin, such I believe to be the fact. In a very long conversation of a general nature upon the course of my studies, and the present direction of my reading, Dr. Cyril Jackson treated me just as he would have done his equal in station and in age. Coming, at length, to the particular purpose of my visit at this time to himself, he assumed a little more of his official stateliness. He condescended to say that it would have given him pleasure to reckon me amongst his flock; "But, sir," he said, in a tone of some sharpness, "your guardians have acted improperly. It was their duty to have given me at least one year's notice of their intention to place you at Christ Church. At present I have not a dog-kennel in my college untenanted." Upon this, I observed that nothing remained for me to do but to apologize for having occupied so much of his time; that, for myself, I now first heard of this preliminary application; and that, as to my guardians, I was bound to acquit them of all oversight in this instance, they being no parties to my present scheme. The Dean expressed his astonishment at this statement. I, on my part, was just then making my parting bows, and had reached the door, when a gesture of the Dean's, courteously waving me back to the sofa I had quitted, invited me to resume my explanations; and I had a conviction at the moment that the interview would have terminated in the Dean's suspending his standing rule in my favor. But, just at that moment, the thundering heralds of the Dean's hall announced some man of high rank: the sovereign of Christ Church seemed distressed for a moment; but then recollecting himself, bowed in a way to indicate that I was dismissed. And thus it happened that I did not become a member of Christ Church.

A few days passed in thoughtless indecision. At the end of that time, a trivial difficulty arose to settle my determination. I had brought about fifty guineas to Oxford; but the expenses of an Oxford inn, with almost daily entertainments to young friends, had made such inroads upon this sum, that, after allowing for the contingencies incident to a college initiation, enough would not remain to meet the usual demand for what is called "caution money." This is a small sum, properly enough demanded of every student, when matriculated, as a pledge for meeting any loss from unsettled arrears, such as his sudden death or his unannounced departure might else continually be inflicting upon his college. By releasing the college, therefore, from all necessity for degrading vigilance or persecution, this demand does, in effect, operate beneficially to the feelings of all parties. In most colleges it amounts to twenty-five pounds: in one only it was considerably less. And this trifling consideration it was, concurring with a reputation *at that time* for relaxed discipline, which finally determined me in preferring W—- College to all others. This college had the capital disadvantage, in my eyes, that its chapel possessed no organ, and no musical service. But any other choice would have driven me to an instant call for more money—a measure which, as too flagrantly in contradiction to the whole terms on which I had volunteered to undertake an Oxford life, I could not find nerves to face.

At W—— College, therefore, I entered: and here arises the proper occasion for stating the true costs of an Oxford education. First comes the question of *lodging*. This item varies, as may be supposed; but my own case will place on record the two extremes of cost in one particular college, nowadays differing, I believe, from the general standard. The first rooms assigned me, being small and ill-lighted, as part of an old Gothic building, were charged at four guineas a year. These I soon exchanged for others a little better, and for them I paid six guineas. Finally, by privilege of seniority, I obtained a handsome set of well-proportioned rooms, in a modern section of the college, charged at ten guineas a year. This set was composed of three rooms; namely, an airy bedroom, a study, and a spacious room for receiving visitors. This range of accommodation is pretty general in Oxford, and, upon the whole, may be taken perhaps as representing the average amount of luxury in this respect, and at the average amount of cost. The furniture and the fittings up of these rooms cost me about twenty-five guineas; for the Oxford rule is, that if you take the rooms (which is at your own option), in that case, you *third* the furniture and the embellishments—that is, you succeed to the total cost diminished by one third. You pay, therefore, two guineas out of each three to your *immediate* predecessor. But, as he also may have succeeded to the furniture upon the same terms, whenever there happens to have been a rapid succession of occupants, the original cost to a remote predecessor is sometimes brought down, by this process of diminution, to a mere fraction of the true value; and yet no individual occupant can complain of any heavy loss. Whilst upon this subject, I may observe that, in the seventeenth century, in Milton's time, for example (about 1624), and for more than sixty years after that era, the practice of *chumship* prevailed: every set of chambers was possessed by two cooccupants; they had generally the same bed-room, and a common study; and they were called *chums*. This practice, once all but universal, is now entirely extinct; and the extinction serves to mark the advance of the country, not so much in luxury as in refinement.

The next item which I shall notice is that which in college bills is expressed by the word *Tutorage*. This is the same in all colleges, I believe, namely, ten guineas per annum. And this head suggests an explanation which is most important to the reputation of Oxford, and fitted to clear up a very extensive delusion. Some years ago, a most elaborate statement was circulated of the number and costly endowment of the Oxford professorships. Some thirty or more there were, it was alleged, and five or six only which were not held as absolute sinecures. Now, this is a charge which I am not here meaning to discuss. Whether defensible or not, I do not now inquire. It is the practical interpretation and construction of this charge which I here wish to rectify. In most universities, except those of England, the professors are the body on whom devolves the whole duty and burthen of teaching; they compose the sole fountains of instruction; and if these fountains fail, the fair inference is, that the one great purpose of the institution is defeated. But this inference, valid for all other places, is not so for Oxford and Cambridge. And here, again, the difference arises out of the peculiar distribution of these bodies into separate and independent colleges. Each college takes upon itself the regular instruction of its separate inmates—of these and of no others; and for this office it appoints, after careful selection, trial, and probation, the best qualified amongst those of its senior members who choose to undertake a trust of such heavy responsibility. These officers are called Tutors; and they are connected by duties and by accountability, not with the university at all, but with their own private colleges. The professors, on the other hand, are *public* functionaries, not connected (as respects the exercise of their duties) with any college whatsoever—not even with their own—but altogether and exclusively with the whole university. Besides the public tutors appointed in each college, on the scale of one to each dozen or score of students, there are also tutors strictly private, who attend any students in search of special and extraordinary aid, on terms settled privately by themselves. Of these persons, or their existence, the college takes no cognizance; but between the two classes of tutors, the most studious young men—those who would be most likely to avail themselves of the lectures read by the professors—have their whole time pretty severely occupied: and the inference from all this is, not only that the course of Oxford education would suffer little if no professors at all existed, but also that, if the existing professors were *ex abundanti* to volunteer the most exemplary spirit of exertion, however much this spectacle of conscientious dealing might edify the university, it would contribute but little to the promotion of academic purposes. The establishment of professors is, in fact, a thing of ornament and pomp. Elsewhere, they are the working servants; but, in Oxford, the ministers corresponding to them bear another name, — they are called *Tutors*. These are the working agents in the Oxford system; and the professors, with salaries in many cases merely nominal, are persons sequestered, and properly sequestered, to the solitary cultivation and advancement of knowledge, which a different order of men is appointed to communicate.

Here let us pause for one moment, to notice another peculiarity in the Oxford system, upon the tendency of which I shall confidently make my appeal to the good sense of all unprejudiced readers. I have said that the *tutors* of Oxford correspond to the *professors* of other universities. But this correspondence, which is absolute and unquestionable as regards the point then at issue, — namely, where we are to look for that limb of the establishment on which rests the main teaching agency, — is liable to considerable qualification, when we examine the mode of their teaching. In both cases, this is conveyed by what is termed "lecturing;"—but what is the meaning of a lecture in Oxford and elsewhere? Elsewhere, it means a solemn dissertation, read, or sometimes histrionically declaimed, by the professor. In Oxford, it means an exercise performed orally by the students, occasionally assisted by the tutor, and subject, in its whole course, to his corrections, and what may be called his *scholia*, or collateral suggestions and improvements. Now, differ as men may as to other features of the Oxford, compared with the hostile system, here I conceive that there is no room for doubt or demur. An Oxford lecture imposes a real, *bona fide* task upon the student; it will not suffer him to fall asleep, either literally or in the energies of his understanding; it is a real drill, under the excitement, perhaps, of personal competition, and under the review of a superior scholar. But, in Germany, under the declamations of the professor, the young men are often literally sleeping; nor is it easy to see how the attention can be kept from wandering, on this plan, which subjects the auditor to no risk of sudden question or personal appeal. As to the prizes given for essays, etc., by the professors, these have the effect of drawing forth latent talent, but they can yield no criterion of the attention paid to the professor; not to say that the competition for these prizes is a matter of choice. Sometimes it is true that examinations take place; but the Oxford lecture is a daily examination; and, waiving *that*, what chance is there (I would ask) for searching examinations, for examinations conducted with the requisite *auctoritas* (or weight of influence derived from personal qualities), if—which may Heaven prevent!—the German tenure of professorships were substituted for our British one: that is, if for independent and liberal teachers were substituted poor mercenary haberdashers of knowledge—cap in hand to opulent students—servile to their caprices—and, at one blow, degrading the science they profess, the teacher, and the pupil? Yet I hear that such advice *was* given to a Royal Commission, sent to investigate one or more of the Scottish universities. In the German universities, every professor holds his situation, not in his good behavior, but on the capricious pleasure of the young men who resort to his market. He opens a shop, in fact: others, without limit, generally men of no credit or known respectability, are allowed to open rival shops; and the result is, sometimes, that the whole kennel of scoundrel professors ruin one another; each standing with his mouth open, to leap at any bone thrown amongst them, from the table of the "Burschen;" all hating, fighting, calumniating each other, until the land is sick of its base knowledge-mongers,

and would vomit the loathsome crew, were any natural
channel open to their instincts of abhorrence. The most
important of the Scottish professorships—those which are
fundamentally morticed to the moral institutions of the land
—are upon the footing of Oxford tutorships, as regards
emoluments; that is, they are not suffered to keep up a
precarious mendicant existence, upon the alms of the
students, or upon their fickle admirations. It is made
imperative upon a candidate for admission into the ministry
of the Scottish Kirk, that he shall show a certificate of
attendance through a given number of seasons at given
lectures.

The next item in the quarterly (or, technically, the *term*) bills
of Oxford is for servants. This, in my college, and, I believe,
in all others, amounted, nominally, to two guineas a year.
That sum, however, was paid to a principal servant, whom,
perhaps, you seldom or never saw; the actual attendance
upon yourself being performed by one of his deputies; and
to this deputy—who is, in effect, a *factotum*, combining in
his single person all the functions of chambermaid, valet,
waiter at meals, and porter or errand-boy—by the custom of
the place and your own sense of propriety, you cannot but
give something or other in the shape of perquisites. I was
told, on entering, that half a guinea a quarter was the
customary allowance,—the same sum, in fact, as was levied
by the college for his principal; but I gave mine a guinea a
quarter, thinking that little enough for the many services he
performed; and others, who were richer than myself, I dare
say, often gave much more. Yet, sometimes, it struck me,
from the gratitude which his looks testified, on my punctual
payment of this guinea,—for it was the only bill with regard
to which I troubled myself to practise any severe
punctuality,—that perhaps some thoughtless young man
might give him less, or might even forget to give anything;

and, at all events, I have reason to believe that half that sum
would have contented him. These minutiae I record
purposely; my immediate object being to give a rigorous
statement of the real expenses incident to an English
university education, partly as a guide to the calculations of
parents, and partly as an answer to the somewhat libellous
exaggerations which are current on this subject, in times
like these, when even the truth itself, and received in a spirit
of candor the most indulgent, may be all too little to defend
these venerable seats of learning from the ruin which seems
brooding over them. Yet, no! Abominable is the language of
despair even in a desperate situation. And, therefore,
Oxford, ancient mother! and thou, Cambridge, twin-light of
England! be vigilant and erect, for the enemy stands at all
your gates! Two centuries almost have passed since the boar
was within your vineyards, laying waste and desolating
your heritage. Yet that storm was not final, nor that eclipse
total. May this also prove but a trial and a shadow of
affliction! which affliction, may it prove to you, mighty
incorporations, what, sometimes, it is to us, poor, frail
homunculi—a process of purification, a solemn and oracular
warning! And, when that cloud is overpast, then, rise,
ancient powers, wiser and better—ready, like the
lampudéphoroi of old, to enter upon a second *stadium*, and to
transmit the sacred torch through a second period of twice
[Footnote: Oxford may confessedly claim a duration of that
extent; and the pretensions of Cambridge, in that respect, if
less aspiring, are, however, as I believe, less accurately
determined.] five hundred years. So prays a loyal *alumnus*,
whose presumption, if any be, in taking upon himself a
monitory tone, is privileged by zeal and filial anxiety.

To return, however, into the track from which I have
digressed. The reader will understand that any student is at
liberty to have private servants of his own, as many and of

what denomination he pleases. This point, as many others
of a merely personal bearing, when they happen to stand in
no relation to public discipline, neither the university nor
the particular college of the student feels summoned or even
authorized to deal with. Neither, in fact, does any other
university in Europe; and why, then, notice the case?
Simply thus: if the Oxford discipline, in this particular
chapter, has nothing special or peculiar about it, yet the case
to which it applies *has*, and is almost exclusively found in
our universities. On the continent it happens most rarely
that a student has any funds disposable for luxuries so
eminently such as grooms or footmen; but at Oxford and
Cambridge the case occurs often enough to attract notice
from the least vigilant eye. And thus we find set down to
the credit account of other universities the non-existence of
luxury in this or other modes, whilst, meantime, it is well
known to the fair inquirer that each or all are indulgences,
not at all or so much as in idea proscribed by the sumptuary
edicts of those universities; but, simply, by the lower scale of
their general revenues. And this lower scale, it will be said—
how do you account for that? I answer, not so much by the
general inferiority of continental Europe to Great Britain in
diffusive wealth (though that argument goes for something,
it being notorious that, whilst immoderate wealth,
concentrated in a small number of hands, exists in various
continental states upon a larger scale than with us,
moderately large estates, on the other hand, are, with them,
as one to two hundred, or even two hundred and fifty, in
comparison of ours), but chiefly upon this fact, which is too
much overlooked, that the foreign universities are not
peopled from the wealthiest classes, which are the class
either already noble, or wishing to become such. And why
is that? Purely from the vicious constitution of society on
the continent, where all the fountains of honor lie in the
military profession or in the diplomatic. We English, haters

and revilers of ourselves beyond all precedent, disparagers of
our own eminent advantages beyond all sufferance of honor
or good sense, and daily playing into the hands of foreign
enemies, who hate us out of mere envy or shame, have
amongst us some hundreds of writers who will die or suffer
martyrdom upon this proposition—that aristocracy, and the
spirit and prejudices of aristocracy, are more operative (more
effectually and more extensively operative) amongst
ourselves, than in any other known society of men. Now, I,
who believe all errors to arise in some narrow, partial, or
angular view of truth, am seldom disposed to meet any
sincere affirmation by a blank, unmodified denial. Knowing,
therefore, that some acute observers do really believe this
doctrine as to the aristocratic forces, and the way in which
they mould English society, I cannot but suppose that some
symptoms do really exist of such a phenomenon; and the
only remark I shall here make on the case is this, that, very
often, where any force or influence reposes upon deep
realities, and upon undisturbed foundations, *there* will be
the least heard of loquacious and noisy expressions of its
power; which expressions arise most, not where the current
is most violent, but where (being possibly the weakest) it is
most fretted with resistance.

In England, the very reason why the aristocratic feeling
makes itself so sensibly felt and so distinctly an object of
notice to the censorious observer is, because it maintains a
troubled existence amongst counter and adverse influences,
so many and so potent. This might be illustrated
abundantly. But, as respects the particular question before
me, it will be sufficient to say this: With us the profession
and exercise of knowledge, as a means of livelihood, is
honorable; on the continent it is not so. The knowledge, for
instance, which is embodied in the three learned professions,
does, with us, lead to distinction and civil importance; no

man can pretend to deny this; nor, by consequence, that the professors personally take rank with the highest order of gentlemen. Are they not, I demand, everywhere with us on the same footing, in point of rank and consideration, as those who bear the king's commission in the army and navy? Can this be affirmed of the continent, either generally, or, indeed, partially? I say, *no*. Let us take Germany, as an illustration. Many towns (for anything I know, all) present us with a regular bisection of the resident *notables*, or wealthier class, into two distinct (often hostile) coteries: one being composed of those who are "*noble*;" the other, of families equally well educated and accomplished, but *not*, in the continental sense, "noble." The meaning and value of the word is so entirely misapprehended by the best English writers, being, in fact, derived from our own way of applying it, that it becomes important to ascertain its true value. A "nobility," which is numerous enough to fill a separate ball-room in every sixth-rate town, it needs no argument to show, cannot be a nobility in any English sense. In fact, an *edelmann* or nobleman, in the German sense, is strictly what we mean by a *born gentleman*; with this one only difference, that, whereas, with us, the rank which denominates a man such passes off by shades so insensible, and almost infinite, into the ranks below, that it becomes impossible to assign it any strict demarkation or lines of separation; on the contrary, the continental noble points to certain fixed barriers, in the shape of privileges, which divide him, *per saltum*, from those who are below his own order. But were it not for this one legal benefit of accurate circumscription and slight favor, the continental noble, whether Baron of Germany, Count of France, or Prince of Sicily and of Russia, is simply on a level with the common landed *esquire* of Britain, and *not* on a level in very numerous cases.

Such being the case, how paramount must be the spirit of aristocracy in continental society! Our *haute noblesse*—our genuine nobility, who are such in the general feeling of their compatriots—will do *that* which the phantom of nobility of the continent will not: the spurious nobles of Germany will not mix, on equal terms, with their untitled fellow-citizens, living in the same city and in the same style as themselves; they will not meet them in the same ball or concert-room. Our great territorial nobility, though sometimes forming exclusive circles (but not, however, upon any principle of high birth), do so daily. They mix as equal partakers in the same amusements of races, balls, musical assemblies, with the baronets (or *elite* of the gentry); with the landed esquires (or middle gentry); with the superior order of tradesmen (who, in Germany, are absolute ciphers, for political weight, or social consideration, but, with us, constitute the lower and broader stratum of the nobilitas, [Footnote: It may be necessary to inform some readers that the word *noble*, by which so large a system of imposition and fraud, as to the composition of foreign society, has long been practised upon the credulity of the British, corresponds to our word *gentlemanly* (or, rather, to the vulgar word *genteel*, if that word were ever used legally, or *extra gradum*), not merely upon the argument of its *virtual* and operative value in the general estimate of men (that is, upon the argument that a count, baron, &c., does not, *qua* such, command any deeper feeling of respect or homage than a British esquire), but also upon the fact, that, originally, in all English registers, as, for instance, in the Oxford matriculation registers, all the upper gentry (knights, esquires, &c.) are technically designated by the word *nobiles.—See Chambeilayuc,* &c.] or gentry). The obscure baronage of Germany, it is undeniable, insist upon having "an atmosphere of their own;" whilst the Howards, the Stanleys, the Talbots, of England; the Hamiltons, the

Douglases, the Gordons, of Scotland, are content to acknowledge a sympathy with the liberal part of their untitled countrymen, in that point which most searchingly tries the principle of aristocratic pride, namely, in their pleasures. To have the same pursuits of business with another, may be a result of accident or position; to have the same pleasures, being a matter of choice, argues a community of nature in the *moral* sensibilities, in that part of our constitution which differences one man from another in the capacities of greatness and elevation. As with their amusements, so with their graver employments; the same mutual repulsion continues to divide the two orders through life.

The nobles either live in gloomy seclusion upon their private funds, wherever the privilege of primogeniture has enabled them to do so; or, having no funds at all (the case of ninety-nine in one hundred), they go into the army; that profession, the profession of arms, being regarded as the only one compatible with an *edelmann's* pretensions. Such was once the feeling in England; such is still the feeling on the continent. It is a prejudice naturally clinging to a semi-barbarous (because growing out of a barbarous) state, and, in its degree, clinging to every stage of imperfect civilization; and, were there no other argument, this would be a sufficient one, that England, under free institutions, has outrun the continent, in real civilization, by a century; a fact which is concealed by the forms of luxurious refinement in a few exclusive classes, too often usurping the name and honors of radical civilization.

From the super-appreciation of the military profession arises a corresponding contempt of all other professions whatsoever *paid by fellow-citizens*, and not by the king or the state. The clerical profession is in the most abject degradation throughout Southern Germany; and the reason why this forces itself less imperiously upon the public notice is, that, in rural situations, from the absence of a resident gentry (speaking generally), the pastor is brought into rare collision with those who style themselves *noble*; whilst, in towns, the clergy find people enough to countenance those who, being in the same circumstances as to comfort and liberal education, are also under the same ban of rejection from the "nobility," or born gentry. The legal profession is equally degraded; even a barrister or advocate holds a place in the public esteem little differing from that of an Old Bailey attorney of the worst class. And this result is the less liable to modification from personal qualities, inasmuch as there is no great theatre (as with us) for individual display. Forensic eloquence is unknown in Germany, as it is too generally on the continent, from the defect of all popular or open judicatures. A similar defect of deliberative assemblies—such, at least, as represent any popular influences and debate with open doors—intercepts the very possibility of senatorial eloquence. [Footnote: The subject is amusingly illustrated by an anecdote of Goethe, recorded by himself in his autobiography. Some physiognomist, or phrenologist, had found out, in Goethe's structure of head, the sure promise of a great orator. "Strange infatuation of nature!" observes Goethe, on this assurance, "to endow me so richly and liberally for that particular destination which only the institutions of my country render impossible. Music for the deaf! Eloquence without an audience!"] That of the pulpit only remains. But even of this—whether it be from want of the excitement and contagious emulation from the other fields of oratory, or from the peculiar genius of Lutheranism—no models have yet arisen that could, for one moment, sustain a comparison with those of England or France. The highest names in this department would not, to a foreign ear, carry with them

any of that significance or promise which surrounds the
names of Jeremy Taylor or Barrow, Bossuet or Bourdaloue,
to those even who have no personal acquaintance with
their works. This absence of all fields for gathering public
distinctions cooperates, in a very powerful way, with the
contempt of the born gentry, to degrade these professions;
and this double agency is, a third time, reinforced by those
political arrangements which deny every form of state
honor or conspicuous promotion to the very highest
description of excellence, whether of the bar, the pulpit, or
the civic council. Not "the fluent Murray," or the
accomplished Erskine, from the English bar—not Pericles or
Demosthenes, from the fierce democracies of Greece—not
Paul preaching at Athens—could snatch a wreath from
public homage, nor a distinction from the state, nor found
an influence, nor leave behind them an operative model, in
Germany, as now constituted. Other walks of emolument
are still more despised. Alfieri, a continental "noble," that is,
a born gentleman, speaks of bankers as we in England
should of a Jewish usurer, or tricking money-changer. The
liberal trades, such as those which minister to literature or
the fine arts, which, with us, confer the station of
gentleman upon those who exercise them, are, in the
estimate of a continental "noble," fitted to assign a certain
rank or place in the train and equipage of a gentleman, but
not to entitle their most eminent professors to sit down,
except by sufferance, in his presence. And, upon this point,
let not the reader derive his notions from the German
books: the vast majority of German authors are not "noble;"
and, of those who are, nine tenths are liberal in this respect,
and speak the language of liberality, not by sympathy with
their own order, or as representing *their* feelings, but in
virtue of democratic or revolutionary politics.

Such as the rank is, and the public estimation of the leading professions, such is the natural condition of the universities which rear them. The "nobles" going generally into the army, or leading lives of indolence, the majority by far of those who resort to universities do so as a means of future livelihood. Few seek an academic life in Germany who have either money to throw away on superfluities and external show, or who have such a rank to support as might stimulate their pride to expenses beyond their means. Parsimony is, therefore, in these places, the governing law; and pleasure, not less fervently wooed than at Oxford or at Cambridge, putting off her robes of elegance and ceremony, descends to grossness, and not seldom to abject brutality.

The sum of my argument is—that, because, in comparison of the army, no other civil profession is, in itself, held of sufficient dignity; and not less, perhaps, because, under governments essentially unpopular, none of these professions has been so dignified artificially by the state, or so attached to any ulterior promotion, either through the state or in the state, as to meet the demands of aristocratic pride—none of them is cultivated as a means of distinction, but originally as a means of livelihood; that the universities, as the nurseries of these unhonored professions, share naturally in *their* degradation; and that, from this double depreciation of the place and its final objects, few or none resort thither who can be supposed to bring any extra funds for supporting a system of luxury; that the general temperance, or sobriety of demeanor, is far enough, however, from keeping pace with the absence of costly show; and that, for this absence even, we are to thank their poverty rather than their will. It is to the great honor, in my opinion, of our own country, that those often resort to her fountains who have no motive but that of disinterested reverence for knowledge; seeking, as all men perceive, neither emolument directly from university funds, nor knowledge as the means of emolument. Doubtless, it is neither dishonorable, nor, on a large scale, possible to be otherwise, that students should pursue their academic career chiefly as ministerial to their capital object of a future livelihood. But still I contend that it is for the interest of science and good letters that a considerable body of volunteers should gather about their banners, without pay or hopes of preferment. This takes place on a larger scale at Oxford and Cambridge than elsewhere; and it is but a trivial concession in return, on the part of the university, that she should allow, even if she had the right to withhold, the privilege of living within her walls as they would have lived at their fathers' seats; with one only reserve, applied to all modes of expense that are, in themselves, immoral excesses, or occasions of scandal, or of a nature to interfere too much with the natural hours of study, or specially fitted to tempt others of narrower means to ruinous emulation.

Upon these principles, as it seems to me, the discipline of the university is founded. The keeping of hunters, for example, is unstatutable. Yet, on the other hand, it is felt to be inevitable that young men of high spirit, familiar with this amusement, will find means to pursue it in defiance of all the powers, however exerted, that can properly be lodged in the hands of academic officers. The range of the proctor's jurisdiction is limited by positive law; and what should hinder a young man, bent upon his pleasure, from fixing the station of his hunter a few miles out of Oxford, and riding to cover on a hack, unamenable to any censure? For, surely, in this age, no man could propose so absurd a thing as a general interdiction of riding. How, in fact, does the university proceed? She discountenances the practice; and, if forced upon her notice, she visits it with censure, and that sort of punishment which lies within her means. But she takes no pains to search out a trespass, which, by the mere

act of seeking to evade public display in the streets of the
university, already tends to limit itself; and which, besides,
from its costliness, can never become a prominent nuisance.
This I mention as illustrating the spirit of her legislation;
and, even in this case, the reader must carry along with him
the peculiar distinction which I have pressed with regard to
English universities, in the existence of a large volunteer
order of students seeking only the liberalization, and not
the profits, of academic life. In arguing upon their case, it is
not the fair logic to say: These pursuits taint the decorum of
the studious character; it is not fair to calculate how much
is lost to the man of letters by such addiction to fox-
hunting; but, on the contrary, what is gained to the fox-
hunter, who would, at any rate, be such, by so considerable
a homage paid to letters, and so inevitable a commerce with
men of learning. Anything whatsoever attained in this
direction, is probably so much more than would have been
attained under a system of less toleration. *Lucro ponamus*, we
say, of the very least success in such a case. But, in speaking
of toleration as applied to acts or habits positively against
the statutes, I limit my meaning to those which, in their
own nature, are morally indifferent, and are
discountenanced simply as indirectly injurious, or as
peculiarly open to excess. Because, on graver offences (as
gambling, &c.), the malicious impeachers of Oxford must
well have known that no toleration whatsoever is practised
or thought of. Once brought under the eye of the university
in a clear case and on clear evidence, it would be punished
in the most exemplary way open to a limited authority; by
rustication, at least—that is, banishment for a certain number
of terms, and consequent loss of these terms—supposing the
utmost palliation of circumstances; and, in an aggravated
case, or in a second offence, most certainly by final
expulsion.

But it is no part of duty to serve the cause even of good
morals by impure means; and it is as difficult beforehand to
prevent the existence of vicious practices so long as men
have, and ought to have, the means of seclusion liable to no
violation, as it is afterwards difficult, without breach of
honor, to obtain proof of their existence. Gambling has been
known to exist in some dissenting institutions; and, in my
opinion, with no blame to the presiding authorities. As to
Oxford in particular, no such habit was generally prevalent
in my time; it is not an English vice; nor did I ever hear of
any great losses sustained in this way. But, were it
otherwise, I must hold, that, considering the numbers,
rank, and great opulence, of the students, such a habit
would impeach the spirit and temper of the age rather than
the vigilance or magisterial fidelity of the Oxford authorities.
They are limited, like other magistrates, by honor and
circumstances, in a thousand ways; and if a knot of students
will choose to meet for purposes of gaming, they must
always have it in their power to baffle every honorable or
becoming attempt at detecting them. But upon this subject I
shall make two statements, which may have some effect in
moderating the uncharitable judgments upon Oxford
discipline. The first respects the age of those who are the
objects of this discipline; on which point a very grave error
prevails. In the last Parliament, not once, but many times
over, Lord Brougham and others assumed that the students
of Oxford were chiefly *boys*; and this, not idly or casually,
but pointedly, and with a view to an ulterior argument; for
instance, by way of proving how little they were entitled to
judge of those thirty-nine articles to which their assent was
demanded. Now, this argued a very extraordinary
ignorance; and the origin of the error showed the levity in
which their legislation was conducted. These noble lords
had drawn their ideas of a university exclusively from
Glasgow. Here, it is well known, and I mention it neither

for praise nor blame, that students are in the habit of
coming at the early age of fourteen. These may allowably be
styled *boys*. But, with regard to Oxford, eighteen is about
the *earliest* age at which young men begin their residence:
twenty and upwards is, therefore, the age of the majority;
that is, twenty is the *minimum* of age for the vast majority; as
there must always be more men of three years' standing,
than of two or of one. Apply this fact to the question of
discipline: young men beyond twenty, generally,—that is to
say, of the age which qualifies men for seats in the national
council,—can hardly, with decency, either be called or
treated as boys; and many things become impossible as
applied to *them*, which might be of easy imposition upon an
assemblage *really* childish. In mere justice, therefore, when
speculating upon this whole subject of Oxford discipline,
the reader must carry along with him, at every step, the
recollection of that signal difference as to age, which I have
now stated, between Oxonians and those students whom
the hostile party contemplate in their arguments. [Footnote:
Whilst I am writing, a debate of the present Parliament,
reported on Saturday, March 7, 1835, presents us with a
determinate repetition of the error which I have been
exposing; and, again, as in the last Parliament, this error is
not *inert*, but is used for a hostile (apparently a malicious)
purpose; nay, which is remarkable, it is the *sole* basis upon
which the following argument reposes. Lord Radnor again
assumes that the students of Oxford are "boys;" he is again
supported in this misrepresentation by Lord Brougham;
and again the misrepresentation is applied to a purpose of
assault upon the English universities, but especially upon
Oxford. And the nature of the assault does not allow any
latitude in construing the word *boys*, nor any room for
evasion as respects the total charge, except what goes the
length of a total retraction. The charge is, that, in a

requisition made at the very threshold of academic life, upon the under standing and the honor of the students, the university burdens their consciences to an extent, which, in after life, when reflection has enlightened them to the meaning of their engagements, proves either a snare to those who trifle with their engagements, or an insupportable burden to those who do not. For the inculpation of the party imposing such oaths, it is essential that the party taking them should be in a childish condition of the moral sense, and the sense of responsibility; whereas, amongst the Oxonian *under*-graduates, I will venture to say that the number is larger of those who rise above than of those who fall below twenty; and, as to sixteen (assumed as the representative age by Lord Radnor), in my time, I heard of only one student, amongst, perhaps, sixteen hundred, who was so young. I grieve to see that the learned prelate, who replied to the assailants, was so much taken by surprise; the defence might have been made triumphant. With regard to oaths incompatible with the spirit of modern manners, and yet formally unrepealed—*that* is a case of neglect and indolent oversight. But the *gravamen* of that reproach does not press exclusively upon Oxford; all the ancient institutions of Europe are tainted in the same way, more especially the monastic orders of the Romish church.] Meantime, to show that, even under every obstacle presented by this difference of age, the Oxford authorities do, nevertheless, administer their discipline with fidelity, with intrepidity, and with indifference as respects the high and the low, I shall select from a crowd of similar recollections two anecdotes, which are but trifles in themselves, and yet are not such to him who recognizes them as expressions of a uniform system of dealing.

A great whig lord (Earl C— —) happened (it may be ten years ago) to present himself one day at Trinity (the leading

college of Cambridge), for the purpose of introducing Lord F
— —ch, his son, as a future member of that splendid society.
Possibly it mortified his aristocratic feelings to hear the head
of the college, even whilst welcoming the young nobleman
in courteous terms, yet suggesting, with some solemnity,
that, before taking any final resolution in the matter, his
lordship would do well to consider whether he were fully
prepared to submit himself to college discipline; for that,
otherwise, it became his own duty frankly to declare that
the college would not look upon his accession to their
society as any advantage. This language arose out of some
recent experience of refractory and turbulent conduct upon
the part of various young men of rank; but it is very
possible that the noble earl, in his surprise at a salutation so
uncourtly, might regard it, in a tory mouth, as having some
lurking reference to his own whig politics. If so, he must
have been still more surprised to hear of another case,
which would meet him before he left Cambridge, and which
involved some frank dealing as well as frank speaking,
when a privilege of exception might have been presumed, if
tory politics, or services the most memorable, could ever
create such a privilege. The Duke of W— —had two sons at
Oxford. The affair is now long past; and it cannot injure
either of them to say, that one of the brothers trespassed
against the college discipline, in some way, which compelled
(or was thought to compel) the presiding authorities into a
solemn notice of his conduct. Expulsion appeared to be the
appropriate penalty of his offences: but, at this point, a just
hesitation arose. Not in any servile spirit, but under a
proper feeling of consideration for so eminent a public
benefactor as this young nobleman's father, the rulers
paused—and at length signified to him that he was at liberty
to withdraw himself privately from the college, but also, and
at the same time, from the university. He did so; and his
brother, conceiving him to have been harshly treated,

withdrew also; and both transferred themselves to Cambridge. That could not be prevented: but there they were received with marked reserve. One was *not* received, I believe, in a technical sense; and the other was received conditionally; and such restrictions were imposed upon his future conduct as served most amply, and in a case of great notoriety, to vindicate the claims of discipline, and, in an extreme case, a case so eminently an extreme one that none like it is ever likely to recur, to proclaim the footing upon which the very highest rank is received at the English universities. Is that footing peculiar *to them*? I willingly believe that it is not; and, with respect to Edinburgh and Glasgow, I am persuaded that their weight of dignity is quite sufficient, and would be exerted to secure the same subordination from men of rank, if circumstances should ever bring as large a number of that class within their gates, and if their discipline were equally applicable to the habits of students not domiciled within their walls. But, as to the smaller institutions for education within the pale of dissent, I feel warranted in asserting, from the spirit of the anecdotes which have reached me, that they have not the *auctoritas* requisite for adequately maintaining their dignity.

So much for the aristocracy of our English universities: their glory is, and the happiest application of their vast influence, that they have the power to be republican, as respects their internal condition. Literature, by substituting a different standard of rank, tends to republican equality; and, as one instance of this, properly belonging to the chapter of *servants*, which originally led to this discussion, it ought to be known that the class of "servitors," once a large body in Oxford, have gradually become practically extinct under the growing liberality of the age. They carried in their academic dress a mark of their inferiority; they waited at dinner on those of higher rank, and performed other menial services, humiliating to themselves, and latterly felt as no less humiliating to the general name and interests of learning. The better taste, or rather the relaxing pressure of aristocratic prejudice, arising from the vast diffusion of trade and the higher branches of mechanic art, have gradually caused these functions of the order (even where the law would not permit the extinction of the order) to become obsolete. In my time, I was acquainted with two servitors: but one of them was rapidly pushed forward into a higher station; and the other complained of no degradation, beyond the grievous one of exposing himself to the notice of young women in the streets, with an untasselled cap; but this he contrived to evade, by generally going abroad without his academic dress. The *servitors* of Oxford are the *sizars* of Cambridge; and I believe the same changes [Footnote: These changes have been accomplished, according to my imperfect knowledge of the case, in two ways: first, by dispensing with the services whenever that could be done; and, secondly, by a wise discontinuance of the order itself in those colleges which were left to their own choice in this matter.] have taken place in both.

One only account with the college remains to be noticed; but this is the main one. It is expressed in the bills by the word *battels*, derived from the old monkish word *patella* (or batella), a plate; and it comprehends whatsoever is furnished for dinner and for supper, including malt liquor, but not wine, as well as the materials for breakfast, or for any casual refreshment to country visitors, excepting only groceries. These, together with coals and fagots, candles, wine, fruit, and other more trifling *extras*, which are matters of personal choice, form so many private accounts against your name, and are usually furnished by tradesmen living near to the college, and sending their servants daily to receive orders. Supper, as a meal not universally taken, in many colleges is served privately in the student's own room; though some colleges still retain the ancient custom of a public supper. But dinner is, in all colleges, a public meal, taken in the refectory or "hall" of the society; which, with the chapel and library, compose the essential public *suite* belonging to every college alike. No absence is allowed, except to the sick, or to those who have formally applied for permission to give a dinner-party. A fine is imposed on all other cases of absence. Wine is not generally allowed in the public hall, except to the "high table," that is, the table at which the fellows and some other privileged persons are entitled to dine. The head of the college rarely dines in public. The other tables, and, after dinner, the high table, usually adjourn to their wine, either upon invitations to private parties, or to what are called the "common rooms" of the several orders—graduates and undergraduates, &c. The dinners are always plain, and without pretensions—those, I mean, in the public hall; indeed, nothing *can* be plainer in most colleges—a simple choice between two or three sorts of animal food, and the common vegetables. No fish, even as a regular part of the fare; no soups, no game; nor, except on some very rare festivity, did I ever see a variation from this plain fare at Oxford. This, indeed, is proved sufficiently by the average amount of the *battels*. Many men "battel" at the rate of a guinea a week: I did so for years: that is, at the rate of three shillings a day for everything connected with meals, excepting only tea, sugar, milk, and wine. It is true that wealthier men, more expensive men, and more careless men, often "battelled" much higher; but, if they persisted in this excess, they incurred censures, more and more urgent, from the head of the college.

Now, let us sum up; premising that the extreme duration of residence in any college at Oxford amounts to something under thirty weeks. It is possible to keep "short terms," as the phrase is, by a residence of thirteen weeks, or ninety-one days; but, as this abridged residence is not allowed, except in here and there a college, I shall assume—as something beyond the strict *maximum* of residence—thirty weeks as my basis. The account will then stand thus:

1. Rooms,.. Ł10 10 0
2. Tutorage,................. .... 10 10 0
3. Servants (subject to the explanations made above),
   say.. 5 5 0
4. Battels (allowing one shilling a day beyond what
   I and others spent in much dearer times; that is,
   allowing twenty-eight shillings weekly), for
   thirty weeks,................................. 40 4 0
                          −−−−− Ł66 9 0

This will be a liberal calculation for the college bill. What remains? 1. Candles, which the reader will best calculate upon the standard of his own general usage in this particular. 2. Coals, which are remarkably dear at Oxford—dearer, perhaps, than anywhere else in the island; say, three times as dear as at Edinburgh. 3. Groceries. 4. Wine. 5. Washing. This last article was, in my time, regulated by the college, as there were certain privileged washer-women, between whom and the students it was but fair that some proper authority should interfere to prevent extortion, in return for the monopoly granted. Six guineas was the regulated sum; but this paid for everything,—table-linen, &c., as well as for wearing apparel; and it was understood to cover the whole twenty-eight or thirty weeks. However, it was open to every man to make his own arrangements, by insisting on a separate charge for each separate article. All other expenses of a merely personal nature, such as postage, public amusements, books, clothes, &c., as they have no special connection with Oxford, but would, probably, be balanced by corresponding, if not the very same, expenses in any other place or situation, I do not calculate. What I have specified are the expenses which would accrue to a student in consequence of leaving his father's house. The rest would, in these days, be the same, perhaps, everywhere. How much, then, shall we assume as the total charge on account of Oxford? Candles, considering the quantity of long days amongst the thirty weeks, may be had for one shilling and sixpence a week; for few students—unless they have lived in India, after which a physical change occurs in the sensibility of the nostrils—are finical enough to burn wax-lights. This will amount to two pounds, five shillings. Coals, say sixpence a day; for threepence a day will amply feed one grate in Edinburgh; and there are many weeks in the thirty which will demand no fire at all. Groceries and

wine, which are all that remain, I cannot calculate. But
suppose we allow for the first a shilling a day, which will be
exactly ten guineas for thirty weeks; and for the second,
nothing at all. Then the extras, in addition to the college
bills, will stand thus:

Washing for thirty weeks, at the privileged rate, .. Ł6 6 0
Candles, ... 2 5 0
Fire, ... 5 5 0
Groceries, ... 10 10 0
       — — — —- Total, ... Ł24 6
0

The college bills, therefore, will be sixty-six pounds, nine
shillings; the extras, not furnished by the college, will be
about twenty-four pounds, six shillings, — making a total
amount of ninety pounds, fifteen shillings. And for this
sum, annually, a man may defray *every* expense incident to
an Oxford life, through a period of weeks (namely, thirty)
something more than he will be permitted to reside. It is
true, that, for the *first* year, there will be, in addition to this,
his outfit: and for *every* year there will be his journeys.
There will also be twenty-two weeks uncovered by this
estimate; but for these it is not my business to provide, who
deal only with Oxford.

That this estimate is true, I know too feelingly. Would that it
were *not*! would that it were false! Were it so, I might the
better justify to myself that commerce with fraudulent Jews
which led me so early to commence the dilapidation of my
small fortune. It *is* true; and true for a period (1804-8) far
dearer than this. And to any man who questions its
accuracy I address this particular request—that he will lay
his hand upon the special item which he disputes. I
anticipate that he will answer thus: "I dispute none: it is not

174

by positive things that your estimate errs, but by negations. It is the absence of all allowance for indispensable items that vitiates the calculation." Very well: but to this, as to other things, we may apply the words of Dr. Johnson — "Sir, the reason I drink no wine, is because I can practise abstinence, but not temperance." Yes: in all things, abstinence is easier than temperance; for a little enjoyment has invariably the effect of awaking the sense of enjoyment, irritating it, and setting it on edge. I, therefore, recollecting my own case, have allowed for *no* wine-parties. Let our friend, the abstraction we are speaking of, give breakfast-parties, if he chooses to give any; and certainly to give none at all, unless he were dedicated to study, would seem very churlish. Nobody can be less a friend than myself to monkish and ascetic seclusion, unless it were for twenty-three hours out of the twenty-four.

But, however this be settled, let no mistake be made; nor let that be charged against the system which is due to the habits of individuals. Early in the last century, Dr. Newton, the head of a college in Oxford, wrote a large book against the Oxford system, as ruinously expensive. But then, as now, the real expense was due to no cause over which the colleges could exercise any effectual control. It is due exclusively to the habits of social intercourse amongst the young men; from which *he* may abstain who chooses. But, for any academic authorities to interfere by sumptuary laws with the private expenditure of grown men, many of them, in a legal sense, *of age*, and all near it, must appear romantic and extravagant, for this (or, indeed, any) stage of society. A tutor being required, about 1810, to fix the amount of allowance for a young man of small fortune, nearly related to myself, pronounced three hundred and twenty pounds little enough. He had this allowance, and was ruined in consequence of the credit which it procured for him, and the society it connected him with. The majority have two hundred pounds a year: but my estimate stands good, for all that.

Having stated, generally, the expenses of the Oxford system, I am bound, in candor, to mention one variety in the mode of carrying this system into effect, open to every man's adoption, which confers certain privileges, but, at the same time (by what exact mode, I know not), considerably increases the cost, and in that degree disturbs my calculation. The great body of undergraduates, or students, are divided into two classes—*Commoners*, and *Gentlemen Commoners*. Perhaps nineteen out of twenty belong to the former class; and it is for that class, as having been my own, that I have made my estimate. The other class of *Gentlemen Commoners* (who, at Cambridge, bear the name of *Fellow Commoners*) wear a peculiar dress, and have some privileges which naturally imply some corresponding increase of cost; but why this increase should go to the extent of doubling the total expense, as it is generally thought to do, or how it *can* go to that extent, I am unable to explain. The differences which attach to the rank of "Gentlemen Commoners" are these: At his entrance he pays double "caution money;" that is, whilst Commoners in general pay about twenty-five guineas, he pays fifty; but this can occur only once; and, besides, in strict point of right, this sum is only a deposit, and is liable to be withdrawn on leaving the university, though it is commonly enough finally presented to the college in the shape of plate. The next difference is, that, by comparison with the Commoner, he wears a much more costly dress. The Commoner's gown is made of what is called *prince's stuff*; and, together with the cap, costs about five guineas. But the Gentleman Commoner has two gowns —an undress for the morning, and a full dress-gown for the evening; both are made of silk, and the latter is very elaborately ornamented. The cap also is more costly, being covered with velvet instead of cloth. At Cambridge, again, the tassel is made of gold fringe or bullion, which, in Oxford, is peculiar to the caps of noblemen; and there are many other varieties in that university, where the dress for "pensioners" (that is, the Oxford "Commoners") is specially varied in almost every college; the object being, perhaps, to give a ready means to the academic officers for ascertaining, at a glance, not merely the general fact that such or such a delinquent is a gownsman (which is all that can be ascertained at Oxford), but also the particular college to which he belongs. Allowance being made for these two items of "dress" and "caution-money," both of which apply only to the original outfit, I know of no others in which the expenditure of a Gentleman Commoner ought to exceed, or could with propriety exceed, those of a Commoner. He has, indeed, a privilege as regards the choice of rooms; he chooses first, and probably chooses those rooms which, being best, are dearest; that is, they are on a level with the best; but usually there are many sets almost equally good; and of these the majority will be occupied by Commoners. So far, there is little opening for a difference. More often, again, it will happen that a man of this aristocratic class keeps a private servant; yet this happens also to Commoners, and is, besides, no properly college expense. Tutorage is charged double to a Gentleman Commoner — namely, twenty guineas a year: this is done upon a fiction (as it sometimes turns out) of separate attention, or aid given in a private way to his scholastic pursuits. Finally, there arises naturally another and peculiar source of expense to the "Gentleman Commoner," from a fact implied in his Cambridge designation of "*Fellow* Commoner," *commensalis* — namely, that he associates at meals with the "fellows" and other authorities of the college. Yet this again expresses rather the particular shape which his expenditure assumes

than any absolute increase in its amount. He subscribes to a
regular mess, and pays, therefore, whether present or not;
but so, in a partial sense, does the Commoner, by his forfeits
for "absent commons." He subscribes also to a regular fund
for wine; and, therefore, he does not enjoy that immunity
from wine-drinking which is open to the Commoner. Yet,
again, as the Commoner does but rarely avail himself of this
immunity, as he drinks no less wine than the Gentleman
Commoner, and, generally speaking, wine not worse in
quality, it is difficult to see any ground for a regular
assumption of higher expenditure in the one class than the
other. However, the universal impression favors that
assumption. All people believe that the rank of Gentleman
Commoner imposes an expensive burden, though few
people ever ask why. As a matter of fact, I believe it to be
true that Gentlemen Commoners spend more by a third, or
a half, than any equal number of Commoners, taken
without selection. And the reason is obvious: those who
become Gentlemen Commoners are usually determined to
that course by the accident of having very large funds; they
are eldest sons, or only sons, or men already in possession
of estates, or else (which is as common a case as all the rest
put together) they are the heirs of newly-acquired wealth —
sons of the *nouveaux riches* — a class which often requires a
generation or two to rub off the insolence of a too conscious
superiority. I have called them an "aristocratic" class; but, in
strictness, they are not such; they form a privileged class,
indeed, but their privileges are few and trifling, not to add
that these very privileges are connected with one or two
burdens, more than outweighing them in the estimate of
many; and, upon the whole, the chief distinction they enjoy
is that of advertising themselves to the public as men of
great wealth, or great expectations; and, therefore, as
subjects peculiarly adapted to fraudulent attempts.
Accordingly, it is not found that the sons of the nobility are

much inclined to enter this order: these, if they happen to be the eldest sons of earls, or of any peers above the rank of viscount, so as to enjoy a title themselves by the courtesy of England, have special privileges in both universities as to length of residence, degrees, &c.; and their rank is ascertained by a special dress. These privileges it is not usual to forego; though sometimes that happens, as, in my time, in the instance of Lord George Grenville (now Lord Nugent); he neither entered at the aristocratic college (Christ Church), nor wore the dress of a nobleman. Generally, however, an elder son appears in his true character of nobleman; but the younger sons rarely enter the class of Gentlemen Commoners. They enter either as "Commoners," or under some of those various designations ("scholars," "demies," "students," "junior fellows") which imply that they stand upon the foundation of the college to which they belong, and are aspirants for academic emoluments.

Upon the whole, I am disposed to regard this order of Gentlemen Commoners as a standing temptation held out by authority to expensive habits, and a very unbecoming proclamation of honor paid to the aristocracy of wealth. And I know that many thoughtful men regard it in the same light with myself, and regret deeply that any such distribution of ranks should be authorized, as a stain upon the simplicity and general manliness of the English academic laws. It is an open profession of homage and indulgence to wealth, *as* wealth—to wealth disconnected from everything that might ally it to the ancestral honors and heraldries of the land. It is also an invitation, or rather a challenge, to profuse expenditure. Regularly, and by law, a Gentleman Commoner is liable to little heavier burdens than a Commoner; but, to meet the expectations of those around him, and to act up to the part he has assumed, he must spend more, and he must be more careless in controlling his expenditure, than a moderate and prudent Commoner. In every light, therefore, I condemn the institution, and give it up to the censures of the judicious. So much in candor I concede. But, to show equal candor on the other side, it must be remembered that this institution descends to us from ancient times, when wealth was not so often divided from territorial or civic honors, conferring a real precedency.

III.

OXFORD.

There was one reason why I sought solitude at that early age, and sought it in a morbid excess, which must naturally have conferred upon my character some degree of that interest which belongs to all extremes. My eye had been couched into a secondary power of vision, by misery, by solitude, by sympathy with life in all its modes, by experience too early won, and by the sense of danger critically escaped. Suppose the case of a man suspended by some colossal arm over an unfathomed abyss,—suspended, but finally and slowly withdrawn,—it is probable that he would not smile for years. That was my case: for I have not mentioned, in the "Opium Confessions," a thousandth part of the sufferings I underwent in London and in Wales; partly because the misery was too monotonous, and, in that respect, unfitted for description; but, still more, because there is a mysterious sensibility connected with real suffering which recoils from circumstantial rehearsal or delincation, as from violation offered to something sacred, and which is, or should be, dedicated to privacy. Grief does not parade its pangs, nor the anguish of despairing hunger

willingly count again its groans or its humiliations. Hence
it was that Ledyard, the traveller, speaking of his Russian
experiences, used to say that some of his miseries were such,
that he never *would* reveal them. Besides all which, I really
was not at liberty to speak, without many reserves, on this
chapter of my life, at a period (1821) not twenty years
removed from the actual occurrences, unless I desired to
court the risk of crossing at every step the existing law of
libel, so full of snares and man-traps, to the careless equally
with the conscientious writer. This is a consideration which
some of my critics have lost sight of in a degree which
surprises me. One, for example, puts it to his readers
whether any house such as I describe as the abode of my
money-lending friend could exist "*in* Oxford-street;" and, at
the same time, he states, as circumstances drawn from my
description, but, in fact, pure coinages of his own, certain
romantic impossibilities, which, doubtless, could as little
attach to a house in Oxford-street as they could to a house
in any other quarter of London. Meantime, I had
sufficiently indicated that, whatsoever street *was* concerned
in that affair, Oxford-street was *not*; and it is remarkable
enough, as illustrating this amiable reviewer's veracity, that
no one street in London was absolutely excluded but one;
and that one, Oxford-street. For I happened to mention
that, on such a day (my birth-day), I had turned aside *from*
Oxford-street to look at the house in question. I will now
add that this house was in Greek-street: so much it may be
safe to say. But every candid reader will see that both
prudential restraints, and also disinterested regard to the
feelings of possibly amiable descendants from a vicious man,
would operate with any thoughtful writer, in such a case,
to impose reserve upon his pen. Had my guardians, had my
money-lending friend of Jewry, and others concerned in my
memoirs, been so many shadows, bodiless abstractions, and
without earthly connections, I might readily have given my

own names to my own creations, and have treated them as
unceremoniously as I pleased. Not so under the real
circumstances of the case. My chief guardian, for instance,
though obstinate to a degree which risked the happiness
and the life of his ward, was an upright man otherwise; and
his children are entitled to value his memory.

Again, my Greek-street *trapexités*, the "*foenerator Alpheus*,"
who delighted to reap where he had not sown, and too
often (I fear) allowed himself in practices which not
impossibly have long since been found to qualify him for
distant climates and "Botanic" regions,—even he, though I
might truly describe him as a mere highwayman, whenever
he happened to be aware that I had received a friendly loan,
yet, like other highwaymen of repute, and "gentle thieves,"
was not inexorable to the petitions of his victim: he would
sometimes toss back what was required for some instant
necessity of the road; and at *his* breakfast-table it was, after
all, as elsewhere recorded, that I contrived to support life;
barely, indeed, and most slenderly, but still with the final
result of escaping absolute starvation. With that recollection
before me, I could not allow myself to probe his frailties too
severely, had it even been certainly safe to do so. But
enough; the reader will understand that a year spent either
in the valleys of Wales, or upon the streets of London, a
wanderer, too often houseless in both situations, might
naturally have peopled the mind of one constitutionally
disposed to solemn contemplations with memorials of
human sorrow and strife too profound to pass away for
years.

Thus, then, it was—past experience of a very peculiar kind,
the agitations of many lives crowded into the compass of a
year or two, in combination with a peculiar structure of
mind—offered one explanation of the very remarkable and

unsocial habits which I adopted at college; but there was another not less powerful, and not less unusual. In stating this, I shall seem, to some persons, covertly designing an affront to Oxford. But that is far from my intention. It is noways peculiar to Oxford, but will, doubtless, be found in every university throughout the world, that the younger part of the members—the undergraduates, I mean, generally, whose chief business must have lain amongst the great writers of Greece and Rome—cannot have found leisure to cultivate extensively their own domestic literature. Not so much that time will have been wanting; but that the whole energy of the mind, and the main course of the subsidiary studies and researches, will naturally have been directed to those difficult languages amongst which lie their daily tasks. I make it no subject of complaint or scorn, therefore, but simply state it as a fact, that few or none of the Oxford undergraduates, with whom parity of standing threw me into collision at my first outset, knew anything at all of English literature. The *Spectator* seemed to me the only English book of a classical rank which they had read; and even this less for its inimitable delicacy, humor, and refined pleasantry in dealing with manners and characters, than for its insipid and meagre essays, ethical or critical. This was no fault of theirs: they had been sent to the book chiefly as a subject for Latin translations, or of other exercises; and, in such a view, the vague generalities of superficial morality were more useful and more manageable than sketches of manner or character, steeped in national peculiarities. To translate the terms of whig politics into classical Latin, would be as difficult as it might be for a whig himself to give a consistent account of those politics from the year 1688. Natural, however, and excusable, as this ignorance might be, to myself it was intolerable and incomprehensible. Already, at fifteen, I had made myself familiar with the great English poets. About sixteen, or not long after, my interest in the story of Chatterton had carried me over the whole ground of the Rowley controversy; and that controversy, by a necessary consequence, had so familiarized me with the "Black Letter," that I had begun to find an unaffected pleasure in the ancient English metrical romances; and in Chaucer, though acquainted as yet only with part of his works, I had perceived and had felt profoundly those divine qualities, which, even at this day, are so languidly acknowledged by his unjust countrymen. With this knowledge, and this enthusiastic knowledge of the elder poets—of those most remote from easy access—I could not well be a stranger in other walks of our literature, more on a level with the general taste, and nearer to modern diction, and, therefore, more extensively multiplied by the press.

Yet, after all—as one proof how much more commanding is that part of a literature which speaks to the elementary affections of men, than that which is founded on the mutable aspects of manners—it is a fact that, even in our elaborate system of society, where an undue value is unavoidably given to the whole science of social intercourse, and a continual irritation applied to the sensibilities which point in that direction; still, under all these advantages, Pope himself is less read, less quoted, less thought of, than the elder and graver section of our literature. It is a great calamity for an author such as Pope, that, generally speaking, it requires so much experience of life to enjoy his peculiar felicities as must argue an age likely to have impaired the general capacity for enjoyment. For my part, I had myself a very slender acquaintance with this chapter of our literature; and what little I had was generally, at that period of my life, as, with most men, it continues to be to the end of life, a reflex knowledge, acquired through those pleasant miscellanies, half gossip, half criticism—such as Warton's Essay on Pope, Boswell's Johnson, Mathias'

Pursuits of Literature, and many scores beside of the same indeterminate class; a class, however, which do a real service to literature, by diffusing an indirect knowledge of fine writers in their most effective passages, where else, in a direct shape, it would often never extend.

In some parts, then, having even a profound knowledge of our literature, in all parts having some, I felt it to be impossible that I should familiarly associate with those who had none at all; not so much as a mere historical knowledge of the literature in its capital names and their chronological succession. Do I mention this in disparagement of Oxford? By no means. Among the undergraduates of higher standing, and occasionally, perhaps, of my own, I have since learned that many might have been found eminently accomplished in this particular. But seniors do not seek after juniors; they must be sought; and, with my previous bias to solitude, a bias equally composed of impulses and motives, I had no disposition to take trouble in seeking any man for any purpose.

But, on this subject, a fact still remains to be told, of which I am justly proud; and it will serve, beyond anything else that I can say, to measure the degree of my intellectual development. On coming to Oxford, I had taken up one position in advance of my age by full thirty years: that appreciation of Wordsworth, which it has taken full thirty years to establish amongst the public, I had already made, and had made operative to my own intellectual culture in the same year when I clandestinely quitted school. Already, in 1802, I had addressed a letter of fervent admiration to Mr. Wordsworth. I did not send it until the spring of 1803; and, from misdirection, it did not come into his hands for some months. But I had an answer from Mr. Wordsworth before I was eighteen; and that my letter was thought to express the homage of an enlightened admirer, may be inferred from the fact that his answer was long and full. On this anecdote I do not mean to dwell; but I cannot allow the reader to overlook the circumstances of the case. At this day, it is true, no journal can be taken up which does not habitually speak of Mr. Wordsworth as of a great if not *the* great poet of the age. Mr. Bulwer, living in the intensest pressure of the world, and, though recoiling continually from the judgments of the world, yet never in any violent degree, ascribes to Mr. Wordsworth (in his *England and the English*, p. 308) "an influence of a more noble and purely intellectual character, than *any* writer of our age or nation has exercised." Such is the opinion held of this great poet in 1835; but what were those of 1805-15,—nay, of 1825? For twenty years after the date of that letter to Mr. Wordsworth above referred to, language was exhausted, ingenuity was put on the rack, in the search after images and expressions vile enough—insolent enough—to convey the unutterable contempt avowed for all that he had written, by the fashionable critics. One critic—who still, I believe, edits a rather popular journal, and who belongs to that class, feeble, fluttering, ingenious, who make it their highest ambition not to lead, but, with a slave's adulation, to obey and to follow all the caprices of the public mind—described Mr. Wordsworth as resembling, in the quality of his mind, an old nurse babbling in her paralytic dotage to sucking babies. If this insult was peculiarly felt by Mr. Wordsworth, it was on a consideration of the unusual imbecility of him who offered it, and not because in itself it was baser or more insolent than the language held by the majority of journalists who then echoed the public voice. *Blackwood's Magazine* (1817) first accustomed the public ear to the language of admiration coupled with the name of Wordsworth. This began with Professor Wilson; and well I remember—nay, the proofs are still easy to hunt up—that, for eight or ten years, this singularity of opinion, having no countenance from other journals, was treated as a whim, a paradox, a bold extravagance, of the *Blackwood* critics. Mr. Wordsworth's neighbors in Westmoreland, who had (generally speaking) a profound contempt for him, used to rebut the testimony of *Blackwood* by one constant reply —"Ay, *Blackwood* praises Wordsworth, but who else praises him?" In short, up to 1820, the name of Wordsworth was trampled under foot; from 1820 to 1830, it was militant; from 1830 to 1835, it has been triumphant. In 1803, when I entered at Oxford, that name was absolutely unknown; and the finger of scorn, pointed at it in 1802 by the first or second number of the *Edinburgh Review*, failed to reach its mark from absolute defect of knowledge in the public mind. Some fifty beside myself knew who was meant by "that poet who had cautioned his friend against growing double," etc.; to all others it was a profound secret.

These things must be known and understood properly to value the prophetic eye and the intrepidity of two persons, like Professor Wilson and myself, who, in 1802-3, attached themselves to a banner not yet raised and planted; who outran, in fact, their contemporaries by one entire generation; and did *that* about 1802 which the rest of the world are doing in chorus about 1832.

Professor Wilson's period at Oxford exactly coincided with my own; yet, in that large world, we never met. I know, therefore, but little of his policy in regard to such opinions or feelings as tended to dissociate him from the mass of his coevals. This only I know, that he lived as it were in public; and must, therefore, I presume, have practised a studied reserve as to his deepest admirations; and, perhaps, at that day (1803-8) the occasions would be rare in which much dissimulation would be needed. Until Lord Byron had

begun to pilfer from Wordsworth and to abuse him,
allusions to Wordsworth were not frequent in conversation;
and it was chiefly on occasion of some question arising
about poetry in general, or about the poets of the day, that
it became difficult to dissemble. For my part, hating the
necessity for dissimulation as much as the dissimulation
itself, I drew from this peculiarity also of my own mind a
fresh reinforcement of my other motives for sequestering
myself; and, for the first two years of my residence in
Oxford, I compute that I did not utter one hundred words.

I remember distinctly the first (which happened also to be
the last) conversation that I ever held with my tutor. It
consisted of three sentences, two of which fell to his share,
one to mine. On a fine morning, he met me in the
Quadrangle, and, having then no guess of the nature of my
pretensions, he determined (I suppose) to probe them.
Accordingly, he asked me, "What I had been lately reading?"
Now, the fact was, that I, at that time immersed in
metaphysics, had really been reading and studying very
closely the *Parmenides*, of which obscure work some Oxford
men, early in the last century, published a separate edition.
Yet, so profound was the benignity of my nature, that, in
those days, I could not bear to witness, far less to cause, the
least pain or mortification to any human being. I recoiled,
indeed, from the society of most men, but not with any
feelings of dislike. On the contrary, in order that I *might* like
all men, I wished to associate with none. Now, then, to have
mentioned the *Parmenides* to one who, fifty thousand to one,
was a perfect stranger to its whole drift and purpose, looked
too *méchant*, too like a trick of malice, in an age when such
reading was so very unusual. I felt that it would be taken
for an express stratagem for stopping my tutor's mouth. All
this passing rapidly through my mind, I replied, without
hesitation, that I had been reading Paley. My tutor's

rejoinder I have never forgotten: "Ah! an excellent author; excellent for his matter; only you must be on your guard as to his style; he is very vicious *there*." Such was the colloquy; we bowed, parted, and never more (I apprehend) exchanged one word. Now, trivial and trite as this comment on Paley may appear to the reader, it struck me forcibly that more falsehood, or more absolute falsehood, or more direct inversion of the truth, could not, by any artifice of ingenuity, have been crowded into one short sentence. Paley, as a philosopher, is a jest, the disgrace of the age; and, as regards the two universities, and the enormous responsibility they undertake for the books which they sanction by their official examinations for degrees, the name of Paley is their great opprobrium. But, on the other hand, for style, Paley is a master. Homely, racy, vernacular English, the rustic vigor of a style which intentionally foregoes the graces of polish on the one hand, and of scholastic precision on the other—that quality of merit has never been attained in a degree so eminent. This first interchange of thought upon a topic of literature did not tend to slacken my previous disposition to retreat into solitude; a solitude, however, which at no time was tainted with either the moroseness or the pride of a cynic.

Neither must the reader suppose that, even in that day, I belonged to the party who disparage the classical writers, or the classical training of the great English schools. The Greek drama I loved and revered. But, to deal frankly, because it is a subject which I shall hereafter bring before the public, I made great distinctions. I was not that indiscriminate admirer of Greek and Roman literature, which those too generally are who admire it at all. This protesting spirit, against a false and blind idolatry, was with me, at that time, a matter of enthusiasm—almost of bigotry. I was a bigot against bigots. Let us take the Greek oratory, for example:—

What section of the Greek literature is more fanatically exalted, and studiously in depreciation of our own? Let us judge of the sincerity at the base of these hollow affectations, by the downright facts and the producible records. To admire, in any sense which can give weight and value to your admiration, presupposes, I presume, some acquaintance with its object. As the earliest title to an opinion, one way or other, of the Greek eloquence, we ought to have studied some of its most distinguished artists; or, say *one*, at least; and this one, we may be sure, will be, as it ought to be, Demosthenes. Now, it is a fact, that all the copies of Demosthenes sold within the last hundred years would not meet the demand of one considerable town, were that orator a subject of study amongst even classical scholars. I doubt whether, at this day, there exist twenty men in Europe who can be said to have even once read Demosthenes; and, therefore, it was that, when Mr. Mitford, in his "History of Greece," took a new view of this orator's political administration—a view which lowered his character for integrity—he found an unresisting acceder to his doctrines in a public having no previous opinion upon the subject, and, therefore, open to any casual impression of malice or rash judgment. Had there been any acquaintance with the large remains which we still possess of this famous orator, no such wrong could have been done. I, from my childhood, had been a reader, nay, a student of Demosthenes; and, simply, for this reason, that, having meditated profoundly on the true laws and philosophy of diction, and of what is vaguely denominated style, and finding nothing of any value in modern writers upon this subject, and not much as regards the grounds and ultimate principles even in the ancient rhetoricians, I have been reduced to collect my opinions from the great artists and practitioners, rather than from the theorists; and, among those artists, in the most plastic of languages, I hold

Demosthenes to have been the greatest.

The Greek is, beyond comparison, the most plastic of languages. It was a material which bent to the purposes of him who used it beyond the material of other languages; it was an instrument for a larger compass of modulations; and it happens that the peculiar theme of an orator imposes the very largest which is consistent with a prose diction. One step further in passion, and the orator would become a poet. An orator can exhaust the capacities of a language—an historian, never. Moreover, the age of Demosthenes was, in my judgment, the age of highest development for arts dependent upon social refinement. That generation had fixed and ascertained the use of words; whereas, the previous generation of Thucydides, Xenophon, Plato, &c., was a transitional period: the language was still moving, and tending to a meridian not yet attained; and the public eye had been directed consciously upon language, as in and for itself an organ of intellectual delight, for too short a time, to have mastered the whole art of managing its resources. All these were reasons for studying Demosthenes, as the one great model and standard of Attic prose; and, studied him I *had*, more than any other prose writer whatever. *Paripassu*, I had become sensible that others had *not* studied him. One monotonous song of applause I found raised on every side; something about being "like a torrent, that carries everything before it." This original image is all we get in the shape of criticism; and never any attempt even at illustrating what is greatest in him, or characterizing what is most peculiar. The same persons who discovered that Lord Brougham was the modern Bacon have also complimented him with the title of the English Demosthenes. Upon this hint, Lord Brougham, in his address to the Glasgow students, has deluged the great Athenian with wordy admiration. There is an obvious prudence in lodging your praise upon an object from which you count upon a rebound to yourself. But here, as everywhere else, you look in vain for any marks or indications of a personal and *direct* acquaintance with the original orations. The praise is built rather upon the popular idea of Demosthenes, than upon the real Demosthenes. And not only so, but even upon style itself, and upon the art of composition *in abstracto*, Lord Brougham does not seem to have formed any clear conceptions—principles he has none. Now, it is useless to judge of an artist until you have some principles on the art. The two capital secrets in the art of prose composition are these: 1st, The philosophy of transition and connection, or the art by which one step in an evolution of thought is made to arise out of another: all fluent and effective composition depends on the *connections*; —2dly, The way in which sentences are made to modify each other; for, the most powerful effects in written eloquence arise out of this reverberation, as it were, from each other in a rapid succession of sentences; and, because some limitation is necessary to the length and complexity of sentences, in order to make this interdependency felt, hence it is that the Germans have no eloquence. The construction of German prose tends to such immoderate length of sentences, that no effect of intermodification can ever be apparent. Each sentence, stuffed with innumerable clauses of restriction, and other parenthetical circumstances, becomes a separate section —an independent whole. But, without insisting on Lord Brougham's oversights, or errors of defect, I will digress a moment to one positive caution of his, which will measure the value of his philosophy on this subject. He lays it down for a rule of indefinite application, that the Saxon part of our English idiom is to be favored at the expense of that part which has so happily coalesced with the language from the Latin or Greek. This fancy, often patronized by other writers, and even acted upon, resembles that restraint which some metrical writers have imposed upon themselves —of writing a long copy of verses, from which some particular letter, or from each line of which some different letter, should be carefully excluded. What followed? Was the reader sensible, in the practical effect upon his ear, of any beauty attained? By no means; all the difference, sensibly perceived, lay in the occasional constraints and affectations to which the writer had been driven by his self-imposed necessities. The same chimera exists in Germany; and so much further is it carried, that one great puritan in this heresy (Wolf) has published a vast dictionary, the rival of Adelung's, for the purpose of expelling every word of foreign origin and composition out of the language, by assigning some equivalent term spun out from pure native Teutonic materials. *Bayonet*, for example, is patriotically rejected, because a word may be readily compounded tantamount to *musket-dirk*; and this sort of composition thrives showily in the German, as a language running into composition with a fusibility only surpassed by the Greek.

But what good purpose is attained by such caprices? In three sentences the sum of the philosophy may be stated. It has been computed (see *Duclos*) that the Italian opera has not above six hundred words in its whole vocabulary: so narrow is the range of its emotions, and so little are these emotions disposed to expand themselves into any variety of thinking. The same remark applies to that class of simple, household, homely passion, which belongs to the early ballad poetry. Their passion is of a quality more venerable, it is true, and deeper than that of the opera, because more permanent and coextensive with human life; but it is not much wider in its sphere, nor more apt to coalesce with contemplative or philosophic thinking. Pass from these narrow fields of the intellect, where the relations of the

objects are so few and simple, and the whole prospect so
bounded, to the immeasurable and sea-like arena upon
which Shakspeare careers—co-infinite with life itself—yes,
and with something more than life. Here is the other pole,
the opposite extreme. And what is the choice of diction?
What is the *lexis*? Is it Saxon exclusively, or is it Saxon by
preference? So far from that, the Latinity is intense—not,
indeed, in his construction, but in his choice of words; and
so continually are these Latin words used, with a critical
respect to their earliest (and, where *that* happens to have
existed, to their unfigurative) meaning, that, upon this one
argument I would rely for upsetting the else impregnable
thesis of Dr. Farmer as to Shakspeare's learning. Nay, I will
affirm that, out of this regard to the Latin acceptation of
Latin words, may be absolutely explained the Shakspearian
meaning of certain words, which has hitherto baffled all his
critics. For instance, the word *modern*, of which Dr. Johnson
professes himself unable to explain the *rationale* or principle
regulating its Shakspearian use, though he felt its value, it is
to be deduced thus: First of all, change the pronunciation a
little, by substituting for the short *o*, as we pronounce it in
modern, the long *o*, as heard in *modish*, and you will then,
perhaps, perceive the process of analogy by which it passed
into the Shakspearian use. The *matter* or substance of a
thing is, usually, so much more important than its fashion
or *manner*, that we have hence adopted, as one way for
expressing what is important as opposed to what is trivial,
the word *material*. Now, by parity of reason, we are entitled
to invert this order, and to express what is unimportant by
some word indicating the mere fashion or external manner
of an object as opposed to its substance. This is effected by
the word *modal* or *modern*, as the adjective from *modus*, a
fashion or manner; and in that sense Shakspeare employs
the word. Thus, Cleopatra, undervaluing to Caesar's agent

the bijouterie which she has kept back from inventory, and which her treacherous steward had betrayed, describes them as mere trifles

"Such gifts as we greet modern friends withal;"

where all commentators have *felt* that modern must form the position, mean, slight, and inconsiderable, though perplexed to say how it came by such a meaning. A *modern* friend is, in the Shakspearian sense, with relation to a real and serviceable friend, that which the fashion of a thing is, by comparison with its substance. But a still better illustration may be taken from a common line, quoted every day, and ludicrously misinterpreted. In the famous picture of life—"All the world's a stage"—the justice of the piece is described as

"Full of wise saws and modern instances;"

which (*horrendum dictu!*) has been explained, and, I verily believe, is generally understood to mean, *full of wise sayings and modern illustrations*. The true meaning is—full of proverbial maxims of conduct and of trivial arguments; that is, of petty distinctions, or verbal disputes, such as never touch the point at issue. The word *modern* I have already deduced; the word *instances* is equally Latin, and equally used by Shakspeare in its Latin sense. It is originally the word *instantia*, which, by the monkish and scholastic writers, is uniformly used in the sense of an argument, and originally of an argument urged in objection to some previous argument. [Footnote: I cannot for a moment believe that the original and most eloquent critic in *Blackwood* is himself the dupe of an argument, which he has alleged against this passage, under too open a hatred of

Shakspeare, as though it involved a contradiction to common sense, by representing *all* human beings of such an age as school-boys, all of such another age as soldiers, of such another as magistrates, &c. Evidently the logic of the famous passage is this that whereas every age has its peculiar and appropriate temper, that profession or employment is selected for the exemplification which seems best fitted, in each case, to embody the characteristic or predominating quality. Thus, because impetuosity, self-esteem, and animal or irreflective courage, are qualities most intense in youth, next it is considered in what profession those qualities find their most unlimited range; and because that is obviously the military profession, therefore it is that the soldier is selected as the representative of young men. For the same reason, as best embodying the peculiar temper of garrulous old age, the magistrate comes forward as supporting the part of that age. Not that old men are not also soldiers; but that the military profession, so far from strengthening, moderates and tempers the characteristic temper of old age.]

I affirm, therefore, that Lord Brougham's counsel to the Glasgow students is not only bad counsel,—and bad counsel for the result, as well as for the grounds, which are either capricious or nugatory,—but also that, in the exact proportion in which the range of thought expands, it is an impossible counsel, an impracticable counsel—a counsel having for its purpose to embarrass and lay the mind in fetters, where even its utmost freedom and its largest resources will be found all too little for the growing necessities of the intellect. "Long-tailed words in *osity* and *ation*!" What does *that* describe? Exactly the Latin part of our language. Now, those very terminations speak for themselves:—All high abstractions end in *ation*; that is, they are Latin; and, just in proportion as the abstracting power

extends and widens, do the circles of thought widen, and
the horizon or boundary (contradicting its own Grecian
name) melts into the infinite. On this account it was that
Coleridge (*Biographia Literaria*) remarks on Wordsworth's
philosophical poetry, that, in proportion as it goes into the
profound of passion and of thought, do the words increase
which are vulgarly called "*dictionary* words." Now, these
words, these "dictionary" words, what are they? Simply
words of Latin or Greek origin: no other words, no Saxon
words, are ever called by illiterate persons dictionary words.
And these dictionary words are indispensable to a writer,
not only in the proportion by which he transcends other
writers as to extent and as to subtility of thinking, but also
as to elevation and sublimity. Milton was not an extensive
or discursive thinker, as Shakspeare was; for the motions of
his mind were slow, solemn, sequacious, like those of the
planets; not agile and assimilative; not attracting all things
within its own sphere; not multiform: repulsion was the
law of his intellect—he moved in solitary grandeur. Yet,
merely from this quality of grandeur, unapproachable
grandeur, his intellect demanded a larger infusion of
Latinity into his diction.

For the same reason (and, without such aids, he would
have had no proper element in which to move his wings) he
enriched his diction with Hellenisms and with Hebraisms;
[Footnote: The diction of Milton is a case absolutely unique
in literature: of many writers it has been said, but of him
only with truth, that he created a peculiar language. The
value must be tried by the result, not by inferences from *a
priori* principles; such inferences might lead us to anticipate
an unfortunate result; whereas, in fact, the diction of Milton
is such that no other could have supported his majestic style
of thinking. The final result is a *transcendant* answer to all
adverse criticism; but still it is to be lamented that no man

properly qualified has undertaken the examination of the Miltonic diction as a separate problem. Listen to a popular author of this day (Mr. Bulwer). He, speaking on this subject, asserts (*England and the English*, p. 329), that, *"There is scarcely an English idiom which Milton has not violated, or a foreign one which he has not borrowed."* Now, in answer to this extravagant assertion, I will venture to say that the two following are the sole cases of questionable idiom throughout Milton:—1st, "Yet virgin of Proserpine from Jove;" and, in this case, the same thing might be urged in apology which Aristotle urges in another argument, namely, that *anonymon to pathos*, the case is unprovided with *any* suitable expression. How would it be possible to convey in good English the circumstances here indicated—namely, that Ceres was yet in those days of maiden innocence, when she had borne no daughter to Jove? Second, I will cite a case which, so far as I remember, has been noticed by no commentator; and, probably, because they have failed to understand it. The case occurs in the "Paradise Regained;" but where I do not at this moment remember. "Will they *transact* with God?" This is the passage; and a most flagrant instance it offers of pure Latinism. *Transigere*, in the language of the civil law, means to make a compromise; and the word *transact* is here used in that sense—a sense utterly unknown to the English language. This is the worst case in Milton; and I do not know that it has been ever noticed. Yet even here it may be doubted whether Milton is not defensible; asking if they proposed to terminate their difference with God after the fashion in use amongst courts of law, he points properly enough to these worldly settlements by the technical term which designated them. Thus, might a divine say: Will he arrest the judgments of God by a *demurrer*? Thus, again, Hamlet apostrophizes the lawyer's skull by the technical terms used in actions for assault, &c. Besides, what proper term is there in English for expressing a compromise? Edmund Burke, and other much older authors, express the idea by the word *temperament*; but that word, though a good one, was at one time considered an exotic term—equally a Gallicism and a Latinism.] but never, as could be easy to show, without a full justification in the result. Two things may be asserted of all his exotic idioms—1st, That they express what could not have been expressed by any native idiom; 2d, That they harmonize with the English language, and give a coloring of the antique, but not any sense of strangeness to the diction. Thus, in the double negative, "Nor did they not perceive," &c., which is classed as a Hebraism—if any man fancy that it expresses no more than the simple affirmative, he shows that he does not understand its force; and, at the same time, it is a form of thought so natural and universal, that I have heard English people, under corresponding circumstances, spontaneously fall into it. In short, whether a man differ from others by greater profundity or by greater sublimity, and whether he write as a poet or as a philosopher, in any case, he feels, in due proportion to the necessities of his intellect, an increasing dependence upon the Latin section of the English language; and the true reason why Lord Brougham failed to perceive this, or found the Saxon equal to his wants, is one which I shall not scruple to assign, inasmuch as it does not reflect personally on Lord Brougham, or, at least, on him exclusively, but on the whole body to which he belongs. That thing which he and they call by the pompous name of statesmanship, but which is, in fact, *statescraft*—the art of political intrigue—deals (like the opera) with ideas so few in number, and so little adapted to associate themselves with other ideas, that, possibly, in the one case equally as in the other, six hundred words are sufficient to meet all their demands.

I have used my privilege of discursiveness to step aside from
Demosthenes to another subject, no otherwise connected
with the Attic orator than, first, by the common reference of
both subjects to rhetoric; but, secondly, by the accident of
having been jointly discussed by Lord Brougham in a paper,
which (though now forgotten) obtained, at the moment,
most undue celebrity. For it is one of the infirmities of the
public mind with us, that whatever is said or done by a
public man, any opinion given by a member of Parliament,
however much out of his own proper jurisdiction and range
of inquiry, commands an attention not conceded even to
those who speak under the known privilege of professional
knowledge. Thus, Cowper was not discovered to be a poet
worthy of any general notice, until Charles Fox, a most
slender critic, had vouchsafed to quote a few lines, and that,
not so much with a view to the poetry, as to its party
application. But now, returning to Demosthenes, I affirm
that his case is the case of nearly all the classical writers,—at
least, of all the prose writers. It is, I admit, an extreme one;
that is, it is the general case in a more intense degree. Raised
almost to divine honors, never mentioned but with affected
rapture, the classics of Greece and Rome are seldom read,
most of them never; are they, indeed, the closet companions
of any man? Surely it is time that these follies were at an
end; that our practice were made to square a little better
with our professions; and that our pleasures were sincerely
drawn from those sources in which we pretend that they lie.

The Greek language, mastered in any eminent degree, is the
very rarest of all accomplishments, and precisely because it is
unspeakably the most difficult. Let not the reader dupe
himself by popular cant. To be an accomplished Grecian,
demands a very peculiar quality of talent; and it is almost
inevitable that one who is such should be vain of a
distinction which represents so much labor and difficulty

overcome. For myself, having, as a school-boy, attained to a
very unusual mastery over this language, and (though as
yet little familiar with the elaborate science of Greek metre)
moving through all the obstacles and resistances of a Greek
book with the same celerity and ease as through those of the
French and Latin, I had, in vanquishing the difficulties of
the language, lost the main stimulus to its cultivation. Still,
I read Greek daily; but any slight vanity which I might
connect with a power so rarely attained, and which, under
ordinary circumstances, so readily transmutes itself into a
disproportionate admiration of the author, in me was
absolutely swallowed up in the tremendous hold taken of
my entire sensibilities at this time by our own literature.
With what fury would I often exclaim: He who loveth not
his brother whom he hath seen, how shall he love God
whom he hath not seen? You, Mr. A, L, M, O, you who care
not for Milton, and value not the dark sublimities which
rest ultimately (as we all feel) upon dread realities, how can
you seriously thrill in sympathy with the spurious and
fanciful sublimities of the classical poetry—with the nod of
the Olympian Jove, or the seven-league strides of Neptune?
Flying Childers had the most prodigious stride of any horse
on record; and at Newmarket that is justly held to be a great
merit; but it is hardly a qualification for a Pantheon. The
parting of Hector and Andromache—that is tender,
doubtless; but how many passages of far deeper, far diviner
tenderness, are to be found in Chaucer! Yet in these cases we
give our antagonist the benefit of an appeal to what is really
best and most effective in the ancient literature. For, if we
should go to Pindar, and some other great names, what a
revelation of hypocrisy as respects the *fade* enthusiasts for
the Greek poetry!

Still, in the Greek tragedy, however otherwise embittered
against ancient literature by the dismal affectations current

in the scenical poetry, at least I felt the presence of a great
and original power. It might be a power inferior, upon the
whole, to that which presides in the English tragedy; I
believed that it was; but it was equally genuine, and
appealed equally to real and deep sensibilities in our nature.
Yet, also, I felt that the two powers at work in the two forms
of the drama were essentially different; and without having
read a line of German at that time, or knowing of any such
controversy, I began to meditate on the elementary grounds
of difference between the Pagan and the Christian forms of
poetry. The dispute has since been carried on extensively in
France, not less than in Germany, as between the *classical*
and the *romantic*. But I will venture to assert that not one
step in advance has been made, up to this day. The shape
into which I threw the question it may be well to state;
because I am persuaded that out of that one idea, properly
pursued, might be evolved the whole separate characteristics
of the Christian and the antique: Why is it, I asked, that the
Christian idea of *sin* is an idea utterly unknown to the
Pagan mind? The Greeks and Romans had a clear
conception of a moral ideal, as we have; but this they
estimated by a reference to the will; and they called it virtue,
and the antithesis they called vice. The *lacheté* or relaxed
energy of the will, by which it yielded to the seductions of
sensual pleasure, that was vice; and the braced-up tone by
which it resisted these seductions was virtue. But the idea of
holiness, and the antithetic idea of sin, as a violation of this
awful and unimaginable sanctity, was so utterly
undeveloped in the Pagan mind, that no word exists in
classical Greek or classical Latin which approaches either
pole of this synthesis; neither the idea of *holiness*, nor of its
correlate, *sin*, could be so expressed in Latin as at once to
satisfy Cicero and a scientific Christian. Again (but this was
some years after), I found Schiller and Goethe applauding
the better taste of the ancients, in symbolizing the idea of

death by a beautiful youth, with a torch inverted, &c., as
compared with the Christian types of a skeleton and hour-
glasses, &c. And much surprised I was to hear Mr. Coleridge
approving of this German sentiment. Yet, here again I felt
the peculiar genius of Christianity was covertly at work
moving upon a different road, and under opposite ideas, to
a just result, in which the harsh and austere expression yet
pointed to a dark reality, whilst the beautiful Greek
adumbration was, in fact, a veil and a disguise. The
corruptions and the other "dishonors" of the grave, and
whatsoever composes the sting of death in the Christian
view, is traced up to sin as its ultimate cause. Hence, besides
the expression of Christian humility, in thus nakedly
exhibiting the wrecks and ruins made by sin, there is also a
latent profession indicated of Christian hope. For the
Christian contemplates steadfastly, though with trembling
awe, the lowest point of his descent; since, for him, that
point, the last of his fall, is also the first of his reäscent, and
serves, besides, as an exponent of its infinity; the infinite
depth becoming, in the rebound, a measure of the infinite
reäscent. Whereas, on the contrary, with the gloomy
uncertainties of a Pagan on the question of his final
restoration, and also (which must not be overlooked) with
his utter perplexity as to the nature of his restoration, if any
were by accident in reserve, whether in a condition tending
downwards or upwards, it was the natural resource to
consult the general feeling of anxiety and distrust, by
throwing a thick curtain and a veil of beauty over the
whole too painful subject. To place the horrors in high
relief, could here have answered no purpose but that of
wanton cruelty; whereas, with the Christian hopes, the very
saddest memorials of the havocs made by death are
antagonist prefigurations of great victories in the rear.

These speculations, at that time, I pursued earnestly; and I then believed myself, as I yet do, to have ascertained the two great and opposite laws under which the Grecian and the English tragedy has each separately developed itself. Whether wrong or right in that belief, sure I am that those in Germany who have treated the case of classical and romantic are not entitled to credit for any discovery at all. The Schlegels, who were the hollowest of men, the windiest and wordiest (at least, Frederic was so), pointed to the distinction; barely indicated it; and that was already some service done, because a presumption arose that the antique and the modern literatures, having clearly some essential differences, might, perhaps, rest on foundations originally distinct, and obey different laws. And hence it occurred that many disputes, as about the unities, etc., might originate in a confusion of these laws. This checks the presumption of the shallow criticism, and points to deeper investigations. Beyond this, neither the German nor the French disputers on the subject have talked to any profitable purpose.

I have mentioned Paley as accidentally connected with my *début* in literary conversation; and I have taken occasion to say how much I admired his style and its unstudied graces, how profoundly I despised his philosophy. I shall here say a word or two more on that subject. As respects his style, though secretly despising the opinion avowed by my tutor (which was, however, a natural opinion for a stiff lover of the artificial and the pompous), I would just as unwillingly be supposed to adopt the extravagant opinions, in the other extreme, of Dr. Parr and Mr. Coleridge. These two gentlemen, who privately hated Paley, and, perhaps, traduced him, have hung like bees over one particular paragraph in his Evidences, as though it were a flower transplanted from Hymettus. Dr. Parr pronounced it the finest sentence in the English language. It is a period (that is, a cluster of sentences) moderately well, but not *too* well constructed, as the German nurses are accustomed to say. Its felicity depends on a trick easily imitated—on a balance happily placed (namely, *"in which the wisest of mankind would rejoice to find an answer to their doubts, and rest to their inquiries"*). As a *bravura*, or *tour de force*, in the dazzling fence of rhetoric, it is surpassed by many hundreds of passages which might be produced from rhetoricians; or, to confine myself to Paley's contemporaries, it is very far surpassed by a particular passage in Burke's letter upon the Duke of Bedford's base attack upon him in the House of Lords; which passage I shall elsewhere produce, because I happen to know, on the authority of Burke's executors, that Burke himself considered it the finest period which he had ever written. At present, I will only make one remark, namely, that it is always injudicious, in the highest degree, to cite for admiration that which is not a *representative* specimen of the author's manner. In reading Lucian, I once stumbled on a passage of German pathos, and of German effect. Would it have been wise, or would it have been intellectually just, to quote this as the text of an eulogium on Lucian? What false criticism it would have suggested to every reader! what false anticipations! To quote a formal and periodic pile of sentences, was to give the feeling that Paley was what the regular rhetorical artists designate as a periodic writer, when, in fact, no one conceivable character of style more pointedly contradicted the true description of his merits.

But, leaving the style of Paley, I must confess that I agree with Mr. Bulwer (*England and the English*) in thinking it shocking and almost damnatory to an English university, the great well-heads of creeds, moral and evangelical, that authors such in respect of doctrine as Paley and Locke should hold that high and influential station as teachers, or rather oracles of truth, which has been conceded to them. As to Locke, I, when a boy, had made a discovery of one

blunder full of laughter and of fun, which, had it been
published and explained in Locke's lifetime, would have
tainted his whole philosophy with suspicion. It relates to
the Aristotelian doctrine of syllogism, which Locke
undertook to ridicule. Now, a flaw, a hideous flaw, in the *soi-
disant* detecter of flaws, a ridicule in the exposer of the
ridiculous—*that* is fatal; and I am surprised that Lee, who
wrote a folio against Locke in his lifetime, and other
examiners, should have failed in detecting this. I shall
expose it elsewhere; and, perhaps, one or two other
exposures of the same kind will give an impetus to the
descent of this falling philosophy. With respect to Paley, and
the naked *prudentialism* of his system, it is true that in a
longish note Paley disclaims that consequence. But to this
we may reply, with Cicero, *Non quoero quid neget Epicurus, sed
quid congruenter neget.* Meantime, waiving all this as too
notorious, and too frequently denounced, I wish to recur to
this trite subject, by way of stating an objection made to the
Paleyan morality in my seventeenth year, and which I have
never since seen reason to withdraw. It is this:—I affirm that
the whole work, from first to last, proceeds upon that sort
of error which the logicians call *ignoratio elenchi*, that is,
ignorance of the very question concerned—of the point at
issue. For, mark, in the very vestibule of ethics, two
questions arise—two different and disconnected questions,
A and B; and Paley has answered the wrong one. Thinking
that he was answering A, and meaning to answer A, he
has, in fact, answered B. One question arises thus: Justice is
a virtue; temperance is a virtue; and so forth. Now, what is
the common principle which ranks these several species
under the same genus? What, in the language of logicians,
is the common differential principle which determines these
various aspects of moral obligation to a common genius?
Another question, and a more interesting question to men
in general, is this,—What is the motive to virtue? By what

impulse, law, or motive, am I impelled to be virtuous rather than vicious? Whence is the motive derived which should impel me to one line of conduct in preference to the other? This, which is a practical question, and, therefore, more interesting than the other, which is a pure question of speculation, was that which Paley believed himself to be answering. And his answer was,—That utility, a perception of the resulting benefit, was the true determining motive. Meantime, it was objected that often the most obvious results from a virtuous action were far otherwise than beneficial. Upon which, Paley, in the long note referred to above, distinguished thus: That whereas actions have many results, some proximate, some remote, just as a stone thrown into the water produces many concentric circles, be it known that he, Dr. Paley, in what he says of utility, contemplates only the final result, the very outermost circle; inasmuch as he acknowledges a possibility that the first, second, third, including the penultimate circle, may all happen to clash with utility; but then, says he, the outermost circle of all will never fail to coincide with the absolute maximum of utility. Hence, in the first place, it appears that you cannot apply this test of utility in a practical sense; you cannot say, This is useful, *ergo*, it is virtuous; but, in the inverse order, you must say, This is virtuous, *ergo*, it is useful. You do not rely on its usefulness to satisfy yourself of its being virtuous; but, on the contrary, you rely on its virtuousness, previously ascertained, in order to satisfy yourself of its usefulness. And thus the whole practical value of this test disappears, though in that view it was first introduced; and a vicious circle arises in the argument; as you must have ascertained the virtuousness of an act, in order to apply the test of its being virtuous. But, *secondly*, it now comes out that Paley was answering a very different question from that which he supposed himself answering. Not any practical question as to the motive or impelling force in being virtuous, rather than vicious,—that is, to the *sanctions* of virtue,—but a purely speculative question, as to the issue of virtue, or the common *vinculum* amongst the several modes or species of virtue (justice, temperance, etc.)—this was the real question which he was answering. I have often remarked that the largest and most subtle source of error in philosophic speculations has been the confounding of the two great principles so much insisted on by the Leibnitzians, namely, the *ratio cognoscendi* and the *ratio essendi*. Paley believed himself to be assigning—it was his full purpose to assign—the *ratio cognoscendi*; but, instead of that, unconsciously and surreptitiously, he has actually assigned the *ratio essendi*; and, after all, a false and imaginary *ratio essendi*.

THE PAGAN ORACLES

It is remarkable—and, without a previous explanation, it might seem paradoxical to say it—that oftentimes under a continual accession of light important subjects grow more and more enigmatical. In times when nothing was explained, the student, torpid as his teacher, saw nothing which called for explanation—all appeared one monotonous blank. But no sooner had an early twilight begun to solicit the creative faculties of the eye, than many dusky objects, with outlines imperfectly defined, began to converge the eye, and to strengthen the nascent interest of the spectator. It is true that light, in its final plenitude, is calculated to disperse all darkness. But this effect belongs to its consummation. In its earlier and *struggling* states, light does but reveal darkness. It makes the darkness palpable and "visible." Of which we may see a sensible illustration in a gloomy glass-house, where the sullen lustre from the furnace does but mass and accumulate the thick darkness in the rear upon which the moving figures are relieved. Or we may see an intellectual illustration in the mind of the savage, on whose blank surface there exists no doubt or perplexity at all, none of the pains connected with ignorance; he is conscious of no darkness, simply because for *him* there exists no visual ray of speculation—no vestige of prelusive light.

Similar, and continually more similar, has been the condition of ancient history. Once yielding a mere barren crop of facts and dates, slowly it has been kindling of late years into life and deep interest under superior treatment. And hitherto, as the light has advanced, *pari passu* have the masses of darkness strengthened. Every question solved has been the parent of three new questions unmasked. And the power of breathing life into dry bones has but seemed to multiply the skeletons and lifeless remains; for the very natural reason—that these dry bones formerly (whilst viewed as incapable of revivification) had seemed less numerous, because everywhere confounded to the eye with stocks and stones, so long as there was no motive of hope for marking the distinction between them.

Amongst all the illustrations which might illuminate this truth, none is so instructive as the large question of PAGAN ORACLES. Every part, indeed, of the Pagan religion, the course, geographically or ethnographically, of its traditions, the vast labyrinth of its mythology, the deductions of its contradictory genealogies, the disputed meaning of its many secret "mysteries" [*teletai*—symbolic rites or initiations], all these have been submitted of late years to the scrutiny of glasses more powerful, applied under more combined arrangements, and directed according to new principles more comprehensively framed. We cannot in sincerity affirm—always with immediate advantage. But even where the individual effort may have been a failure as regarded the immediate object, rarely, indeed, it has happened but that much indirect illumination has resulted —which, afterwards entering into combination with other scattered currents of light, has issued in discoveries of value; although, perhaps, any one contribution, taken separately, had been, and would have remained, inoperative. Much has been accomplished, chiefly of late years; and, confining our view to ancient history, almost exclusively amongst the Germans—by the Savignys, the Niebuhrs, the Otfried

Muellers. And, if that *much* has left still more to do, it has also brought the means of working upon a scale of far accelerated speed.

The books now existing upon the ancient oracles, above all, upon the Greek oracles, amount to a small library. The facts have been collected from all quarters,—examined, sifted, winnowed. Theories have been raised upon these facts under every angle of aspect; and yet, after all, we profess ourselves to be dissatisfied. Amongst much that is sagacious, we feel and we resent with disgust a taint of falsehood diffused over these recent speculations from vulgar and even counterfeit incredulity; the one gross vice of German philosophy, not less determinate or less misleading than that vice which, heretofore, through many centuries, had impoverished this subject, and had stopped its discussion under the anile superstition of the ecclesiastical fathers.

These fathers, both Greek and Latin, had the ill fortune to be extravagantly esteemed by the church of Rome; whence, under a natural reaction, they were systematically depreciated by the great leaders of the Protestant Reformation. And yet hardly in a corresponding degree. For there was, after all, even among the reformers, a deep-seated prejudice in behalf of all that was "primitive" in Christianity; under which term, by some confusion of ideas, the fathers often benefited. Primitive Christianity was reasonably venerated; and, on this argument, that, for the first three centuries, it was necessarily more sincere. We do not think so much of that sincerity which affronted the fear of persecution; because, after all, the searching persecutions were rare and intermitting, and not, perhaps, in any case, so fiery as they have been represented. We think more of that gentle but insidious persecution which lay in the

solicitations of besieging friends, and more still of the
continual temptations which haunted the irresolute
Christian in the fascinations of the public amusements. The
theatre, the circus, and, far beyond both, the cruel
amphitheatre, constituted, for the ancient world, a
passionate enjoyment, that by many authors, and especially
through one period of time, is described as going to the
verge of frenzy. And we, in modern times, are far too little
aware in what degree these great carnivals, together with
another attraction of great cities, the pomps and festivals of
the Pagan worship, broke the monotony of domestic life,
which, for the old world, was even more oppressive than it
is for us. In all principal cities, so as to be within the reach
of almost all provincial inhabitants, there was a
hippodrome, often uniting the functions of the circus and
the amphitheatre; and there was a theatre. From all such
pleasures the Christian was sternly excluded by his very
profession of faith. From the festivals of the Pagan religion
his exclusion was even more absolute; against them he was
a sworn militant protester from the hour of his baptism.
And when these modes of pleasurable relaxation had been
subtracted from ancient life, what could remain? Even less,
perhaps, than most readers have been led to consider. For
the ancients had no such power of extensive locomotion, of
refreshment for their wearied minds, by travelling and
change of scene, as we children of modern civilization
possess. No ships had then been fitted up for passengers,
nor public carriages established, nor roads opened
extensively, nor hotels so much as imagined hypothetically;
because the relation of *xenia*, or the obligation to reciprocal
hospitality, and latterly the Roman relation of patron and
client, had stifled the first motions of enterprise of the
ancients; in fact, no man travelled but the soldier, and the
man of political authority. Consequently, in sacrificing
public amusements, the Christians sacrificed *all* pleasure

whatsoever that was not rigorously domestic; whilst in facing the contingencies of persecutions that might arise under the rapid succession of changing emperors, they faced a perpetual *anxiety* more trying to the fortitude than any fixed and measurable evil. Here, certainly, we have a guarantee for the deep faithfulness of early Christians, such as never can exist for more mixed bodies of professors, subject to no searching trials.

Better the primitive Christians were (by no means individually better, but better on the total body), yet they were not in any intellectual sense wiser. Unquestionably the elder Christians participated in the local follies, prejudices, superstitions, of their several provinces and cities, except where any of these happened to be too conspicuously at war with the spirit of love or the spirit of purity which exhaled at every point from the Christian faith; and, in all intellectual features, as were the Christians generally, such were the fathers. Amongst the Greek fathers, one might be unusually learned, as Clement of Alexandria; and another might be reputed unusually eloquent, as Gregory Nazianzen, or Basil. Amongst the Latin fathers, one might be a man of admirable genius, as far beyond the poor, vaunted Rousseau in the impassioned grandeur of his thoughts, as he was in truth and purity of heart; we speak of St. Augustine (usually called St. Austin), and many might be distinguished by various literary merits. But could these advantages anticipate a higher civilization? Most unquestionably some of the fathers were the *élite* of their own age, but not in advance of their age. They, like all their contemporaries, were besieged by errors, ancient, inveterate, traditional; and accidentally, from one cause special to themselves, they were not merely liable to error, but usually prone to error. This cause lay in the *polemic* form which so often they found a necessity, or a convenience, or a temptation for assuming, as teachers or defenders of the truth.

He who reveals a body of awful truth to a candid and willing auditory is content with the grand simplicities of truth in the quality of his proofs. And truth, where it happens to be of a high order, is generally its own witness to all who approach it in the spirit of childlike docility. But far different is the position of that teacher who addresses an audience composed in various proportions of sceptical inquirers, obstinate opponents, and malignant scoffers. Less than an apostle is unequal to the suppression of all human reactions incident to wounded sensibilities. Scorn is too naturally met by retorted scorn: malignity in the Pagan, which characterized all the known cases of signal opposition to Christianity, could not but hurry many good men into a vindictive pursuit of victory. Generally, where truth is communicated *polemically* (this is, not as it exists in its own inner simplicity, but as it exists in external relation to error), the temptation is excessive to use those arguments which will tell at the moment upon the crowd of bystanders, by preference to those which will approve themselves ultimately to enlightened disciples. Hence it is, that, like the professional rhetoricians of Athens, not seldom the Christian fathers, when urgently pressed by an antagonist equally mendacious and ignorant, could not resist the human instinct for employing arguments such as would baffle and confound the unprincipled opponent, rather than such as would satisfy the mature Christian. If a man denied himself all specious arguments, and all artifices of dialectic subtlety, he must renounce the hopes of a *present* triumph; for the light of absolute truth on moral or on spiritual themes is too dazzling to be sustained by the diseased optics of those habituated to darkness. And hence we explain not only the many gross delusions of the fathers,

their sophisms, their errors of fact and chronology, their
attempts to build great truths upon fantastic etymologies, or
upon popular conceits in science that have long since
exploded, but also their occasional unchristian tempers. To
contend with an unprincipled and malicious liar, such as
Julian the Apostate, in its original sense the first deliberate
miscreant, offered a dreadful snare to any man's charity. And
he must be a furious bigot who will justify the rancorous
lampoons of Gregory Nazianzen. Are we, then, angry on
behalf of Julian? So far as *he* was interested, not for a
moment would we have suspended the descending scourge.
Cut him to the bone, we should have exclaimed at the time!
Lay the knout into every "raw" that can be found! For we
are of opinion that Julian's duplicity is not yet adequately
understood. But what was right as regarded the claims of
the criminal, was *not* right as regarded the duties of his
opponent. Even in this mischievous renegade, trampling
with his orangoutang hoofs the holiest of truths, a
Christian bishop ought still to have respected his sovereign,
through the brief period that he *was* such, and to have
commiserated his benighted brother, however wilfully
astray, and however hatefully seeking to quench that light
for other men, which, for his own misgiving heart, we
could undertake to show that he never *did* succeed in
quenching. We do not wish to enlarge upon a theme both
copious and easy. But here, and everywhere, speaking of the
fathers as a body, we charge them with anti-christian
practices of a two-fold order: sometimes as supporting their
great cause in a spirit alien to its own, retorting in a temper
not less uncharitable than that of their opponents;
sometimes, again, as adopting arguments that are
unchristian in their ultimate grounds; resting upon errors
the reputation of errors; upon superstitions the overthrow
of superstitions; and drawing upon the armories of
darkness for weapons that, to be durable, ought to have

been of celestial temper. Alternately, in short, the fathers trespass against those affections which furnish to Christianity its moving powers, and against those truths which furnish to Christianity its guiding lights. Indeed, Milton's memorable attempt to characterize the fathers as a body, contemptuous as it is, can hardly be challenged as overcharged.

Never in any instance were these aberrations of the fathers more vividly exemplified than in their theories upon the Pagan Oracles. On behalf of God, they were determined to be wiser than God; and, in demonstration of scriptural power, to advance doctrines which the Scriptures had nowhere warranted. At this point, however, we shall take a short course; and, to use a vulgar phrase, shall endeavor to "kill two birds with one stone." It happens that the earliest book in our modern European literature, which has subsequently obtained a station of authority on the subject of the ancient Oracles, applied itself entirely to the erroneous theory of the fathers. This is the celebrated *Antonii Van Dale, "De Ethnicorum Oraculis Dissertationes,"* which was published at Amsterdam *at least* as early as the year 1682; that is, one hundred and sixty years ago. And upon the same subject there has been no subsequent book which maintains an equal rank. Van Dale might have treated his theme simply with a view to the investigation of the truth, as some recent inquirers have preferred doing; and, in that case, the fathers would have been noticed only as incidental occasions might bring forward their opinions—true or false. But to this author the errors of the fathers seemed capital; worthy, in fact, of forming his *principal* object; and, knowing their great authority in the Papal church, he anticipated, in the plan of attaching his own views to the false views of the fathers, an opening to a double patronage—that of the Protestants, in the first place, as interested in all doctrines seeming to be anti-papal; that of the sceptics, in the second place, as interested in the exposure of whatever had once commanded, but subsequently lost, the superstitious reverence of mankind. On this policy, he determined to treat the subject polemically. He fastened, therefore, upon the fathers with a deadly *acharnement*, that evidently meant to leave no arrears of work for any succeeding assailant; and it must be acknowledged that, simply in relation to this purpose of hostility, his work is triumphant. So much was not difficult to accomplish; for barely to enunciate the leading doctrine of the fathers is, in the ear of any chronologist, to overthrow it. But, though successful enough in its functions of destruction, on the other hand, as an affirmative or constructive work, the long treatise of Van Dale is most unsatisfactory. It leaves us with a hollow sound ringing in the ear, of malicious laughter from gnomes and imps grinning over the weaknesses of man—his paralytic facility in believing—his fraudulent villany in abusing this facility—but in no point accounting for those real effects of diffusive social benefits from the Oracle machinery, which must arrest the attention of candid students, amidst some opposite monuments of incorrigible credulity, or of elaborate imposture.

As a book, however, belonging to that small cycle (not numbering, perhaps, on *all* subjects, above three score), which may be said to have moulded and controlled the public opinion of Europe through the last five generations, already for itself the work of Van Dale merits a special attention. It is confessedly the *classical* book—the original *fundus* for the arguments and facts applicable to this question; and an accident has greatly strengthened its authority. Fontenelle, the most fashionable of European authors, at the opening of the eighteenth century, writing in a language at that time even more predominant than at present, did in effect employ all his advantages to propagate and popularize the views of Van Dale. Scepticism naturally courts the patronage of France; and in effect that same remark which a learned Belgian (Van Brouwer) has found frequent occasion to make upon single sections of Fontenelle's work, may be fairly extended into a representative account of the whole—"*L'on trouve les mêmes arguments chez Fontenelle, mais dégagés des longueurs du savant Van Dale, et exprimés avec plus d'élégance.*" This *rifaccimento* did not injure the original work in reputation: it caused Van Dale to be less read, but to be more esteemed; since a man confessedly distinguished for his powers of composition had not thought it beneath his ambition to adopt and recompose Van Dale's theory. This important position of Van Dale with regard to the effectual creed of Europe—so that, whether he were read directly or were slighted for a more fashionable expounder, equally in either case it was *his* doctrines which prevailed—must always confer a circumstantial value upon the original dissertations, "*De Ethnicorum Oraculis.*"

This original work of Van Dale is a book of considerable extent. But, in spite of its length, it divides substantially into two great chapters, and no more, which coincide, in fact, with the two separate dissertations. The first of these dissertations, occupying one hundred and eighty-one pages, inquires into the failure and extinction of the Oracles; when they failed, and under what circumstances. The second of these dissertations inquires into the machinery and resources of the Oracles during the time of their prosperity. In the first dissertation, the object is to expose the folly and gross ignorance of the fathers, who insisted on representing the history of the case roundly in this shape—as though all had prospered with the Oracles up to the nativity of Christ; but that, after his crucifixion, and simultaneously with the first promulgation of Christianity, all Oracles had suddenly drooped; or, to tie up their language to the rigor of their theory, had suddenly expired. All this Van Dale peremptorily denies; and, in these days, it is scarcely requisite to add, triumphantly denies; the whole hypothesis of the fathers having literally not a leg to stand upon; and being, in fact, the most audacious defiance to historical records that, perhaps, the annals of human folly present.

In the second dissertation, Van Dale combats the other notion of the fathers—that, during their prosperous ages, the Oracles had moved by an agency of evil spirits. He, on the contrary, contends that, from the first hour to the last of their long domination over the minds and practice of the Pagan world, they had moved by no agencies whatever, but those of human fraud, intrigue, collusion, applied to human blindness, credulity, and superstition.

We shall say a word or two upon each question. As to the first, namely, *when* it was that the Oracles fell into decay and silence, thanks to the headlong rashness of the Fathers, Van Dale's assault cannot be refused or evaded. In reality, the evidence against them is too flagrant and hyperbolical. If we were to quote from Juvenal—"Delphis et Oracula cessant," in that case, the fathers challenge it as an argument on *their* side, for that Juvenal described a state of things immediately posterior to Christianity; yet even here the word *cessant* points to a distinction of cases which already in itself is fatal to their doctrine. By *cessant* Juvenal means evidently what we, in these days, should mean in saying of a ship in action that her fire was slackening. This powerful poet, therefore, wiser so far than the Christian fathers, distinguishes two separate cases: first, the state of torpor and languishing which might be (and in fact was) the predicament of many famous Oracles through centuries not fewer than five, six,

or even eight; secondly, the state of absolute dismantling
and utter extinction which, even before his time, had
confounded individual Oracles of the inferior class, not from
changes affecting religion, whether true or false, but from
political revolutions. Here, therefore, lies the first blunder of
the fathers, that they confound with total death the long
drooping which befell many great Oracles from languor in
the popular sympathies, under changes hereafter to be
noticed; and, consequently, from revenues and machinery
continually decaying. That the Delphic Oracle itself—of all
oracles the most illustrious—had not expired, but simply
slumbered for centuries, the fathers might have been
convinced themselves by innumerable passages in authors
contemporary with themselves; and that it was continually
throwing out fitful gleams of its ancient power, when any
very great man (suppose a Caesar) thought fit to stimulate
its latent vitality, is notorious from such cases as that of
Hadrian. He, in his earlier days, whilst yet only dreaming of
the purple, had not found the Oracle superannuated or
palsied. On the contrary, he found it but too clear-sighted;
and it was no contempt in him, but too ghastly a fear and
jealousy, which labored to seal up the grander ministrations
of the Oracle for the future. What the Pythia had foreshown
to himself, she might foreshow to others; and, when
tempted by the same princely bribes, she might authorize
and kindle the same aspiring views in other great officers.
Thus, in the new condition of the Roman power, there was
a perpetual peril, lest an oracle, so potent as that of Delphi,
should absolutely create rebellions, by first suggesting
hopes to men in high commands. Even as it was, all
treasonable assumptions of the purple, for many
generations, commenced in the hopes inspired by auguries,
prophecies, or sortileges. And had the great Delphic Oracle,
consecrated to men's feelings by hoary superstition, and
privileged by secrecy, come forward to countersign such hopes,

many more would have been the wrecks of ambition, and even bloodier would have been the blood-polluted line of the imperial successions. Prudence, therefore, it was, and state policy, not the power of Christianity, which gave the *final* shock (of the *original* shock we shall speak elsewhere) to the grander functions of the Delphic Oracle. But, in the mean time, the humbler and more domestic offices of this oracle, though naturally making no noise at a distance, seem long to have survived its state relations. And, apart from the sort of galvanism notoriously applied by Hadrian, surely the fathers could not have seen Plutarch's account of its condition, already a century later than our Saviour's nativity. The Pythian priestess, as we gather from *him*, had by that time become a less select and dignified personage; she was no longer a princess in the land—a change which was proximately due to the impoverished income of the temple; but she was still in existence; still held in respect; still trained, though at inferior cost, to her difficult and showy ministrations. And the whole establishment of the Delphic god, if necessarily contracted from that scale which had been suitable when great kings and commonwealths were constant suitors within the gates of Delphi, still clung (like the Venice of modern centuries) to her old ancestral honors, and kept up that decent household of ministers which corresponded to the altered ministrations of her temple. In fact, the evidences on behalf of Delphi as a princely house, that had indeed partaken in the decaying fortunes of Greece, but naturally was all the prouder from the irritating contrast of her great remembrances, are so plentifully dispersed through books, that the fathers must have been willingly duped. That in some way they *were* duped is too notorious from the facts, and might be suspected even from their own occasional language; take, as one instance, amongst a whole *harmony* of similar expressions, this short passage from Eusebius—*hoi Hellenes*

homologentes ekleloipenai auton ta chresteria: the Greeks
admitting that their Oracles have failed. (There is, however,
a disingenuous vagueness in the very word *ekleloipenai*), *ed'
allote pote ex aionos* — and when? why, at no other crisis
through the total range of their existence — *e kata tes chrones
tes euangelikes didaskalias* — than precisely at the epoch of the
evangelical dispensation, etc. Eusebius was a man of too
extensive reading to be entirely satisfied with the Christian
representations upon this point. And in such indeterminate
phrases as *kata tes chrones* (which might mean indifferently
the entire three centuries then accomplished from the first
promulgation of Christianity, or specifically that narrow
punctual limit of the earliest promulgation), it is easy to
trace an ambidextrous artifice of compromise between what
would satisfy his own brethren, on the one hand, and
what, on the other hand, he could hope to defend against
the assaults of learned Pagans.

In particular instances it is but candid to acknowledge that
the fathers may have been misled by the remarkable
tendencies to error amongst the ancients, from their want of
public journals, combined with territorial grandeur of
empire. The greatest possible defect of harmony arises
naturally in this way amongst ancient authors, locally
remote from each other; but more especially in the post-
christian periods, when reporting any aspects of change, or
any results from a revolution variable and advancing under
the vast varieties of the Roman empire. Having no
newspapers to effect a level amongst the inequalities and
anomalies of their public experience in regard to the
Christian revolution, when collected from innumerable
tribes so widely differing as to civilization, knowledge,
superstition, &c.; hence it happened that one writer could
report with truth a change as having occurred within
periods of ten to sixty years, which for some other province

would demand a circuit of six hundred. For example, in Asia Minor, all the way from the sea coast to the Euphrates, towns were scattered having a dense population of Jews. Sometimes these were the most malignant opponents of Christianity; that is, wherever they happened to rest in the *letter* of their peculiar religion. But, on the other hand, where there happened to be a majority (or, if not numerically a majority, yet influentially an overbalance) in that section of the Jews who were docile children of their own preparatory faith and discipline, no bigots, and looking anxiously for the fulfilment of their prophecies (an expectation at that time generally diffused),—under those circumstances, the Jews were such ready converts as to account naturally for sudden local transitions, which in other circumstances or places might not have been credible.

This single consideration may serve to explain the apparent contradictions, the irreconcilable discrepancies, between the statements of contemporary Christian bishops, locally at a vast distance from each other, or (which is even more important) reporting from communities occupying different stages of civilization. There was no harmonizing organ of interpretation, in Christian or in Pagan newspapers, to bridge over the chasms that divided different provinces. A devout Jew, already possessed by the purest idea of the Supreme Being, stood on the very threshold of conversion: he might, by one hour's conversation with an apostle, be transfigured into an enlightened Christian; whereas a Pagan could seldom in one generation pass beyond the infirmity of his novitiate. His heart and affections, his will and the habits of his understanding, were too deeply diseased to be suddenly transmuted. And hence arises a phenomenon, which has too languidly arrested the notice of historians; namely, that already, and for centuries before the time of Constantine, wherever the Jews had been thickly sown as

colonists, the most potent body of Christian zeal stood
ready to kindle under the first impulse of encouragement
from the state; whilst in the great capitals of Rome and
Alexandria, where the Jews were hated and neutralized
politically by Pagan forces, not for a hundred years later
than Constantine durst the whole power of the government
lay hands on the Pagan machinery, except with timid
precautions, and by graduations so remarkably adjusted to
the circumstances, that sometimes they wear the shape of
compromises with idolatry. We must know the ground, the
quality of the population, concerned in any particular
report of the fathers, before we can judge of its probabilities.
Under local advantages, insulated cases of Oracles suddenly
silenced, of temples and their idol-worship overthrown, as
by a rupture of new-born zeal, were not less certain to arise
as rare accidents from rare privileges, or from rare
coincidences of unanimity in the leaders of the place, than
on the other hand they were certain *not* to arise in that
unconditional universality pretended by the fathers.
Wheresoever Paganism was interwoven with the whole
moral being of a people, as it was in Egypt, or with the
political tenure and hopes of a people, as it was in Rome,
there a long struggle was inevitable before the revolution
could be effected. Briefly, as against the fathers, we find a
sufficient refutation in what *followed* Christianity. If, at a
period five, or even six hundred years after the birth of
Christ, you find people still consulting the local Oracles of
Egypt, in places sheltered from the point-blank range of the
state artillery,—there is an end, once and forever, to the
delusive superstition that, merely by its silent presence in
the world, Christianity must instantaneously come into
fierce activity as a reägency of destruction to all forms of
idolatrous error. That argument is multiplied beyond all
power of calculation; and to have missed it is the most
eminent instance of wilful blindness which the records of

human folly can furnish. But there is another refutation lying in an opposite direction, which presses the fathers even more urgently in the rear than this presses them in front; any author posterior to Christianity, who should point to the decay of Oracles, they would claim on their own side. But what would they have said to Cicero, — by what resource of despair would they have parried his authority, when insisting (as many times he does insist), forty and even fifty years before the birth of Christ, on the languishing condition of the Delphic Oracle? What evasion could they imagine here? How could that languor be due to Christianity, which far anticipated the very birth of Christianity? For, as to Cicero, who did not "far anticipate the birth of Christianity." we allege *him* rather because his work *De Divinatione* is so readily accessible, and because his testimony on any subject is so full of weight, than because other and much older authorities cannot be produced to the same effect. The Oracles of Greece had lost their vigor and their palmy pride full two centuries before the Christian era. Historical records show this *ŕ posteriori*, whatever were the cause; and the cause, which we will state hereafter, shows it *ŕ priori*, apart from the records.

Surely, therefore, Van Dale needed not to have pressed his victory over the helpless fathers so unrelentingly, and after the first ten pages by cases and proofs that are quite needless and *ex abundanti*; simply the survival of any one distinguished Oracle upwards of four centuries *after* Christ —that is sufficient. But if with this fact we combine the other fact, that all the principal Oracles had already begun to languish, more than two centuries *before* Christianity, there can be no opening for a whisper of dissent upon any real question between Van Dale and his opponents; namely, both as to the possibility of Christianity coexisting with such forms of error, and the possibility that oracles should be overthrown by merely Pagan, or internal changes. The less plausible, however, that we find this error of the fathers, the more curiosity we naturally feel about the source of that error; and the more so, because Van Dale never turns his eyes in that direction.

This source lay (to speak the simple truth) in abject superstition. The fathers conceived of the enmity between Christianity and Paganism, as though it resembled that between certain chemical poisons and the Venetian wine-glass, which (according to the belief [Footnote: Which belief we can see no reason for rejecting so summarily as is usually done in modern times. It would be absurd, indeed, to suppose a kind of glass qualified to expose all poisons indifferently, considering the vast range of their chemical differences. But, surely, as against that one poison then familiarly used for domestic murders, a chemical reagency might have been devised in the quality of the glass. At least, there is no *prima facie* absurdity in such a supposition.] of three centuries back) no sooner received any poisonous fluid, than immediately it shivered into crystal splinters. They thought to honor Christianity, by imaging it as some exotic animal of more powerful breed, such as we English have witnessed in a domestic case, coming into instant collision with the native race, and exterminating it everywhere upon the first conflict. In this conceit they substituted a foul fiction of their own, fashioned on the very model of Pagan fictions, for the unvarying analogy of the divine procedure. Christianity, as the last and consummate of revelations, had the high destination of working out its victory through what was greatest in a man—through his reason, his will, his affections. But, to satisfy the fathers, it must operate like a drug—like sympathetic powders—like an amulet—or like a conjurer's charm. Precisely the monkish effect of a Bible when hurled at an evil spirit—not the true rational effect of that profound oracle read, studied, and laid to heart—was that which the fathers ascribed to the mere proclamation of Christianity, when first piercing the atmosphere circumjacent to any oracle; and, in fact, to their gross appreciations, Christian truth was like the scavenger bird in Eastern climates, or the stork in Holland, which signalizes its presence by devouring all the native brood of vermin, or nuisances, as fast as they reproduce themselves under local distemperatures of climate or soil.

It is interesting to pursue the same ignoble superstition, which, in fact, under Romish hands, soon crept like a parasitical plant over Christianity itself, until it had nearly strangled its natural vigor, back into times far preceding that of the fathers. Spite of all that could be wrought by Heaven, for the purpose of continually confounding the local vestiges of popular reverence which might have gathered round stocks and stones, so obstinate is the hankering after this mode of superstition in man that his heart returns to it with an elastic recoil as often as the openings are restored. Agreeably to this infatuation, the temple of the true God—even its awful *adytum*—the holy of holies—or the places where the ark of the covenant had rested in its migrations—all were conceived to have an eternal and a self-vindicating sanctity. So thought man: but God himself, though to man's folly pledged to the vindication of his own sanctities, thought far otherwise; as we know by numerous profanations of all holy places in Judea, triumphantly carried through, and avenged by no plausible judgments. To speak only of the latter temple, three men are memorable as having polluted its holiest recesses: Antiochus Epiphanes, Pompey about a century later, and Titus pretty nearly by the same exact interval later than Pompey. Upon which of these three did any judgment descend? Attempts have been made to impress that coloring

of the sequel in two of these cases, indeed, but without effect
upon *any* man's mind. Possibly in the case of Antiochus,
who seems to have moved under a burning hatred, not so
much of the insurgent Jews as of the true faith which
prompted their resistance, there is some colorable argument
for viewing him in his miserable death as a monument of
divine wrath. But the two others had no such malignant
spirit; they were tolerant, and even merciful; were
authorized instruments for executing the purposes of
Providence; and no calamity in the life of either can be
reasonably traced to his dealings with Palestine. Yet, if
Christianity could not brook for an instant the mere
coëxistence of a Pagan oracle, how came it that the Author
of Christianity had thus brooked (nay, by many signs of
coöperation, had promoted) that ultimate desecration,
which planted "the abomination of desolation" as a
victorious crest of Paganism upon his own solitary altar?
The institution of the Sabbath, again—what part of the
Mosaic economy could it more plausibly have been expected
that God should vindicate by some memorable interference,
since of all the Jewish institutions it was that one which
only and which frequently became the occasion of wholesale
butchery to the pious (however erring) Jews? The scruple of
the Jews to fight, or even to resist an assassin, on the
Sabbath, was not the less pious in its motive because
erroneous in principle; yet no miracle interfered to save
them from the consequences of their infatuation. And this
seemed the more remarkable in the case of their war with
Antiochus, because *that* (if any that history has recorded)
was a holy war. But, after one tragical experience, which
cost the lives of a thousand martyrs, the Maccabees—quite
as much on a level with their scrupulous brethren in piety
as they were superior in good sense—began to reflect that
they had no shadow of a warrant from Scripture for
counting upon any miraculous aid; that the whole

expectation, from first to last, had been human and presumptuous; and that the obligation of fighting valiantly against idolatrous compliances was, at all events, paramount to the obligation of the Sabbath. In one hour, after unyoking themselves from this monstrous millstone of their own forging, about their own necks, the cause rose buoyantly aloft as upon wings of victory; and, as their very earliest reward—as the first fruits from thus disabusing their minds of windy presumptions—they found the very case itself melting away which had furnished the scruple; since their cowardly enemies, now finding that they would fight on all days alike, had no longer any motive for attacking them on the Sabbath; besides that their own astonishing victories henceforward secured to them often the choice of the day not less than of the ground.

But, without lingering on these outworks of the true religion, namely, 1st, the Temple of Jerusalem; 2dly, the Sabbath,—both of which the divine wisdom often saw fit to lay prostrate before the presumption of idolatrous assaults, on principles utterly irreconcilable with the Oracle doctrine of the fathers,—there is a still more flagrant argument against the fathers, which it is perfectly confounding to find both them and their confuter overlooking. It is this. Oracles, take them at the very worst, were no otherwise hostile to Christianity than as a branch of Paganism. If, for instance, the Delphic establishment were hateful (as doubtless it was) to the holy spirit of truth which burned in the mind of an apostle, *why* was it hateful? Not primarily in its character of Oracle, but in its universal character of Pagan temple; not as an authentic distributor of counsels adapted to the infinite situations of its clients—often very wise counsels; but as being ultimately engrafted on the stem of idolatrous religion —as deriving, in the last resort, their sanctions from Pagan deities, and, therefore, as sharing *constructively* in all the

pollutions of that tainted source. Now, therefore, if
Christianity, according to the fancy of the fathers, could not
tolerate the co-presence of so much evil as resided in the
Oracle superstition, —that is, in the derivative, in the
secondary, in the not unfrequently neutralized or even
redundantly compensated mode of error, —then, *á fortiori*,
Christianity could not have tolerated for an hour the parent
superstition, the larger evil, the fontal error, which diseased
the very organ of vision—which not merely distorted a few
objects on the road, but spread darkness over the road itself.
Yet what is the fact? So far from any mysterious repulsion
externally between idolatrous errors and Christianity, as
though the two schemes of belief could no more coexist in
the same society than two queen-bees in a hive, —as though
elementary nature herself recoiled from the abominable
concursus, —do but open a child's epitome of history, and you
find it to have required four entire centuries before the
destroyer's hammer and crowbar began to ring loudly
against the temples of idolatrous worship; and not before
five, nay, locally six, or even seven centuries had elapsed,
could the better angel of mankind have sung gratulations
announcing that the great strife was over—that man was
inoculated with the truth; or have adopted the impressive
language of a Latin father, that "the owls were to be heard
in *every* village hooting from the dismantled fanes of
heathenism, or the gaunt wolf disturbing the sleep of
peasants as he yelled in winter from the cold, dilapidated
altars." Even this victorious consummation was true only
for the southern world of civilization. The forests of
Germany, though pierced already to the south in the third
and fourth centuries by the torch of missionaries, —though
already at that time illuminated by the immortal Gothic
version of the New Testament preceding Ulppilas, and still
surviving, —sheltered through ages in the north and east
vast tribes of idolaters, some awaiting the baptism of

Charlemagne in the eighth century and the ninth, others
actually resuming a fierce countenance of heathenism for the
martial zeal of crusading knights in the thirteenth and
fourteenth. The history of Constantine has grossly misled
the world. It was very early in the fourth century (313 A.
D.) that Constantine found himself strong enough to take
his *earliest* steps for raising Christianity to a privileged
station; which station was not merely an effect and
monument of its progress, but a further cause of progress.
In this latter light, as a power advancing and moving, but
politically still militant, Christianity required exactly one
other century to carry out and accomplish even its eastern
triumph. Dating from the era of the very inaugurating and
merely local acts of Constantine, we shall be sufficiently
accurate in saying that the corresponding period in the fifth
century (namely, from about 404 to 420 A. D.) first
witnessed those uproars of ruin in Egypt and Alexandria—
fire racing along the old carious timbers, battering-rams
thundering against the ancient walls of the most horrid
temples—which rang so searchingly in the ears of Zosimus,
extorting, at every blow, a howl of Pagan sympathy from
that ignorant calumniator of Christianity. So far from the
fact being, according to the general prejudice, as though
Constantine had found himself able to destroy Paganism,
and to replace it by Christianity; on the contrary, it was
both because he happened to be far too weak, in fact, for
such a mighty revolution, and because he *knew* his own
weakness, that he fixed his new capital, as a preliminary
caution, upon the Propontis.

There were other motives to this change, and particularly
(as we have attempted to show in a separate dissertation)
motives of high political economy, suggested by the relative
conditions of land and agriculture in Thrace and Asia
Minor, by comparison with decaying Italy; but a paramount

motive, we are satisfied, and the earliest motive, was the incurable Pagan bigotry of Rome. Paganism for Rome, it ought to have been remembered by historians, was a mere necessity of her Pagan origin. Paganism was the fatal dowry of Rome from her inauguration; not only she had once received a retaining fee on behalf of Paganism, in the mysterious *Ancile,* supposed to have fallen from heaven, but she actually preserved this bribe amongst her rarest jewels. She possessed a palladium, such a national amulet or talisman as many Grecian or Asiatic cities had once possessed—a *fatal* guarantee to the prosperity of the state. Even the Sibylline books, whatever ravages they might be supposed by the intelligent to have sustained in a lapse of centuries, were popularly believed, in the latest period of the Western empire, to exist as so many charters of supremacy. Jupiter himself in Rome had put on a peculiar Roman physiognomy, which associated him with the destinies of the gigantic state. Above all, the solemn augury of the twelve vultures, so memorably passed downwards from the days of Romulus, through generations as yet uncertain of the event, and, therefore, chronologically incapable of participation in any fraud—an augury *always* explained as promising twelve centuries of supremacy to Rome, from the year 748 or 750 B. C.—coöperated with the endless other Pagan superstitions in anchoring the whole Pantheon to the Capitol and Mount Palatine. So long as Rome had a worldly hope surviving, it was impossible for her to forget the Vestal Virgins, the College of Augurs, or the indispensable office and the *indefeasible* privileges of the *Pontifex Maximus,* which (though Cardinal Baronius, in his great work, for many years sought to fight off the evidences for that fact, yet afterwards partially he confessed his error) actually availed—historically and *medallically* can be demonstrated to have availed—for the temptation of Christian Cæsars into collusive adulteries with heathenism.

Here, for instance, came an emperor that timidly recorded his scruples—feebly protested, but gave way at once as to an ugly necessity. There came another, more deeply religious, or constitutionally more bold, who fought long and strenuously against the compromise. "What! should he, the delegate of God, and the standard-bearer of the true religion, proclaim himself officially head of the false? No; that was too much for his conscience." But the fatal meshes of prescription, of superstitions ancient and gloomy, gathered around him; he heard that he was no perfect Cćsar without this office, and eventually the very same reason which had obliged Augustus not to suppress, but himself to assume, the tribunitian office, namely, that it was a popular mode of leaving democratic organs untouched, whilst he neutralized their democratic functions by absorbing them into his own, availed to overthrow all Christian scruples of conscience, even in the most Christian of the Cćsars, many years *after* Constantine. The pious Theodosius found himself literally compelled to become a Pagan pontiff. A *bon mot* [Footnote: "A *bon mot*."—This was built on the accident that a certain *Maximus* stood in notorious circumstances of rivalship to the emperor [Theodosius]: and the bitterness of the jest took this turn that if the emperor should persist in declining the office of _Pont. *Maximus*, in that case, "erit Pontifex Maximus;" that is, Maximus (the secret aspirant) shall be our Pontifex. *So* the words sounded to those in the secret [*synetoisi*], whilst to others they seemed to have no meaning at all.] circulating amongst the people warned him that, if he left the cycle of imperial powers incomplete, if he suffered the galvanic battery to remain imperfect in its circuit of links, pretty soon he would tempt treason to show its head, and would even for the present find but an imperfect obedience. Reluctantly therefore the emperor gave way: and perhaps soothed his fretting conscience, by offering to heaven, as a penitential litany, that same petition which Naaman the

Syrian offered to the prophet Elijah as a reason for a
personal dispensation. Hardly more possible it was that a
camel should go through the eye of a needle, than that a
Roman senator should forswear those inveterate
superstitions with which his own system of aristocracy had
been riveted for better and worse. As soon would the
Venetian senator, the gloomy "magnifico" of St. Mark, have
consented to Renounce the annual wedding of his republic
with the Adriatic, as the Roman noble, whether senator, or
senator elect, or of senatorial descent, would have dissevered
his own solitary stem from the great forest of his ancestral
order; and this he must have done by doubting the legend
of Jupiter Stator, or by withdrawing his allegiance from
Jupiter Capitolinus. The Roman people universally became
agitated towards the opening of the fifth century after
Christ, when their own twelfth century was drawing near
to its completion. Rome had now reached the very condition
of Dr. Faustus—having originally received a known term of
prosperity from some dark power; but at length hearing the
hours, one after the other, tolling solemnly from the
church-tower, as they exhausted the waning minutes of the
very final day marked down in the contract. The more
profound was the faith of Rome in the flight of the twelve
vultures, once so glorious, now so sad, an augury, the
deeper was the depression as the last hour drew near that
had been so mysteriously prefigured. The reckoning, indeed,
of chronology was slightly uncertain. The Varronian
account varied from others. But these trivial differences
might tell as easily against them as for them, and did but
strengthen the universal agitation. Alaric, in the opening of
the fifth century [about 410]—Attila, near the middle [445]—
already seemed prelusive earthquakes running before the
final earthquake. And Christianity, during this era of public
alarm, was so far from assuming a more winning aspect to
Roman eyes, as a religion promising to survive their own,

that already, under that character of reversionary triumph, this gracious religion seemed a public insult, and this meek religion a perpetual defiance; pretty much as a king sees with scowling eyes, when revealed to him in some glass of Cornelius Agrippa, the portraits of that mysterious house which is destined to supplant his own.

Now, from this condition of feeling at Rome, it is apparent not only as a fact that Constantine did not overthrow Paganism, but as a possibility that he could not have overthrown it. In the fierce conflict he would probably have been overthrown himself; and, even for so much as he *did* accomplish, it was well that he attempted it at a distance from Rome. So profoundly, therefore, are the fathers in error, that instead of that instant victory which they ascribe to Christianity, even Constantine's revolution was merely local. Nearly five centuries, in fact, it cost, and not three, to Christianize even the entire Mediterranean empire of Rome; and the premature effort of Constantine ought to be regarded as a mere *fluctus decumanus* in the continuous advance of the new religion, —one of those ambitious billows which sometimes run far ahead of their fellows in a tide steadily gaining ground, but which inevitably recede in the next moment, marking only the strength of that tendency which sooner or later is destined to fill the whole capacity of the shore.

To have proved, therefore, if it could have been proved, that Christianity had been fatal in the way of a magical charm to the Oracles of the world, would have proved nothing but a perplexing inconsistency, so long as the fathers were obliged to confess that Paganism itself, as a gross total, as the parent superstition (sure to reproduce Oracles faster than they could be extinguished), had been suffered to exist for many centuries concurrently with Christianity, and had finally

been overthrown by the simple majesty of truth that courts
the light, as matched against falsehood that shuns it.

As applied, therefore, to the first problem in the whole
question upon Oracles, — *When, and under what circumstances,
did they cease?* — the *Dissertatio* of Van Dale, and the *Histoire des
Oracles* by Fontenelle, are irresistible, though not written in
a proper spirit of gravity, nor making use of that
indispensable argument which we have ourselves derived
from the analogy of all scriptural precedents.

But the case is far otherwise as concerns the second
problem, — *How, and by what machinery, did the Oracles, in the
days of their prosperity, conduct their elaborate ministrations?* To
this problem no justice at all is done by the school of Van
Dale. A spirit of mockery and banter is ill applied to
questions that at any time have been centres of fear, and
hope, and mysterious awe, to long trains of human
generations. And the coarse assumption of systematic fraud
in the Oracles is neither satisfactory to the understanding,
as failing to meet many important aspects of the case, nor is
it at all countenanced by the kind of evidences that have
been hitherto alleged. The fathers had taken the course—
vulgar and superstitious—of explaining everything
sagacious, everything true, everything that by possibility
could seem to argue prophetic functions in the greater
Oracles, as the product indeed of inspiration, but of
inspiration emanating from an evil spirit. This hypothesis of
a diabolic inspiration is rejected by the school of Van Dale.
Both the power of at all looking into the future, and the
fancied source of that power, are dismissed as contemptible
chimeras. Upon the first of these dark pretensions we shall
have occasion to speak at another point. Upon the other we
agree with Van Dale. Yet, even here, the spirit of triumphant
ridicule, applied to questions not wholly within the

competence of human resources, is displeasing in grave discussions: grave they are by necessity of their relations, howsoever momentarily disfigured by levity and the unseasonable grimaces of self-sufficient "philosophy." This temper of mind is already advertised from the first to the observing reader of Van Dale by the character of his engraved frontispiece. Men are there exhibited in the act of juggling, and still more odiously as exulting over their juggleries by gestures of the basest collusion, such as protruding the tongue, inflating one cheek by means of the tongue, grinning, and winking obliquely. These vilenesses are so ignoble, that for his own sake a man of honor (whether as a writer or a reader) shrinks from dealing with any case to which they do really adhere; such a case belongs to the province of police courts, not of literature. But, in the ancient apparatus of the Oracles although frauds and *espionage* did certainly form an occasional resource, the artifices employed were rarely illiberal in their mode, and always ennobled by their motive. As to the mode, the Oracles had fortunately no temptation to descend into any tricks that could look like "thimble-rigging;" and as to the motive, it will be seen that this could never be dissociated from some regard to public or patriotic objects in the first place; to which if any secondary interest were occasionally attached, this could rarely descend so low as even to an ordinary purpose of gossiping curiosity, but never to a base, mercenary purpose of fraud. Our views, however, on this phasis of the question, will speedily speak for themselves.

Meantime, pausing for one moment to glance at the hypothesis of the fathers, we confess ourselves to be scandalized by its unnecessary plunge into the ignoble. Many sincere Christian believers have doubted altogether of any evil spirits, as existences, warranted by Scripture, that is, as beings whose principle was evil ["evil, be thou my good:" P. L.]; others, again, believing in the possibility that spiritual beings had been (in ways unintelligible to us) seduced from their state of perfection by temptations analogous to those which had seduced man, acquiesced in the notion of spirits tainted with evil, but not therefore (any more than man himself) essentially or causelessly malignant. Now, it is well known, and, amongst others, Eichhorn _(Einletung in das alte Testament) has noticed the fact, which will be obvious, on a little reflection, to any even unlearned student of the Scriptures who can throw his memory back through a real familiarity with those records, that the Jews derived their obstinate notions of fiends and demoniacal possessions (as accounting even for bodily affections) entirely from their Chaldean captivity. Not before that great event in Jewish history, and, therefore, in consequence of that event, were the Jews inoculated with this Babylonian, Persian, and Median superstition. Now, if Eichhorn and others are right, it follows that the elder Scriptures, as they ascend more and more into the purer atmosphere of untainted Hebrew creeds, ought to exhibit an increasing freedom from all these modes of demoniacal agency. And accordingly so we find it. Messengers of God are often concerned in the early records of Moses; but it is not until we come down to Post-Mosaical records, Job, for example (though that book is doubtful as to its chronology), and the chronicles of the Jewish kings (*Judaic or Israelitish*), that we first find any allusion to malignant spirits. As against Eichhorn, however, though readily conceding that the agency is not often recognized, we would beg leave to notice, that there is a three-fold agency of evil, relatively to man, ascribed to certain spirits in the elder Scriptures, namely: 1, of *misleading* (as in the case of the Israelitish king seduced into a fatal battle by a falsehood originating with a spiritual being); 2, of *temptation*; 3, of calumnious *accusation* directed against absent parties. It is not absolutely an untenable hypothesis, that these functions of malignity to man, as at first sight they appear, may be in fact reconcilable with the general functions of a being not malignant, and not evil in any sense, but simply obedient to superior commands: for none of us supposes, of course, that a "destroying angel" must be an evil spirit, though sometimes appearing in a dreadful relation of hostility to *all* parties (as in the case of David's punishment). But, waiving all these speculations, one thing is apparent, that the negative allowance, the toleration granted to these later Jewish modes of belief by our Saviour, can no more be urged as arguing any positive sanction to such existences (to *demons* in the bad sense), than his toleration of Jewish errors and conceits in questions of science. Once for all, it was no purpose of his mission to expose errors in matters of pure curiosity, and in speculations *not* moral, but exclusively intellectual. And, besides the ordinary argument for rejecting such topics of teaching, as not necessarily belonging to any known purpose of the Christian revelation (which argument is merely negative, and still leaves it open to have regarded such communications as a possible *extra* condescension, as a *lucro ponatur*, not absolutely to have been expected, but if granted as all the more meritorious in Christianity), we privately are aware of an argument, far more rigorous and coërcive, which will place this question upon quite another basis. This argument, which, in a proper situation, and with ampler disposable space, we shall expose in its strength, will show that it was not that neutral possibility which men have supposed, for the founder of our faith to have granted light, casually or indirectly, upon questions of curiosity. One sole revelation was made by Him, as to the nature of the intercourse and the relations in another world; but *that* was for the purpose of forestalling a vile, unspiritual notion, already current amongst the childish Jews, and sure to propagate itself even to our own days, unless an utter *averruncatio* were applied to it. This was its purpose, and not any purpose of gratification to unhallowed curiosity; we speak of the question about the reversionary rights of marriage in a future state. This memorable case, by the way, sufficiently exposes the gross, infantine sensualism of the Jewish mind at that period, and throws an indirect light on their creed as to demons. With this one exception, standing by itself and self-explained, there never was a gleam of revelation granted by any authorized prophet to speculative curiosity, whether pointing to science, or to the mysteries of the spiritual world. And the true argument on this subject would show that this abstinence was not accidental; was not merely on a motive of convenience, as evading any needless extension of labors in teaching, which is the furthest point attained by any existing argument; but, on the contrary, that there was an obligation of consistency, stern, absolute, insurmountable, which made it *essential* to withhold such revelations; and that had but one such condescension, even to a harmless curiosity, been conceded, there would have arisen instantly a rent—a fracture—a schism—in another vast and collateral purpose of Providence.

From all considerations of the Jewish condition at the era of Christianity, the fathers might have seen the license for doubt as to the notions of a diabolic inspiration. Why must the prompting spirits, if really assumed to be the efficient agency behind the Oracles, be figured as holding any relation at all to moral good or moral evil? Why not allow of demoniac powers, excelling man in beauty, power, prescience, but otherwise neutral as to all purposes of man's moral nature? Or, if revolting angels were assumed, why degrade their agency in so vulgar and unnecessary a way, by adopting the vilest relation to man which can be imputed

to a demon—his function of secret *calumnious accusation*; from
which idea, lowering the Miltonic "archangel ruined" into
the assessor of thieves, as a private slanderer (*diabolos*),
proceeds, through the intermediate Italian *diavolo*, our own
grotesque vulgarism of the *devil*; [Footnote: But, says an
unlearned man, Christ uses the word *devil*. Not so. The
word used is *diabolos*. Translate v. g. "The accuser and his
angels."] an idea which must ever be injurious, in common
with all base conceptions, to a grand and spiritual religion.
If the Oracles *were* supported by mysterious agencies of
spiritual beings, it was still open to have distinguished
between mere modes of power or of intelligence, and modes
of illimitable evil. The *results* of the Oracles were beneficent:
that was all which the fathers had any right to know: and
their unwarranted introduction of wicked or rebel angels
was as much a surreptitious fraud upon their audiences, as
their neglect to distinguish between the conditions of an
extinct superstition and a superstition dormant or decaying.

To leave the fathers, and to state our own views on the final
question argued by Van Dale—"What was the essential
machinery by which the Oracles moved?"—we shall inquire,

1. What was the relation of the Oracles (and we would wish
to be understood as speaking particularly of the Delphic
Oracle) to the credulity of Greece?

2. What was the relation of that same Oracle to the absolute
truth?

3. What was its relation to the public welfare of Greece?

Into this trisection we shall decompose the coarse unity of
the question presented by Van Dale and his Vandals, as
though the one sole "issue," that could be sent down for
trial before a jury, were the likelihoods of fraud and gross

swindling. It is not with the deceptions or collusions of the Oracles, as mere matters of fact, that we in this age are primarily concerned, but with those deceptions as they affected the contemporary people of Greece. It is important to know whether the general faith of Greece in the mysterious pretensions of Oracles were unsettled or disturbed by the several agencies at work that naturally tended to rouse suspicion; such, for instance, as these four which follow:—1. Eminent instances of scepticism with regard to the oracular powers, from time to time circulating through Greece in the shape of *bon mots*; or, 2, which silently amounted to the same virtual expression of distrust, Refusals (often more speciously wearing the name of *neglects*) to consult the proper Oracle on some hazardous enterprize of general notoriety and interest; 3. Cases of direct failure in the event, as understood to have been predicted by the Oracle, not unfrequently accompanied by tragical catastrophes to the parties misled by this erroneous construction of the Oracle; 4. (which is, perhaps, the climax of the exposures possible under the superstitions of Paganism), A public detection of known oracular temples doing business on a considerable scale, as accomplices with felons.

Modern appraisers of the oracular establishments are too commonly in all moral senses anachronists. We hear it alleged with some plausibility against Southey's portrait of Don Roderick, though otherwise conceived in a spirit proper for bringing out the whole sentiment of his pathetic situation, that the king is too Protestant, and too evangelical, after the model of 1800, in his modes of penitential piety. The poet, in short, reflected back upon one who was too certain in the eighth century to have been the victim of dark popish superstitions, his own pure and enlightened faith. But the anachronistic spirit in which modern sceptics react upon the Pagan Oracles is not so elevating as the English poet's. Southey reflected his own superiority upon the Gothic prince of Spain. But the sceptics reflect their own vulgar habits of mechanic and compendious office business upon the large institutions of the ancient Oracles. To satisfy them, the Oracle should resemble a modern coach-office—where undoubtedly you would suspect fraud, if the question "How far to Derby?" were answered evasively, or if the grounds of choice between two roads were expressed enigmatically. But the *to loxon*, or mysterious indirectness of the Oracle, was calculated far more to support the imaginative grandeur of the unseen God, and was designed to do so, than to relieve the individual suitor in a perplexity seldom of any capital importance. In this way every oracular answer operated upon the local Grecian neighborhood in which it circulated as one of the impulses which, from time to time, renewed the sense of a mysterious involution in the invisible powers, as though they were incapable of direct correspondence or parallelism with the monotony and slight compass of human ideas. As the symbolic dancers of the ancients, who narrated an elaborate story, *Saltando Hecubam*, or *Saltando Loadamiam*, interwove the passion of the advancing incidents into the intricacies of the figure—something in the same way, it was understood by all men, that the Oracle did not so much evade the difficulty by a dark form of words, as he revealed his own hieroglyphic nature. All prophets, the true equally with the false, have felt the instinct for surrounding themselves with the majesty of darkness. And in a religion like the Pagan, so deplorably meagre and starved as to most of the draperies connected with the mysterious and sublime, we must not seek to diminish its already scanty wardrobe. But let us pass from speculation to illustrative anecdotes. We have imagined several cases which might seem fitted for giving a shock to the general Pagan confidence in Oracles. Let us review them.

The first is the case of any memorable scepticism published in a pointed or witty form; as Demosthenes avowed his suspicions "that the Oracle was *Philippizing*." This was about 344 years B.C. Exactly one hundred years earlier, in the 444th year B.C., or the *locus* of Pericles, Herodotus (then forty years old) is universally supposed to have read, which for *him* was publishing, his history. In this work two insinuations of the same kind occur: during the invasion of Darius the Mede (about 490 B.C.) the Oracle was charged with *Medizing*; and in the previous period of Pisistratus (about 555 B.C.) the Oracle had been almost convicted of *Alcmonidizing*. The Oracle concerned was the same, —namely, the Delphic, —in all three cases. In the case of Darius, fear was the ruling passion; in the earlier case, a near self-interest, but not in a base sense selfish. The Alemonidae, an Athenian house hostile to Pisistratus, being exceedingly rich, had engaged to rebuild the ruined temple of the Oracle; and had fulfilled their promise with a munificence outrunning the letter of their professions, particularly with regard to the quality of marble used in facing or "veneering" the front elevation. Now, these sententious and rather witty expressions gave wings and buoyancy to the public suspicions, so as to make them fly from one end of Greece to the other; and they continued in lively remembrance for centuries. Our answer we reserve until we have illustrated the other heads.

In the second case, namely, that of sceptical slights shown to the Oracle, there are some memorable precedents on record. Everybody knows the ridiculous stratagem of Crsus, the Lydian king, for trying the powers of the Oracle, by a monstrous culinary arrangement of pots and pans, known (as he fancied) only to himself. Generally the course of the

Delphic Oracle under similar insults was—warmly to resent them. But Crsus, as a king, a foreigner, and a suitor of unexampled munificence, was privileged, especially because the ministers of the Delphic temple had doubtless found it easy to extract the secret by bribery from some one of the royal mission. A case, however, much more interesting, because arising between two leading states of Greece, and in the century subsequent to the ruder age of Crsus (who was about coeval with Pisistratus, 555 B. C.), is reported by Xenophon of the Lacedćmonians and Thebans. They concluded a treaty of peace without any communication, not so much as a civil notification to the Oracle; *to men Teo ouden ekoinosanto, hopis hć eirpnp genoito*—to the god (the Delphic god) they made no communication at all as to the terms of the peace; *outoi de ebeleuonto*, but they personally pursued their negotiations in private. That this was a very extraordinary reach of presumption, is evident from the care of Xenophon in bringing it before his readers; it is probable, indeed, that neither of the high contracting parties had really acted in a spirit of religious indifference, though it is remarkable of the Spartans, that of all Greek tribes they were the most facile and numerous delinquents under all varieties of foreign temptations to revolt from their hereditary allegiance—a fact which measures the degree of unnatural constraint and tension which the Spartan usages involved; but in this case we rather account for the public outrage to religion and universal usage, by a strong political jealousy lest the provisions of the treaty should transpire prematurely amongst states adjacent to Botia.

Whatever, meantime, were the secret motive to this policy, it did not fail to shock all Greece profoundly. And, in a slighter degree, the same effect upon public feeling followed the act of Agesipolis, who, after obtaining an answer from the Oracle of Delphi, carried forward his suit to the more awfully ancient Oracle of Dodona; by way of trying, as he alleged, "whether the child agreed with its papa." These open expressions of distrust were generally condemned; and the irresistible proof that they were, lies in the fact that they led to no imitations. Even in a case mentioned by Herodotus, when a man had the audacity to found a colony without seeking an oracular sanction, no precedent was established; though the journey to Delphi must often have been peculiarly inconvenient to the founders of colonies moving westwards from Greece; and the expenses of such a journey, with the subsequent offerings, could not but prove unseasonable at the moment when every drachma was most urgently needed. Charity begins at home, was a thought quite as likely to press upon a Pagan conscience, in those circumstances, as upon our modern Christian consciences under heavy taxation; yet, for all that, such was the regard to a pious inauguration of all colonial enterprises, that no one provision or pledge of prosperity was held equally indispensable by all parties to such hazardous speculations. The merest worldly foresight, indeed, to the most irreligious leader, would suggest this sanction as a necessity, under the following reason:—colonies the most enviably prosperous upon the whole, have yet had many hardships to contend with in their noviciate of the first five years; were it only from the summer failure of water under circumstances of local ignorance, or from the casual failure of crops under imperfect arrangements of culture. Now, the one great qualification for wrestling strenuously with such difficult contingencies in solitary situations, is the spirit of cheerful hope; but, when any room had been left for apprehending a supernatural curse resting upon their efforts—equally in the most thoughtfully pious man and the most crazily superstitious—all spirit of hope would be blighted at once; and the religious neglect would, even in a common human way, become its own certain executor, through mere depression of spirits and misgiving of expectations. Well, therefore, might Cicero in a tone of defiance demand, "Quam vero Grćcia coloniam misit in Ćtoliam, Ioniam, Asiam, Siciliam, Italiam, sine Pythio (the Delphic), aut Dodonseo, aut Hammonis oraculo?" An oracular sanction must be had, and from a leading oracle—the three mentioned by Cicero were the greatest; [Footnote: To which at one time must be added, as of equal rank, the Oracle of the Branchides, in Asia Minor. But this had been destroyed by the Persians, in retaliation of the Athenian outrages at Sardis.] and, if a minor oracle could have satisfied the inaugurating necessities of a regular colony, we may be sure that the Dorian states of the Peloponnesus, who had twenty-five decent oracles at home (that is, within the peninsula), would not so constantly have carried their money to Delphi. Nay, it is certain that even where the colonial counsels of the greater oracles seemed extravagant, though a large discretion was allowed to remonstrance, and even to very homely expostulations, still, in the last resort, no doubts were felt that the oracle must be right. Brouwer, the Belgic scholar, who has so recently and so temperately treated these subjects (Histoire de la Civilisation Morale et Religieuse chez les Grecs: 6 tomes: Groningue—1840), alleges a case (which, however, we do not remember to have met) where the client ventured to object:—"*Mon roi Apollon, je crois que tu es fou.*" But cases are obvious which look this way, though not going so far as to charge lunacy upon the lord of prophetic vision. Battus, who was destined to be the eldest father of Cyrene, so memorable as the first ground of Greek intercourse with the African shore of the Mediterranean, never consulted the Delphic Oracle in reference to his eyes, which happened to be diseased, but that he was admonished to prepare for colonizing Libya. —"Grant me patience," would Battus reply; "here am I getting into years, and never do I consult the Oracle about

my precious sight, but you, King Phbus, begin your old
yarn about Cyrene. Confound Cyrene! Nobody knows
where it is. But, if you are serious, speak to my son—he's a
likely young man, and worth a hundred of old rotten
hulks, like myself." Battus was provoked in good earnest;
and it is well known that the whole scheme went to sleep
for several years, until King Phoebus sent in a gentle
refresher to Battus and his islanders, in the shape of failing
crops, pestilence, and his ordinary chastisements. The people
were roused—the colony was founded—and, after utter
failure, was again re-founded, and the results justified the
Oracle. But, in all such cases, and where the remonstrances
were least respectful, or where the resistance of *inertia* was
longest, we differ altogether from M. Brouwer in his belief,
that the suitors fancied Apollo to have gone distracted. If
they ever said so, this must have been merely by way of
putting the Oracle on its mettle, and calling forth some
plainer—not any essentially different—answer from the
enigmatic god; for there it was that the doubts of the clients
settled, and on that it was the practical demurs hinged. Not
because even Battus, vexed as he was about his precious
eyesight, distrusted the Oracle, but because he felt sure that
the Oracle had not spoken out freely; therefore, had he and
many others in similar circumstances presumed to delay. A
second edition was what they waited for, corrected and
enlarged. We have a memorable instance of this policy in the
Athenian envoys, who, upon receiving a most ominous
doom, but obscurely expressed, from the Delphic Oracle,
which politely concluded by saying, "And so get out, you
vagabonds, from my temple—don't cumber my decks any
longer;" were advised to answer sturdily—"No!—we shall
not get out—we mean to sit here forever, until you think
proper to give us a more reasonable reply." Upon which
spirited rejoinder, the Pythia saw the policy of revising her
truly brutal rescript as it had stood originally.

The necessity, indeed, was strong for not acquiescing in the Oracle, until it had become clearer by revision or by casual illustrations, as will be seen even under our next head. This head concerns the case of those who found themselves deceived by the *event* of any oracular prediction. As usual, there is a Spartan case of this nature. Cleomenes complained bitterly that the Oracle of Delphi had deluded him by holding out as a possibility, and under given conditions as a certainty, that he should possess himself of Argos. But the Oracle was justified: there was an inconsiderable place outside the walls of Argos which bore the same name. Most readers will remember the case of Cambyses, who had been assured by a legion of oracles that he should die at Ecbatana. Suffering, therefore, in Syria from a scratch inflicted upon his thigh by his own sabre, whilst angrily sabring a ridiculous quadruped whom the Egyptian priests had put forward as a god, he felt quite at his ease so long as he remembered his vast distance from the mighty capital of Media, to the eastward of the Tigris. The scratch, however, inflamed, for his intemperance had saturated his system with combustible matter; the inflammation spread; the pulse ran high: and he began to feel twinges of alarm. At length mortification commenced: but still he trusted to the old prophecy about Ecbatana, when suddenly a horrid discovery was made—that the very Syrian village at his own head-quarters was known by the pompous name of Ecbatana. Josephus tells a similar story of some man contemporary with Herod the Great. And we must all remember that case in Shakspeare, where the first king of the *red* rose, Henry IV., had long fancied his destiny to be that he should meet his death in Jerusalem; which naturally did not quicken his zeal for becoming a crusader. "All time enough," doubtless he used to say; "no hurry at all, gentlemen!" But at length, finding himself pronounced by the doctor ripe for dying, it became a question whether the prophet were a false prophet, or the doctor a false doctor. However, in such a case, it is something to have a collision of opinions—a prophet against a doctor. But, behold, it soon transpired that there was no collision at all. It was the Jerusalem chamber, occupied by the king as a bed-room, to which the prophet had alluded. Upon which his majesty reconciled himself at once to the ugly necessity at hand

"In that Jerusalem shall Harry die."

The last case—that of oracular establishments turning out to be accomplices of thieves—is one which occurred in Egypt on a scale of some extent; and is noticed by Herodotus. This degradation argued great poverty in the particular temples: and it is not at all improbable that, amongst a hundred Grecian Oracles, some, under a similar temptation, would fall into a similar disgrace. But now, as regards even this lowest extremity of infamy, much more as regards the qualified sort of disrepute attending the three minor cases, one single distinction puts all to rights. The Greeks never confounded the temple, and household of officers attached to the temple service, with the dark functions of the presiding god. In Delphi, besides the Pythia and priests, with their train of subordinate ministers directly billeted on the temple, there were two orders of men outside, Delphic citizens, one styled *Arizeis*, the other styled *Hosioi*,—a sort of honorary members, whose duty was probably *inter alia*, to attach themselves to persons of corresponding rank in the retinues of the envoys or consulting clients, and doubtless to collect from them, in convivial moments, all the secrets or general information which the temple required for satisfactory answers. If they personally went too far in their intrigues or stratagems of decoy, the disgrace no more recoiled on the god, than, in modern times, the vices or crimes of a priest can affect the pure religion at whose altars he officiates.

Meantime, through these outside ministers—though unaffected by their follies or errors as trepanners—the Oracle of Delphi drew that vast and comprehensive information, from every local nook or recess of Greece, which made it in the end a blessing to the land. The great error is, to suppose the majority of cases laid before the Delphic Oracle strictly questions for *prophetic* functions. Ninety-nine in a hundred respected marriages, state-treaties, sales, purchases, founding of towns or colonies, &c., which demanded no faculty whatever of divination, but the nobler faculty (though unpresumptuous) of sagacity, that calculates the natural consequences of human acts, cooperating with elaborate investigation of the local circumstances. If, in any paper on the general civilization of Greece (that great mother of civilization for all the world), we should ever attempt to trace this element of Oracles, it will not be difficult to prove that Delphi discharged the office of a central *bureau d'administration*, a general depot of political information, an organ of universal combination for the counsels of the whole Grecian race. And that which caused the declension of the Oracles was the loss of political independence and autonomy. After Alexander, still more after the Roman conquest, each separate state, having no powers and no motive for asking counsel on state measures, naturally confined itself more and more to its humbler local interests of police, or even at last to its family arrangements.

THE REVOLUTION OF GREECE.

[1833.]

It is falsely charged upon itself by this age, in its character of *censor morum*, that effeminacy in a practical sense lies either amongst its full-blown faults, or amongst its lurking tendencies. A rich, a polished, a refined age, may, by mere necessity of inference, be presumed to be a luxurious one; and the usual principle, by which moves the whole trivial philosophy which speculates upon the character of a particular age or a particular nation, is first of all to adopt some one central idea of its characteristics, and then without further effort to pursue its integration; that is, having assumed (or, suppose even having demonstrated) the existence of some great influential quality in excess sufficient to overthrow the apparent equilibrium demanded by the common standards of a just national character, the speculator then proceeds, as in a matter of acknowledged right, to push this predominant quality into all its consequences, and all its closest affinities. To give one illustration of such a case, now perhaps beginning to be forgotten: Somewhere about the year 1755, the once celebrated Dr. Brown, after other little attempts in literature and paradox, took up the conceit that England was ruined at her heart's core by excess of luxury and sensual self-indulgence. He had persuaded himself that the ancient activities and energies of the country were sapped by long habits of indolence, and by a morbid plethora of enjoyment in every class. Courage, and the old fiery spirit of the people, had gone to wreck with the physical qualities which had sustained them. Even the faults of the public mind had given way under its new complexion of character; ambition and civil dissension were extinct. It was questionable whether a good hearty assault and battery, or a respectable knock-down blow, had been dealt by any man in London for one or two generations. The doctor carried his reveries so far, that he even satisfied himself and one or two friends (probably by looking into the parks at hours propitious to his hypothesis) that horses were seldom or ever used for riding; that, in fact, this accomplishment was too boisterous or too perilous for the gentle propensities of modern Britons; and that, by the best accounts, few men of rank or fashion were now seen on horseback. This pleasant collection of dreams did Doctor Brown solemnly propound to the English public, in two octavo volumes, under the title of "An Estimate of the Manners and Principles of the Times;" and the report of many who lived in those days assures us that for a brief period the book had a prodigious run. In some respects the doctor's conceits might seem too startling and extravagant; but, to balance *that,* every nation has some pleasure in being heartily abused by one of its own number; and the English nation has always had a special delight in being alarmed, and in being clearly convinced that it is and ought to be on the brink of ruin. With such advantages in the worthy doctor's favor, he might have kept the field until some newer extravaganza had made his own obsolete, had not one ugly turn in political affairs given so smashing a refutation to his practical conclusions, and called forth so sudden a rebound of public feeling in the very opposite direction, that a bomb-shell descending right through the whole impression of his book could not more summarily have laid a chancery "injunction" upon its further sale. This

arose under the brilliant administration of the first Mr. Pitt:
England was suddenly victorious in three quarters of the
globe; land and sea echoed to the voice of her triumphs; and
the poor Doctor Brown, in the midst of all this hubbub, cut
his own throat with his own razor. Whether this dismal
catastrophe were exactly due to his mortification as a baffled
visionary, whose favorite conceit had suddenly exploded like
a rocket into smoke and stench, is more than we know. But,
at all events, the sole memorial of his hypothesis which now
reminds the English reader that it ever existed is one solitary
notice of good-humored satire pointed at it by Cowper.
[Footnote: "The Inestimable Estimate of Brown."] And the
possibility of such exceeding folly in a man otherwise of
good sense and judgment, not depraved by any brain-fever
or enthusiastic infatuation, is to be found in the vicious
process of reasoning applied to such estimates; the doctor,
having taken up one novel idea of the national character,
proceeded afterwards by no tentative inquiries, or
comparison with actual facts and phenomena of daily
experience, but resolutely developed out of his one idea all
that it appeared analytically to involve; and postulated
audaciously as a solemn fact whatsoever could be exhibited
in any possible connection with his one central principle,
whether in the way of consequence or of affinity.

Pretty much upon this unhappy Brunonian mode of
deducing our national character, it is a very plausible
speculation, which has been and will again be chanted, that
we, being a luxurious nation, must by force of good logical
dependency be liable to many derivative taints and
infirmities which ought of necessity to besiege the blood of
nations in that predicament. All enterprise and spirit of
adventure, all heroism and courting of danger for its own
attractions, ought naturally to languish in a generation
enervated by early habits of personal indulgence. Doubtless

they *ought;* *a priori,* it seems strictly demonstrable that such consequences should follow. Upon the purest forms of inference in *Barbara* or *Celarent,* it can be shown satisfactorily that from all our tainted classes, *a fortiori* then from our most tainted classes—our men of fashion and of opulent fortunes—no description of animal can possibly arise but poltroons and *fainéans.* In fact, pretty generally, under the known circumstances of our modern English education and of our social habits, we ought, in obedience to all the *precognita* of our position, to show ourselves rank cowards; yet, in spite of so much excellent logic, the facts are otherwise. No age has shown in its young patricians a more heroic disdain of sedentary ease; none in a martial support of liberty or national independence has so gayly volunteered upon services the most desperate, or shrunk less from martyrdom on the field of battle, whenever there was hope to invite their disinterested exertions, or grandeur enough in the cause to sustain them. Which of us forgets the gallant Mellish, the frank and the generous, who reconciled himself so gayly to the loss of a splendid fortune, and from the very bosom of luxury suddenly precipitated himself upon the hardships of Peninsular warfare? Which of us forgets the adventurous Lee of Lime, whom a princely estate could not detain in early youth from courting perils in Nubia and Abyssinia, nor (immediately upon his return) from almost wooing death as a volunteer aide-de-camp to the Duke of Wellington at Waterloo? So again of Colonel Evans, who, after losing a fine estate long held out to his hopes, five times over put himself at the head of *forlorn hopes.* Such cases are memorable, and were conspicuous at the time, from the lustre of wealth and high connections which surrounded the parties; but many thousand others, in which the sacrifices of personal ease were less noticeable from their narrower scale of splendor, had equal merit for the cheerfulness with which those sacrifices were made.

[Footnote: History of the Greek Revolution, by Thomas Gordon.] Here, again, in the person of the author before us, we have another instance of noble and disinterested heroism, which, from the magnitude of the sacrifices that it involved, must place him in the same class as the Mellishes and the Lees. This gallant Scotsman, who was born in 1788, or 1789, lost his father in early life. Inheriting from him a good estate in Aberdeenshire, and one more considerable in Jamaica, he found himself, at the close of a long minority, in the possession of a commanding fortune. Under the vigilant care of a sagacious mother, Mr. Gordon received the very amplest advantages of a finished education, studying first at the University of Aberdeen, and afterwards for two years at Oxford; whilst he had previously enjoyed as a boy the benefits of a private tutor from Oxford. Whatever might be the immediate result from this careful tuition, Mr. Gordon has since completed his own education in the most comprehensive manner, and has carried his accomplishments as a linguist to a point of rare excellence. Sweden and Portugal excepted, we understand that he has personally visited every country in Europe. He has travelled also in Asiatic Turkey, in Persia, and in Barbary. From this personal residence in foreign countries, we understand that Mr. Gordon has obtained an absolute mastery over certain modern languages, especially the French, the Italian, the modern Greek, and the Turkish.[Footnote: Mr. Gordon is privately known to be the translator of the work written by a Turkish minister, "*Tchebi Effendi*" published in the Appendix to Wilkinson's Wallachia, and frequently referred to by the *Quarterly Review* in its notices of Oriental affairs.] Not content, however, with this extensive education in a literary sense, Mr. Gordon thought proper to prepare himself for the part which he meditated in public life, by a second, or military education, in two separate services;— first, in the British, where he served in the Greys, and in the forty-third regiment; and subsequently, during the campaign of 1813, as a captain on the Russian staff.

Thus brilliantly accomplished for conferring lustre and benefit upon any cause which he might adopt amongst the many revolutionary movements then continually emerging in Southern Europe, he finally carried the whole weight of his great talents, prudence, and energy, together with the unlimited command of his purse, to the service of Greece in her heroic struggle with the Sultan. At what point his services and his countenance were appreciated by the ruling persons in Greece, will be best collected from the accompanying letter, translated from the original, in modern Greek, addressed to him by the provisional government of Greece, in 1822. It will be seen that this official document notices with great sorrow Mr. Gordon's absence from Greece, and with some surprise, as a fact at that time unexplained and mysterious; but the simple explanation of this mystery was, that Mr. Gordon had been brought to the very brink of the grave by a contagious fever, at Tripolizza, and that his native air was found essential to his restoration. Subsequently, however, he returned, and rendered the most powerful services to Greece, until the war was brought to a close, as much almost by Turkish exhaustion, as by the armed interference of the three great conquerors of Navarino.

"The government of Greece to the SIGNOR GORDON, a man worthy of all admiration, and a friend of the Grecians, health and prosperity.

"It was not possible, most excellent sir, nor was it a thing endurable to the descendants of the Grecians, that they should be deprived any longer of those imprescriptible rights which belong to the inheritance of their birth—rights which a barbarian of a foreign soil, an anti-christian tyrant, issuing from the depths of Asia, seized upon with a robber's hand, and, lawlessly trampling under foot, administered up to this time the affairs of Greece, after his own lust and will. Needs it was that we, sooner or later, shattering this iron and heavy sceptre, should recover, at the price of life itself (if *that* were found necessary), our patrimonial heritage, that thus our people might again be gathered to the family of free and self-legislating states. Moving, then, under such impulses, the people of Greece advanced with one heart, and perfect unanimity of council, against an oppressive despotism, putting their hands to an enterprise beset with difficulties, and hard indeed to be achieved, yet, in our present circumstances, if any one thing in this life, most indispensable. This, then, is the second year which we are passing since we have begun to move in this glorious contest, once again struggling, to all appearance, upon unequal terms, but grasping our enterprise with the right hand and the left, and with all our might stretching forward to the objects before us.

"It was the hope of Greece that, in these seasons of emergency, she would not fail of help and earnest resort of friends from the Christian nations throughout Europe. For it was agreeable neither to humanity nor to piety, that the rights of nations, liable to no grudges of malice or scruples of jealousy, should be surreptitiously and wickedly filched away, or mocked with outrage and insult; but that they should be settled firmly on those foundations which Nature herself has furnished in abundance to the condition of man in society. However, so it was, that Greece, cherishing these most reasonable expectations, met with most unmerited disappointments.

"But you, noble and generous Englishman, no sooner heard the trumpet of popular rights echoing melodiously from the summits of Taygetus, of Ida, of Pindus, and of Olympus, than, turning with listening ears to the sound, and immediately renouncing the delights of country, of family ties, and (what is above all) of domestic luxury and ease, and the happiness of your own fireside, you hurried to our assistance. But suddenly, and in contradiction to the universal hope of Greece, by leaving us, you have thrown us all into great perplexity and amazement, and that at a crisis when some were applying their minds to military pursuits, some to the establishment of a civil administration, others to other objects, but all alike were hurrying and exerting themselves wherever circumstances seemed to invite them.

"Meantime, the government of Greece having heard many idle rumors and unauthorized tales disseminated, but such as seemed neither in correspondence with their opinion of your own native nobility from rank and family, nor with what was due to the newly-instituted administration, have slighted and turned a deaf ear to them all, coming to this resolution—that, in absenting yourself from Greece, you are doubtless obeying some strong necessity; for that it is not possible nor credible of a man such as you displayed yourself to be whilst living amongst us, that he should mean to insult the wretched—least of all, to insult the unhappy and much-suffering people of Greece. Under these circumstances, both the deliberative and the executive bodies of the Grecian government, assembling separately, have come to a resolution, without one dissentient voice, to invite you back to Greece, in order that you may again take a share in the Grecian contest—a contest in itself glorious, and not alien from your character and pursuits. For the liberty of any one nation cannot be a matter altogether indifferent to the rest, but naturally it is a common and diffusive interest; and nothing can be more reasonable than that the Englishman and the Grecian, in such a cause, should make themselves yoke-fellows, and should participate as brothers in so holy a struggle. Therefore, the Grecian government hastens, by this present distinguished expression of its regard, to invite you to the soil of Greece, a soil united by such tender memorials with yourself; confident that you, preferring glorious poverty and the hard living of Greece to the luxury and indolence of an obscure seclusion, will hasten your return to Greece, agreeably to your native character, restoring to us our valued English connection. Farewell!

"The Vice-president of the Executive,

"**ATHANASIUS KANAKARES.**

"The Chief-Secretary, Minister of Foreign Relations, NEGENZZ."

Since then, having in 1817 connected himself in marriage with a beautiful young lady of Armenian Greek extraction, and having purchased land and built a house in Argos, Mr. Gordon may be considered in some sense as a Grecian citizen. Services in the field having now for some years been no longer called for, he has exchanged his patriotic sword for a patriotic pen—judging rightly that in no way so effectually can Greece be served at this time with Western Europe, as by recording faithfully the course of her revolution, tracing the difficulties which lay or which arose in her path, the heroism with which she surmounted them, and the multiplied errors by which she raised up others to herself. Mr. Gordon, of forty authors who have partially treated this theme, is the first who can be considered either impartial or comprehensive; and upon his authority, not seldom using his words, we shall now present to our readers the first continuous abstract of this most interesting and romantic war:

GREECE, in the largest extent of that term, having once belonged to the Byzantine empire, is included, by the misconception of hasty readers, in the great wreck of 1453. They take it for granted that, concurrently with Constantinople, and the districts adjacent, these provinces passed at that disastrous era into the hands of the Turkish conqueror; but this is an error. Parts of Greece, previously to that era, had been dismembered from the Eastern empire; —other parts did not, until long *after* it, share a common fate with the metropolis. Venice had a deep interest in the Morea; *in* that, and *for* that, she fought with various success for generations; and it was not until the year 1717, nearly three centuries from the establishment of the crescent in Europe, that "the banner of St. Mark, driven finally from the Morea and the Archipelago," was henceforth exiled (as respected Greece) to the Ionian Islands.

In these contests, though Greece was the prize at issue, the children of Greece had no natural interest, whether the cross prevailed or the crescent; the same, for all substantial results, was the fate which awaited themselves. The Moslem might be the more intolerant by his maxims, and he might be harsher in his professions; but a slave is not the less a slave, though his master should happen to hold the same creed with himself; and towards a member of the Greek church one who looked westward to Rome for his religion was likely to be little less of a bigot than one who looked to Mecca. So that we are not surprised to find a Venetian rule of policy recommending, for the daily allowance of these Grecian slaves, "a *little* bread, and a liberal application of the cudgel"! Whichever yoke were established was sure to be hated; and, therefore, it was fortunate for the honor of the Christian name, that from the year 1717 the fears and the enmity of the Greeks were to be henceforward pointed exclusively towards *Mahometan* tyrants.

To be hated, however, sufficiently for resistance, a yoke must have been long and continuously felt. Fifty years might be necessary to season the Greeks with a knowledge of Turkish oppression; and less than two generations could hardly be supposed to have manured the whole territory with an adequate sense of the wrongs they were enduring, and the withering effects of such wrongs on the sources of public prosperity. Hatred, besides, without hope, is no root out of which an effective resistance can be expected to grow; and fifty years almost had elapsed before a great power had arisen in Europe, having in any capital circumstance a joint interest with Greece, or specially authorized, by visible right and power, to interfere as her protector. The semi-Asiatic power of Russia, from the era of the Czar Peter the Great, had arisen above the horizon with the sudden sweep and splendor of a meteor. The arch described by her ascent was as vast in compass as it was rapid; and, in all history, no political growth, not that of our own Indian empire, had travelled by accelerations of speed so terrifically marked. Not that even Russia could have really grown in strength according to the *apparent* scale of her progress. The strength was doubtless there, or much of it, before Peter and Catherine; but it was latent: there had been no such sudden growth as people fancied; but there had been a sudden evolution. Infinite resources had been silently accumulating from century to century; but, before the Czar Peter, no mind had come across them of power sufficient to reveal their situation, or to organize them for practical effects. In some nations, the manifestations of power are coincident with its growth; in others, from vicious institutions, a vast crystallization goes on for ages blindly and in silence, which the lamp of some meteoric mind is required to light up into brilliant display. Thus it had been in Russia; and hence, to the abused judgment of all Christendom, she had seemed to leap like Pallas from the brain of Jupiter—gorgeously endowed, and in panoply of civil array, for all purposes of national grandeur, at the *fiat* of one coarse barbarian. As the metropolitan home of the Greek church, she could not disown a maternal interest in the humblest of the Grecian tribes, holding the same faith with herself, and celebrating their worship by the same rites. This interest she could, at length, venture to express in a tone of sufficient emphasis; and Greece became aware that she could, about the very time when Turkish oppression had begun to unite its victims in aspirations for redemption, and had turned their eyes abroad in search of some great standard under whose shadow they could flock for momentary protection, or for future hope. What cabals were reared upon this condition of things by Russia, and what premature dreams of independence were encouraged throughout Greece in the reign of Catherine II., may be seen amply developed, in the once celebrated work of Mr. William Eton.

Another great circumstance of hope for Greece, coinciding with the dawn of her own earliest impetus in this direction, and travelling *puri passu* almost with the growth of her mightiest friend, was the advancing decay of her oppressor. The wane of the Turkish crescent had seemed to be in some secret connection of fatal sympathy with the growth of the Russian cross. Perhaps the reader will thank us for rehearsing the main steps by which the Ottoman power had flowed and ebbed. The foundations of this empire were laid in the thirteenth century, by Ortogrul, the chief of a Turkoman tribe, residing in tents not far from Dorylćum, in Phrygia (a name so memorable in the early crusades), about the time when Jenghiz had overthrown the Seljukian dynasty. His son Osman first assumed the title of Sultan;

and, in 1300, having reduced the city of Prusa, in Bithynia, he made it the capital of his dominions. The Sultans who succeeded him for some generations, all men of vigor, and availing themselves not less of the decrepitude which had by that time begun to palsy the Byzantine sceptre, than of the martial and religious fanaticism which distinguished their own followers, crossed the Hellespont, conquering Thrace and the countries up to the Danube. In 1453, the most eminent of these Sultans, Mahomet II., by storming Constantinople, put an end to the Roman empire; and before his death he placed the Ottoman power in Europe pretty nearly on that basis to which it had again fallen back by 1821. The long interval of time between these two dates involved a memorable flux and reflux of power, and an oscillation between two extremes of panic-striking grandeur, in the ascending scale (insomuch that the Turkish Sultan was supposed to be charged in the Apocalypse with the dissolution of the Christian thrones), and in the descending scale of paralytic dotage tempting its own instant ruin. In speculating on the causes of the extraordinary terror which the Turks once inspired, it is amusing, and illustrative of the revolutions worked by time, to find it imputed, in the first place, to superior discipline; for, if their discipline was imperfect, they had, however, a *standing* army of Janissaries, whilst the whole of Christian Europe was accustomed to fight merely summer campaigns with hasty and untrained levies; a second cause lay in their superior finances, for the Porte had a regular revenue, when the other powers of Europe relied upon the bounty of their vassals and clergy; and, thirdly, which is the most surprising feature of the whole statement, the Turks were so far ahead of others in the race of improvement, that to them belongs the credit of having first adopted the extensive use of gunpowder, and of having first brought battering-trains against fortified places. To his artillery and his musketry it was that Selim the

Ferocious (grandson of that Sultan who took Constantinople) was indebted for his victories in Syria and Egypt. Under Solyman the Magnificent (the well-known contemporary of the Emperor Charles Y.) the crescent is supposed to have attained its utmost altitude; and already for fifty years the causes had been in silent progress which were to throw the preponderance into the Christian scale. In the reign of his son, Selim the Second, this crisis was already passed; and the battle of Lepanto, in 1571, which crippled the Turkish navy in a degree never wholly recovered, gave the first overt signal to Europe of a turn in the course of their prosperity. Still, as this blow did not equally affect the principal arm of their military service, and as the strength of the German empire was too much distracted by Christian rivalship, the *prestige* of the Turkish name continued almost unbroken until their bloody overthrow in 1664, at St. Gothard, by the imperial General Montecuculi. In 1673 they received another memorable defeat from Sobieski, on which occasion they lost twenty-five thousand men. In what degree, however, the Turkish Samson had been shorn of his original strength, was not yet made known to Europe by any adequate expression, before the great catastrophe of 1683. In that year, at the instigation of the haughty vizier, Kara Mustafa, the Turks had undertaken the siege of Vienna; and great was the alarm of the Christian world. But, on the 12th of September, their army of one hundred and fifty thousand men was totally dispersed by seventy thousand Poles and Germans, under John Sobieski—"He conquering *through* God, and God by him." [Footnote: See the sublime Sonnet of Chiabrora on this subject, as translated by Mr. Wordsworth.] Then followed the treaty of Carlovitz, which stripped the Porte of Hungary, the Ukraine, and other places; and "henceforth" says Mr. Gordon, "Europe ceased to dread the Turks; and began even to look upon their existence as a necessary element of the balance of power among its states." Spite of their losses, however, during the first half of the eighteenth century, the Turks still maintained a respectable attitude against Christendom. But the wars of the Empress Catherine II., and the French invasion of Egypt, demonstrated that either their native vigor was exhausted and superannuated, or, at least, that the institutions were superannuated by which their resources had been so long administered. Accordingly, at the commencement of the present century, the Sultan Selim II. endeavored to reform the military discipline; but in the first collision with the prejudices of his people, and the interest of the Janissaries, he perished by sedition. Mustafa, who succeeded to the throne, in a few months met the same fate. But then (1808) succeeded a prince formed by nature for such struggles,— cool, vigorous, cruel, and intrepid. This was Mahmoud the Second. He perfectly understood the crisis, and determined to pursue the plans of his uncle Selim, even at the hazard of the same fate. Why was it that Turkish soldiers had been made ridiculous in arms, as often as they had met with French troops, who yet were so far from being the best in Christendom, that Egypt herself, and the beaten Turks, had seen *them* in turn uniformly routed by the British? Physically, the Turks were equal, at the very least, to the French. In what lay their inferiority? Simply in discipline, and in their artillery. And so long as their constitution and discipline continued what they had been, suited (that is) to centuries long past and gone, and to a condition of Christendom obsolete for ages, so long it seemed inevitable that the same disasters should follow the Turkish banners. And to this point, accordingly, the Sultan determined to address his earliest reforms. But caution was necessary; he waited and watched. He seized all opportunities of profiting by the calamities or the embarrassments of his potent neighbors. He put down all open revolt. He sapped the authority of all the great families in Asia Minor, whose hereditary influence could be a counterpoise to his own. Mecca and Medina, the holy cities of his religion, he brought again within the pale of his dominions. He augmented and fostered, as a counterbalancing force to the Janissaries, the corps of the Topjees or artillery-men. He amassed preparatory treasures. And, up to the year 1820, "his government," says Mr. Gordon, "was highly unpopular; but it was strong, stern, and uniform; and he had certainly removed many impediments to the execution of his ulterior projects."

Such was the situation of Turkey at the moment when her Grecian vassal prepared to trample on her yoke. In her European territories she reckoned, at the utmost, eight millions of subjects. But these, besides being more or less in a semi-barbarous condition, and scattered over a very wide surface of country, were so much divided by origin, by language, and religion, that, without the support of her Asiatic arm, she could not, according to the general opinion, have stood at all. The rapidity of her descent, it is true, had been arrested by the energy of her Sultans during the first twenty years of the nineteenth century. But for the last thirty of the eighteenth she had made a headlong progress downwards. So utterly, also, were the tables turned, that, whereas in the fifteenth century her chief superiority over Christendom had been in the three points of artillery, discipline, and fixed revenue, precisely in these three she had sunk into utter insignificance, whilst all Christendom had been continually improving. Selim and Mahmoud indeed had made effectual reforms in the corps of gunners, as we have said, and had raised it to the amount of sixty thousand men; so that at present they have respectable field-artillery, whereas previously they had only heavy battering-trains. But the defects in discipline cannot be

remedied, so long as the want of a settled revenue obliges
the Sultan to rely upon hurried levies from the provincial
militias of police. Turkey, however, might be looked upon as
still formidable for internal purposes, in the haughty and
fanatical character of her Moslem subjects. And we may add,
as a concluding circumstance of some interest, in this sketch
of her modern condition, that pretty nearly the same
European territories as were assigned to the eastern Roman
empire at the time of its separation from the western,
[Footnote: "The vitals of the monarchy lay within that vast
triangle circumscribed by the Danube, the Save, the
Adriatic, Euxine, and Egean Seas, whose altitude may be
computed at five hundred, and the length of its base at
seven hundred geographical miles."—GORDON.] were
included within the frontier line of Turkey, on the first of
January, 1821.

Precisely in this year commenced the Grecian revolution.
Concurrently with the decay of her oppressor the Sultan,
had been the prodigious growth of her patron the Czar. In
what degree she looked up to that throne, and the intrigues
which had been pursued with a view to that connection,
may be seen (as we have already noticed) in Eton's Turkey—
a book which attracted a great deal of notice about thirty
years ago. Meantime, besides this secret reliance on Russian
countenance or aid, Greece had since that era received great
encouragement to revolt from the successful experiment in
that direction made by the Turkish province of Servia. In
1800, Czerni George came forward as the asserter of Servian
independence, and drove the Ottomans out of that province.
Personally he was not finally successful. But his example
outlived him; and, after fifteen years' struggle, Servia (says
Mr. Gordon) offered "the unwonted spectacle of a brave and
armed Christian nation living under its own laws in the
heart of Turkey," and retaining no memorial of its former

servitude, but the payment of a slender and precarious tribute to the Sultan, with a *verbal* profession of allegiance to his sceptre. Appearances were thus saved to the pride of the haughty Moslem by barren concessions which cost no real sacrifice to the substantially victorious Servian.

Examples, however, are thrown away upon a people utterly degraded by long oppression. And the Greeks were pretty nearly in that condition. "It would, no doubt," says Mr. Gordon, "be possible to cite a more *cruel* oppression than that of the Turks towards their Christian subjects, but none *so fitted to break men's spirit*." The Greeks, in fact (under which name are to be understood, not only those who speak Greek, but the Christian Albanians of Roumelia and the Morea, speaking a different language, but united with the Greeks in spiritual obedience to the same church), were, in the emphatic phrase of Mr. Gordon, "the slaves of slaves:" that is to say, not only were they liable to the universal tyranny of the despotic Divan, but "throughout the empire they were in the habitual intercourse of life subjected to vexations, affronts, and exactions, from Mahometans of every rank. Spoiled of their goods, insulted in their religion and domestic honor, they could rarely obtain justice. The slightest flash of courageous resentment brought down swift destruction on their heads; and cringing humility alone enabled them to live in ease, or even in safety." Stooping under this iron yoke of humiliation, we have reason to wonder that the Greeks preserved sufficient nobility of mind to raise so much as their wishes in the direction of independence. In a condition of abasement, from which a simple act of apostasy was at once sufficient to raise them to honor and wealth, "and from the meanest serfs gathered them to the caste of oppressors," we ought not to wonder that some of the Greeks should be mean, perfidious, and dissembling, but rather that any (as Mr. Gordon says) "had courage to adhere to their religion, and to eat the bread of affliction." But noble aspirations are fortunately indestructible in human nature. And in Greece the lamp of independence of spirit had been partially kept alive by the existence of a native militia, to whom the Ottoman government, out of mere necessity, had committed the local defence. These were called *Armatoles* (or Gendarmerie); their available strength was reckoned by Pouqueville (for the year 1814) at ten thousand men; and, as they were a very effectual little host for maintaining, from age to age, the "true faith militant" of Greece, namely, that a temporary and a disturbed occupation of the best lands in the country did not constitute an absolute conquest on the part of the Moslems, most of whom flocked for security with their families into the stronger towns; and, as their own martial appearance, with arms in their hands, lent a very plausible countenance to their insinuations that they, the Christian Armatoles, were the true *bona fide* governors and possessors of the land under a Moslem Suzerain; and, as the general spirit of hatred to Turkish insolence was not merely maintained in their own local stations, [Footnote: Originally, it seems, there were fourteen companies (or *capitanerias*) settled by imperial diplomas in the mountains of Olympus, Othryx, Pindus, and ta; and distinct appropriations were made by the Divan for their support. *Within* the Morea, the institution of the Armatoles was never tolerated; but there the same spirit was kept alive by tribes, such as the Mainatts, whose insurmountable advantages of natural position enabled them eternally to baffle the most powerful enemy.] but also propagated thence with activity to every part of Greece;—it may be interesting to hear Mr. Gordon's account of their peculiar composition and habits.

"The Turks," says he, "from the epoch of Mahommed the Second, did not (unless in Thessaly) generally settle there.

Beyond Mount ta, although they seized the best lands, the Mussulman inhabitants were chiefly composed of the garrisons of towns with their families. Finding it impossible to keep in subjection with a small force so many rugged cantons, peopled by a poor and hardy race, and to hold in check the robbers of Albania, the Sultans embraced the same policy which has induced them to court the Greek hierarchy, and respect ecclesiastical property,—by enlisting in their service the armed bands that they could not destroy. When wronged or insulted, these Armatoles threw off their allegiance, infested the roads, and pillaged the country; while such of the peasants as were driven to despair by acts of oppression joined their standard; the term Armatole was then exchanged for that of Klefthis [*Kleptćs*] or Thief, a profession esteemed highly honorable, when it was exercised sword in hand at the expense of the Moslems. [Footnote: And apparently, we may add, when exercised at the expense of whomsoever at sea. The old Grecian instinct, which Thucydides states so frankly, under which all seafarers were dedicated to spoil as people who courted attack, seems never to have been fully rooted out from the little creeks and naval fastnesses of the Morea, and of some of the Egean islands. Not, perhaps, the mere spirit of wrong and aggression, but some old traditionary conceits and maxims, brought on the great crisis of piracy, which fell under no less terrors than of the triple thunders of the great allies.] Even in their quietest mood, these soldiers curbed Turkish tyranny; for, the captains and Christian primates of districts understanding each other, the former, by giving to some of their men a hint to desert and turn Klefts, could easily circumvent Mahometans who came on a mission disagreeable to the latter. The habits and manners of the Armatoles, living among forests and in mountain passes, were necessarily rude and simple: their magnificence consisted in adorning with silver their guns, pistols, and daggers; their

amusements, in shooting at a mark, dancing, and singing
the exploits of the most celebrated chiefs. Extraordinary
activity, and endurance of hardships and fatigue, made them
formidable light troops in their native fastnesses; wrapped
in shaggy cloaks, they slept on the ground, defying the
elements; and the pure mountain air gave them robust
health. Such were the warriors that, in the very worst
times, kept alive a remnant of Grecian spirit."

But all these facts of history, or institutions of policy, nay,
even the more violent appeals to the national pride in such
memorable transactions as the expatriation of the illustrious
Suliotes (as also of some eminent predatory chieftains from
the Morea), were, after all, no more than indirect
excitements of the insurrectionary spirit. If it were possible
that any adequate occasion should arise for combining the
Greeks in one great movement of resistance, such continued
irritations must have the highest value, as keeping alive the
national spirit, which must finally be relied on to improve it
and to turn it to account; but it was not to be expected that
any such local irritations could ever of themselves avail to
create an occasion of sufficient magnitude for imposing
silence on petty dissensions, and for organizing into any
unity of effort a country so splintered and naturally cut into
independent chambers as that of Greece. That task,
transcending the strength (as might seem) of any real
agencies or powers then existing in Greece, was assumed by
a mysterious, [Footnote: Epirus and Acarnania, etc., to the
north-west; Roumelia, Thebes, Attica, to the east; the
Morea, or Peloponnesus, to the south-west; and the islands
so widely dispersed in the Egean, had from position a
separate interest over and above their common interest as
members of a Christian confederacy. And in the absence of
some great representative society, there was no voice
commanding enough to merge the local interest in the

universal one of Greece. The original (or *Philomuse* society), which adopted literature for its ostensible object, as a mask to its political designs, expired at Munich in 1807; but not before it had founded a successor more directly political. Hence arose a confusion, under which many of the crowned heads in Europe were judged uncharitably as dissemblers or as traitors to their engagements. They had subscribed to the first society; but they reasonably held that this did not pledge them to another, which, though inheriting the secret purposes of the first, no longer masked or disavowed them.] and, in some sense, a fictitious society of corresponding members, styling itself the *Hetćria*. A more astonishing case of mighty effects prepared and carried on to their accomplishment by small means, magnifying their own extent through great zeal and infinite concealment, and artifices the most subtle, is not to be found in history. The *secret tribunal* of the middle ages is not to be compared with it for the depth and expansion of its combinations, or for the impenetrability of its masque. Nor is there in the whole annals of man a manoeuvre so admirable as that, by which this society, silently effecting its own transfiguration, and recasting as in a crucible its own form, organs, and most essential functions, contrived, by mere force of seasonable silence, or by the very pomp of mystery, to carry over from the first or innoxious model of the Hetćria, to its new organization, all those weighty names of kings or princes who would not have given their sanction to any association having political objects, however artfully veiled. The early history of the Hetćria is shrouded in the same mystery as the whole course of its political movements. Some suppose that Alexander Maurocordato, ex-Hospodar of Wallachia, during his long exile in Russia, founded it for the promotion of education, about the beginning of the present century. Others ascribe it originally to Riga. At all events, its purposes were purely intellectual in its earliest form. In

1815, in consequence chiefly of the disappointment which
the Greeks met with in their dearest hopes from the
Congress of Vienna, the Hetćria first assumed a political
character under the secret influence of Count Capodistria, of
Corfu, who, having entered the Russian service as mere
private secretary to Admiral Tchitchagoff, in 1812, had, in a
space of three years, insinuated himself into the favor of the
Czar, so far as to have become his private secretary, and a
cabinet minister of Russia. He, however, still masked his
final objects under plans of literature and scientific
improvement. In deep shades he organized a vast apparatus
of agents and apostles; and then retired behind the curtain
to watch or to direct the working of his blind machine. It is
an evidence of some latent nobility in the Greek character, in
the midst of that levity with which all Europe taxes it, that
never, except once, were the secrets of the society betrayed;
nor was there the least ground for jealousy offered either to
the stupid Moslems, in the very centre of whom, and round
about them, the conspiracy was daily advancing, or even to
the rigorous police of Moscow, where the Hetćria had its
head-quarters. In the single instance of treachery which
occurred, it happened that the Zantiote, who made the
discovery to Ali Pacha on a motion of revenge, was himself
too slenderly and too vaguely acquainted with the final
purposes of the Hetćria for effectual mischief, having been
fortunately admitted only to its lowest degree of initiation;
so that all passed off without injury to the cause, or even
personally to any of its supporters. There were, in fact, five
degrees in the Hetćria. A candidate of the lowest class (styled
Adelphoi, or brothers), after a minute examination of his past
life and connections, and after taking a dreadful oath, under
impressive circumstances, to be faithful in all respects to the
society and his afflicted country, and even to assassinate his
nearest and dearest relation, if detected in treachery, was
instructed only in the general fact that a design was on foot

to ameliorate the condition of Greece. The next degree of *Systimenoi,* or bachelors, who were selected with more anxious discrimination, were informed that this design was to move towards its object *by means of a revolution.* The third class, called *Priests of Eleusis,* were chosen from the aristocracy; and to them it was made known that *this revolution was near at hand*; and, also, that there were in the society higher ranks than their own. The fourth class was that of the *prelates*; and to this order, which never exceeded the number of one hundred and sixteen, and comprehended the leading men of the nation, the most unreserved information was given upon all the secrets of the Hetćria; after which they were severally appointed to a particular district, as superintendent of its interests, and as manager of the whole correspondence on its concerns with the Grand Arch. This, the crowning order and key-stone of the society, was reputed to comprehend sixteen "mysterious and illustrious names," amongst which were obscurely whispered those of the Czar, the Crown Prince of Bavaria and of Wurtemburg, of the Hospodar of Wallachia, of Count Capodistria, and some others. The orders of the Grand Arch were written in cipher, and bore a seal having in sixteen compartments the same number of initial letters. The revenue which it commanded must have been considerable; for the lowest member, on his noviciate, was expected to give at least fifty piastres (at this time about two pounds sterling); and those of the higher degrees gave from three hundred to one thousand each. The members communicated with each other, in mixed society, by masonic signs.

It cannot be denied that a secret society, with the grand and almost awful purposes of the Hetćria, spite of some taint which it had received in its early stages from the spirit of German mummery, is fitted to fill the imagination, and to command homage from the coldest. Whispers circulating from mouth to mouth of some vast conspiracy mining subterraneously beneath the very feet of their accursed oppressors; whispers of a great deliverer at hand, whose mysterious *Labarum*, or mighty banner of the Cross, was already dimly descried through northern mists, and whose eagles were already scenting the carnage and "savor of death" from innumerable hosts of Moslems; whispers of a revolution which was again to call, as with the trumpet of resurrection, from the grave, the land of Timoleon and Epaminondas; such were the preludings, low and deep, to the tempestuous overture of revolt and patriotic battle which now ran through every nook of Greece, and caused every ear to tingle.

The knowledge that this mighty cause must be sowed in dishonor, —propagated, that is, in respect to the knowledge of its plans, by redoubled cringings to their brutal masters, in order to shield it from suspicion, —but that it would probably be reaped in honor; the belief that the poor Grecian, so abject and trampled under foot, would soon reappear amongst the nations who had a name, in something of his original beauty and power; these dim but elevating perceptions, and these anticipations, gave to every man the sense of an ennobling secret confided to his individual honor, and, at the same time, thrilled his heart with sympathetic joy, from approaching glories that were to prove a personal inheritance to his children. Over all Greece a sense of power, dim and vast, brooded for years; and a mighty phantom, under the mysterious name of *Arch*, in whose cloudy equipage were descried, gleaming at intervals, the crowns and sceptres of great potentates, sustained, whilst it agitated their hearts. *London* was one of the secret watchwords in their impenetrable cipher; *Moscow* was a countersign; Bavaria and Austria bore mysterious parts in the drama; and, though no sound was heard, nor voice given to the powers that were working, yet, as if by mere force of secret sympathy, all mankind who were worthy to participate in the enterprise seemed to be linked in brotherhood with Greece. These notions were, much of them, mere phantasms and delusions; but they were delusions of mighty efficacy for arming the hearts of this oppressed country against the terrors that must be faced; and for the whole of them Greece was indebted to the Hetćria, and to its organized agency of apostles (as they were technically called), who compassed land and sea as pioneers for the coming crusade. [Footnote: Considering how very much the contest did finally assume a religious character (even Franks being attached, not as friends of Greece, but simply as Christians), one cannot but wonder that this romantic term has not been applied to the Greek war in Western Europe.]

By 1820 Greece was thoroughly inoculated with the spirit of resistance; all things were ready, so far, perhaps, as it was possible that they should ever be made ready under the eyes and scimitars of the enemy. Now came the question of time, —*when* was the revolt to begin? Some contend, says Mr. Gordon, that the Hetćria should have waited for a century, by which time they suppose that the growth of means in favor of Greece would have concurred with a more than corresponding decay in her enemy. But, to say nothing of the extreme uncertainty which attends such remote speculation, and the utter impossibility of training men with no personal hopes to labor for the benefit of distant generations, there was one political argument against that course, which Mr. Gordon justly considers unanswerable. It is this: Turkey in Europe has been long tottering on its basis. Now, were the attempt delayed until Russia had displaced her and occupied her seat, Greece would then have received her liberty as a boon from the conqueror; and the construction would have been that she held it by sufferance, and under a Russian warrant. This argument is conclusive. But others there were who fancied that 1825 was the year at which all the preparations for a successful revolt could have been matured. Probably some gain in such a case would have been balanced against some loss. But it is not necessary to discuss that question. Accident, it was clear, might bring on the first hostile movement at any hour, when the *minds* of all men were prepared, let the means in other respects be as deficient as they might. Already, in 1820, circumstances made it evident that the outbreak of the insurrection could not long be delayed. And, accordingly, in the following year all Greece was in flames.

This affair of 1820 has a separate interest of its own, connected with the character of the very celebrated person to whom it chiefly relates; but we notice it chiefly as the real occasion, the momentary spark, which, alighting upon the combustibles, by this time accumulated everywhere in Greece, caused a general explosion of the long-hoarded insurrectionary fury. Ali Pacha, the far-famed vizier of Yannina, had long been hated profoundly by the Sultan, who in the same proportion loved and admired his treasures. However, he was persuaded to wait for his death, which could not (as it seemed) be far distant, rather than risk anything upon the chances of war. And in this prudent resolution he would have persevered, but for an affront which he could not overlook. An Albanian, named Ismael Pasho Bey, once a member of Ali's household, had incurred his master's deadly hatred; and, flying from his wrath to various places under various disguises, had at length taken refuge in Constantinople, and there sharpened the malice of Ali by attaching himself to his enemies. Ali was still further provoked by finding that Ismael had won the Sultan's favor, and obtained an appointment in the palace. Mastered by his fury, Ali hired assassins to shoot his enemy in the very midst of Constantinople, and under the very eyes of imperial protection. The assassins failed, having only wounded him; they were arrested, and disclosed the name of their employer.

Here was an insult which could not be forgiven: Ali Pacha was declared a rebel and a traitor; and solemnly excommunicated by the head of the Mussulman law. The Pachas of Europe received orders to march against him; and a squadron was fitted out to attack him by sea.

In March, 1820, Ali became acquainted with these strong measures; which at first he endeavored to parry by artifice and bribery. But, finding *that* mode of proceeding absolutely without hope, he took the bold resolution of throwing himself, in utter defiance, upon the native energies of his own ferocious heart. Having, however, but small reliance on his Mahometan troops in a crisis of this magnitude, he applied for Christian succors, and set himself to *court* the Christians generally. As a first step, he restored the Armatoles—that very body whose suppression had been so favorite a measure of his policy, and pursued so long, so earnestly, and so injuriously to his credit amongst the Christian part of the population. It happened, at the first opening of the campaign, that the Christians were equally courted by the Sultan's generalissimo, Solyman, the Pacha of Thessaly. For this, however, that Pacha was removed and decapitated; and a new leader was now appointed in the person of that very enemy, Ismael Pasho, whose attempted murder had brought the present storm upon Ali. Ismael was raised to the rank of Serasker (or generalissimo), and was also made Pacha of Yannina and Del vino. Three other armies, besides a fleet under the Captain Bey, advanced upon Ali's territories simultaneously from different quarters. But at that time, in defiance of these formidable and overwhelming preparations, bets were strongly in Ali's favor amongst all who were acquainted with his resources: for he had vast treasures, fortresses of great strength, inexhaustible supplies of artillery and ammunition, a country almost inaccessible, and fifteen thousand light troops, whom Mr. Gordon, upon personal knowledge, pronounces "excellent."

Scarcely had the war commenced, when Ali was abandoned by almost the whole of his partisans, in mere hatred of his execrable cruelty and tyrannical government. To Ali, however, this defection brought no despondency; and with unabated courage he prepared to defend himself to the last, in three castles, with a garrison of three thousand men. That he might do so with entire effect, he began by destroying his own capital of Yannina, lest it should afford shelter to the enemy. Still his situation would have been most critical, but for the state of affairs in the enemy's camp. The Serasker was attended by more than twenty other Pashas. But they were all at enmity with each other. One of them, and the bravest, was even poisoned by the Serasker. Provisions were running short, in consequence of their own dissensions. Winter was fast approaching; the cannonading had produced no conspicuous effect; and the soldiers were disbanding. In this situation, the Sultan's lieutenants again saw the necessity of courting aid from the Christian population of the country. Ali, on his part, never scrupled to bid against them at any price; and at length, irritated by the ill-usage of the Turks on their first entrance, and disgusted with the obvious insincerity of their reluctant and momentary kindness, some of the bravest Christian tribes (especially the celebrated Suliotes) consented to take Ali's bribes, forgot his past outrages and unnumbered perfidies, and, reading his sincerity in the extremity of his peril, these bravest of the brave ranged themselves amongst the Sultan's enemies. During the winter they gained some splendid successes; other alienated friends came back to Ali; and even some Mahometan Beys were persuaded to take up arms in his behalf. Upon the whole, the Turkish Divan was very seriously alarmed; and so much so, that it superseded the Serasker Ismael, replacing him with the famous Kourshid Pacha, at that time viceroy of the Morea. And so ended the year 1820.

This state of affairs could not escape the attention of the vigilant Hetćria. Here was Ali Pacha, hitherto regarded as an insurmountable obstacle in their path, absolutely compelled by circumstances to be their warmest friend. The Turks again, whom no circumstances could entirely disarm, were yet crippled for the time, and their whole attention preoccupied by another enemy, most alarming to their policy, and most tempting to their cupidity. Such an opportunity it seemed unpardonable to neglect. Accordingly, it was resolved to begin the insurrection. At its head was placed Prince Alexander Ypsilanti, a son of that Hospodar of Wallachia whose deposition by the Porte had produced the Russian war of 1806. This prince's qualifications consisted in his high birth, in his connection with Russia (for he had risen to the rank of major-general in that service), and, finally (if such things can deserve a mention), in an agreeable person and manners. For all other and higher qualifications he was wholly below the situation and the urgency of the crisis. His first error was in the choice of his ground. For some reasons, which are not sufficiently explained,—possibly on account of his family connection with those provinces,—he chose to open the war in Moldavia and Wallachia. This resolution he took in spite of every warning, and the most intelligent expositions of the absolute necessity that, to be at all effectual, the first stand should be made in Greece. He thought otherwise; and, managing the campaign after his own ideas, he speedily involved himself in quarrels, and his army, through the perfidy of a considerable officer, in ruinous embarrassments. This unhappy campaign is circumstantially narrated by Mr. Gordon in his first book; but, as it never crossed the Danube, and had no connection with Greece except by its purposes, we shall simply rehearse the great outline of its course. The signal for insurrection was given in January, 1821; and Prince Ypsilanti took the field, by crossing the Pruth in March. Early in April he received a communication from the Emperor of Russia, which at once prostrated his hopes before an enemy was seen. He was formally disavowed by that prince, erased from his army-list, and severely reproached for his *folly and ingratitude,*" in letters from two members of the Russian cabinet; and on the 9th of April this fact was publicly notified in Yassy, the capital of Moldavia, by the Russian consul-general. His army at this time consisted of three thousand men, which, however, was afterwards reinforced, but with no gunpowder except what was casually intercepted, and no lead except some that had been stripped from the roof of an ancient cathedral. On the 12th of May the Pacha of Ibrail opened the campaign. A few days after, the Turkish troops began to appear in considerable force; and on the 8th of June an alarm was suddenly given "that the white turbans were upon them." In the engagement which followed, the insurgent army gave way; and, though their loss was much smaller than that of the Turks, yet, from the many blunders committed, the consequences were disastrous; and, had the Turks pursued, there would on that day have been an end of the insurrection. But far worse and more decisive was the subsequent disaster of the 17th. Ypsilanti had been again reinforced; and his advanced guard had surprised a Turkish detachment of cavalry in such a situation that their escape seemed impossible. Yet all was ruined by one officer of rank, who got drunk, and advanced with an air of bravado — followed, on a principle of honor, by a sacred battalion [*hieros lochos*], composed of five hundred Greek volunteers, of birth and education, the very *élite* of the insurgent infantry. The Turks gave themselves up for lost; but, happening to observe that this drunkard seemed unsupported by other parts of the army, they suddenly mounted, came down upon the noble young volunteers before they could even form in square; and nearly the whole, disdaining to fly, were cut to pieces on the ground. An officer of rank, and a brave man, appalled by this hideous disaster, the affair of a few moments, rode up to the spot, and did all he could to repair it. But the cowardly drunkard had fled at the first onset, with all his Arnauts; panic spread rapidly; and the whole force of five thousand men fled before eight hundred Turks, leaving four hundred men dead on the field, of whom three hundred and fifty belonged to the sacred battalion.

The Turks, occupied with gathering a trophy of heads, neglected to pursue. But the work was done. The defeated advance fell back upon the main body; and that same night the whole army, panic-struck, ashamed, and bewildered, commenced a precipitate retreat. From this moment Prince Ypsilanti thought only of saving himself. This purpose he effected in a few days, by retreating into Austria, from which territory he issued his final order of the day, taxing his army, in violent and unmeasured terms, with cowardice and disobedience. This was in a limited sense true; many distinctions, however, were called for in mere justice; and the capital defects, after all, were in himself. His plan was originally bad; and, had it been better, he was quite unequal to the execution of it. The results were unfortunate to all concerned in it. Ypsilanti himself was arrested by Austria, and thrown into the unwholesome prison of Mongatz, where, after languishing for six years, he perished miserably. Some of the subordinate officers prolonged the struggle in a guerilla style for some little time; but all were finally suppressed. Many were put to death; many escaped into neutral ground; and it is gratifying to add, that of two traitors amongst the higher officers, one was detected and despatched in a summary way of vengeance by his own associates; the other, for some unexplained reason, was beheaded by his Turkish friends at the very moment when he had put himself into their power, in fearless obedience to their own summons to *come and receive his well-merited reward*, and under an express assurance from the Pacha of Silistria that he was impatiently waiting to invest him with a pelisse of honor. Such faith is kept with traitors; such faith be ever kept with the betrayers of nations and their holiest hopes! Though in this instance the particular motives of the Porte are still buried in mystery.

Thus terminated the first rash enterprise, which resulted from the too tempting invitation held out in the rebellion then agitating Epirus, locking up, as it did, and neutralizing, so large a part of the disposable Turkish forces. To this we return. Kourshid Pacha quitted the Morea with a large body of troops, in the first days of January, 1821, and took the command of the army already before Yannina. But, with all his great numerical superiority to the enemy with whom he contended, and now enjoying undisturbed union in his own camp, he found it impossible to make his advances rapidly. Though in hostility to the Porte, and though now connected with Christian allies, Ali Pacha was yet nominally a Mahometan. Hence it had been found impossible as yet to give any color of an anti-Christian character to the war; and the native Mahometan chieftains had therefore no scruple in coalescing with the Christians of Epirus, and making joint cause with Ali. Gradually, from

the inevitable vexations incident to the march and residence
of a large army, the whole population became hostile to
Kourshid; and their remembrance of Ali's former
oppressions, if not effaced, was yet suspended in the
presence of a nuisance so immediate and so generally
diffused; and most of the Epirots turned their arms against
the Porte. The same feelings which governed *them* soon
spread to the provinces of Etolia and Acarnania; or rather,
perhaps, being previously ripe for revolt, these provinces
resolved to avail themselves of the same occasion.
Missolonghi now became the centre of rebellion; and
Kourshid's difficulties were daily augmenting. In July of this
year (1821) these various insurgents, actively cooperating,
defeated the Serasker in several actions, and compelled a
Pacha to lay down his arms on the road between Yannina
and Souli. It was even proposed by the gallant partisan,
Mark Bozzaris, that all should unite to hem in the Serasker;
but a wound, received in a skirmish, defeated this plan. In
September following, however, the same Mark intercepted
and routed Hassan Pacha in a defile on his march to
Yannina; and in general the Turks were defeated everywhere
except at the headquarters of the Serasker, and with losses
in men enormously disproportioned to the occasions. This
arose partly from the necessity under which they lay of
attacking expert musketeers under cover of breastworks,
and partly from their own precipitance and determination to
carry everything by summary force; "whereas," says Mr.
Gordon, "a little patience would surely have caused them to
succeed, and at least saved them much dishonor, and
thousands of lives thrown away in mere wantonness." But,
in spite of all blunders, and every sort of failure elsewhere,
the Serasker was still advancing slowly towards his main
objects—the reduction of Ali Pacha. And by the end of
October, on getting possession of an important part of Ali's
works, he announced to the Sultan that he should soon be

able to send him the traitor's head, for that he was already reduced to six hundred men. A little before this, however, the celebrated Maurocordato, with other persons of influence, had arrived at Missolonghi with the view of cementing a general union of Christian and Mahometan forces against the Turks. In this he was so far successful, that in November a combined attack was made upon Ismael, the old enemy of Ali, and three other Pachas, shut up in the town of Arta. This attack succeeded partially; but it was attempted at a moment dramatically critical, and with an effect ruinous to the whole campaign, as well as that particular attack. The assailing party, about thirty-four hundred men, were composed in the proportion of two Christians to one Mahometan. They had captured one half of the town; and, Mark Bozzaris having set this on fire to prevent plundering, the four Pachas were on the point of retreating under cover of the smoke. At that moment arrived a Mahometan of note, instigated by Kourshid, who was able to persuade those of his own faith that the Christians were not fighting with any sincere views of advantage to Ali, but with ulterior purposes hostile to Mahometanism itself. On this, the Christian division of the army found themselves obliged to retire without noise, in order to escape their own allies, now suddenly united with the four Pachas. Nor, perhaps, would even this have been effected, but for the precaution of Mark Bozzaris in taking hostages from two leading Mahometans. Thus failed the last diversion in favor of Ali Pacha, who was henceforward left to his own immediate resources. All the Mahometan tribes now ranged themselves on the side of Kourshid; and the winter of 1821-2 passed away without further disturbance in Epirus.

Meantime, during the absence of Kourshid Pacha from the Morea, the opportunity had not been lost for raising the insurrection in that important part of Greece. Kourshid had marched early in January, 1821; and already in February symptoms of the coming troubles appeared at Patrass, "the most flourishing and populous city of the Peloponnesus, the emporium of its trade, and residence of the foreign consuls and merchants." Its population was about eighteen thousand, of which number two thirds were Christian. In March, when rumors had arrived of the insurrection beyond the Danube, under Alexander Ypsilanti, the fermentation became universal; and the Turks of Patrass hastily prepared for defence. By the twenty-fifth, the Greeks had purchased all the powder and lead which could be had; and about the second of April they raised the standard of the Cross. Two days after this, fighting began at Patrass. The town having been set on fire, "the Turkish castle threw shot and shells at random; the two parties fought amongst the ruins, and massacred each other without mercy; the only prisoners that were spared owed their lives to fanaticism; some Christian youths being circumcised by the Mollahs, and some Turkish boys baptized by the priests."

"While the commencement of the war," says Mr. Gordon, "was thus signalized by the ruin of a flourishing city, the insurrection gained ground with wonderful rapidity; and from mountain to mountain, and village to village, propagated itself to the furthest corner of the Peloponnesus. Everywhere the peasants flew to arms; and those Turks who resided in the open country or unfortified towns were either cut to pieces, or forced to fly into strongholds." On the second of April, the flag of independence was hoisted in Achaia. On the ninth, a Grecian senate met at Calamata, in Messenia, having for its president Mavromichalis, Prince or Bey of Maina, a rugged territory in the ancient Sparta, famous for its hardy race of robbers and pirates. [Footnote: These Mainates have been supposed to be of Sclavonian origin; but Mr. Gordon, upon the authority of the Emperor Constantine Porphyrogenitos, asserts that they are of pure Laconian blood, and became Christians in the reign of that emperor's grandfather, Basil the Macedonian. They are, and ever have been, robbers by profession; robbers by land, pirates by sea; for which last branch of their mixed occupation they enjoy singular advantages in their position at the point of junction between the Ionian and Egean seas. To illustrate their condition of perpetual warfare, Mr. Gordon mentions that there were very lately individuals who had lived for twenty years in towers, not daring to stir out lest their neighbors should shoot them. They were supplied with bread and cartridges by their wives; for the persons of women are sacred in Maina. Two other good features in their character are their hospitality and their indisposition to bloodshed. They are in fact *gentle thieves* — the Robin Hoods of Greece.]

On the sixth of April, the insurrection had spread to the narrow territory of Megaris, situated to the north of the isthmus. The Albanian population of this country, amounting to about ten thousand, and employed by the Porte to guard the defiles of the entrance into Peloponnesus, raised the standard of revolt, and marched to invest the Acrocorinthus. In the Messenian territory, the Bishop of Modon, having made his guard of Janissaries drunk, cut the whole of them to pieces; and then encamping on the heights of Navarin, his lordship blockaded that fortress. The abruptness of these movements, and their almost simultaneous origin at distances so considerable, sufficiently prove how ripe the Greeks were for this revolt as respected temper; and in other modes of preparation they never *could* have been ripe whilst overlooked by Turkish masters. That haughty race now retreated from all parts of the Morea, within the ramparts of Tripolizza.

In the first action which occurred, the Arcadian Greeks did not behave well; they fled at the very sound of the Moslem tread. Colocotroni commanded; and he rallied them again; but again they deserted him at the sight of their oppressors; "and I," said Colocotroni afterwards, when relating the circumstances of this early affair, "having with me only ten companions including my horse, sat down in a bush and wept."

Meantime, affairs went ill at Patrass. Yussuf Pacha, having been detached from Epirus to Euba by the Scrasker, heard on his route of the insurrection in Peloponnesus. Upon which, altering his course, he sailed to Patrass, and reached it on the fifteenth of April. This was Palm Sunday, and it dawned upon the Greeks with evil omens. First came a smart shock of earthquake; next a cannonade announcing the approach of the Pacha; and, lastly, an Ottoman brig of war, which saluted the fort and cast anchor before the town.

The immediate consequences were disastrous. The Greeks retreated; and the Pacha detached Kihaya-Bey, a Tartar officer of distinguished energy, with near three thousand men, to the most important points of the revolt. On the fifth of May, the Tartar reached Corinth, but found the siege already raised. Thence he marched to Argos, sending before him a requisition for bread. He was answered by the men of Argos that they had no bread, but only powder and ball at his service. This threat, however, proved a gasconade; the Kihaya advanced in three columns; cavalry on each wing, and infantry in the centre; on which, after a single discharge, the Argives fled. [Footnote: It has a sublime effect in the record of this action to hear that the Argives were drawn up behind a wall originally raised as a defence *against the deluge of Inachus*.] Their general, fighting bravely, was killed, together with seven hundred others, and fifteen hundred women captured. The Turks, having sacked and burned Argos, then laid siege to a monastery, which surrendered upon terms; and it is honorable to the memory of this Tartar general, that, according to the testimony of Mr. Gordon, at a time when the war was managed with merciless fury and continual perfidies on both sides, he observed the terms with rigorous fidelity, treated all his captives with the utmost humanity, and even liberated the women.

Thus far the tide had turned against the Greeks; but now came a decisive reaction in their favor; and, as if forever to proclaim the folly of despair, just at the very crisis when it was least to have been expected, the Kihaya was at this point joined by the Turks of Tripolizza, and was now reputed to be fourteen thousand strong. This proved to be an exaggeration; but the subsequent battle is the more honorable to those who believed it. At a council of war, in the Greek camp, the prevailing opinion was that an action could not prudently be risked. One man thought otherwise; this was Anagnostoras; he, by urging the desolations which would follow a retreat, brought over the rest to his opinion; and it was resolved to take up a position at Valtezza, a village three hours' march from Tripolizza. Thither, on the twenty-seventh of May, the Kihaya arrived with five thousand men, in three columns, having left Tripolizza at dawn; and immediately raised redoubts opposite to those of the Greeks, and placed three heavy pieces of cannon in battery. He hoped to storm the position; but, if he should fail, he had a reason for still anticipating a victory, and *that* was the situation of the fountains, which must soon have drawn the Greeks out of their position, as they had water only for twenty-four hours' consumption.

The battle commenced: and the first failure of the Kihaya was in the cannonade; for his balls, passing over the Greeks, fell amongst a corps of his own troops. These now made three assaults; but were repulsed in all. Both sides kept up a fire till night; and each expected that his enemy would retire in the darkness. The twenty-eighth, however, found the two armies still in the same positions. The battle was renewed for five hours; and then the Kihaya, finding his troops fatigued, and that his retreat was likely to be intercepted by Nikitas (a brave partisan officer bred to arms in the service of England), who was coming up by forced marches from Argos with eight hundred men, gave the signal for retreat. This soon became a total rout; the Kihaya lost his horse; and the Greeks, besides taking two pieces of cannon, raised a trophy of four hundred Moslem heads.

Such was the battle of Yaltezza, the inaugural performance of the insurrection; and we have told it thus circumstantially, because Mr. Gordon characterizes it as "remarkable for the moral effect it produced;" and he does not scruple to add, that it "certainly decided the campaign in Peloponnesus, *and perhaps even the fate of the revolution.*"

Three days after, that is, on the last day of May, 1821, followed the victory of Doliana, in which the Kihaya, anxious to recover his lost ground, was encountered by Nikitas. The circumstances were peculiarly brilliant. For the Turkish general had between two and three thousand men, besides artillery; whereas Nikitas at first sustained the attack in thirteen barricaded houses, with no more than ninety-six soldiers, and thirty armed peasants. After a resistance of eleven hours, he was supported by seven hundred men; and in the end he defeated the Kihaya with a very considerable loss.

These actions raised the enthusiasm of the Morea to a high point; and in the mean time other parts of Greece had joined in the revolt. In the first week of April an insurrection burst out in the eastern provinces of Greece, Attica, Boeotia, and Phocis. The insurgents first appeared near Livadia, one of the best cities in northern Greece. On the thirteenth, they occupied Thebes without opposition. Immediately after, Odysseus propagated the revolt in Phocis, where he had formerly commanded as a lieutenant of Ali Pacha's. Next arose the Albanian peasantry of Attica, gathering in armed bodies to the west of Athens. Towards the end of April, the

Turks, who composed one fifth of the Athenian population (then rated at ten thousand), became greatly agitated; and twice proposed a massacre of the Christians. This was resisted by the humane Khadi; and the Turks, contenting themselves with pillaging absent proprietors, began to lay up stores in the Acropolis. With ultra Turkish stupidity, however, out of pure laziness, at this critical moment, they confided the night duty on the ramparts of the city to Greeks. The consequence may be supposed. On the eighth of May, the Ottoman standard had been raised and blessed by an Tman. On the following night, a rapid discharge of musketry, and the shouts of *Christ has risen! Liberty! Liberty!* proclaimed the capture of Athens. Nearly two thousand peasants, generally armed with clubs, had scaled the walls and forced the gates. The prisoners taken were treated with humanity. But, unfortunately, this current of Christian sentiment was immediately arrested by the conduct of the Turks in the Acropolis, in killing nine hostages, and throwing over the walls some naked and headless bodies.

The insurrection next spread to Thessaly; and at last even to Macedonia, from the premature and atrocious violence of the Pacha of Salonika. Apprehending a revolt, he himself drew it on, by cutting off the heads of the Christian merchants and clergy (simply as a measure of precaution), and enforcing his measures on the peasantry by military execution. Unfortunately, from its extensive plains, this country is peculiarly favorable to the evolutions of the Turkish cavalry; the insurgents were, therefore, defeated in several actions; and ultimately took refuge in great numbers amongst the convents on Mount Athos, which also were driven into revolt by the severity of the Pacha. Here the fugitives were safe from the sabres of their merciless pursuers; but, unless succored by sea, ran a great risk of perishing by famine. But a more important accession to the cause of independence, within one month from its first outbreak in the Morea, occurred in the Islands of the Archipelago. The three principal of these in modern times, are Hydra, Spezzia, and Psarra. [Footnote: Their insignificance in ancient times is proclaimed by the obscurity of their ancient names—Aperopia, Tiparenus, and Psyra.] They had been colonized in the preceding century, by some poor families from Peloponnesus and Ionia. At that time they had gained a scanty subsistence as fishermen. Gradually they became merchants and seamen. Being the best sailors in the Sultan's dominions, they had obtained some valuable privileges, amongst which was that of exemption from Turkish magistrates; so that, if they could not boast of *autonomy*, they had at least the advantage of executing the bad laws of Turkish imposition by chiefs of their own blood. And they had the further advantage of paying but a moderate tribute to the Sultan. So favored, their commerce had flourished beyond all precedent. And latterly, when the vast extension of European warfare had created first-rate markets for grain, selecting, of course, those which were highest at the moment, they sometimes doubled their capitals in two voyages; and seven or eight such trips in a year were not an unusual instance of good fortune. What had been the result, may be collected from the following description, which Mr. Gordon gives us, of Hydra: "Built on a sterile rock, which does not offer, at any season, the least trace of vegetation, it is one of the best cities in the Levant, and *infinitely superior to any other in Greece*; the houses are all constructed of white stone; and those of the aristocracy—erected at an immense expense, floored with costly marbles, and splendidly furnished—*might pass for palaces even in the capitals of Italy*. Before the revolution, poverty was unknown; all classes being comfortably lodged, clothed, and fed. Its inhabitants at this epoch exceeded twenty thousand, of whom four thousand were able-bodied seamen."

The other islands were, with few exceptions, arid rocks; and most of them had the inestimable advantage of being unplagued with a Turkish population. Enjoying that precious immunity, it may be wondered why they should have entered into the revolt. But for this there were two great reasons: they were ardent Christians in the first place, and disinterested haters of Mahometanism on its own merits; secondly, as the most powerful [Footnote: Mr. Gordon says that "they could, without difficulty, fit out a hundred sail of ships, brigs, and schooners, armed with from twelve to twenty-four guns each, and manned by seven thousand stout and able sailors." Pouqueville ascribes to them, in 1813, a force considerably greater. But the peace of Paris (one year after Pouqueville's estimates) naturally reduced their power, as their extraordinary gains were altogether dependent on war and naval blockades.] nautical confederacy in the Levant, they anticipated a large booty from captures at sea. In that expectation, at first, they were not disappointed. But it was a source of wealth soon exhausted; for, naturally, as soon as their ravages became known, the Mussulmans ceased to navigate. Spezzia was the first to hoist the independent flag; this was on the ninth of April, 1821. Psarra immediately followed her example. Hydra hesitated, and at first even declined to do so; but, at last, on the 28th of April, this island also issued a manifesto of adherence to the patriotic cause. On the third of May, a squadron of eleven Hydriot and seven Spezzia vessels sailed from Hydra, having on the mainmast "an address to the people of the Egean sea, inviting them to rally round the national standard: an address that was received with enthusiasm in every quarter of the Archipelago where the Turks were not numerous enough to restrain popular feeling."

"The success of the Greek marine in this first expedition,"
says Mr. Gordon, "was not confined to merely spreading the
insurrection throughout the Archipelago: a swarm of swift
armed ships swept the sea from the Hellespont to the waters
of Crete and Cyprus; captured every Ottoman trader they
met with, and put to the sword, or flung overboard, the
Mahometan crews and passengers; for the contest already
assumed a character of terrible ferocity. It would be vain to
deny that they were guilty of shocking barbarities; at the
little island of Castel Rosso, on the Karamanian shore, they
butchered, in cold blood, several beautiful Turkish females;
and a great number of defenceless pilgrims (mostly old men),
who, returning from Mecca, fell into their power, off
Cyprus, were slain without mercy, because they would not
renounce their faith." Many such cases of hideous barbarity
had already occurred, and did afterwards occur, on the
mainland. But this is the eternal law and providential
retribution of oppression. The tyrant teaches to his slave the
crimes and the cruelties which he inflicts; blood will have
blood; and the ferocious oppressor is involved in the natural
reaction of his own wickedness, by the frenzied retaliation
of the oppressed. Now was indeed beheld the realization of
the sublime imprecation in Shakspeare: "one spirit of the
first-born Cain" did indeed reign in the hearts of men; and
now, if ever upon this earth, it seemed likely, from the
dreadful *acharnement* which marked the war on both sides,—
the *acharnement* of long-hoarded vengeance and maddening
remembrances in the Grecian, of towering disdain in the
alarmed oppressor,—that, in very simplicity of truth,
"Darkness would be the burier of the dead."

Such was the opening scene in the astonishing drama of the
Greek insurrection, which, through all its stages, was
destined to move by fire and blood, and beyond any war in
human annals to command the interest of mankind

through their sterner affections. We have said that it was
eminently a romantic war; but not in the meaning with
which we apply that epithet to the semi-fabulous wars of
Charlemagne and his Paladins, or even to the Crusaders.
Here are no memorable contests of generosity; no triumphs
glorified by mercy; no sacrifices of interest the most basely
selfish to martial honor; no ear on either side for the
pleadings of desolate affliction; no voice in any quarter of
commanding justice; no acknowledgment of a common
nature between the belligerents; nor sense of a participation
in the same human infirmities, dangers, or necessities. To
the fugitive from the field of battle there was scarcely a
retreat; to the prisoner there was absolutely no hope. Stern
retribution, and the very rapture of vengeance, were the
passions which presided on the one side; on the other,
fanaticism and the cruelty of fear and hatred, maddened by
old hereditary scorn. Wherever the war raged there followed
upon the face of the land one blank Aceldama. A desert
tracked the steps of the armies, and a desert in which was no
oasis; and the very atmosphere in which men lived and
breathed was a chaos of murderous passions. Still it is true
that the war was a great romance. For it was filled with
change, and with elastic rebound from what seemed final
extinction; with the spirit of adventure carried to the utmost
limits of heroism; with self-devotion on the sublimest scale,
and the very frenzy of patriotic martyrdom; with
resurrection of everlasting hope upon ground seven times
blasted by the blighting presence of the enemy; and with
flowers radiant in promise springing forever from under the
very tread of the accursed Moslem.

NOTE.—We have thought that we should do an acceptable
service to the reader by presenting him with a sketch of the
Suliotes, and the most memorable points in their history. We

have derived it (as to the facts) from a little work originally composed by an Albanian in modern Greek, and printed at Venice in 1815. This work was immediately translated into Italian, by Gherardini, an Italian officer of Milan; and, ten years ago, with some few omissions, it was reproduced in an English version; but in this country it seems never to have attracted public notice, and is probably now forgotten.

With respect to the name of Suli, the Suliotes themselves trace it to an accident:—"Some old men," says the Albanian author, reciting his own personal investigations amongst the oldest of the Suliotes, "replied that they did not remember having any information from their ancestors concerning the first inhabitants of Suli, except this only: that some goat and swine herds used to lead their flocks to graze on the mountains where Suli and Ghiafa now stand; that these mountains were not only steep and almost inaccessible, but clothed with thickets of wood, and infested by wild boars; that these herdsmen, being oppressed by the tyranny of the Turks of a village called to this day Gardichi, took the resolution of flying for a distance of six hours' journey to this sylvan and inaccessible position, of sharing in common the few animals which they had, and of suffering voluntarily every physical privation, rather than submit to the slightest wrong from their foreign tyrants. This resolution, they added, must be presumed to have been executed with success; because we find that, in the lapse of five or six years, these original occupants of the fastness were joined by thirty other families. Somewhere about that time it was that they began to awaken the jealousy of the Turks; and a certain Turk, named Suli, went in high scorn and defiance, with many other associates, to expel them from this strong position; but our stout forefathers met them with arms in their hands. Suli, the leader and inciter of the Turks, was killed outright upon the ground; and, on the very spot where he fell, at this day stands the centre of our modern Suli, which took its name, therefore, from that same slaughtered Turk, who was the first insolent and malicious enemy with whom our country in its days of infancy had to contend for its existence."

Such is the most plausible account which can now be obtained of the *incunabula* of this most indomitable little community, and of the circumstances under which it acquired its since illustrious name. It was, perhaps, natural that a little town, in the centre of insolent and bitter enemies, should assume a name which would long convey to their whole neighborhood a stinging lesson of mortification, and of prudential warning against similar molestations. As to the *chronology* of this little state, the Albanian author assures us, upon the testimony of the same old Suliotes, that "seventy years before" there were barely one hundred men fit for the active duties of war, which, in ordinary states of society, would imply a total population of four hundred souls. That may be taken, therefore, as the extreme limit of the Suliote population at a period of seventy years antecedently to the date of tke conversation on which he founds his information. But, as he has unfortunately omitted to fix the exact era of these conversations, the whole value of his accuracy is neutralized by his own carelessness. However, it is probable, from the internal evidence of his book, which brings down affairs below the year 1812, that his information was collected somewhere about 1810. We must carry back the epoch, therefore, at which Suli had risen to a population of four hundred, pretty nearly to the year 1740; and since, by the same traditionary evidence, Suli had then accomplished an independent existence through a space of eighty years, we have reason to conclude that the very first gatherings of poor Christian herdsmen to this sylvan sanctuary, when stung to madness by Turkish insolence and persecution, would take place about the era of the Restoration (of our Charles II.), that is, in 1660.

In more modern times, the Suliotes had expanded into four separate little towns, peopled by five hundred and sixty families, from which they were able to draw one thousand first-rate soldiers. But, by a very politic arrangement, they had colonized with sixty-six other families seven neighboring towns, over which, from situation, they had long been able to exercise a military preponderance. The benefits were incalculable which they obtained by this connection. At the first alarm of war the fighting men retreated with no incumbrances but their arms, ammunition, and a few days' provision, into the four towns of Suli proper, which all lay within that ring fence of impregnable position from which no armies could ever dislodge them; meantime, they secretly drew supplies from the seven associate towns, which were better situated than themselves for agriculture, and which (apparently taking no part in the war) pursued their ordinary labors unmolested. Their tactics were simple, but judicious; if they saw a body of five or six thousand advancing against their position, knowing that it was idle for them to meet such a force in the open field, they contented themselves with detaching one hundred and fifty or two hundred men to skirmish on their flanks, and to harass them according to the advantages of the ground; but if they saw no more than five hundred or one thousand in the hostile column, they then issued in equal or superior numbers, in the certainty of beating them, striking an effectual panic into their hearts, and also of profiting largely by plunder and by ransom.

In so small and select a community, where so much must continually depend upon individual qualities and personal heroism, it may readily be supposed that the women would play an important part; in fact, "the women carry arms and fight bravely. When the men go to war, the women bring them food and provisions; when they see their strength declining in combat, they run to their assistance, and fight along with them; but, if by any chance their husbands behave with cowardice, they snatch their arms from them, and abuse them, calling them mean, and unworthy of having a wife." Upon these feelings there has even been built a law in Suli, which must deeply interest the pride of women in the martial honor of their husbands; agreeably to this law, any woman whose husband has distinguished himself in battle, upon going to a fountain to draw water, has the liberty to drive away another woman whose husband is tainted with the reproach of cowardice; and all who succeed her, "from dawn to dewy eve," unless under the ban of the same withering stigma, have the same privilege of taunting her with her husband's baseness, and of stepping between her or her cattle until their own wants are fully supplied.

This social consideration of the female sex, in right of their husbands' military honors, is made available for no trifling purposes; on one occasion it proved the absolute salvation of the tribe. In one of the most desperate assaults made by Ali Pacha upon Suli, when that tyrant was himself present at the head of eight thousand picked men, animated with the promise of five hundred piastres a man, to as many as should enter Suli, after ten hours' fighting under an enfeebling sun, and many of the Suliote muskets being rendered useless by continual discharges, a large body of the enemy had actually succeeded in occupying the sacred interior of Suli itself. At that critical moment, when Ali was in the very paroxysms of frantic exultation, the Suliote women, seeing that the general fate hinged upon the next five minutes, turned upon the Turks *en masse*, and with such a rapture of sudden fury, that the conquering army was instantly broken—thrown into panic, pursued; and, in that state of ruinous disorder, was met and flanked by the men, who were now recovering from their defeat. The consequences, from the nature of the ground, were fatal to the Turkish army and enterprise; the whole camp equipage was captured; none saved their lives but by throwing away their arms; one third of the Turks (one half by some accounts) perished on the retreat; the rest returned at intervals as an unarmed mob; and the bloody, perfidious Pacha himself saved his life only by killing two horses in his haste. So total was the rout, and so bitter the mortification of Ali, who had seen a small band of heroic women snatch the long-sought prize out of his very grasp, that for some weeks he shut himself up in his palace at Yannina, would receive no visits, and issued a proclamation imposing instant death upon any man detected in looking out at a window or other aperture—as being *presumably* engaged in noticing the various expressions of his defeat which were continually returning to Yannina.

The wars, in which the adventurous courage of the Suliotes (together with their menacing position) could not fail to involve them, were in all eleven. The first eight of these occurred in times before the French Revolution, and with Pachas who have left no memorials behind them of the terrific energy or hellish perfidy which marked the character of Ali Pacha. These Pachas, who brought armies at the lowest of five thousand, and at the most of twelve thousand men, were uniformly beaten; and apparently were content to be beaten. Sometimes a Pacha was even made prisoner; but, as the simple [Footnote: On the same occasion the Pacha's son, and sixty officers of the rank of *Aga*, were also made prisoners by a truly rustic mode of assault. The Turks had shut themselves up in a church; into this, by night, the

Suliotes threw a number of hives, full of bees, whose insufferable stings soon brought the haughty Moslems into the proper surrendering mood. The whole body were afterwards ransomed for so trifling a sum as one thousand sequins.] Suliotes little understood the art of improving advantages, the ransom was sure to be proportioned to the value of the said Pacha's sword-arm in battle, rather than to his rank and ability to pay; so that the terms of liberation were made ludicrously easy to the Turkish chiefs.

These eight wars naturally had no other ultimate effect than to extend the military power, experience, and renown, of the Suliotes. But their ninth war placed them in collision with a new and far more perilous enemy than any they had yet tried; above all, he was so obstinate and unrelenting an enemy, that, excepting the all-conquering mace of death, it was certain that no obstacles born of man ever availed to turn him aside from an object once resolved on. The reader will understand, of course, that this enemy was Ali Pacha. Their ninth war was with him; and he, like all before him, was beaten; but *not* like all before him did Ali sit down in resignation under his defeat. His hatred was now become fiendish; no other prosperity or success had any grace in his eyes, so long as Suli stood, by which he had been overthrown, trampled on, and signally humbled. Life itself was odious to him, if he must continue to witness the triumphant existence of the abhorred little mountain village which had wrung laughter at his expense from every nook of Epirus. *Delenda est Carthago! Suli must be exterminated!* became, therefore, from this time, the master watchword of his secret policy. And on the 1st of June, in the year 1792, he commenced his second war against the Suliotes, at the head of twenty-two thousand men. This was the second war of Suli with Ali Pacha; but it was the tenth war on their annals; and, as far as their own exertions were concerned, it had the same result as all the rest. But, about the sixth year of the war, in an indirect way, Ali made one step towards his final purpose, which first manifested its disastrous tendency in the new circumstances which succeeding years brought forward. In 1797 the French made a lodgment in Corfu; and, agreeably to their general spirit of intrigue, they had made advances to Ali Pacha, and to all other independent powers in or about Epirus. Amongst other states, in an evil hour for that ill-fated city, they wormed themselves into an alliance with Prevesa; and in the following year their own quarrel with Ali Pacha gave that crafty robber a pretence, which he had long courted in vain, for attacking the place with his overwhelming cavalry, before they could agree upon the mode of defence, and long before *any* mode could have been tolerably matured. The result was one universal massacre, which raged for three days, and involved every living Prevesan, excepting some few who had wisely made their escape in time, and excepting those who were reserved to be tortured for Ali's special gratification, or to be sold for slaves in the shambles. This dreadful catastrophe, which in a few hours rooted from the earth an old and flourishing community, was due in about equal degrees to the fatal intriguing of the interloping French, and to the rankest treachery in a quarter where it could least have been held possible; namely, in a Suliote, and a very distinguished Suliote, Captain George Botzari; but the miserable man yielded up his honor and his patriotism to Ali's bribe of one hundred purses (perhaps at that time equal to twenty-five hundred pounds sterling). The way in which this catastrophe operated upon Ali's final views was obvious to everybody in that neighborhood. Parga, on the sea-coast, was an indispensable ally to Suli; now, Prevesa stood in the same relation to Parga, as an almost indispensable ally, that Parga occupied towards Suli.

This shocking tragedy had been perpetrated in the October of 1798; and, in less than two years from that date, namely, on the 2d of June, 1800, commenced the eleventh war of the Suliotes; being their third with Ali, and the last which, from their own guileless simplicity, meeting with the craft of the most perfidious amongst princes, they were ever destined to wage. For two years, that is, until the middle of 1802, the war, as managed by the Suliotes, rather resembles a romance, or some legend of the acts of Paladins, than any grave chapter in modern history. Amongst the earliest victims it is satisfactory to mention the traitor, George Botzari, who, being in the power of the Pacha, was absolutely compelled to march with about two hundred of his kinsmen, whom he had seduced from Suli, against his own countrymen, under whose avenging swords the majority of them fell, whilst the arch-traitor himself soon died of grief and mortification. After this, Ali himself led a great and well-appointed army in various lines of assault against Suli. But so furious was the reception given to the Turks, so deadly and so uniform their defeat, that panic seized on the whole army, who declared unanimously to Ali that they would no more attempt to contend with the Suliotes—"Who," said they, "neither sit nor sleep, but are born only for the destruction of men." Ali was actually obliged to submit to this strange resolution of his army; but, by way of compromise, he built a chain of forts pretty nearly encircling Suli; and simply exacted of his troops that, being forever released from the dangers of the open field, they should henceforward shut themselves up in these forts, and constitute themselves a permanent blockading force for the purpose of bridling the marauding excursions of the Suliotes. It was hoped that, from the close succession of these forts, the Suliotes would find it impossible to slip between the cross fires of the Turkish musketry; and that, being thus absolutely cut off from their common resources

of plunder, they must at length be reduced by mere
starvation. That termination of the contest was in fact
repeatedly within a trifle of being accomplished; the poor
Suliotes were reduced to a diet of acorns; and even of this
food had so slender a quantity that many died, and the rest
wore the appearance of blackened skeletons. All this misery,
however, had no effect to abate one jot of their zeal and their
undying hatred to the perfidious enemy who was bending
every sinew to their destruction. It is melancholy to record
that such perfect heroes, from whom force the most
disproportioned, nor misery the most absolute, had ever
wrung the slightest concession or advantage, were at length
entrapped by the craft of their enemy; and by their own
foolish confidence in the oaths of one who had never been
known to keep any engagement which he had a momentary
interest in breaking. Ali contrived first of all to trepan the
matchless leader of the Suliotes, Captain Foto Giavella, who
was a hero after the most exquisite model of ancient Greece,
Epaminondas, or Timoleon, and whose counsels were
uniformly wise and honest. After that loss, all harmony of
plan went to wreck amongst the Suliotes; and at length,
about the middle of December, 1803, this immortal little
independent state of Suli solemnly renounced by treaty to
Ali Pacha its sacred territory, its thrice famous little towns,
and those unconquerable positions among the crests of
wooded inaccessible mountains which had baffled all the
armies of the crescent, led by the most eminent of the
Ottoman Pachas, and not seldom amounting to twenty,
twenty-five, and in one instance even to more than thirty
thousand men. The articles of a treaty, which on one side
there never was an intention of executing, are scarcely
worth repeating; the amount was—that the Suliotes had
perfect liberty to go whither they chose, retaining the whole
of their arms and property, and with a title to payment in
cash for every sort of warlike store which could not be

carried off. In excuse for the poor Suliotes in trusting to treaties of any kind with an enemy whom no oaths could bind for an hour, it is but fair to mention that they were now absolutely without supplies either of ammunition or provisions; and that, for seven days, they had suffered under a total deprivation of water, the sources of which were now in the hands of the enemy, and turned into new channels. The winding up of the memorable tale is soon told:—the main body of the fighting Suliotes, agreeably to the treaty, immediately took the route to Parga, where they were sure of a hospitable reception, that city having all along made common cause with Suli against their common enemy, Ali. The son of Ali, who had concluded the treaty, and who inherited all his father's treachery, as fast as possible despatched four thousand Turks in pursuit, with orders to massacre the whole. But in this instance, through the gallant assistance of the Parghiotes, and the energetic haste of the Suliotes, the accursed wretch was disappointed of his prey. As to all the other detachments of the Suliotes, who were scattered at different points, and were necessarily thrown everywhere upon their own resources without warning or preparation of any kind,—they, by the terms of the treaty, had liberty to go away or to reside peaceably in any part of Ali's dominions. But as these were mere windy words, it being well understood that Ali's fixed intention was to cut every throat among the Suliotes, whether of man, woman, or child,—nay, as he thought himself dismally ill-used by every hour's delay which interfered with the execution of that purpose,—what rational plan awaited the choice of the poor Suliotes, finding themselves in the centre of a whole hostile nation, and their own slender divisions cut off from communication with each other? What could people so circumstanced propose to themselves as a suitable resolution for their situation? Hope there was none; sublime despair was all that their case allowed; and, considering the

unrivalled splendors of their past history for more than one
hundred and sixty years, perhaps most readers would reply,
in the famous words of Corneille—*Qu'ils mourussent*. That
was their own reply to the question now so imperatively
forced upon them; and die they all did. It is an argument of
some great original nobility in the minds of these poor
people, that none disgraced themselves by useless
submissions, and that all alike, women as well as men,
devoted themselves in the "high Roman fashion" to the now
expiring cause of their country. The first case which
occurred exhibits the very perfection of *nonchalance* in
circumstances the most appalling. Samuel, a Suliote monk,
of somewhat mixed and capricious character, and at times
even liable to much suspicion amongst his countrymen, but
of great name, and of unquestionable merit in his military
character, was in the act of delivering over to authorized
Turkish agents a small outpost, which had greatly annoyed
the forces of Ali, together with such military stores as it still
contained. By the treaty, Samuel was perfectly free, and
under the solemn protection of Ali; but the Turks, with the
utter shamelessness to which they had been brought by
daily familiarity with treachery the most barefaced, were
openly descanting to Samuel upon the unheard-of tortures
which must be looked for at the hands of Ali, by a soldier
who had given so much trouble to that Pacha as himself.
Samuel listened coolly; he was then seated on a chest of
gunpowder, and powder was scattered about in all
directions. He watched in a careless way until he observed
that all the Turks, exulting in their own damnable perfidies,
were assembled under the roof of the building. He then
coolly took the burning snuff of a candle, and threw it into
a heap of combustibles, still keeping his seat upon the chest
of powder. It is unnecessary to add that the little fort, and
all whom it contained, were blown to atoms. And with
respect to Samuel in particular, no fragment of his skeleton

could ever be discovered. [Footnote: The deposition of two Suliote sentinels at the door, and of a third person who escaped with a dreadful scorching, sufficiently established the facts; otherwise the whole would have been ascribed to the treachery of Ali or his son.] After this followed as many separate tragedies as there were separate parties of Suliotes; when all hope and all retreat were clearly cut off, then the women led the great scene of self-immolation, by throwing their children headlong from the summit of precipices; which done, they and their husbands, their fathers and their sons, hand in hand, ran up to the brink of the declivity, and followed those whom they had sent before. In other situations, where there was a possibility of fighting with effect, they made a long and bloody resistance, until the Turkish cavalry, finding an opening for their operations, made all further union impossible; upon which they all plunged into the nearest river, without distinction of age or sex, and were swallowed up by the merciful waters. Thus, in a few days, from the signing of that treaty, which nominally secured to them peaceable possession of their property, and paternal treatment from the perfidious Pacha, none remained to claim his promises or to experience his abominable cruelties. In their native mountains of Epirus, the name of Suliote was now blotted from the books of life, and was heard no more in those wild sylvan haunts, where once it had filled every echo with the breath of panic to the quailing hearts of the Moslems. In the most "palmy" days of Suli, she never had counted more than twenty-five hundred fighting men; and of these no considerable body escaped, excepting the corps who hastily fought their way to Parga. From that city they gradually transported themselves to Corfu, then occupied by the Russians. Into the service of the Russian Czar, as the sole means left to a perishing corps of soldiers for earning daily bread, they naturally entered; and when Corfu afterwards passed from Russian to English masters, it was equally inevitable that for the same urgent purposes they should enter the military service of England. In that service they received the usual honorable treatment, and such attention as circumstances would allow to their national habits and prejudices. They were placed also, we believe, under the popular command of Sir R. Church, who, though unfortunate as a supreme leader, made himself beloved in a lower station by all the foreigners under his authority. These Suliotes have since then returned to Epirus and to Greece, the peace of 1815 having, perhaps, dissolved their connection with England, and they were even persuaded to enter the service of their arch-enemy, Ali Pacha. Since his death, their diminished numbers, and the altered circumstances of their situation, should naturally have led to the extinction of their political importance. Yet we find them in 1832 still attracting (or rather concentrating) the wrath of the Turkish Sultan, made the object of a separate war, and valued (as in all former cases) on the footing of a distinct and independent nation. On the winding up of this war, we find part of them at least an object of indulgent solicitude to the British government, and under their protection transferred to Cephalonia. Yet again, others of their scanty clan meet us at different points of the war in Greece; especially at the first decisive action with Ibrahim, when, in the rescue of Costa Botzaris, every Suliote of his blood perished on the spot; and again, in the fatal battle of Athens (May 6, 1827), Mr. Gordon assures us that "almost all the Suliotes were exterminated." We understand him to speak not generally of the Suliotes, as of the total clan who bear that name, but of those only who happened to be present at that dire catastrophe. Still, even with this limitation, such a long succession of heavy losses descending upon a people who never numbered above twenty-five hundred fighting men, and who had passed through the furnace, seven times heated, of Ali Pacha's

wrath, and suffered those many and dismal tragedies which
we have just recorded, cannot but have brought them
latterly to the brink of utter extinction.